THE FEUD

GEMMA ROGERS

Boldwood

First published in Great Britain in 2022 by Boldwood Books Ltd.

Copyright © Gemma Rogers, 2022

Cover Photography: Shutterstock

A CIP catalogue record for this book is available from the British Library.

Paperback ISBN 978-1-80048-689-8

Large Print ISBN 978-1-80048-690-4

Hardback ISBN 978-1-80426-231-3

Ebook ISBN 978-1-80048-692-8

Kindle ISBN 978-1-80048-691-1

Audio CD ISBN 978-1-80048-684-3

MP3 CD ISBN 9978-1-80048-685-0

Digital audio download ISBN 978-1-80048-687-4

Boldwood Books Ltd
23 Bowerdean Street
London SW6 3TN
www.boldwoodbooks.com

For Buster
Our Best Friend

PROLOGUE

The metal key was cold in my hand as I crouched, one knee pressed against the damp tarmac of the driveway, moisture seeping into my leggings. I shivered; drizzle hung in the air, the constant threat of October's persistent heavy rain. It was not a night to be out for a walk.

Hamstrings twitched of their own accord as I stayed rooted to the spot; neglected muscles stretched into positions I was unaccustomed to. I had to get on with it, I'd get seen from the road if someone came past. If they innocently glanced through the open gates and found me squatted on someone's driveway in the dark. Thankfully, the weather had meant the streets were quiet.

Shielded from view of the large double-fronted house, I was hidden by the F-Pace Jaguar I was yet to touch. Lights from inside glowed brightly through the open blinds into the darkness, but there was no movement from the front of the house, no sound carried on the still night air either. The motion sensor of the security light obviously didn't reach the back of the large driveway which extended around twenty-five feet. Although I bet it would after today.

A bitter aftertaste of cheap vodka clung to my tongue which, combined with my heart racing, made my stomach swim. Through my single AirPod, I could hear the Teams meeting with the Americans I was supposed to be attending. Lisa's Texan drawl grating, using her chance to speak as an opportunity for a sales pitch. I'd done my bit already and turned the volume right down. I wasn't required to talk, but I had no idea if I'd be called upon again. I had to move fast while I had my chance.

I chewed on my lip as the muscles in my thighs pinged. I'd been in the same position too long, my legs protesting despite the adrenaline coursing around my body. Was I really going to do it? What would it be classed as? Criminal damage? I'd never so much as had a parking ticket, but I wasn't putting up with shit from anyone. Not any more. Nothing came from playing by the rules. You got treated like a doormat. *He* needed to be taught a lesson and I'd bet the brand-spanking-new 71-plate Jaguar hiding me was his pride and joy.

Staying low, I rounded the side of the car, the bordering fence to his neighbour on my right. With one swift motion, I dragged my key from the back wing all the way to the bonnet, relishing the squeaking sound as it cut into the paintwork. The satisfying noise as the key sliced down to the metal. A rush of euphoria hit me as the alarm sounded, a loud, high-pitched squeal disturbing the peace.

Orange indicator lights flashed accusingly in time with the shrill siren, illuminating my presence beside the car as I stood, ready to make my escape. The security light flooded the space instantly, so bright it hurt my eyes, and I could hear a dog barking from inside the house. Before I had a chance to turn, a shadowy figure appeared at the window, their frame filling the space, looming large. It seemed to stare straight at me.

I froze, shivers shooting down my spine, unsure whether I'd been seen and not wanting to draw attention by moving. The shape in the window shifted and, jolted to my senses, I ignored the shooting pains in my legs and broke into a run; unable to contain the smile forming on my face. Payback was a bitch.

1

THE DAY BEFORE

'I'm really sorry, Kay, I'm not sure how they can justify it, but you know how it is.' Ed shrugged, his brown blazer crumpling at the shoulders as he leant over the microwave, waiting for it to ping. He didn't care, he worked in Operations. Who was appointed in the Human Resources department was of no consequence to him. I scowled into my coffee, seeing my reflection swim. It tasted as bitter as my mood.

Behind me, the door to the small kitchenette was thrown open, knocking my elbow just as I took a sip, hot liquid escaping the mug and sloshing down the front of my cream blouse.

'Fuck!' I winced as the brown stain blossomed, causing the fabric to stick like molten lava to my skin.

Ed turned around at my curse, eyes wide, his mouth forming an oval. 'Language, Kay!'

A silk-like voice came from the doorway as I gingerly peeled the searing chiffon from my chest and reached for the kitchen roll. I didn't even bother to look up, let alone respond. I knew from the voice it was Tim, and he was on my shit list today.

Tim was the Global HR Manager of Winston's Transport. A

haulage company that covered the United Kingdom, with major hubs in Gatwick, as well as Birmingham and Newcastle, and a small head office in Tunbridge Wells. Tim was the most senior member of staff in the Gatwick hub, something he loved reminding everyone on a regular basis.

'Here, let me help.' Ed dived in, handing me reams of kitchen towel, all the time trying to avert his eyes from the lace of my bra on full display through the now transparent material.

My skin was on fire and, ignoring the audience, I ran the sheets under the cold tap and dabbed at my chest. Relief was instantaneous, its bliss swiftly broken by the sound of Tim clearing his throat.

'Kay, I'd like to introduce you to the new HR Manager for the South. This is Liam Shepherds, previously from our Tunbridge Wells office; I don't believe you two have met.' It wasn't a question.

I turned and pulled my lips into a tight smile while sizing up the man who had shuffled into the cramped space, back pressed against the worktop.

He looked in his early thirties, easily ten years younger than me. Dark green eyes framed by strawberry-blond eyelashes. His skin was pale and freckled, but he looked smart in a taupe suit teamed with a soft pink shirt. He thrust his hand forward, an innocent smile warmed his face.

'Lovely to meet you,' he said.

'This is Kay Massingham, she's our Contract Manager based here in Gatwick. Like you, Kay reports to me with a dotted line to our legal department.' Tim's deep voice seemed to boom around the tiny kitchen. With four people inside, the space had been absorbed, atmosphere claustrophobic.

I gave Liam a damp but firm handshake, hoping he didn't notice my nails bitten to the quick.

'Welcome to the team,' I said crisply, anger bubbling in my

stomach. Tim knew we'd never met. I'd not heard of him before, let alone seen him. I'd bet my last month's salary he didn't hold the CIPD qualification that was supposedly the prerequisite for the Human Resources Manager role. The qualification I'd spent months working towards in my own time, in the hope of adding another string to my bow.

'Ed, would you mind introducing Liam to the Operations Department,' Tim said. It was an instruction not a request, as was Tim's way.

Ed and Liam exited the kitchen as the microwave announced Ed's lunch was done – it would be cold by the time he ate it.

I turned my back on Tim, leaning over the sink, still trying to rescue my blouse which was now only fit for the bin.

'I know this isn't the outcome you hoped for, Kay,' Tim said stiffly.

I clenched my jaw tight, but it wasn't enough to stop the words escaping like projectile vomit. Pushed-down resentment rising and spilling out. 'Five bloody years I've worked here, Tim. I've gone above and beyond for this company. Extra hours, weekends. I'm the only female who's managed to claw their way into the management team,' I went on, interrupted by Tim waving his hands like he was trying to slow a herd of rampaging buffalo.

'Liam's been earmarked for fast-track promotion by the powers that be. You know how it is. I didn't have a choice.'

'Oh, grow a pair, that job should have been mine and you know it,' I snapped.

Tim's eyes darkened; a shadow crossing his face. I'd overstepped the mark, but I couldn't help myself.

'Careful, I understand you're upset. We might be friends, Kay, but remember I'm still your boss, for the time being anyway.' He crossed his arms and I noticed dandruff speckling the shoulder of his blazer, fallen from his perfectly coiffed Just for Men hair. He should have gone grey years ago, well into his fifties now, and it was obvious he dyed it.

'You're not my friend, Tim, friends don't screw each other over. We're colleagues, and that's all we'll ever be,' I retorted. He looked wounded, but I didn't stop. 'I'm taking the afternoon off; I need a fresh shirt. You can put it down as hours owed.'

I stormed past him and back to my office. In my peripheral vision through the glass-panelled wall, I could see Liam shaking hands with Gav and Sarge over in Operations.

'All fucking lads together,' I muttered as I pushed my half-eaten sandwich into the bin and switched off my computer. I should have got out of this company a long time ago. I was never going to get anywhere, not here.

Winston's Transport was a haulage firm stuck in the dark ages, headed up by an old fart with prehistoric values who thought women should be relegated to answering phones and looking pretty. There were few females in management positions and to make it into one your face had to fit.

I'd started as a HR Assistant to Tim five years ago, my first full-time job after having the twins. When they both started at high school, they needed me less and I was ready to pick up my career again. It was hard, but I clawed my way up to Contract Manager three years after joining Winston's, a few weeks shy of my forty-first birthday. I'd learnt I had to work harder than anyone else to get noticed. In the early days, I wore skirts and stiletto heels, which were quickly replaced by trouser suits and flatter shoes. It seemed the less feminine I looked, the more I was taken seriously.

A howl of laughter came from the open-plan area. Sarge was throwing his head back, bulbous stomach jiggling as he let out a loud guffaw at one of Tim's jokes. They stood in a circle, peacocking, slapping each other on the back and rearranging their crotches while no one batted an eyelid. I only had to reposition a bra strap before the lewd comments started. Fucking men.

I should have been used to the male comradery, but even so, I'd been the first to apply for the HR Manager position covering the southern region when Martin left to work for the logistics giant Eddie Stobart in September. Going to a competitor meant he'd gone straight on gardening leave, leaving the role wide open.

Tim knew how much I wanted that job, how I needed the bump in salary now I was a single parent, trying to manage the bills by myself. I'd been open about the difficulties I was having at home, but now I wished more than anything I'd kept my mouth shut. It had made me look weak when I was already at a disadvantage just for being a woman.

Liam being appointed was a massive kick in the teeth. The announcement had come out via email that morning, sent to the whole company. Hearing whispers around the office about who the new HR Manager for the South was had been humiliating. It was no secret I'd applied, that I'd been interviewed officially almost a month ago. I'd enquired only last week as to if there would be a second interview but was told management were still reviewing candidates. It seemed they'd just been waiting for Liam's replacement to slot into his previous sales role, freeing him up to move to Gatwick. The least Tim could have done was told me I'd been rejected. He was a coward and had only got to the position he had because his face had fit. Mine, it appeared, did not.

To add insult to injury, I heard my name mentioned as I stalked out of the office with my bag.

'Don't worry about Kay, she's a little hormonal sometimes.' It preceded a loud snigger from the group, but I wasn't sure who'd said it – Sarge or Gav most likely.

'Careful, lads, I'd hate to have to report you,' Tim chortled. *As if.*

I sat in the car, biting back angry tears, trying to console myself, it was nothing new. I'd have to pick myself up and keep plugging away. Although what was the point, it was like wading through treacle. There was no future for me in haulage, not at Winston's anyway.

I turned on the engine and switched the blowers on to clear the windscreen, ignoring the sounds of the planes coming in to land. A noise I was so accustomed to, I barely even registered we were so close to the airport.

It was only October, but my life had unravelled since the spring. My husband, Jonathan, moved out of the three-bed detached home we'd saved so hard for, a separation which had become increasingly nasty. Our sixteen-year-old twins, Rachel and Ryan, seemed keen to live with him and his relaxed parenting manner. Currently they were floating between us both, while we existed in limbo. Meanwhile, I was struggling to cope with their rejection, Jonathan's too. We'd been happy, or so I'd been led to believe, although he'd admitted he hadn't been for a while. He'd denied there was another woman, but I couldn't honestly say I believed him.

I'd started drinking more to get by, the extra calories of a bottle of wine almost every night had taken a toll on my waistline. Personally, life was a mess, but professionally I had it together. I was good at my job; the promotion, I felt, was guaranteed and now that rug had been pulled out from beneath me too. At least I was over the hump of the week, there were only two more days to drag myself through and then the weekend to decide on the future.

It looked as though I was going to have to sell the house. I couldn't afford to remortgage and buy Jonathan out, not without the HR Manager salary I coveted. Letting tears escape, I thrust my fingers into my hair, pulling tight at the scalp, and screamed into my lap, knowing I wouldn't be heard from the office. No longer was I going to be ridiculed and trodden on by the misogynists of the world. Something had to give.

2

I arrived at St James's Senior School at two in the afternoon, managing to get the last space before the double yellow lines. I'd been lucky, with the threat of an autumnal rain shower prominent in the gunmetal sky, parents lined the narrow road almost an hour before their little darlings finished for the day. All so they wouldn't get wet.

Around 1,400 students attended, including those in sixth form, which meant the school run was notoriously busy. The building was situated on a no through road with a small roundabout at the end. The idea was that parents could drop off their children at the kerb, drive around the roundabout and easily leave without there being too much congestion. However, the limited number of spaces meant parents parked pretty much wherever they liked, and each drop-off and pick-up was chaos, especially when it was raining.

Normally, the twins walked home, sometimes together, sometimes with their friends. It took them around twenty-five minutes up a long hill towards our house, and being in their last year of high school, they both had a key to let themselves in. Jonathan and I worked full-time, although I was able to drop them off on the way to work. Meaning I could guarantee they weren't late for school, but it was a nice surprise for them to be picked up.

Something positive to come out of a shitty Wednesday and I needed to build bridges with both of them. To try to repair the cracks left by Jonathan leaving, something they blamed me for, although I had no idea why. I'd sent a text to let them know I was outside, but I wouldn't get a response yet; they weren't supposed to have their phones switched on during school hours.

I stared out of the window, shivering. The coffee stain on my blouse was yet to dry, the material now cold and damp, spreading through my skin and chilling the blood in my veins. My chest was still an angry red, throbbing as if to remind me of my humiliating day. I didn't bother to turn on the engine, the heater of my Skoda was rubbish when the car wasn't in motion, blowing tepid air would only add to my discomfort. Not even my resentment about the missed promotion could keep me warm.

Damn Tim and his eager-to-please personality. Liam had been selected by the upper management team and my boss was hardly going to argue my case. What the hell was a fast-track promotion anyway, it wasn't a scheme I'd ever heard mentioned in any of the HR meetings. They just made it up as they went along. Conspiring against anyone with breasts, that was how it felt. It hadn't been easy for me to gain the trust of the employees, the drivers and warehouse operatives. Even the office-based men had been a challenge, so ingrained was the chauvinism. The amount of casual sexism, Freudian slips and disparaging remarks I'd endured over the years. Not letting it chip away at me, brushing it off, as Tim suggested. It was clear from the start it was a put-up-or-ship-out situation. So, I put up with it, ignored them and rose above it. Until today.

Not getting the promotion changed everything. I couldn't stomach grovelling to Tim for a raise which would no doubt be dismissed, especially after our exchange in the kitchen. I was on my own and had to deal with it.

Cars began to filter down the road, those hopeful they would get a space in the dedicated lines, driving away disappointed. Others already stopping on the double yellows, half on the kerb as though the rules didn't apply to them.

'There's another one,' I muttered to myself as a large grey F-Pace Jaguar passed, swinging in front of me and reversing back, too close to my car. I tutted and glared through the window into the dark tinted glass, hoping the driver would see my expression in their rear-view mirror, but they didn't move forward. Honestly, it was like the normal Highway Code didn't apply at pick-up and drop-off. It was every parent for themselves.

Hordes of school children in their purple uniforms poured from the school entrance. I craned my neck looking for Ryan or Rachel, they rarely came out together. Tall, long-limbed and athletic-looking, Ryan had light brown hair, whereas Rachel had highlighted hers blonde. They looked similar, both having my height and angular jaw, as well as Jonathan's high forehead and wide-set blue eyes.

I saw Ryan first, eyes down, scanning his phone. He walked right past the car. I hurried to open my door and clamber out.

'Ryan,' I called, but he didn't turn around.

'Ryan!' I shouted again, seeing the children around me snigger.

Ryan heard the second time and turned around, frowning when he saw me.

'What are you doing here?' he asked, striding towards me, brow furrowed.

'I thought I'd pick you both up, save you walking,' I replied, bewildered at his surliness.

'Dad's here, we're going back to his.'

I looked around for Jonathan's car, spying the Mazda further down the road. I watched as Rachel climbed in the passenger seat, the glare on the glass prevented me seeing inside. Why was he picking them up?

'What happened to you anyway? You look awful!' Ryan wrinkled his nose, his disdain obvious. A trait he'd inherited from his father.

I turned to look at my reflection in the Skoda window. Hair wild, mascara smudges on my face that I hadn't noticed. Not to mention the large brown smear down my top. Cheeks flushing red, I baulked. How had I not realised what a state I looked.

'Bad day at work,' I replied, but Ryan was already backing away.

'See you later, Mum. Dad's taking us to Nan's early for the weekend. I'll get him to ring you.' Then he turned and walked on.

'What? What about school?' I shouted after him, but he shrugged.

'It's Nan's seventieth, remember?'

I watched as he got in the back of the Mazda and Jonathan pulled away, passing me slowly. I recognised the sneer on his face, the look of victory, the game of one-upmanship we'd entered that I'd never wanted to be a part of. He always won. He wanted the children, and they were leaning towards living with him. Apparently he was more fun, more chilled, didn't moan and there was little push for chores or homework. Jonathan had become the cool dad. I barely recognised him any more but I couldn't deny the void he'd left behind in our family home.

With only me, there was no reason to keep the three-bedroomed house, better to sell and split the proceeds. I couldn't afford to live there alone, not without Jonathan paying the mortgage, and he wasn't coming back; he'd made that abundantly clear. He'd continued to pay it since leaving, but his generosity wouldn't last forever. In fact, I was sure he was twisting the twins against me, feeding them just enough information to form the opinion he wanted them to have. Painting himself as the victim in the break-down of our marriage when it couldn't have been further from the truth.

Rachel told me she knew I'd driven him out, but it was untrue: Jonathan had got up one morning in late March, packed a bag and left, telling me he no longer loved me. I'd sat in shock, staring out of the window all day, waiting for him to return. That was the end of our eighteen-year marriage, over in a couple of sentences, no discussion. I'd been the one to make excuses for him to the kids as I fought to patch things back together. Finding out he'd rented a flat less than a mile away. Sure it wouldn't be long before he moved in a younger model. Perhaps it was a midlife crisis, and he'd start driving around in a two-seater sports car.

A horn beeped as I opened my door to get back in, the anger in my stomach bubbling away again. I bit the inside of my cheek, as the text from Jonathan came through.

Taking twins to Mum's for the weekend, 70th birthday on Friday. I did tell you! You must have forgotten. Squared it with the school.

His mum, June, lived in an enormous barn conversion in Suffolk, and despite it being cold, the twins would enjoy being by the coast. Jonathan's dad had died in an accident at work years ago when we first moved in together. He'd worked in a large warehouse, moving stock around by forklift when a large load had got loose and fallen on top of him. He'd died from internal bleeding before the ambulance got him to the hospital. June received an enormous payout from the company and bought the barn in Suffolk to be nearer her sister.

I hadn't seen June for months, not since last Christmas when we'd visited as a family over the festivities. I was hurt by her lack of contact after she'd found out Jonathan and I were no longer together; I'd been her daughter-in-law for eighteen years, but that didn't seem to matter. Both of us had stepped up when Jonathan's dad died, gave her support and comfort, helped sort out the finances. All that had been forgotten because Jonathan was her blue-eyed boy, and he could do no wrong. If he didn't want me in his life, then she didn't want me in hers.

I was sure he hadn't told me he was taking the twins to visit her. I would have remembered it, although I had forgotten it was June's seventieth birthday. I doubted he'd 'squared' the absence with the school though. He'd probably sent an email informing the office they wouldn't be in for whatever reason. The twins were in their GCSE year, any removal from their classes was frowned upon, even one day for a jolly in Suffolk, let alone two. I was the only one doing any parenting now, an easy target to be the bad guy to the twins.

My phone chimed again with another message from Jonathan.

Enjoy your dinner for one 😊

My fingers tingled, pulses firing beneath my skin. That smug bastard.

3

I threw the car into reverse, trying to fight the urge to scream, as the lights of the Jaguar in front of me sprang to life. I'd seen a tall honey-blonde pupil, similar age to the twins, climb into the car and knew it would be pulling out shortly. Indicating for a second, I swung the Skoda out into the slow-moving procession towards the roundabout, heat radiating through my pores.

Jonathan had to goad me, he enjoyed it, provoking a reaction. He was lucky he'd stayed in the car, otherwise I would have given him a mouthful. We were supposed to coordinate the twins together: what they were doing, who was picking up who and where. They were teenagers but not yet adults. It was like my opinion no longer mattered; I'd be informed when they'd decided what they wanted between them and their dad.

My fingers gripped the steering wheel, knuckles white. Blood pressure shot up, the skin blotchy at my neck. I ground my teeth, a volcano ready to erupt. After what happened at work, I was close to losing it. Irritation gushed through my veins as I recalled the jibes that nudged me towards the edge.

'Don't worry about Kay, she's a little hormonal sometimes.' The words rang out in my head, followed by a cacophony of sniggering. Jonathan's condescending '*enjoy your dinner for one.*' Then Tim's patronising tone, fake sympathy radiating off him, '*I know this isn't the outcome you were hoping for...*' The voices repeated themselves on loop inside my brain until I could no longer stand it and I turned the radio on to drown out the taunts.

Screw them. Screw them all. The kids had deserted me in favour of their dad, and I needed company, someone to offload onto. I was going to drive to the off-licence, grab a couple of bottles of wine and call Claire, invite her round for dinner. She was my best mate; we could put the world to rights over a couple of glasses and I'd be ready to fight another day tomorrow.

Despite my plan, the swirl of annoyance lingered, unwilling to disperse as I queued around the roundabout and back towards the main road. There was a sea of purple uniforms milling about, their breath tiny wisps in the air, but my children had gone. My car was empty. There was no point to my journey to the school – what a waste of time. My resentment simmered, like a pot ready to boil. It had nowhere to go, no way to expend it and I stewed in its heat.

After a few minutes, I was out of the school queue and on my way home. It was always slow-going at those times of the day, so many cars on the road. Everyone in a hurry. No one had any patience. I indicated left at the junction where mine and Jonathan's favourite local pub, The Hillside, was situated. Back when things were good, we ate there every other weekend, but I hadn't been there in months. I carried on past; the detour to the off-licence would only take five minutes. There was no need to rush, I was going home to an empty house.

Traffic lights ahead switched to red, and I waited, mine the first car in the left-hand lane. I hated getting caught by the lights as two lanes went into one almost immediately afterwards and there was always some dickhead who thought he had the right to jump the queue. It irked me no end.

To my right, a Mini Cooper's engine purred. I could already tell it was going to be quick to accelerate. I blew out a long breath and made my peace that it would go ahead. As the lights turned amber, the driver of the Mini sped forwards.

I put my foot down so as not to leave a large gap when a grey Jaguar flew past, a man at the wheel. The girl I'd seen outside the school sat in the passenger seat; her phone glued to her ear. It was the car that had parked in front of me earlier, the one that had reversed too close.

Inches from my bumper, the Jaguar ran out of road and had to swing in front tightly. I slammed on the brakes, heart in my mouth. They'd almost hit my car!

'Arsehole!' I shouted out of the window and flashed my lights.

The driver of the Jag ignored me. I imagined him laughing, the young girl tossing back her golden hair, beaming at how fast her daddy's car was.

The vein in my temple throbbed, irrational hatred towards the man in front consumed me. Fired stoked in my gut, flames rising. What right did he have to drive like that? How dare he cut me up, all because he had a larger car, a newer, better, more expensive one?

I put my foot on the accelerator, driving as close to him as I safely could. Glaring through the windscreen, eyes locked on, my death stare. Hoping he would see, hoping he could feel the rage pulsating from me.

Wine now forgotten, I ignored the turning for the road where the off-licence was and tailed the Jag instead, realising I'd seen the car before. The owner lived on Dene Hill, a house directly facing the entrance to the road where I lived.

It was a quiet part of town, the local shop at least a ten-minute walk away. A central parish church sat on top of Dene Hill, surrounded by lots of small cul-de-sacs. It had a real community feel. There wasn't a lot of through traffic, so you only came this way if you lived here or were visiting. Non-residents sometimes likened the area to a maze, because each road was lined with similar three- and four-bedroom homes, built with a Georgian feel to them. Every house had leaded windows, the larger ones were double-fronted, painted white or cream, with well-kept lawns and paved driveways.

Over the past year, I'd watched as the owner of the Jag bought and renovated the house after it went up for sale. I'd driven by most days and seen the man and his daughter occasionally. The house was beautiful, double-fronted and now painted a crisp white. An archway with pillars had been built over the entrance. Large navy UPVC windows matched the composite door. It was a massive improvement on what it looked like before.

Jonathan and I had watched with interest, admiring the alterations and seeing the workmen come and go. Commenting when something new had been added. Then we saw a company outside tarmacking the drive. We couldn't believe it. A stunningly renovated house, large automatic wooden gates installed, and the owner had tarmacked the drive. We assumed he'd run out of budget, unable to understand why he'd neglected to lay a bricked or resin driveway to complement the facelift. We'd lost interest after that, the show home we'd coveted had become a disappointment.

Still, I saw the owner sometimes, usually in the morning on the school run. He drove like he owned the road, refusing to wait for oncoming traffic down the hill despite them having right of way. Today he'd picked the wrong day – and the wrong person. I followed him up the hill, watching as he indicated at the last minute and pulled into the open gates on his driveway. I stopped abruptly across the entrance to the drive and leapt out of the car with no idea what I was going to do.

'Where the hell do you get off driving like that. You almost hit my car!' I shouted at the man climbing out of the Jaguar.

He frowned in surprise at first, then appeared mildly amused as he took me in. I no longer cared about my appearance, whether I looked a mess with my make-up smudged and stained blouse.

'Excuse me?' he said politely, lip curling up at the side.

I wanted to slap the smile off his face. He was tall, well-kempt, with slicked-back salt-and-pepper hair and a healthy glow that in October could only be fake tan or the result of an early autumn holiday in the sun. Good-looking but he knew it, in his navy blazer and light blue shirt. He pulled at the sleeve, twisting a cufflink as he looked me up and down.

His daughter got out, nose wrinkling at my presence, staring at me as though I was a circus freak.

I balled my hands into fists, not in control as the words flew out. 'You cut me up at the lights, driving like a dickhead in your big fancy car. You don't own the road, you know.'

'Okay, okay. I apologise if I cut you up, although I don't remember doing so.' He sighed, turning to his daughter. 'Ava, go inside would you.'

She sloped away. He turned back to look at me, eyes narrowed, able to speak freely without his daughter overhearing.

'Look, I can't help it if you don't know the rules of the road. If that's the case perhaps you shouldn't be driving.' His voice was light, non-threatening.

I could tell he was enjoying the confrontation, the chance to belittle me. I opened my mouth to speak, but nothing came out. I was so incensed my brain wouldn't focus. Instead, I just stood there, pushing my nails into the flesh of my palm.

'Are we done?' he asked, eyebrows raised, a smirk on his lips.

'How dare you!' I managed, but it sounded weak.

He merely shook his head and laughed. 'Get off my driveway,

you silly woman, before I remove you myself,' he said, before turning back to the house, leaving me ranting wordlessly to his back.

My eyes blazed with rage, he'd dismissed me, made me feel foolish. Called me a 'silly woman'. How dare he speak to me like that. What was it with men? What made them feel they had the right to talk down to me, as if I was inferior? As if I was nothing but an irritating stone in their shoe, or bug on their windscreen. I had a voice and demanded it be heard.

I climbed back in my car, electrified, panting like an overheated dog. I wanted to rip his condescending face off. It wasn't over. He was going to learn some manners and I was going to be the one to teach him.

4

Five minutes later, off-licence forgotten, I was in the house, pacing the kitchen. Adrenaline surged as my mind ran through all the things I should have said. Not remotely helpful now. He was a condescending flash bastard, rolling in cash and thinking he was the top of the food chain. Treating the rest of us like peasants.

They were *all* bastards, the lot of them. How many times would I allow myself to be treated like something scraped off someone's shoe?

A nerve snapped inside me, and I dashed upstairs, ripping off my blouse, buttons flying in all directions. I stared at my reflection in the full-length mirror. A version of Medusa looked back, dishevelled hair, crazed eyes. Unhinged.

I no longer recognised myself, turning away, repulsed. Removing my wide-legged trousers, I threw on a pair of leggings and a sweatshirt, carefully dabbing my chest with some antiseptic cream. The skin stinging.

Once dressed, I texted Claire.

Shit day! Dinner and vino tonight? Please say yes…

I waited for the usual swift response and wasn't disappointed. Claire worked for a recruitment agency and her phone, which she used for both work and personal, was glued to her permanently.

Yes! Wednesday night though, so not too heavy. Be over at six. I'll bring the wine. x

That was usually the way: I'd cook for Claire and she'd bring the wine. Claire lived alone and never bothered to cook for herself. She lived on microwave meals for one from Marks and Spencer and was always grateful for the offer of a home-cooked meal. Tonight, it would have to be stir-fry, I had zero motivation for anything else.

Great, see you then. x

It was almost half past three, so I had a few hours to fill. I set about giving the house a general tidy, pushing the hoover around and disinfecting the toilets. I had to go through the mortgage statements for the house but had been putting it off, knowing there was no way I could make the maths work, not without the promotion. I was too angry to deal with being forced to give up our home.

Jonathan had told me I wouldn't be able to afford it by myself and I'd have to sell. Insisting he wouldn't be able to pay the mortgage on the house and the rental of his flat for much longer. I had been determined to prove him wrong, that I would be able to manage, so it was a blow to admit defeat.

I'd sought advice, but without initiating divorce proceedings, there wasn't much I could do. If I dug my heels in, he would have to get an order of sale from the court to sell the house as it was jointly mine. It would cost me money I didn't have in legal fees to fight him and what would be the point if I couldn't afford to live here anyway. Not getting the promotion had ruined everything.

I had a contract to go through for work, which was what I had intended to do in the office this afternoon – going through the terms and conditions between Winston's and our auto-parts supplier, Allegra, as the contract was up for renewal. They had made a few suggestions to the document, mainly on the second-ment of some staff to work out of the Birmingham hub for the short term. However, I had no intention of touching that today. They could sing for it.

Instead, I put my AirPods in and played some classic Aerosmith at full volume and wheeled the hoover around like it was a weapon. It helped expend the energy and the rage lodged inside for the past couple of hours, releasing it like a pin to a balloon. The altercation with Jaguar man had left me frustrated, not satiated. It hadn't been as liberating as I thought to speak up. If anything, it – or rather he – had wound me up more. It churned in my stomach like something I couldn't digest, so I tried to keep myself busy, distracted.

I lingered in each of the twin's bedrooms, picking up discarded, barely worn clothes and hanging them back in their wardrobes. Arranging books tossed onto the floor and pushing open windows to air their rooms. It was as though a switch was flicked, upon turning into teenagers. Boys' bedrooms became smelly and musty overnight, whereas girls' bedrooms stank of cheap perfume, sprayed relentlessly. Make-up was spread over every surface, like a bomb had gone off at the Rimmel stand in Boots.

I sat on Rachel's bed, touching the soft cotton covers, baby pink patterned with large winking eyelashes. How had it come to this? They were out more than they were home and now with Jonathan renting his new place, it was only going to get worse. He could do no wrong in their eyes and I cringed when I thought of the lies I was sure he'd spun them.

The truth will out, my mum used to say when she was alive, and I hoped she was right. I didn't want to be the one to tell them their dad was a lying shitbag. I was trying to avoid bad-mouthing him at all. Being the better person and showing them maturity, but it seemed to do me little favours.

Jonathan didn't want to go through the courts for mediation, said it was pointless paying solicitors hundreds or even thousands of pounds for things we could decide ourselves amicably. He liked to remind me that *he* wasn't insisting on custody of the twins and that we'd both have equal amounts of time, but he would prefer to leave it up to them to decide who they wanted to live with permanently. Currently he only had a two-bed flat and had to sleep on a double sofa bed in the lounge when the kids came to stay. I could already tell all of them were getting weary with that set-up but despite the squeeze they still preferred his company to mine.

Getting up, I switched songs when Aerosmith's 'Don't Wanna Miss a Thing' came on. I didn't want to listen to any ballads; I had to hold on to my anger, because without it, I had nothing left.

I finished cleaning and at half past five I chopped vegetables in preparation for the stir-fry, defrosting what I had already frozen. Rummaging around in the cupboard, I discovered noodles and soy sauce and even found Quorn pieces at the back of the freezer. Claire was a vegetarian, and ate spinach with everything, like Popeye, throwing handfuls of it onto her plate alongside every meal she microwaved.

When Claire arrived, bang on six, she clutched a bottle of chilled Chardonnay and a packet of cigarettes in one hand, a bunch of keys and trademark bag of spinach in the other.

'I have arrived!' she announced, brandishing her goods as she crossed the threshold.

Claire had been my best friend since high school – the same school the twins now attended. We'd stayed in Crawley, both of us working at Gatwick in our twenties, flight attendants and check-in staff, revelling in the booming airport town. Our careers had taken a different direction after that. I'd decided to move into human resources, and she'd wanted to try recruitment.

Claire could sell ice to Eskimos; she was funny, charming and still a knockout in her forties. Full lips and a button nose, her hair dyed jet black in contrast to my highlights. We were polar opposites: she was petite, and I was tall, she was skinny and angular whereas I'd become more rounder, softer, since having the twins.

'Thank God you're here. What a shit day!' I said, rolling my eyes and closing the door after her.

She strode right through to the kitchen, dumping everything on the table and immediately opening the wine. We were so used to the routine, we did it wordlessly. I grabbed two glasses, she poured and then unwrapped the cellophane of the cigarettes.

'Are the kids here, as it sounds like you might need one of these as well?' she said, taking two from the packet and looking over her shoulder as if expecting to see Rachel or Ryan any second.

'No, they're with Jonathan,' I replied, rolling my eyes and opening the back door.

We stood outside, shivering in the afternoon chill as we smoked, both of us pulling a face at the first drag as we always did. Always questioning why we did it. Whenever we were together, and we'd had a drink, we'd always smoke but rarely separately. It was part of our ritual.

I told Claire about the promotion awarded to Liam, Tim's limp apology and how I was scared I'd have to sell the house.

'It's the kids' home, the one they've grown up in. I don't want to sell it, but I can't afford to buy Jonathan out,' I moaned.

Claire sucked on her cigarette, a stream of smoke escaping from her nose.

'Maybe you can get a lodger?'

'Not without declaring it as a sublet and I think that makes the mortgage even more difficult to get.'

'You don't have to declare everything, Kay. I know you're as straight as a die, but you don't need to play by the rules all the time, you know. No one does!' she admonished.

It was true, I always did everything I was supposed to: I paid bills on time, parked only where I was allowed, stayed within the speed limit. Claire always teased me that I was the angel to her devil.

'I know. It's not done me much good, has it? Everything is a mess and it's all down to men.'

'Is Jonathan still being a dick?' Claire asked.

I nodded, flicking my ash onto the patio, and watching it get whisked away. 'Yep, he's taken the kids to his mum's today for the weekend, no notice, no warning. Then sent me a text saying "enjoy your dinner for one." Tosser.' I watched Claire's mouth gape.

'Jesus, there's no need for that. What a shithead.'

We extinguished our cigarettes and went back inside. Claire sat at the table and watched me move around the kitchen, pulling out the wok and sesame oil.

'Then on the way home, I had a go at a guy who cut me up at the lights and he patronised me like I was some idiot, told me I was a silly woman!'

'So many men think they own the road,' Claire said, taking a large gulp of her wine.

'I know. I was livid. I still am.'

Two glasses later and the wine was already running low. I'd cooked the stir-fry which Claire devoured, but I pushed mine around my plate, eating only the noodles.

'You should have slashed Jaguar man's tyres.' Claire laughed as our conversation fell back to him. We'd already verbally annihilated flighty Jonathan and gutless Tim.

'Maybe I should have. What an arse.'

We didn't mean it; it was just talk, but the idea fizzed in my mind. Something so out of character for me but that would make me smile every time I drove past, instead of reminding me how he'd made me feel. Small, stupid and insignificant.

5

Claire left around eight, the bottle of wine chucked in the recycling bin on the way out. She had a date tomorrow night; someone she'd been chatting to on the dating app Hinge was taking her for a drink. We planned to meet on Saturday, so she could fill me in. Normally, on a weekend, if she was free, we went for a hike and had lunch afterwards. Without the kids at home, it would be quiet, and she knew I'd be rattling around.

I couldn't deny I was disappointed they were away. I'd hoped to spend some time with them, perhaps take them out somewhere, but they were at that age where they wanted to spend most of their time with their friends and not their mum. I couldn't compete however keen I was to build bridges between us.

I crawled into bed at ten, after clearing the kitchen, and sent a goodnight text to the twins before scrolling through Facebook. I froze when Jonathan's name came up, my thumb lingering over the screen. He'd posted a photo of him and the kids out for dinner. Each had an enormous sundae in front of them and were smiling for the camera. Rachel, I could see, was a second away from rolling her eyes. She hated having her photo taken.

My stomach hardened at the perfect family shot – the only one missing was me. We'd never have that again. Jonathan had made it so and even though I'd accepted he no longer loved me, I missed the connection we used to have. The bond over the shared parenting of the twins. We were a team, the four of us, and now I was out in the cold.

He swore there was no one else, but I didn't believe it. How could there not be? Someone was taking the photo. Was I so awful he couldn't bear to be with me any more, live under the same roof, sleep in the same bed? Without Claire for support, I would have fallen into a pit of wallowing. I knew I was drinking too much as it was, but life was so bloody hard at times.

I put my phone on the bedside table and closed my eyes, wishing for sleep, to fall into blissful unconsciousness. The only time I didn't feel like I wasn't enough.

The alarm was a rude awakening, having tossed and turned all night, stewing on the job, the failure of my marriage and the run-in with Jaguar man. My thoughts had been consumed by fantastical ideas of tyre slashing, public shaming and verbal annihilation of Jonathan, Tim and Jaguar man altogether. I was anything but refreshed, but for once I felt determined. From now on, I'd be different, fight my corner and stand up for myself. Starting with my job at Winston's.

When I arrived shortly before nine, Liam was in his office, next to mine, tapping away at his keyboard. He smiled and waved in greeting and I raised a hand back, forcing a smile. As soon as I logged on, I opened our intranet site and searched for Liam Shepherds. The paged loaded and his photo filled the screen. I glanced through the glass partition, but Liam was still typing, focused on his screen and oblivious to my investigation.

He looked even younger in his profile picture, barely out of university and I saw the page hadn't yet been updated to reflect his new role. Before taking my promotion, he was a Sales Manager looking after Retail at Tunbridge Wells. Seemed an odd jump into Human Resources Management. Earmarked for fast-track, wasn't that what Tim said? Perhaps he was related to someone high up.

'Morning.' As if by magic, Tim appeared at my door, his booming voice made me jump and I scowled, quickly closing the intranet site. He hovered over the threshold like a vampire waiting to be invited in. 'About yesterday...' he began, but I cut him off.

'It's fine, Tim, I understand,' I said brusquely, and his shoulders seemed to loosen. I didn't wait to let him speak. 'I appreciate my options here are...' I paused for effect, 'limited. I'll start looking around for other opportunities.' My voice was clipped, and I watched Tim's mouth twitch at the corner.

'Kay, we don't want to lose you, you know that. You're excellent at what you do.' He lowered his voice to a whisper, grimacing. 'As I said, it was out of my hands.'

'I'll get the Allegra contract over to you today,' I said, changing the subject.

Tim cleared his throat awkwardly.

'Well, actually, Liam will be signing it.'

My jaw clenched; he had the authority to sign contracts now?

'Fine, I'll give it to him when I'm done.'

'Brilliant, appreciate it.'

Tim backed away and shuffled towards Liam's door. I could hear the mumbling of voices but nothing distinct. God, he was so spineless. Irritation radiated off me and I had to stop myself grinding my teeth. I'd done it so much lately, they'd be down to the bone before long.

By lunchtime, my eyes had gone square. I'd been concentrating so hard on fine-tuning the contract for the auto parts supplier I was worried I'd have a permanent squint. I braved the cold for a walk around the car park with a hot chocolate from the machine to keep my hands warm. It was good to stretch my legs and roll the hunched shoulders away.

I finished the contract at three, content I'd done a good job. Steeling myself to be polite, I knocked on Liam's door. He glanced up and beckoned me in, a genuine smile spreading across his freckled face.

'Hey,' he said, like we were bumping into each other at a barbeque.

'I've finished the Allegra contract, it's ready for your signature. I've emailed you the soft copy as well.' I handed the papers to him stiffly, but he didn't seem to notice.

'Brilliant, thank you. There's a call with them tonight, seven o'clock, would you believe, they have American investors and want them to attend.'

I rolled my eyes; it wasn't unusual. He had better get used to it, nine to five didn't exist at this company – it hadn't for me anyway. The silence stretched out between us, and I turned to leave.

'Kay, I couldn't trouble you to jump on the call, could I? If I send you the invite? Just in case there's any contract-related questions.'

I swung back around, ready to tell him I was unavailable, but he looked so earnest, I relented. It wasn't as if I had any plans anyway.

'Sure.' I sighed, leaving the office while he was still thanking me.

After spending the rest of the afternoon perusing recruitment websites, trying to find another job, I shut down at five o'clock, deflated. There didn't seem to be a lot out there as far as HR was concerned. No positions jumped off the page and it dawned on me I may be in for a hunt.

Heading to my car, I dialled Ryan, then Rachel – both phones went to voicemail. The tension in my chest spreading, I tried Jonathan. He picked up on the first ring.

'Hello,' he said abruptly.

'Hi, it's me. I just wanted to check in on the twins. Are they okay?' I kept my voice light, friendly, and he matched it.

'Yeah, sure they're fine. We've been indoor rock climbing this afternoon, they've loved it.'

'That sounds fun. Are they around?'

'They've taken Boris out for a walk. I'll get them to call you when they're back.' Boris was Jonathan's Mum's ancient border terrier who was blind in one eye. The twins adored him.

'Great, thanks,' I said, but Jonathan had already hung up.

Him cutting me off aggravated me, but I didn't let it linger. I'd hate it if he called every five minutes to see what the twins were doing during the week when they were with me. I missed them, was all. The house was too quiet, too big, without them creating noise and mess as they seemed to do effortlessly.

I drove home, a hollow void in my gut that had little to do with hunger. There was nothing to rush for, no one was there waiting for me. It was time to stop burying my head in the sand. I should use the free time to sort out the finances, work out exactly how much I needed to earn to run a house by myself and search for a job that would pay a salary to match it.

Feeling empowered, I approached Jaguar man's house, it coming into view on my left before the turning into my road. His wooden gates were wide open again and his car was nowhere to be seen. Unconsciously, I slowed the car to a stop, gazing at the ugly tarmac, a massive contrast to the attractive entrance where topiary balls hung either side of the door.

A car behind me sounded its horn and I flinched, trying to manoeuvre forward but stalling in my haste. In the rear-view mirror, I saw the large grey bonnet, the car's indicator flashing, trying to turn into the driveway I was blocking.

'Shit,' I muttered and turned the key, relieved when the engine sprang to life and jerked forward.

'You really are nuts, aren't you,' Jaguar man shouted out of his window as he turned left onto his driveway. He gave me a condescending shake of the head as he went, his voice in my head – '*you silly woman*' – and my insides blistered.

6

I arrived home moments later, vision cloudy from tears. The emboldened attitude from minutes before had given way to frustration, which clung to my skin, making me itch. Why hadn't I said anything? Why hadn't I told him to fuck off?

Slamming the car door, I marched into the house, heading straight for the kitchen without bothering to take my shoes off. I had no wine, but I did have vodka – not that I liked it much. It was old, cheap, won in a raffle at work, but I didn't want to go out again and needs must.

The burn of the liquid down my throat took my breath away. It was Thursday night, everyone drank on a Thursday, didn't they? Start-up drinks for the weekend.

I helped myself to another shot, just to take the edge off, wincing as I swallowed. Looking towards the fridge as I contemplated what to have for dinner. *Dinner for one* as Jonathan had sneered yesterday. I had a leftover lasagne I could reheat. It would do, although, in truth, I was too het up to eat anything.

The phone rang as I was getting changed, putting on my comfy leggings, glad to be out of the tailored trousers.

'Hi, Mum,' Rachel said, sounding upbeat. I melted into a puddle of relief hearing her voice.

'Hi, sweetheart, you enjoying your time with your dad?'

'Yeah, it's good, we went rock climbing, it was awesome. We're streaming a movie and ordering pizza tonight.'

'Lucky you! Your nan okay?'

'She's fine, we've just taken Boris out, but now it's raining.'

'Oh, it's just drizzle here, cold though. Have you got enough clothes?'

'We packed a few bits and brought them to school with us,' Rachel's voice was a little shrill. I wouldn't be surprised if Jonathan had told them to do that. I honestly couldn't remember him running the weekend by me.

'I've got to go, here's Ryan. See you Sunday.' With that, she was gone.

'Hiya,' Ryan came on the phone.

'Hello, love, you having a nice time too?'

'Yeah, it's okay, no Xbox though,' Ryan complained. Although he looked athletic he was anything but since the console had come along.

'It'll still be here when you get back. Dad dropping you off Sunday?'

'Yep.' Ryan was mostly monosyllabic, but that was nothing new.

I could hear talking in the background. Jonathan calling out to someone. I struggled to make out the name, Marie perhaps. There was a muffling on the line as though someone was shielding the phone.

'Okay, well I miss you both, I'll see you Sunday. Be good. Love you,' I said, my voice already betraying me.

'Bye, Mum.' Then Ryan was gone too, the phone line dead.

I sat on the bed, in my leggings and bra, blinking back tears as I threw the phone to the floor. That bastard was getting them to lie for him. He had another woman there, at his mother's house, with my children. I bet he thought it was hilarious, laughing because it was so easy to pull the wool over his wife's eyes.

Picking the phone up again, I considered texting him, but what would be the point? He always used it against me, words or texts said in anger. I was neurotic apparently; he had the messages to prove it. Instead, I returned to the kitchen, poured myself a vodka, adding some orange juice this time, and put the lasagne in the oven to reheat. I texted Claire whilst I remembered, to wish her luck for her date.

She'd been single on and off for years, having never met 'the one'. Although she didn't seem bothered and most of the relationships she'd had ended because she missed her freedom. Having children wasn't a priority for her and although I wouldn't have changed having mine for the world, I envied her deviation from what was society's norm.

I had to take a leaf out of her book and be responsible for my own happiness, not having it depend on a man or my children. It wouldn't be long before they'd fly the nest, go to university or abroad to travel. I had to get used to being on my own.

My plan tonight was to stay in and get blotto, perhaps watch a movie, if I could see straight, and fall into bed when I couldn't. I wished I had nothing to get up for and the weekend would hurry up and arrive.

I only managed half the lasagne and threw the rest away. The few vodkas had made me fuzzy, blurred around the edges, and I was toying with the idea of paying Jaguar man a visit under the cover of darkness. The idea excited me, perhaps I could leave a present on his doorstep, some dog shit I collected on the way there. I sniggered to myself as I looked out of my window onto the road outside.

The temperature had dropped, but it was no longer raining, frost already on the windscreens of parked cars, glistening under the orange glow of lamp posts. They'd been on for a while; the autumn sun had set a while ago, making way for the long expanse of night. A stroll would do me good, some fresh air before I settled in for the night. It might sober me up.

I could just walk past, see if Jaguar man was home. Do a stake-out, like they did on television. I chuckled to myself as I slipped on my trainers, hearing my phone chime from the sofa.

A notification popped up from the Teams app, reminding me I was due to attend a call with our supplier, Allegra, and Liam in fifteen minutes.

Shit! I'd forgotten all about it. That screwed up my plans. I wouldn't have had a drink if I'd remembered, but it wasn't as if they were a client, Allegra was a supplier, so it wasn't a big deal. Liam had said he probably wouldn't need me anyway. Surely I could blow it off? Let him struggle on his own. My eyes shone with glee. *Sink or swim, my friend, and don't worry, I'll be there to swoop in and take your spot as soon as everyone realises you're out of your depth.*

I grabbed my house keys and spotted my AirPods on the side, still in their charging case. It occurred to me, with my phone and the Teams app, I could attend the meeting from anywhere. As long as I had an internet connection I could dial in. My phone had 4G and they'd never know I wasn't at home. It wasn't likely I'd have to say much either. In fact, it gave me the perfect alibi. I giggled darkly.

Pushing the AirPods into my ears, I connected them to my phone and left the house, pocketing my keys and raising the hood over my head. I looked like I was going for an evening run – dark leggings, black hoody and trainers. It wasn't late enough to be considered dodgy, skulking around, it was only just coming up to seven o'clock. However, under the veil of darkness, it could have been much later.

Outside was freezing, the air damp. I hadn't put on enough

layers and considered a jog to keep warm, but there was no way I could, not with the vodka swishing around my stomach. Instead, I opted for a brisk walk and found myself at the end of the road as I needed to dial in to the meeting. Dene Hill was empty, bar one dog walker going in the opposite direction down the hill towards the school. I took a right, ignoring Jaguar Man's house directly opposite, and joined the call to hear Liam's chirpy voice.

'Hi, Damien, Liam Shepherds, the new Human Resources Manager here, we're yet to meet. How are you doing?'

'Good to meet you, Liam. I'm fine thanks. On the call we also have Paul Holmes, our Contract Manager, and Lisa Burt from the US office.'

'Nice to meet you all. I believe Kay Massingham has joined us too,' Liam said, introducing me.

I stumbled up the kerb and quickly unmuted myself.

'Good evening, Kay Massingham here, Contract Manager for Winston's,' I said clearly, ensuring I didn't slur before muting myself again. The fresh air had amplified the few vodkas and I became light-headed.

I kept walking, intending to do a loop around the block and back up the hill as I listened to Liam talk about the supplier agreement between Winston's and Allegra. Moving to discuss the secondment of some of their staff to work out of the Birmingham hub for a couple of months. It was the reason he was heading up the call.

A couple of cars passed – a taxi full of teenagers going into town and a lone woman in a Nissan Micra. No one batted an eyelid at me as I strolled along, shivering and wishing I'd brought a coat.

'Kay, can you step in on that one?' Liam prompted when asked a question relating to the contract he'd signed and forwarded to Damien earlier that day.

I unmuted myself again and the words spilled off my tongue

easily, too easily, as though the alcohol had lubricated my lips. I apologised for rambling, glad no one could see my rosy cheeks.

The conversation turned to Lisa, who had some questions for Liam as I found myself at the bottom of the hill.

As I climbed, Jaguar Man's house came into focus on my left, the electric wooden gates wide open. Why didn't he close them? Perhaps so he could show off his swanky house and car to passers-by. The house was set back around twenty-five feet from the gates and the driveway was wide, easily enough space for four cars to park, however I only ever saw the one – his flashy jag. Maybe he lived alone with his daughter. I'd never seen a woman there, although I assumed he had been married once.

I moved closer, amber lights glowed from the ground-floor windows, but I detected no movement. Upstairs was dark and I imagined him and his daughter watching television together. Was the lounge at the back or the front of the house? I had no idea. Scanning the exterior, I saw a security camera positioned on the left of the furthest window, towards the edge of the building, pointing towards the arched entrance, but I had no clue as to the scope it would pick up.

The Jaguar was facing forward, untouched from when he'd driven in earlier. His flippant comment, '*You really are nuts, aren't you,*' grated in my ears.

Liam's voice faded into the distance, sounding like he was underwater as I removed one of the AirPods and focused on the plan. It was risky, but Jaguar Man's jibes spurred me on. I wanted to hurt him, hurt his pride as he'd wounded mine, and his car seemed like a great place to start.

My pulse spiked as I eased my keys out of my pocket and, keeping low, crept onto the tarmac, shielded from view of the house and hopefully the camera by the car. Looking around, I couldn't see or hear anyone approaching, but it was a quiet road, so not unusual. I crouched, my heart pumping like it was going to explode from my chest. At the same time, despite the tremble in my hands, a bolt of exhilaration hit me. Was I actually going to do this?

He deserved it. Jaguar Man needed to learn how to speak to women and stop being an arse. Hopefully it would make him think before driving around in his expensive car like he owned the road, the rest of us peasants moving aside for him. I was incensed by the injustice of being one of the little people, trampled on by those who believed they were higher up in the food chain. What gave them the right to be so superior?

Every nerve ending in my body buzzed, humming with adrenaline as I took a moment to centre myself, the Texan drawl of Lisa's rambling in my right ear. It was one o'clock in the afternoon there, she had all day to kill. Liam would have to cut in soon, close her down, otherwise we'd be on the call all night.

Buoyed by the vodka streaming through my veins I made my decision. I wasn't going to take it lying down. I was going to take a stand and teach Jaguar Man a lesson.

Less than five minutes later I was home, out of breath, cheeks a hot pink. Glad I was on mute. Liam had finally interrupted Lisa and I could tell he was rounding up to finish the call. I put my key in the front door and rushed inside. Heart hammering in my chest, I was delirious.

I'd done it, I'd been bold and got my own back on a tosser who'd belittled me, not once but twice. I'd shown him.

'If there's nothing further, we'll bid you good day. Thanks very much for your time,' Liam said.

'Have a lovely evening,' I chipped in before the call ended, trying to steady my breathing as I slipped off my trainers.

After locking the door, I chucked my keys onto the window ledge in the hall and hurried upstairs to put my pyjamas on.

My muscles tingled with elation. I'd never done anything like that before. Never knowingly broken the law. I hadn't even so much as graffitied a park bench as a teenager. Claire had always teased me because I was so square. The sensation was strange, alien to me, but I couldn't stop giggling. I imagined him examining his car, seething about the damage. I threw my leggings and hoody into the washing basket and, still shivering, I pulled on fleece pyjamas and a dressing gown.

I needed a drink and came down to the kitchen for a vodka. Warmth spread through me with each sip as I visualised Jaguar Man's fury, his finger tracing the scratch running the length of his car. How much would it cost to repair? I hoped it would ruin his day, like he'd added to the misery of mine yesterday. Respect was a two-way street, if you wanted to get it, you had to give it.

Fizzing with the need to tell someone, I yearned to call Claire but didn't want to interrupt her date. It was something I should keep to myself anyway. Committing a crime, going out vandalising on a Thursday night was completely out of character. It was vigilantism of sorts, but Claire probably wouldn't believe me even if I told her.

After a couple more drinks, I snuggled into bed, watching reruns of *Sex and the City* on my tiny television. Carrie and Mr Big falling in and out of love again. The glow of contentment laid upon me like a warm blanket and I slept better than I had in ages. I'd experienced a new me, reborn in some strange way. I was empowered and, for the first time in a while, excited at the prospect of tomorrow.

* * *

The alarm sounded and I got up, groggily pulling on my dressing gown, a dull ache behind the eyes.

'Kids, get up, time for school,' I called out to the silent house before remembering I was alone. Sighing, I went downstairs to make some coffee, smiling as I sat at the table remembering my antics last night. Picturing Jaguar Man coming out of his house this morning to take his princess to school and having to drive his damaged car.

Underneath the surface, a niggling worry I might be discovered flitted through my mind. I pushed it away, no one saw my crime. No one knew what I'd done, including my best friend. She texted me as I rinsed my cup under the sink and placed it on the draining board.

Will ring you later. JW xx

I sniggered, knowing Claire's code. By JW she meant John Wayne, and by that I guessed she'd had a good night. I couldn't remember the last time I'd had sex, probably about nine months ago, despite Jonathan having only been gone for seven.

After a quick shower, I perused my wardrobe, eyes falling on a dress I hadn't worn for ages. I made the decision, if it would fit, I'd wear it.

Despite the few extra pounds I'd put on from drinking every night, it still looked good. I no longer cared about being taken seriously at Winston's. That ship had sailed. I wanted to dress for me, I wanted to dress like a woman, not a man. Why couldn't I wear what I wanted and still get ahead? Although, in truth, I knew my time at Winston's was coming to an end.

Traffic was heavy on the way to work. Jaguar Man's driveway lay empty, his car nowhere to be seen, although he could still be on his way back from the school run. I wasn't looking forward to running into him again, worried my act of vandalism would be written all over my guilty face. I didn't lie often; I was terrible at it, and everyone always saw straight through me.

In the cold light of day, I regretted what I'd done. What I'd lowered myself to. I had no idea why I'd thought it would make a difference, that Jaguar Man would suddenly change his ways because of a scratch in his paintwork. It was irrational. All I'd done was inconvenience him and dented his wallet. I hadn't changed the world for women's rights. My stomach churned with it as I drove, only subsiding when I reached the nearly full car park which was unusual so early.

Most of the staff appeared to be in the office already when I entered, it was a hive of activity. Liam was waiting for me, coming into my office before I'd even switched on my laptop.

'Thanks so much for last night, Kay. I'm really glad you came on the call.'

'No problem,' I replied, awarding him a tight smile.

'That Lisa went on, didn't she! They were happy with the revised contract and I've had it back signed already this morning.'

'That's great,' I said with as much enthusiasm as I could muster.

'You two playing nice?' Tim chortled from my office door.

I rolled my eyes at him, although he wasn't looking at me, instead listening to Liam singing my praises. It appeared to have been a good decision to join the call.

Liam was as eager as a puppy, he seemed nice, but wet behind the ears and I considered whether he'd be chewed up and spit out by Tim in the months to come. However, it appeared he'd fully enrolled in the boys' club as the two of them guffawed over Jeremy Clarkson's new show. My throat tightened as Tim slapped Liam's back heartily. I excused myself as quickly as I could.

'Got a date?' Tim leered as he stepped out of the doorway to let me pass, looking me up and down and winking at Liam. My throat tightened.

'Yes, with a cup of coffee!' I snapped, stalking past them.

In the kitchen, I found Ed stewing his teabag, dunking it in and out of his cup, stifling a yawn. His eyes widened when I came in.

'Nice dress, Kay. Christ we haven't seen those legs for a while. Heels too, check you out.'

'Oh, piss off, Ed, not you too,' I said with a chuckle. 'Tim's already commented!' Ed was harmless, one of the more likeable Winston's employees and I was always happy to banter with him.

Unlike the others, he knew where to draw the line, never saying anything smutty.

'Are you blushing?' he teased.

'No, it's a hot flush, I'm menopausal as well as hormonal, so beware,' I shot back with a smirk.

He held his hands up in surrender, a broad smile across his face.

'Here, I found this on the printer, think it's one of yours, was about to drop it round.' Ed handed me a bunch of papers from the worktop which looked to be the Allegra contract.

'Cheers, I think it's the new boy, Liam's, I'll give them to him.'

Ed finished his tea and left as I waited for the kettle to boil, perusing the contract which now had a signature on it – Liam's, as well as Damien's from Allegra. I frowned at some of the wording, parts I was sure I'd taken out when I looked over the contract.

I made a coffee and took the contract back to my desk, closing my office door so I could concentrate. Something wasn't right and I called up the soft copy of the contract I'd worked on yesterday. The signed one in my hand, Ed had found on the printer, wasn't the latest version, not the one I'd given to Liam. I sipped at the bitter coffee, the vodka fog still clouding my brain. Had I made a mistake? Sent the wrong one across? I checked the attachment on the email I'd sent to Liam. No, the error was his.

Turning the pages, I gasped as I read the stipulations I'd taken out of Allegra's proposed contract on the secondment of their staff. They'd wanted a confirmed six-month secondment, with all expenses paid, plus pension contributions and private medical healthcare as per our own employees. I'd removed those clauses. The secondment would likely run for three to four months as we were taking their workers on a freelance basis and as far as we were concerned their benefits should still be paid by Allegra.

Shit, Liam had signed the wrong one. Our hands were tied now in what we had to offer the staff, impacting greatly on the cost efficiency of the contract. I looked through the glass partition into his office and watched Liam stare intently at his screen. He'd fucked up, his first day on the job and he'd dropped a massive clanger. Should I go directly to Tim? Tell him what the golden boy had done, see if the powers that be would stand by him when they learned what it would cost them?

I rolled my shoulders back and stood from my desk. This was what I wanted after all. For Liam to slip up and show how out of his depth he was, I just wasn't expecting him to do it on his first day.

8

Liam glanced at me standing idly in my office, debating what to do. He smiled ruefully and my stomach plummeted. Who was I kidding? I might have got my own back on Jaguar Man in a vodka-fuelled act of petty vengeance, but I wasn't ruthless enough to destroy Liam's budding career. Deep down, I knew I couldn't throw him under the bus. I didn't have it in me, despite the fact he had the job I was promised.

'Liam, have you got a minute,' I said loudly, beckoning him in.

Without hesitating, he jumped out of his seat and rushed around to my office with the bounce of a springer spaniel.

'What's up,' he said, taking a seat the other side of my desk, legs spread wide as I lowered back into mine.

'I found this on the printer, it's the signed Allegra contract.' I pushed the paper across the desk.

'Oh, right thanks,' he replied, brow furrowed in confusion.

I waited while he leafed through the contract, but he looked back at me questioningly. His olive eyes clueless. I'd have to spell it out.

'It's the wrong version. It's the earlier one before I amended it, the one with Allegra's additions.'

I watched the colour drain from his face as he squinted at the pages.

'No wonder they were keen to sign it. You've given them pension contributions, medical benefits and a six-month minimum contract for the seconded employees.' I clasped my hands together and laid them upon the desk, I should be enjoying the moment, but instead my insides churned.

'Oh my God. This wasn't the one you sent me?' he said, without blame.

I shook my head as a sheen of sweat glistened on his forehead. He wiped it away with the palm of his hand. 'It wasn't the hard copy I handed you yesterday either. You must have printed off the one revised by them before I got to it.' My tone was soft, not judgemental.

'How can I fix it?' he asked, a tremble in his voice.

'I'll see what I can do. No promises though,' I said, knowing full well getting Allegra to renegotiate what was an extremely beneficial contract to something less favourable was going to be a challenge.

'Thanks, Kay, I owe you one. I mean it. You need anything, you let me know.' He stood and left the office, head bowed, a man defeated, and although I should have relished the victory, it left a bitter taste in my mouth.

My phone rang as I perused the contract again, underlining everything in red pen I'd have to try to renegotiate. I had a good working relationship with Damien from Allegra and believed I could get some points retracted. He would drive a hard bargain though, I was sure.

'Hello, you!' I said, answering the phone to a breathless Claire.

'Hi, sorry, just ran up the stairs. Not as fit as I used to be.' Claire hid in the stairwell at the back of her office building to call me as she worked in an open-plan area where everything was overheard.

'Exhausted from last night, eh?' I teased.

'Am I! Who'd have thought someone with a name like Owen could be such a sex god.'

I sniggered as Claire filled me in on the graphic details of her date. After a few drinks at a pub, she and Owen had ended up at a cocktail bar until last orders when she had invited him back to her house for a 'nightcap'.

'I've hardly had any sleep,' she moaned gleefully.

'It's all right for some. I think I've got cobwebs.' I laughed.

'Heard from Jonathan?' Claire asked.

'No, I spoke to the twins last night though. They're fine.' I considered telling Claire what else I'd got up to, the memory of scratching Jaguar Man's car still at the forefront of my mind, but I decided against it.

'I'm definitely having an early night. Do you have any plans?'

'Only Netflix and chill for one,' I mused. 'Oh, and I need to go shopping for wine, I've run out!' I admitted, giggling.

We finished our conversation and said goodbye after arranging to meet on Saturday for a hike up the Worth Way, a seven-mile bridleway linking Crawley to East Grinstead. A walk we did often, as long as the rain stayed away. Claire was a fair-weather walker who didn't own anything waterproof except for the boots I'd made her purchase in the Mountain Warehouse sale, and she'd only bought them because they were pink. I prayed the weather would be kind and stay dry. A bit of fresh air and a chat with Claire would give me something to look forward to, and I needed it to get through the rest of the day at work which would be a slog.

In the afternoon, I spent an hour on the phone to Damien trying to renegotiate the contract. It was hard-going, with Damien proving to be inflexible at first until I reminded him of the longevity of our partnership with Allegra and how that would likely change if we couldn't work together on what had been an oversight of a new employee. Eventually, he saw sense and we ditched the pension contributions and private medical in favour of keeping the six-month minimum secondment. It was a battle we'd won whilst still maintaining the relationship, and I knew fixing Liam's mistake would indeed mean he owed me one.

'That's amazing, thanks, Kay. I can't believe I made such a balls-up. I'm mortified,' he admitted when I went to explain the revised deal.

'It happens,' I said as I gave Liam the new contract to sign with Damien's signature already on it.

'I honestly appreciate it. I know you went for the job – there's been nothing but whispers about it since I got here.'

'It is what it is, Liam. To be honest, I don't think I'll climb the ladder any further here, I'm missing a certain appendage.' I grimaced, blurting the words out without waiting for Liam to catch up.

'Well, more fool them. You're an integral part of the team and I'll make sure everyone knows it,' he said with conviction, cheeks ruddy.

I left the office at five, waving goodbye to Liam as I went. It felt good, as though I'd been the bigger person. I'd had the chance to play dirty, go over Liam's head and divulge his cock-up to Tim, but I didn't. If I couldn't get ahead at Winston's on merit alone, I'd look somewhere else. I was better than last night's antics, and it wasn't something I was intending to repeat.

I went home via the off-licence, picking up a couple of bottles of wine to see me through the weekend. Jaguar Man was on his driveway as I drove past and I instinctively slowed to get a better look at what he was doing. A black Staffordshire terrier was tied up by the front door, straining on its short lead. It barked at my presence and Jaguar Man's tall, smartly suited frame straightened up and turned to look, pausing his conversation with the man in blue overalls examining the damage to his car. He pointed and swiftly strode towards me.

In a fumble to drive away, I crunched my gears and stalled the Skoda. The dog continued to bark, wanting to see what was going on.

Jaguar Man turned and shouted over his shoulder, 'Shut up, Nero!' But the dog carried on regardless.

I fumbled with the ignition, but before I could start the car, he was banging on my window, eyes flashing incandescent.

'You were on my driveway last night,' he shouted at the passenger window.

'What?' I said, trying to look confused as my heart pounded.

He loomed large over my car, trying to contain his navy blazer billowing in the wind. Instinctively I locked the doors before lowering the window an inch. His eyes were level with the gap, glaring at me.

'It was you. I have you on camera. You scratched my car, you psycho.'

'I'm afraid you're mistaken, I wasn't anywhere near your driveway last night,' I snapped incredulously. Did the camera reach me? I was sure it couldn't have seen much from where I was. It was dark, I'd had my hood up, so surely I couldn't be identified. It was more likely I was the only person he'd pissed off over the past few days, although I found that hard to believe. Despite my reasoning, panic rose in my chest.

He snorted at my response, jaw flexing. 'I've got the police coming around later. I'll be giving them your registration number.' He took a couple of steps back, moving to the rear of the car and holding his phone up to take a photograph of my number plate.

Without bothering to reply, I started the engine and turned

right into my road, knowing it was a dead end and would reveal where I lived. He only had to walk along the street right to the very end and find my car on the driveway to learn exactly which house was mine.

Butterflies beat their wings in my chest as I considered what I'd say if the police came to my door. Visions of being carted away in handcuffs while my neighbours watched through gaps in their curtains engulfed my mind until it was all I could see.

They couldn't prove I'd left the house. I didn't have a fancy smart doorbell to capture my leaving and I didn't believe Jaguar Man had quality footage of me damaging his car.

When I reached home, I stared at the front of the house, as if willing it to give away its secrets. Nausea washed over me as I got out of the car to go inside, the valiant feeling from earlier eradicated. Why had I been so stupid, so reckless? *Because he deserved it*, the voice in my head piped up. I couldn't let Jonathan find out; I'd never hear the end of it. The twins too, what would they think of me? What example was I setting to my children?

It had been a mistake, an error of judgement. What would I get if the footage confirmed it was me? A caution? Or maybe a fine? I had no idea. I'd never even spoken to the police before. Never needed to. Would they take one look at me and assume I was guilty? No, it was innocent until proven guilty. They had to prove I'd committed a crime.

It's nothing, forget it, my inner voice scolded, trying to rein in my panic.

Safely inside, I got changed out of my dress, which had

garnered a couple of comments from the male workforce, but nothing I couldn't handle, to put on jogging bottoms. Dinner consisted of a jacket potato thrown in the oven, covered in a mountain of cheese an hour later, although I couldn't stomach much.

I called Rachel after dinner, who moaned she missed being out with her friends. She, unlike Ryan, was barely ever home. Such a social butterfly, she spent hours at her friends' houses, the cinema or out shopping. Ryan, quite the opposite, was quiet and shut himself in his room with his Xbox playing computer games that nearly always involved killing something. I knew he'd be pining for his console as much as Rachel was missing socialising, but the deal was that Jonathan had the twins at the weekend, and unless they told him they didn't want to go, there wasn't much I could do.

Ryan came on the phone briefly to say hello and I baulked when I heard a female voice in the background. Whoever it was had a high-pitched tinkling voice that was definitely not Jonathan's mum. I swallowed down the grief that flooded in, eyes tearing automatically. Who the hell was she, and why hadn't Jonathan told me he had a new girlfriend? Not only that, but he'd also clearly introduced her to the kids without any prior discussion on it, or any consideration whether they were ready to meet his replacement for me.

Had Jonathan asked them to lie for him, and if he had, how long had it been going on for? The idea boiled my blood, but I didn't want the twins to hear me upset. I was furious Jonathan had involved them in his deceit, swearing loudly when I got off the phone.

To distract myself, I put on a crime documentary I'd wanted to binge, exploiting the opportunity to have the downstairs television to myself with no children around. A man had been accused of throwing his wife down the stairs to collect the insurance money and it was gripping viewing. I struggled to make my mind up by the third consecutive episode whether he was guilty or not.

I'd put off opening the wine until eight, reasoning it was an acceptable time on a Friday night to have a drink, but I'd barely had a sip from the glass before the doorbell rang.

Dread crept over me as I headed for the door, already knowing what I'd find on the other side. I pulled it open to two female police officers on my step.

'Good evening, sorry to disturb you. We're looking for a Mrs Kay Massingham.' They both looked remarkably similar, as though they could be sisters. Dark hair pulled into low ponytails, same height and same slight build despite their bulky uniforms.

'Yes. What's happened? Are the twins okay?' I jumped in, despite having spoken to both of them earlier. The uniform put me on edge. I'd seen too many television programmes where the police knocked on doors to deliver the worst possible news.

'I'm sure they're fine, Mrs Massingham. I'm WPC Baker and this is WPC Richards. We're here about a complaint, may we come in?'

I stepped back, flooded with relief the twins were okay, but the feeling quickly converted to panic, my heart galloping. I knew exactly what the police were here for, but I had to stay calm. I couldn't give myself away. I let them through the door, and they waited patiently in the hallway for me to usher them in.

We stood in the lounge, and I paused the documentary, cheeks burning.

'What sort of complaint?' I stammered, unable to disguise my alarm.

'We've had a complaint of vandalism from a Mr Simon Fox, do you know him?'

I shook my head. So that was what he was called. He looked like a fox, a sly one at that. 'No, I'm afraid I don't. An act of vandalism?' I asked, my voice sounding strangely middle class as if posh people were never criminals.

'Yes, his car was vandalised last night, and he seems to think you, the driver of a red Skoda Fabia,' she checked her notepad, 'GK63 ZUL, are responsible. He told us of an altercation you had at his home.'

'It was hardly an altercation. He cut me up and I told him he was driving like an idiot. That was it.' The middle-class lilt evaporated.

'So, you do know him then?'

'No... yes, of sorts, but I didn't know his name,' I stumbled.

'We've reviewed the footage and we can see you did get out of the car to shout at him.' WPC Baker arched an eyebrow and I felt like a child being scolded for not tidying her toys away.

'I'd had a bad day; I was driving home from work, and he cut me up. We were going in the same direction and when he pulled into his drive, I got out and we had a little set-to, that's all.' If they had the footage from that, what else did they have the footage for? I was sure I was blocked from view by his car last night, plus I was crouched down.

'Okay and you're sure you didn't go back to his house and damage his car?'

'No!' I replied indignantly. 'What time did this happen?' I continued, bolstered by the lie.

'Between seven and half past.'

'Well, I was here, in a Teams meeting for work, it was a call with the US, which is why it was so late.' I moved to grab my handbag and retrieved a business card, scribbling Liam's name, title and email address on the back. He owed me one after all. 'Look, Liam Shepherds was in the meeting, he can vouch I was there,' I said, holding the card out, which WPC Baker took. 'Perhaps Mr Fox has his wires crossed,' I suggested.

'Perhaps he has. Thanks for this, we'll contact Mr Shepherds.'

'Thank you and please let Mr Fox know I'm not the person he's looking for. We live close by, and I don't want any further harassment from him. He flagged down my car earlier and accused me, he was very aggressive,' I added, as they turned to leave.

'Will do, Mrs Massingham, thank you for your time.'

Once they'd gone, I necked the wine and poured another glass, perspiration prickling my back. *That was close.* Hopefully once they'd checked with Liam I was on the call, they'd reiterate that back to Simon Fox and the whole incident would be forgotten.

Surely he could claim the damage on his insurance, he probably only reported it to the police to get a crime number so he could do just that. I remembered how his eyes had blazed as he'd looked through the window of my car. Perhaps the Jaguar truly was his pride and joy. Well, maybe he'd think before driving like he owned the road in future.

I was about to go to bed after watching another two episodes of the crime documentary, the bottle of wine now empty, when my phone flashed up with a notification from Facebook. Jonathan Massingham had posted a photo. Unable to resist, I clicked the link, my heart shattering into a million tiny pieces. It was a photo of him and the twins, but *she* was tagged in it too. Monique Holford, a petite young blonde who had to be early thirties at most. She was tiny, barely five feet tall, and Ryan and Rachel towered over her.

I clicked on her profile picture, another shot of her and Jonathan holding hands across a table at what looked like a candlelight dinner for two. She was my replacement. She was the reason he'd moved out, left me and the twins and was now trying to negotiate his half of the equity of our family home. Things hadn't got nasty, not yet, but they would. Maybe he intended on buying a love nest with Monique.

Tears clouded my vision as the throb in my chest intensified. I couldn't stop staring at her perfect face. Did the twins like her? They were smiling in the photo, and it took all my resolve not to comment on it. To tell Jonathan and Monique to go to hell.

If it wasn't before, it was clear now; Jonathan wasn't coming back. He'd moved on, our marriage was over. It wasn't a blip or a fling, I knew he wouldn't have introduced her to the kids if that was the case. Despite all his faults, they had been his priority since we'd parted, I couldn't deny him that.

As though prodding an open wound, I typed her name into google, my mouth dropping as Monarch Wine Merchants came up as the first hit. The same prestigious wine merchants where Jonathan was a business development manager. I clicked on the link to their website, the *Meet our Staff* page, where the who's who of the company were listed. Monique Holford was halfway down the page as I scrolled. She was the marketing manager. It all made sense, a workplace romance. I imagined their heads bent together; hours spent conjuring up campaigns to snare new clients. Hands brushing, a lingering glance, the suggestion of an after-hours drink. That was how easily it started.

Her bio stated she'd previously worked for an online craft gin club subscription company and enjoyed long country walks and pub lunches. I wanted to vomit. Had he been with her while we were still together? Had he got bored of me? How had it all gone so wrong? My priorities had been skewed, but things would change.

I crawled into bed and wept into my pillow. I'd never felt so alone.

10

'You've got to get back out there. Get on Tinder, or Hinge, that's where I met Owen,' Claire said as we stopped for a break two miles into our hike up the Worth Way. One section of the path was quite high up and you could see miles of green fields in the distance. It was a beautiful sight. I stood with my hands on my hips, panting as she retrieved a bottle of water, took a mouthful and held it out for me. I'd told her all about Monique Holford and showed her the photo Jonathan had posted that had made me cry myself to sleep.

'I don't know, I'm not sure I can be arsed to wade through the crap. How many dates did you go on before Owen? He was the first one you liked in, what, like a hundred!' I laughed, swallowing the lump in my throat. I didn't want Claire to know how much I was hurting, how, deep down, I hoped Jonathan would see sense, come back to me.

Now I knew that was never going to happen. I contemplated fighting for him, reinventing myself with a new job, perhaps losing some weight to show him what he was missing, but what was the point? I couldn't compete with someone ten years younger than me, and now I knew he'd been elsewhere, maybe even cheated, did I really want him back?

'It won't do you any harm to have a bit of fun, go on a few dates. When we get back, I'll sort you a profile out. You never know.' It was easy to get swept up in Claire's enthusiasm to get me back in the game. As if a few dates would fix my broken heart.

She was going out again with Owen tonight and looking forward to her second date to find out more about him. So far, Claire had discovered that he worked in finance and travelled a lot for work. He was divorced and didn't have any children. Not bad for a first-date inquisition. This time, they were going bowling before dinner, so she had to be home early to get ready.

We picked up the pace to bash out the last three miles, talking as we walked despite our legs aching from the incline. All the way, we had to dodge cyclists, joggers and horses on the path.

'It's like a motorway here at times!' I grumbled.

'So, what sort of bloke do you think you're looking for?' she asked, her jet-black ponytail bouncing along with her stride.

'I don't know, a professional maybe, someone who can stand on their own two feet.'

'Hmmm, romantic,' she said sarcastically, and I swiped her arm.

'Tall, obviously – as tall as me at least. I don't know, dark and handsome. I can't remember the last time I fancied anyone.'

'What about that guy in the hard hat at work. You fancied him!'

'That was five years ago when I joined,' I said, remembering Marco and the somersaults my stomach performed when we were introduced.

'He's left now, and yes he was gorgeous. Unfortunately he was also gay!' I laughed, remembering the lads talking about it in the warehouse.

Claire rolled her eyes. 'Always the way.'

* * *

Back at home after lunch, we rested our legs as Claire set up a profile on Hinge, my MacBook upon her thighs, feet up on the pouffe.

'That photo is okay,' I said, choosing one from a holiday in Cyprus over a year ago, me holding a wine glass, skin pink from the sun. The twins were hanging out by the pool eating hotdogs with some other kids they'd met while Jonathan and I went for an early dinner alone. He'd taken the photo of me, and it was a favourite of mine.

'You need six, but we'll put that as your main one.'

My eyes widened and we set about finding some more photos, before entering preferences and conversation starters as prompted by the site.

'Here you go, all done. If you get any messages, they'll pop up here. Let me download the app for you too.' She grabbed my phone and tapped at the screen, waiting a minute before handing it back to me. 'Right, I best be off, thanks for lunch. I'll text you later.'

'Have fun,' I replied with a wink and once again the house was silent.

I hated the quiet, from what had been a bustling home, life had withdrawn from it. I cleared away our plates and put some washing on, knowing there would be more to come tomorrow when the children returned. Sadly, I couldn't wait.

Loading the machine, a single AirPod fell out of the pocket of my black hoody. I pulled everything out again, going through each item of clothing to find the other one, but it was nowhere to be seen. I couldn't find it in the laundry basket either, nor was it in the hallway, in my coat pocket or in my handbag. It was strange, but I figured it would turn up somewhere. At least it wasn't going to break my washing machine.

My mind wandered as I carried on with mundane chores, eventually stopping on Simon Fox. Should I have told Claire what I'd done? Perhaps, but I was hoping to forget my moment of madness. It had been overshadowed by the revelation of Jonathan's mistress. We were separated but still married – for now anyway. I'd have to find out more about Monique. Perhaps see what information the twins volunteered with some gentle prodding. Specifically, how long it had been going on for.

Had tagging Monique in the Facebook post been Jonathan's not-so subtle way of telling me he'd met someone else? All because he was too chickenshit to do it face to face. Was she living with him, could he have moved her into the flat already? In reality, he could have done it months ago; I would never have known if she'd stayed away the weekends the kids visited.

I forced the idea from my mind before it upset me, thoughts returning to Simon. Had the police been back to see him, to clear my name? Guilt niggled at me, but I reminded myself what an arsehole he'd been, and it didn't hang around for long.

After a quick shower, I settled back onto the sofa with the MacBook and put Simon's name into Google. There were so many hits, I resorted to Facebook to search for him.

Surprisingly, he popped up first, although his profile picture was of his car. We had a friend in common – Jonathan, although I wasn't sure if I could call him a friend any more. Did he know Simon? He must do in some capacity. Simon's profile was linked to a business page – Fox Security Solutions based in Crawley. He had his own business near the town centre and their web page displayed every security device you could think of: cameras for houses, for cars, even body-worn ones. As well as those, his company offered motion security lights, fully fitted alarm systems, gate and door operators and a free security assessment for your home.

I shuddered, an icy finger clawing my back. Trust me to trespass on the King Kong of Crawley's home security. Perhaps his footage had been good quality after all. No, I would have been arrested if it had been. Most of the crime would have been shielded by the height of the Jaguar – on that one camera I saw anyway. I wasn't about to go back to get a closer look to find out if there were more.

The doorbell rang, jolting me from my thoughts, and I got up to answer it despite being in my dressing gown with hair still wet from the shower. My eyes widened when I pulled open the door to find Simon Fox standing on the driveway, chestnut eyes glinting as he took in my appearance. I tightened the cord around my middle, unable to comprehend the coincidence I'd been looking him up online while he was stalking up my road trying to find my house. The Staffordshire terrier sat obediently at his feet, shivering. Had he come up here under the guise of an afternoon dog walk?

'Mrs Massingham,' he said, one corner of his mouth turning skyward.

'Can I help you, Mr Fox,' I said, bravado covering the tremble in my voice. I crossed my arms at my chest and leant against the door frame, trying to appear nonchalant.

He took a step towards me, but I refused to flinch.

'The police came to see me, it appears there may have been a misunderstanding.' His voice was smooth, like velvet, hands clasped in front of him in a praying motion. Instead of his blazer, he wore a round-necked burgundy jumper and jeans under a North Face jacket, still managing to look polished despite his casual weekend attire.

I lifted my chin, heart slowing to a normal rhythm. He was here to apologise. 'Yes, I was in a meeting at the time your car was vandalised,' I said stiffly, playing every bit the wronged woman.

'Hmmm, so I hear,' he said, unconvinced, taking another step so he was close enough to reach out an arm and touch me.

I gripped the door, worried for a second he was going to try to force his way in.

'However, we both know it was you on my driveway. All I want is for you to admit it.' He leant in, so his voice was nearly a whisper. I found it more threatening than if he'd shouted and had to stop my knees from knocking together.

'I don't know what you're talking about. Now please leave before I call the police,' I demanded.

He chuckled, running his hand through his hair, as though he was a catalogue model. He could have been, he wasn't unattractive, although his face was long and his eyes too close together. 'There's no need for that, Mrs Massingham, just admit what you did, and we can put all of this behind us.' His tone had a menacing hint to it while remaining playful.

'Goodbye, Mr Fox,' I said as I shut the door, catching his words before it closed fully.

'I'll be seeing you.'

11

I sank back against the door, legs weak. The hallway floor seemed to tilt beneath me. Simon was quietly intimidating, all the more so because he didn't scream and shout obscenities. He'd simply known I'd been the one to scratch his car, certainty plastered across his face. Should I have admitted my crime? Apologised and pulled out my chequebook? Would he have realised it was an error of judgement and agreed I could fix the damage I'd caused?

I rushed to the living-room window and watched him yank the lead of his dog in one sharp movement, practically dragging the poor thing off the driveway. Outside, the light was slowly draining away, giving the sky an ominous feel. Spits of rain began to hit the glass in quick succession, and I remained staring out until I could be sure Simon Fox was gone, and not coming back. The rain carrying him swiftly home.

His demeanour left me uneasy, and keen to know more, I went back to Facebook, but there was no information to be gained there. His profile was locked, other than a link to his company website and photo. I tried Instagram and Twitter, which were the only social media platforms I knew how to operate, but had no joy. I could try LinkedIn, but he'd be able to see I looked at his profile. Perhaps I could ask the twins about Snapchat, maybe his daughter had an account? All the youngsters seemed to be on it.

For the first time since Jonathan had moved out, I felt vulnerable being alone and as outside grew dark, the day turning into night, every sound had me on edge. A creak of the floorboards or a slam of a car door made me jump. I couldn't stop myself replaying our conversation. Had Simon's words been a threat? *'I'll be seeing you.'* He looked as though he would more likely send his solicitor round than a bunch of heavies, not over a scratch on his car. Even if the Jaguar was his pride and joy.

I eventually went to bed, unable to concentrate on the television. I slept badly, tossing, and turning, giving in and getting out of bed at five o'clock in the morning, sleep evading me. Counting down the hours until the kids were back, I had plenty to keep me busy. Ironing shirts for the twins to wear for school and changing the sheets, I had to go food shopping too. Ryan was an eating machine and since he'd hit puberty, our food bill had gone through the roof.

Pushing the trolley around the busy supermarket mid-morning to stock up on their favourites, a text came through from Claire to let me know she was fine and had been with Owen all night. I'd asked her to check in so I knew she was safe. I grinned at my phone, pushing my trolley to the side of the aisle to respond.

I'm glad for you, take care. Speak soon. X

As soon as the text sent, I saw I had a notification on LinkedIn. Opening the app, I found a connection request from Simon Fox. I stared at the screen before realising I was causing a traffic jam and shoved my phone back in my pocket to move down the aisle. Why would he want to connect? I didn't want anything more to do with the man who had intimidated me on my doorstep.

As soon as I got home and unloaded the bags, I checked what was visible on my LinkedIn profile, not much other than my work history and a few posts about Winston's. However, Simon now knew not only where I lived but where I worked too. The notion unsettled me, and I debated whether to open a bottle of wine, but I knew Jonathan would be returning the kids soon and I didn't want him to smell it on my breath. He hated me drinking, it used to be a source of constant arguments. In his eyes, I did it far too much. Despite it not being any of his business what I did any more, I didn't want to give him any excuse not to drop the kids back.

When he arrived, I smiled graciously and kissed the twins as they came in, dragging bags of dirty washing behind them and dumping them on the lounge floor. Ryan barely said hello before he disappeared upstairs and the sound of the Xbox firing up was heard. Rachel at least asked how my weekend had been.

'Do you mind if I come in for a minute?' Jonathan asked, not having crossed the threshold of what was still his house.

'Sure,' I replied, and Rachel went into the kitchen on the hunt for food.

'How have they been?' I asked, awkward with Jonathan there and surprised he'd been so polite. However, he must have known I'd seen the photo on Facebook, perhaps that was why he was wary.

The space seemed odd with him in it, like he didn't belong. Shoving his hand in his pockets, he looked at me, fresh-faced and practically glowing. I gritted my teeth; love did that to a person.

'Fine, had fun, I think. Thanks for letting them come.'

'I had no choice, remember; you didn't tell me you were taking them,' I said, unable to let the bitterness slip out despite my intention to be civil.

'I did!' he began, before deciding not to argue the point further.

'Well, thanks for not making a scene,' he added without so much as flinching.

'If you wanted them to meet your new girlfriend, you should have said,' I shot back, looking to see if my words unbalanced him, but he barely blinked.

'Monique? Well, I guessed it was time they met her.' The implication he'd been seeing her for a while hung in the air, but I didn't give him the satisfaction of asking how long. I kept my head up, not wanting to see how much his words stung. I had no idea if he'd cheated on me or if Monique was the reason he'd left, but it was likely. 'Listen, Kay, I really need to get the house sorted. Have you been to the bank about buying me out?'

'No, I haven't had time,' I lied, stalling.

'Have you even got it valued yet?' he asked, sighing.

I shook my head.

'Well, I'll have to do it if you won't. I need the money tied up in the equity to buy something. My short-term lease is going to run out soon.'

'Can't you move in with Monique?' I snapped the words out before I could stop them.

He didn't answer right away, looking at me like a dog he'd just kicked.

'Monique lives in a bedsit,' he said flatly.

I scoffed. I'd thought she might still live with her parents – she looked young enough. He was such a fucking cliché.

'I'm going to contact a solicitor this week, to get started on divorce proceedings.'

I swallowed hard, knowing it was coming. Like a runaway train, Jonathan couldn't be stopped. I wanted to fold the words up and put them back in his mouth.

'Under what grounds? Adultery?' I snapped, but he just sighed and shrugged.

'Whatever you want, Kay, it just needs to be done.' Should I take that as an admission of guilt?

'Fine,' I replied, although it came out more like a squeak. I wasn't going to let him provoke me. He'd found it amusing initially, enjoyed riling me up so he could tell everyone how difficult I was making our separation. I'd played into his hands at first, the neurotic ex-wife, but it had been exhausting and I'd since learnt not to fall into his trap.

How had the man who had been my rock become a stranger? We'd been married for eighteen years. Happy, or so I'd thought. Only last year on our blissful summer holiday, he'd told me he'd love me forever. What had I done to cause him to change? Was it the drinking?

Jonathan turned to leave, shouting goodbye over his shoulder to the kids.

'Do you know Simon Fox?' I blurted as we got to the door. A pathetic attempt to prolong the agony, to keep him here for a few more minutes. If he was with me, he wasn't with her. It was pitiful that, even now, after everything, I still wanted to keep my husband.

'Yeah, we were at college together years ago, business studies. How do you know him?'

'I don't, not really,' I admitted.

'He's divorced, so you might be in luck there, although I'm not sure if you're his type,' he said, looking me up and down doubtfully.

I shook my head, wounded, and Jonathan chuckled darkly, relishing the cruel things he said that were always in jest but chipped away at my confidence none the less.

'Sorry,' his laugh petered out, 'I'm kidding, but seriously, he runs his own business. I bumped into him in the pub a couple of weeks ago, he was boasting about destroying the local competition and running the leading security firm in Crawley. We didn't talk for long.'

'Okay, thanks.' I deflated behind him as he pulled open the door.

'I'll be in touch about the house,' he said, waving over his shoulder, car keys jingling in his hand as he left. Back to his new life, his new woman.

12

Jonathan talked about our family home like it was a business deal he had to close, as if he had no personal interest. The years of memories, our children learning to walk, their first days at school, summer garden parties in the paddling pool. As though they meant nothing to him. It stung like a slap in the face, but Jonathan had always been able to compartmentalise.

I desperately didn't want to leave this house, but without the promotion and pay rise I had little choice. I'd have to sell up and split the equity.

'Mum,' came Rachel's muffled voice from the kitchen, her mouth full of something.

'Yes,' I called back, closing the front door and forcing the gloom Jonathan's visit had left aside.

'Can you wash my jeans? I'm going to the cinema with Casey after school tomorrow.'

I agreed, my thoughts turning back to Simon Fox.

'Rachel, do you know the girl that lives at the end of our road? Blonde, pretty. Goes to St James's?'

She looked at me blankly, still chewing, Ritz cracker crumbs falling from her hand to the floor.

'You know the house that was done up, opposite the entrance to our road, white, double-fronted. Really lovely, but then they tarmacked the drive.'

Recognition flashed in Rachel's hazel eyes. 'Yeah, that's Ava. She's in my year. She's a bitch,' she stated without blinking.

I grimaced, knowing she was the moment I'd set eyes on her. She looked like the popular girls at high school I remembered. Conveyor-belt pretty, long straight blonde hair, slim and a look of entitlement most girls like her had, as if the top spot had been reserved for them.

Thankfully, Rachel had breezed high school so far. We'd had no instances of bullying, no boyfriends to speak of and she was a good student. Ryan was the more troublesome one, when he wasn't playing Xbox and ventured out with his friends, he'd come home stinking of weed, red-eyed and spaced out. His schoolwork was slipping, but I couldn't get through to him, and neither could Jonathan. I never stopped worrying about him.

It was another weight I carried upon my shoulders. With the house, the separation and now Simon Fox to contend with, the mounting pressure was overwhelming. Not only that, but I had to figure out what to do about my job. Winston's was no longer somewhere I could excel; I'd reached the end of the line, but at the same time I was loath to leave. After putting up with five years' worth of sexist comments, and at times harassment, it shouldn't have been for nothing.

Dinner was awkward, the twins not wanting to talk about their weekend, that they'd spent it with their dad's new girlfriend. The replacement for their mother. Instead, they skirted around the issue until I could bear it no longer. The elephant in the room grown so large it was unavoidable.

'What's Monique like?' I asked, hoping to dispel the tension.

'Nice,' Rachel said diplomatically as Ryan pushed his pasta around his plate. 'It was the first time we'd met her,' she continued.

The atmosphere weighed heavy in the room.

'Did you know about her before the weekend?' I asked, unable to resist.

'No,' Ryan jumped in. So, it was the first they'd heard of Monique too. I took little comfort that they'd had the wool pulled over their eyes as much as I had.

'I'm glad you had a good time.' Forcing a smile onto my face. It was Jonathan's fault he'd put the twins in a difficult position, and I didn't want to make it worse.

'I don't like her,' Ryan said quietly, and I felt a rush of love for my son. Maybe with Monique on the scene, they wouldn't be so keen to stay with Jonathan.

'Is she why Dad left?' Rachel asked, her face looked as though it might crumple.

'I honestly don't know. I didn't know about her until yesterday,' I admitted.

'He told us he couldn't live with you any more, that you weren't the wife he married.'

I choked on a retort, unable to believe what he'd been feeding them. No wonder they resented me.

'They make me sick. All over each other all the time.' Ryan's face darkened and he dropped his fork, it clanging against his bowl.

'You know you don't have to see her if you don't want to. I'll never make you go.' I reached across the table and rested my hand on his forearm. Trying to dispel the images of Jonathan and Monique unable to keep their hands off each other. Nausea washed over me.

'She makes Dad happy, idiot,' Rachel spat at her brother, her words slicing like tiny knives.

I got up to clear the plates, blinking back tears that threatened. *Keep it together, for the kids.* I told myself it was all about them and not about us, although I wished Jonathan felt more like that, but he was selfish. His actions had proved that.

'You've upset Mum now,' Ryan tutted at his sister, who pushed away her plate and stalked upstairs.

'It's okay, it's fine,' I said to her retreating back, before turning to Ryan. 'You all set for school tomorrow?'

'Yeah.'

He finished eating and brought his plate over to the sink, giving me a half-smile before disappearing back upstairs where his Xbox was calling.

I rang Claire and after listening to her gush about how fantastic Owen was, I updated her on the Jonathan situation. It was good to offload some of my worries and Claire was a great listener.

'Fuck him, Kay, he's made his choice and introducing the kids to Monique with no warning is a shitty thing to do. Not to mention lying about why he left. He's just making you the bad guy. You need to move on. A fresh start, maybe moving to a new house will be a good thing. You can take the memories with you.' I tried not to cry, but the tears came anyway.

'You're right, I know you're right. I need to get my shit together and make a plan,' I sniffed. I'd start tomorrow by going to the bank and seeing what I could do about the remortgage. At least then I'd know where I stood.

* * *

The following morning, I dropped the twins off at school, keeping my eye out for Simon Fox, but his Jaguar was nowhere to be seen. Perhaps it was being repaired. I'd been jittery on the drive, the twins picking up on my anxiety, watching my eyes dart around at the other cars on the congested road.

'I'll be home around nine, Mum, remember,' Rachel said, clutching her bag with her change of clothes inside.

I looked at her blankly until I recalled her going to the cinema with Casey.

'Sure, you going to eat at Casey's?' I asked.

'Yep, see ya, Mum,' she said, climbing out of the car.

Ryan nodded a goodbye and got out before I pulled away.

When I got to work, I bumped into Sarge coming out of the kitchen, grease etched into the cracks of skin on his hands, wearing grubby blue overalls. He was a solid unit in his mid-fifties who managed the warehouse.

'Looking good today, Kay,' he said, staring brazenly at my chest.

'Morning, Sarge,' I sighed.

'You know, if you need someone to keep you warm at night now, I'm always available,' he smirked, and my blood ran cold.

'What?'

'Well, now you and Jonathan aren't together, I'm happy to step in if you need a service?' His tone was playful, and he winked. My stomach rolled in response.

'How do you know about that?' I snapped and he held his palms up.

'He happens to be banging my niece; he came round the other day to my sister's. Meeting the parents and all that. She's a bit young for him though, ain't she? She's only twenty-nine!' Sarge had no idea my insides were shrivelling as he went on, offloading information as though we were both impartial spectators.

Now everyone at Winston's would know my marriage was over, the humiliation that Jonathan had left me for another woman, fourteen years his junior. It was unbearable.

'Look, sorry, I didn't think. I was just having a laugh, ya know,' he said, seeing my face drop.

Without answering, I abandoned my coffee and hid in my office for the rest of the morning. A lead weight sat on my chest, refusing to move.

Unable to concentrate on anything, I was glad when lunchtime rolled around and I could leave, gasping in lungfuls of air when I reached the car park. I imagined Sarge and Gav laughing, comparing me and Monique, with me being the loser. I got in my car and drove to the bank ten minutes away in the centre of town, managing to bag a space outside the post office where you could park for free for thirty minutes.

The bank was busy, and I was glad I'd called ahead and booked to see a mortgage advisor. I sat opposite him, in a side room, digging out my account number so the man could look up my details. I spent almost twenty minutes showing bank statements and proof of earnings, but it was to no avail.

'I'm sorry, Mrs Massingham, but increasing your loan to buy your husband out isn't going to be an option in this case. The bank won't guarantee a loan for that sum, because I'm afraid you don't earn enough to secure that amount of money. It would be deemed an unnecessary risk.'

I scowled, shoving the statements back into my bag. So much for being a loyal customer.

'So, I don't have any options at all? What if I went to another bank?'

'You can. However, I believe you'll be told the same thing. At your age, the loan amount and length of repayment terms means it would be unaffordable with your current salary.'

It was a kick in the teeth, but I couldn't deny I hadn't been expecting it. I knew the numbers didn't add up.

I stood outside the bank, shoulders sagging, wishing for a

glimmer of hope to cling on to. I was hanging on by a thread. Across the road, a voice I vaguely recognised made me look up.

Simon Fox was climbing into his shiny Jaguar, talking on his mobile phone. The scratch had disappeared as though it was never there. My crime eradicated. I was impressed how swiftly he'd got it fixed. How much had it cost him? It looked freshly washed and waxed, so he might have had it done that very morning. A man like Simon Fox would hate to drive around in a less than perfect vehicle.

He ended the call, started the car and drove away without spotting me. As the Jaguar moved, I saw what it had been parked in front of. A gleaming shopfront with large glass windows I'd never noticed before. The words 'Fox Security Solutions' in bright orange lettering on a white background. The logo comprising of a fox with the letters FSS inside its body loomed high over the street. I'd found the Fox's den.

13

Curiosity got the better of me and I crossed the road to spy in the window, clocking the security camera over the entrance. I bowed my head, so I wouldn't be easily identified as I looked through the glass. On a modern display were a host of lights, cameras and other devices – I had no idea what they were. A young man in his early twenties stood behind the counter at the back, serving a well-dressed woman. With Simon gone, it was a perfect moment for me to have a look inside. I wanted to find out more about the man who'd intimidated me on my doorstep.

The door had a bell above it, which chimed loudly as I entered, making me start. The man behind the counter looked up and smiled in greeting before going back to his customer. I perused the aisles, looking at all the options available to secure your home. Lingering by a small section of wearable cameras. A large diamond shaped onyx necklace, which looked like dress jewellery, caught my eye. I picked it up and turned it over in my hands, surprised by the weight.

'That's a new bit of kit,' came a friendly voice over my shoulder. 'It has a battery life of thirty hours and a memory of ninety hours.

Activated by sound with a date and timestamp on all recordings.'
The man from the counter met my eye as I turned to find him
standing behind me. Inwardly I jumped, I hadn't noticed the other
customer leave, or heard the bell at the door. 'Light too, isn't it?' His
enthusiasm was infectious, and I smiled.

'How much?' I asked, a speck of an idea forming in my mind.

'Sixty pounds, but we only have three in stock currently.'

I stared at the necklace, unable to believe the pendant was a
working camera. You'd never know.

'I'll take it,' I said impulsively.

The man took the necklace out of my hand and gently put it
back on the display. 'I've got one boxed up under the counter. It
comes with instructions of course, but if you need any help setting
it up, then feel free to pop back and we can assist.'

I smiled politely, impressed by the customer service.

At the desk, I paid with my credit card and put the box in my
handbag.

'How long have you been here?' I asked as we waited for my
receipt to be printed.

'About a year now.'

'Is this your shop?' I asked, knowing full well it wasn't.

'No, Simon Fox owns it. I just work here and help with some of
the installations. Here's a leaflet of the services we offer, if you ever
consider updating your security at home, or perhaps your business,' he said, taking in my tailored suit and skirt I'd worn specifically for my meeting at the bank. 'We offer a free security
assessment of your property and a no-obligation quote.'

'Thank you,' I replied.

The bell chimed from the door, and I whipped around, breath
catching in my throat, not wanting to be caught by Simon on his
property. But two men entered, dressed in sandy jeans and desert
boots, immediately heading for the motion sensor lights.

With no desire to hang around any longer, I left, walking back to my car, only to find a parking ticket on my windscreen.

'Fuck's sake,' I hissed. I'd been ten bloody minutes over the allocated free time. There was no parking warden to be seen, but they were probably hiding in the bushes, with their stopwatches, ready to pounce on the next person late back to their car.

I ripped off the sticker and threw it onto the passenger seat. Another bill to add to the collection.

* * *

Back in the office, I tried to get into the swing of work but was unable to focus. Liam and Tim were both out visiting the Birmingham hub and I was glad of the peace. Would Liam confess his mistake to Tim on the long drive up there? I doubted it, but the error would come out eventually, when the length of the Allegra staff secondment was called into question.

My phone pinged mid-afternoon as I was responding to an email with what I assumed was a text from Claire, but it was a notification from Hinge. Someone had viewed my profile and liked one of my photos. I clicked on the name: Mike Sullivan. His profile popped up, a slim man with dark blond hair swept away from his forehead, smiling at the camera in a shirt and tie. He looked a bit like Daniel Craig, and I stared at the screen dubiously. *He'd liked my photo?*

His profile told me he was forty-five, divorced, lived in Crawley and enjoyed hiking, kayaking and other outdoor pursuits. Four of his other photos showed him running, playing rugby and out on the water, the last one was him sat at the bar of a pub I vaguely recognised.

My face burned as I made the call to Claire, palms clammy. I had no idea what I was supposed to do. Did I message him? Like his photo? Was I supposed to wait a certain amount of time? It was unchartered territory for me, and I didn't want to make a fool of myself.

'Hiya, how are you?' Claire always sounded pleased to hear from me and a warm glow spread from my stomach.

'It's been a weird day,' I mused.

'Oh, tell me about it, mine's been awful, candidates falling out all over the place. Some just can't be arsed to turn up for an interview. So frustrating.'

'I've had someone like one of my photos on Hinge!' I blurted, unable to keep it in any longer.

'Oooh, send me a screenshot,' Claire said.

I did as she asked, my fingers fumbling between the apps as she shouted goodbye to someone in the office.

'He's hot!' she exclaimed when the photo came through her end.

'Out of my league,' I replied, my voice wobbly.

'Don't be ridiculous! No one is out of your league. Right, you need to like one of his photos, then hopefully he'll message you. You can message him of course, but it's always good to be chased,' she said wickedly, and I imagined the corner of her mouth curling upward as it did when she got excited.

'You're the expert.' I clicked back to Hinge and liked the photo of him at the bar.

'Done it?'

'Yep.'

'Right, I've got to go, meeting at three, but ring me if he messages you.' Her voice was shrill, unable to contain her exhilaration before she ended the call.

I looked again at Mike Sullivan's photos, he was attractive, and I was sure if we met, I wouldn't be his type. None the less, it was a confidence boost. Although I hadn't really considered moving on, perhaps there was life after Jonathan.

* * *

At home later, Ryan and I had dinner where we had the longest conversation we'd had in a while without Rachel there. It was nice to spend some time together alone, have him talk about school and his friends without Rachel steering the conversation as she often did. He was more open without her around, and I managed to bring up the deterioration of his schoolwork without sounding judgemental. Ryan told me he was aware his grades had been falling, he was honest about not putting the effort in recently. Was that since his dad had left and life had become unstable? He promised to try harder, and I let him rant about Jonathan and Monique without interruption. It was a relationship he objected to, although I tried to reassure him we both loved him and Rachel the same as we always had. That nothing was going to change between us, and I would always be there if he needed me, whether we were in the same house or not. I was proud of myself for not joining in whilst Ryan was knocking Jonathan off his pedestal. It would have been easy to do so, especially with Jonathan's recent behaviour, but whether we were together or not, we had to parent as a team. Jointly we adored our children, and it didn't do any harm to remind them of that.

Our heart-to-heart over, I cleared away the plates and texted Rachel to make sure she was okay. She responded quickly, her and Casey were already on their way to the cinema and would be home after the showing. Feeling lighter, and with Ryan back upstairs, I retrieved the necklace from my bag and read the instructions to set it up.

It was slightly heavier than normal costume jewellery, but I'd get used to it. Wearing it around the house, I popped into Ryan's room to see if he wanted a drink, using the opportunity to establish if the necklace recorded our exchange. He'd barely grunted at me, but it had showed up on the grainy recording when I'd downloaded the footage, mainly due to Ryan playing Xbox in the dark.

Pleased with my purchase, I sat to watch more of *The Staircase* crime documentary when the Hinge app announced I had a message.

Hi Kay, would love to meet for a coffee this week, perhaps one lunchtime? Mike. X

My mouth filled with saliva and I swallowed, skin tingling with a mix of fear and excitement rolled into one.

I rang Claire immediately, who told me to go for it. Don't hesitate, she'd said, even if nothing comes of it. Get out there, meet new people, get socialising. It was a confidence boost if nothing else. I responded with:

Sound great, is tomorrow too soon? We could meet in Brewers at one?

Brewers was a local coffee shop in town where I often found refuge during my lunch hour.

Stomach churning, I hit send, but a message came back almost straight away agreeing to meet tomorrow. Unable to concentrate on the documentary now, I went upstairs to try to figure out what I was going to wear when Rachel returned home.

'Good movie?' I called as I heard her steps on the stairs.

'Yeah, it was funny. I'm tired though. I've got some homework to do before bed.'

'Okay, I'll be turning in soon. Did you lock the door?' I asked.

'Yep,' she replied, appearing in the doorway. 'That one,' she pointed to one of two dresses I was holding, choosing the green knee-length shift dress I'd only worn once. A flattering empire line ran under the bust pulling in at the waist.

'Okay, that one,' I agreed, and Rachel grinned before disappearing.

I wasn't about to tell the twins I had a date. Jonathan might be free and easy with his newly acquired love life, but I planned to keep my cards close to my chest. No one would know I was dating again. I wasn't going to give Jonathan any fuel to humiliate me with.

14

In the morning, I curled my shoulder-length hair, aware my roots were darker than they should be. I'd have to book in for more high-lights soon. The dress looked nice, snug around my hips, but I could get away with it. I found some black heels at the back of the cupboard and made more effort with my make-up than usual.

'I have a meeting,' I explained to Ryan, who gaped at me momentarily as I ushered the twins into the car.

Simon Fox pulled out of his driveway as I went past and followed me to the school. Perspiration dampened my underarms at the proximity, and I turned off the heat, much to the twins' complaints. Fog hung low in the sky, worse at the bottom of the hill, and I turned on my lights to ensure I was seen by other cars. Rachel was talking to me about her science coursework, but I couldn't focus, condensation lingered on my windscreen and my eyes strayed to the rear-view mirror every few seconds. Watching him, watching me as he followed me turn for turn until we neared the school

'Mum, stop!' Rachel said and my foot hit the brake, coming to an abrupt halt at the crossing as files of purple uniforms swam in front of the car. Some girls stared at us, laughing as they passed, and Rachel sank lower in her seat, her ears pink.

By the time I'd reversed into a space and turned off the ignition, he'd gone round the roundabout and parked up, half on the kerb, opposite me, ignoring the double yellow lines.

I avoided his gaze as long as I could, but when our eyes met, he smiled and gave me a wink. It sent my temperature up a notch.

'Tosser,' I mumbled under my breath as he pulled away and I made my way to work.

I'd worn the necklace, knowing the dress I was wearing was bound to invite some comments. Sarge's eyes bulged when he saw me, but he said nothing, likely still embarrassed from the day before.

'You look nice today, Kay,' Tim said, a wry smile on his face. His gaze penetrated me, as though he could see through my clothes, leaving me naked and exposed. I recalled why I'd started dressing more conservatively in the first place.

'Thanks,' I replied, my voice stilted.

Gav was walking past the kitchen as we exited with our morning coffees and chipped in. 'Careful, lads, she's on the prowl now she's single.'

A few people laughed and I bit my lip, refusing to engage and fighting the urge to tell him to piss off. It seemed news travelled fast.

At five to one, I was sat outside Brewers on a hard wooden chair as there were no tables free inside. I shivered in the cold, pulling my woollen coat around me, and ordered a cappuccino from the waitress.

Sinking lower into my coat, the waitress took pity on me and turned on one of the tall heaters, so at least my back was warm. I saw Mike approach from the other side of the square, squinting as recognition hit and a broad smile developed on his face. Threads of breath floated into the air as he strode towards me.

I stood when he was a few feet away, smoothing my dress, palms damp despite the temperature.

'Kay?' he asked, holding out a hand for me to shake.

'Mike,' I greeted, shaking his hand and hoping he wouldn't recoil from my cold clammy palm.

He pulled out a chair without waiting to be invited and sat. The waitress arrived with my coffee and took Mike's order while I used the opportunity to absorb him fully.

He wore a grey suit, pink shirt and tie, his wavy hair brushed back from his head like his photos. His teeth were perfectly straight, and his smile was large, inviting. He thanked the waitress, a twinkle in his eyes.

My pulse raced as I considered what to say. How to start a conversation. I rarely got tongue-tied, but I hadn't had a date for years and was far out of my comfort zone.

'It's a bit crisp out here, isn't it?' he said, realising we were the only patrons mad enough to sit outside in October.

'I know, I'm sorry, there are no tables free inside, lunchtime rush.' I shifted my chair so I wasn't blocking the heater.

'No bother. Anyway, how's your day going?' His stare was piercing, muddied blue eyes penetrating mine. I told him it had been fine, so far.

'How about you?' I asked, pushing the question back to him to take a sip of my coffee. It was hot and tasted divine.

'Not bad, I've been in meetings since half nine, so it's nice to escape and get some fresh air. How long have you been on Hinge?' His directness startled me, but I explained I'd been separated for a few months and my friend had convinced me to sign up a few days ago. He had a similar story, although he'd been divorced for over six months.

'It's hard to meet people now, not like the old days,' I agreed with a laugh, starting to relax. I crossed my legs, noticing his gaze linger for a split second on my stockinged calf. He had lovely lips, and from the depth of his laughter lines, it looked as though he was always smiling.

Half an hour passed in a flash. We huddled around our coffees, hands on the mugs for warmth, but our conversation didn't linger on the weather. Mike told me he worked in IT for an energy company, spending most of his day in front of a screen. We talked about hiking, he knew the Worth Way well and often rode his mountain bike along the bridle path to the next village. It seemed like we had a lot in common and the attraction grew as I continued to stare at his lips, briefly imagining what they'd feel like to kiss.

At ten to two, I paid the bill, despite Mike's insistence that he should get it. He thanked me for the coffee and said he had to get back but asked if I would like to go out for dinner on Friday night? I was gobsmacked and mumbled I'd love to, before giving him my business card. So much for taking it slow. We'd only exchanged messages via the Hinge app so far but now he'd have my mobile number.

'I haven't got mine on me,' he said, slipping my card into his inside pocket, 'but I'll text you later.'

We stood and he leaned in to brush his lips against my cheek.

'Lovely to meet you, Kay, I'll book us a table on Friday. Any preferences?'

'No, whatever you fancy,' I said, blushing.

He raised a hand to wave and walked back across the square. I watched him go, my chest fluttering.

'I can't believe it, he's lovely,' I said to Claire on the phone as I headed back to the car.

'Told you. Ah I'm glad it went well. Perhaps one night we can all get together, I can't wait for you to meet Owen,' she gushed. I hoped he was the one for her, but Claire had started out this way with men before only to see the flames dwindle as the weeks passed.

'Listen, keep an eye out for anything that comes past your desk that's suitable for me, would you? I'm going to need to find a job with a bigger salary.' Claire often heard about jobs before they were even advertised, so it paid to have her keep me in mind for possible opportunities.

'Will do. No luck at the bank then?' Claire asked.

'Nope, don't earn enough to buy Jonathan out, so it looks as though we'll have to sell. I mean, he's been good to carry on paying the mortgage for as long as he has,' I admitted.

'Yes, but he's keeping a roof over the head of his kids, Kay, remember that. It's not like he's done it for you.'

'I know, I know. Anyway, I better get back. Catch you later,' I said, hanging up.

Back at the office, I got stuck into a proposal for a supplier the sales team had agreed initial terms with, setting up a meeting with Ed to run through the operational side of things. Liam asked if he could sit in on it, wanting to learn as much as he could, and once we were done, Ed left the meeting room to go back to his desk.

'How was Birmingham?' I asked Liam.

'Fine, Tim's got some big ideas about restructuring.'

I rolled my eyes; I'd heard him sound off about that before. 'Nothing new there, he's been talking about restructuring for over a year now.'

'Apparently he's secured management approval, so I guess all will be revealed soon.'

A prickle of unease danced up my back at his words. Were they going to push me out?

'Oh, I had a weird call from the police, wanting to check you were in that meeting on Thursday night?'

I swallowed, my mouth suddenly dry. 'Yes, a misunderstanding. A neighbour complained their car had been vandalised and told the police they thought it was me, can you believe it!' I waffled.

Liam's eyes widened in horror. 'Really?'

'I know, right, it's awful. We've had problems with him for years,' I lied, forcing a dismissive chuckle before changing the subject. 'Did you tell Tim about the Allegra contract?'

'No, not yet. I will,' he replied, eyes darting around the room, looking anywhere but at me.

'It will come up; they'll want to know why the secondment of the staff is six months and not three.'

He looked at the floor. There was no way I was going to be thrown under the bus for his mistake, but at the same time I didn't want to be the one to bring it out into the open. My fingers skimmed my necklace, glad of its comforting weight.

* * *

I left the office on a high later that afternoon, the coffee with Mike having done wonders for my self-esteem, which had ebbed considerably. Jonathan had been chipping away at it for months and work had contributed to me feeling I wasn't enough. It was all going to change though.

My elevated mood plummeted when I arrived home just after five and found a car I didn't recognise on the driveway. Pulling in beside it, I noticed the front door was ajar. Were the kids okay? I climbed out and pushed it open, Jonathan was standing in the hallway.

'Thanks very much for your time, Dean,' he said, shaking the man's hand, who smiled awkwardly at me and walked to his car.

'Who was that?' I asked, jaw tight.

'Dean from Martin's estate agents. I asked them to come around and give us a valuation.'

15

'You could have bloody warned me,' I snapped, annoyed at the intrusion, thinking of the discarded clothes I'd left on the bed and the state of Ryan's room, which smelt like something had died in it.

Jonathan raised his eyebrows. 'You didn't give me much choice, Kay. You need to stop dragging your heels, we have to get this sorted.'

'Oh, piss off,' I said, pushing past him into the lounge.

The twins were sat at the kitchen table, still in their uniform, taking it in turns to eat from a large bag of Doritos.

'You'll ruin your dinner,' I sighed.

'You never said we had to move?' Ryan glared at me, and I turned to Jonathan, who was tapping the screen of his phone.

'See what you've done?' I hissed.

He shrugged, my venom sliding off him.

'Come on, pal, you know we can't keep the house. Your mum and I both need to buy smaller places. It's impossible to stay here.'

Ryan frowned, first at his dad, then back at me, before pushing the crisp packet away and storming upstairs.

I raised my eyes to the ceiling, stretching my neck and counting to ten.

'Can you leave,' I said to Jonathan, frustration threatening to boil over. How dare he blurt it out, not thinking of the repercussions I'd face from the kids.

'See ya, Rach,' he said before disappearing for the door.

'Bye, Dad,' she replied, a hint of sadness in her voice.

I didn't have the energy to argue or explain to the kids that what their dad was doing to them, he was doing to me too. I didn't want to sell the house and move out any more than they did, but he'd left us little choice. They didn't understand that mortgage payments could be a stone around your neck, one that could make you sink under the weight of money you didn't have.

I was trying to shelter them from it as much as possible. Until Jonathan arrived with his size tens, putting his foot well and truly in it, leaving me to pick up the pieces as always. It would have been great if we could have sat down together to tell them about the house. I hadn't mentioned the D word yet either. It was another thing I had to get sorted, a divorce lawyer, but I wasn't in a rush. Jonathan could instigate it. The petition had to come from one party and even though I could claim adultery, I wasn't interested in hurrying through a quickie divorce. Not when he had another woman sniffing around. Why should I make it easy for him to wriggle out of our marriage when he'd messed everything up for me.

I considered opening a bottle of wine, knowing the stress of the situation would float away the more I drank, but it was something I had to get a handle on. Blocking out the problem wouldn't make it go away. Jonathan was right, I was dragging my heels, trying to come up with something to avoid the sale of our family home. But perhaps it was time to admit defeat.

* * *

The week ticked past. Jonathan had been in touch to let me know Martin's estate agents had valued the house at four hundred and fifty-five thousand and it was now on their books. News that was bittersweet in its arrival. It meant more equity to split than we thought but knowing it was on the market made the whole separation real and final.

Work had been uneventful; Liam was avoiding me, I could tell. He kept his head low, office door closed and had barely spoken a word to me. Not wanting to mention the contract again, but with the Allegra secondment coming into effect at the end of October, it would soon come to light. Something wasn't right, but I took comfort in wearing my necklace to work, diligently downloading every day and saving the files on my computer.

I'd replayed my coffee with Mike, cringing at how stilted I'd been. My nerves obvious in the beginning before I eased into the conversation. I hoped our second meeting would be more relaxed. Alcohol always helped, I'd loosen up after a glass of wine, or two. He'd messaged me the day after our coffee to let me know he'd booked a table at Zizzi's for eight on Friday. Since then, we'd exchanged a few texts, a couple of funny memes, all light-hearted.

On Thursday evening, Claire came over for a pre-date pep talk and to help me pick out something to wear. Jonathan was having the kids Friday night and bringing them back on Sunday, so I had the weekend to myself again. I wasn't convinced it was a good thing. The house was too big when it was empty, I hated the quiet.

'I like this one, it's casual, a little sexy but not too much,' Claire said, laying on my bed, a glass of wine in one hand and a polka dot blouse in the other. 'It's got a sweetheart neckline, shows off your collarbones and a bit of skin without being presumptuous,' she carried on.

'Mum, can you sign this form?' Ryan knocked on the door and I let him in. He brandished a sheet of paper and a pen at me.

'What's it for?' I asked, already scanning the page.

'Field trip next week, we're going to visit a working mill for Geography.' He sighed, already bored by the prospect.

I signed the form and handed it back to him, noticing he'd filled in the rest for me, and it was only the parental permission he needed.

'Thanks,' he replied and shuffled back out of the room.

'God, he's getting so tall!' Claire said when he'd gone.

'I know. Scary, isn't it?' I replied and took the blouse out of her hand.

I was so glad Claire had come over, picking out black straight-legged jeans, heeled boots and bringing with her a lipstick for me to wear. She was much better at clothes than I was, knowing exactly how to dress her petite frame and maximise her curves. I mostly wanted to appear shorter, and thinner, although I'd got better at owning my height as the years went by.

'Okay, I'll try it on,' I said, removing my sweatshirt.

'Do you know where you're meeting him yet?'

'Mike's booked a table at Zizzi's, we're meeting there at eight,' I said, pulling on the jeans and nearly toppling over. We'd sunk half a bottle already, the music blaring in my bedroom so the twins wouldn't hear us talking about my upcoming date.

Since she'd arrived to join us for dinner, bringing her spinach with her as always, I'd told Claire about Liam and his contract error and Jonathan inviting the estate agent over. Out of earshot of the kids, she'd shaken her head and hissed, 'He's such a wanker!' A term she frequently used for Jonathan since we'd split.

'The house is worth more than we thought, we might even have enough for around a hundred and fifty grand each, so good for a deposit somewhere else.'

'I don't know why you just don't let me move in,' she mused, 'think of all the great parties we could have.'

'We're not in our twenties any more,' I laughed.

The outfit Claire had chosen looked good and I was pleasantly surprised by my reflection when she applied a coat of her lipstick with perfect precision.

'Gorgeous. He'll be unable to resist,' she said, grinning like a Cheshire cat. I stared at my reflection, apprehensive at such a big step, going on a date with another man. But it would be good to get back in the game as Claire had said, and it would also be a way to show Jonathan I was moving on.

At work on Friday, I'd deliberately orchestrated a quiet day, knowing my concentration levels would be low. I rescheduled my meetings for Monday but got called into the Allegra start-up that Tim put in my diary thirty minutes before it was due. I gathered the paperwork and sat in the meeting room opposite Liam, who smiled tightly at me before averting his gaze. It was as though he was trying to distance himself.

Ed led the meeting, talking through the logistics of the start-up and who was doing what. Liam was going to induct the new employees and go through the contract so everyone knew where they stood. Ed would make sure the workers had a proper training programme and buddy system before they would be allowed to drive any of the forty-foot trailers alone.

I kept expecting Liam to interrupt, to apologise for the error he'd made in the contract, but it never happened. Observing him, he seemed on edge, playing with his pen constantly, unable to stop his hands from moving. Was he expecting me to raise it?

'Maybe we'll send our glamour girl Kay to meet them,' Tim chuckled, eyes glinting, cascading down my body.

'She'll keep them in line wearing those boots. Have you got a riding crop at home?' Ed teased. I didn't mind Ed, his banter was innocent, non-judgemental and without agenda. He usually blushed to high heaven if anything remotely sexual was mentioned. Unlike Tim, whose snake-like eyes stared at my knee-high winter boots as though he was considering getting down on all fours and licking them.

The boots were black, flat-heeled and not at all sexy in my eyes, but the men at Winston's would latch on to anything they could metaphorically rub their crotch on.

'I don't think that's appropriate, do you? Let's get back to the secondment.' Pinched words spilled out of my mouth before I could stop them, steering the meeting back on track.

Liam shifted uncomfortably in his seat. My neck flushed but I ignored the rising burn.

Suitably admonished, my attire wasn't mentioned again. I saw a look pass between Tim and Ed, naughty schoolboys put back in their place. Had I inadvertently sealed my fate? Easy-breezy Kay who would always let things slide and never retaliate had broken her silence. Had I given them an excuse to push me out?

16

'You know we're only kidding.' Tim's posh lilt grated as we stood outside the meeting room, the others already departed. I clutched my papers to my body, a barrier between my boobs and Tim's wandering eyes.

'Yes, I know that, Tim, but it's not always appropriate. Being the *Global* HR Manager, surely you can see that?' I replied, emphasising the 'global'. If he didn't see there was a problem and understand he was contributing to it, what chance did Winston's have?

Tim puffed his chest out like a pigeon; I'd overstepped the mark. 'Now look, Kay, are you saying there's a problem? Because we don't want to open a can of worms here. There's a restructure coming. It's time to keep your head down and not cause a fuss.'

I glared at Tim incredulously but didn't respond. Was that a threat?

'Good, good. Glad to see we're on the same page,' he continued, filling the silence before striding away.

I'd missed my chance to register a formal complaint and perhaps Tim was right, it could be a bad time to raise my head above the parapet.

I touched my neck where the pendant had become a permanent fixture. It gave me comfort and spurred me on at the same time.

* * *

The kids were home when I got there later, packing their things as Jonathan waited on the driveway. He was overseeing the man from the estate agents banging a For Sale board into my flower bed. I scowled at the sign and at them, not bothering to speak as I went inside, hearing Jonathan chuckle before I slammed the door.

'Hi, kids,' I shouted, removing my boots and leaving them on the welcome mat. The twins were upstairs, their rooms a tidal wave of clothes pulled from drawers and wardrobes, but I refused to moan, they weren't going to be home for long and I'd miss them when they left. 'What are you doing this weekend, do you know?' I asked, loitering in the hallway, between the two open doors.

'Not sure. Cinema, I think,' Rachel offered, her voice glum. It was due to rain all weekend and the prospect of being cooped up in Jonathan's flat must have been unappealing.

Ryan seemed to be shoving things into his backpack as though each item had personally offended him.

'What's the matter? Don't you want to go?' I asked, leaning on his door frame.

'I don't see why, every weekend, we have to see him, and now *her*,' he spat.

'You don't have to go *every* weekend. Why don't you stay at home next time, and we'll do something together?'

'It's not that. We don't get to hang out with our mates and stuff, all our time is taken up. Homework and school during the week and Dad all weekend,' Rachel chipped in.

'You went to the cinema with Casey.'

'Okay, once, I went out once. I hardly ever get to do that between the amount of coursework I have to do and then seeing Dad all weekend,' Rachel groaned.

'Well, next weekend, stay here and I won't plan anything. You can both do whatever you like?' I said, buoyed to be the parent they wanted to stay with for a change, even though I knew it was only so they could see their friends.

I understood their frustration, they were sixteen for goodness' sake, wanting to be out. Instead, all their time was planned for them. They didn't spend enough of it doing what they wanted to do, making their own choices and having fun.

Ryan stalked past me, his room resembling a bomb site and smelling like one too. He trotted down the stairs two at a time, his lumbering frame all arms and legs. Rachel rolled her eyes in his direction and gave me a quick peck on the cheek as she passed.

'Bye, Mum. See you Sunday,' she said, swinging her rucksack over her shoulder and following Ryan down the stairs.

I joined them at the front door, where Jonathan was waiting, swinging his keys around his finger like a cowboy.

'Should hopefully have some viewings next week, try and keep it tidy, eh?' he said, and I pressed my lips together, sealing inside the abusive language I wanted to throw at him. I wanted to tell the patronising bastard to fuck off, but I never talked to Jonathan like that in front of the children. Although he seemed to have no qualms putting me down in front of them. What kind of lessons was he teaching them? That it was okay for Ryan to belittle women and Rachel should get used to being spoken to like that by men? It made my blood boil.

'What is that!' Ryan said, booting the base of the For Sale sign and watching it wobble in the wind.

'Don't do that. You can see what it is, Ryan,' Jonathan said icily.

'I don't want to move,' he moaned to his dad. My chest ached for him, I wanted to add, *Me too, kiddo*.

'Yeah well, we all have to do things we don't want to do, son, that's just life,' Jonathan said, ushering him into the car, where Rachel was waiting. I wanted to tell Jonathan that it was an awful year to disrupt the twins, with mock exams coming up, GCSE coursework and revision, but he was already climbing into his car. It would keep for another day.

'Bye, kids, keep in touch,' I called, ignoring Jonathan.

They both waved and I closed the door, anger subsiding. I pitied Monique having to put up with that condescending prick, but she was much younger, and probably accepted it gratefully. I imagined her dressed as Oliver, holding out her hands and saying, 'Please, sir, can I have some more? More please, sir.'

Sniggering at the image, I went back upstairs to air Ryan's room, throwing the window open as wide as it would go. Why did teenage boys' rooms smell so bad? I discovered a few old socks and reams of toilet paper under the bed which I swiftly chucked down the toilet without thinking too much about it.

I should leave his room as it was, that would put off prospective buyers, but I was burying my head in the sand. It might delay things, but it wouldn't stop me losing the house. Plus, I knew I had to show it in the best possible light to ensure offers were as close to the asking price as possible.

Strangers wandering around, looking in every cupboard, judging every corner of my home made me anxious. I was relieved when Jonathan said he'd given Martin's a key so they could come while we were at work and school. At least I wouldn't have to show buyers around, but it did mean keeping on top of the housework every day, so the place looked presentable. It was another thing to add to my already overflowing list.

At least I had the date with Mike to look forward to. I was excited to be out of the house, to take my mind off everything that had been going on. A couple hours' break from the constant worry that life was a precarious house of cards, ready to topple if I made one tiny misstep.

Claire text wishing me good luck and promised to come over tomorrow for another walk, rain depending, suggesting we could sweat out the alcohol from the night before and catch up on gossip.

I got in the shower, washed, shaved and moisturised everywhere before applying my make-up. Black winged eyeliner teamed with Claire's lipstick made my eyes pop. Once I'd finished doing my face, I curled my hair into soft waves that brushed my shoulders. I looked in the mirror when I was dressed, pleased with what I saw as I twirled. I looked nice, trendy even, in my polka dot blouse and jeans.

I bravely snapped a selfie in the mirror and sent it to Claire.

Smokin'

She replied straight away, and I grinned. I'd decided to drive my car into town and get a cab back. There was a car park open twenty-four hours and it only cost two pounds fifty to leave your car there overnight. I could get Claire to drop me off tomorrow, or I could walk into town and pick my car up.

With an empty space in the pit of my stomach that was more about nerves than hunger, I made my way towards the restaurant. Zizzi's was situated in a courtyard, opposite a pub, the Greyhound, and a Chinese restaurant. It wasn't far from the car park and town was already bustling with revellers out to celebrate the end of the week.

As I approached the restaurant, at five to eight, already paranoid Mike wasn't going to turn up and I'd be eating alone, I saw him. He was sat at a table by the window, engrossed in his phone, wearing a teal-coloured shirt open at the neck. A pint of beer stood already on the table, almost half the contents gone.

17

'Hi,' I said, arriving at the table.

Mike jumped up, he looked like a rabbit caught in the headlights before smiling broadly.

'Hello,' he said, taking me by the elbow and leaning in to kiss me on the cheek. He moved around the table, pulling out my chair, and I sat awkwardly, catching my heel on the leg. I couldn't remember the last time anyone had done that. I brushed my fingers through my hair and pointed towards his beer.

'Been here long?'

'I was a bit early, yeah,' he said, clearing his throat and returning to his seat.

I forced my shoulders back. *Relax, you'll be fine.*

'Did you get a cab?' he asked.

'No, I parked over in Bryerly Way, the car park there. I'm going to leave it there though and get a cab home. Did you drive?'

'Nah, I jumped in a cab. Here, let's get you a drink,' Mike said, giving a nod to the waitress.

Within five minutes, I was no longer stumbling over my words or giggling nervously. I had a glass of red in hand and we eased into conversation. Before long, Mike and I talked like we were old friends. We discussed work at first, although he dismissed his job in IT as uninteresting, but by the time the waitress had asked for our main course choices, we'd briefly touched on our marriage breakdowns. Getting it out of the way like it was the elephant in the room.

'He's mentioned divorce, but I've had no papers yet,' I admitted.

'Is it fully over for you?' he asked, his tone light.

I grimaced. 'Definitely. I don't even recognise the man he's become.'

Mike leant back in his seat and took a sip of his beer.

'My wife, Faye, was like that, a totally different person at the end.'

'Well, here's to new beginnings,' I said, raising my glass to clink against his, not wanting to get too maudlin. It was supposed to be a date after all. Even as out of practice as I was, I knew it wasn't good to linger on our exes.

The waitress came over with our food; Mike had chosen a meatball calzone and I had a prawn linguine. Zizzi's food was delicious, and my stomach growled appreciatively. He'd stuck to beer, ordering another pint, but when I'd arrived he'd requested a bottle of Malbec for me when I'd asked for red wine. Before I knew it, half of the bottle was gone, our plates were empty, and the waitress had brought over the dessert menu. Time seemed to be moving too quickly and I wished I could slow it down. Our date was going so well, I was excited to escape to the bathroom and text Claire.

Having a great time! He's lush.

Don't do anything I wouldn't do! 😊

Her reply leaving me open to a world of possibilities.

When I got back to the table, Mike looked sheepish.

'I ordered pistachio gelato, is that okay?'

'Perfect.' I grinned, glowing from the alcohol and the atmosphere.

'I poured you another,' he said, gesturing towards the wine bottle.

'Thank you,' I said, taking a sip. 'Can I just say, I've had a lovely time tonight. My first ever experience of Hinge and it wasn't hideous,' I laughed.

'I'm sure there's a compliment in there somewhere,' Mike cracked, his teeth almost dazzling.

My gaze lingered on his mouth, the urge to press my lips to his consuming me for a second before I forced myself to look away.

'Where did you go just then?' he asked. I must have glazed over.

'That's for me to know and you to find out,' I teased, draining my glass.

Our gelato arrived with two spoons, and we shared it, leant over the table, our heads close. Mike smelled like cedar, clean and fresh. I breathed him in, enjoying the cold gelato on my tongue and the feel of it sliding down my throat.

I asked Mike about his hobbies, the photos he'd posted on Hinge, and he talked animatedly about being out on the water, driving to Amberley and kayaking along the river. He tried to go once a week, usually with his son, Charlie, who was slightly older than the twins. Charlie lived with his mother, but Mike saw him every week. It saddened me my twins were going to become another statistic of a broken home.

'One for the road?' Mike asked, gesturing towards my empty glass. There was at least another in the bottle, but I didn't fancy it. Since finishing eating, my mouth was dry, tongue thick and furry. Bloated from the pasta, my jeans dug annoyingly into my waist.

'Umm, water instead, I think.' I lifted the jug without realising how heavy it was and water sloped over the table.

Mike intervened and poured for me. Had I drank that much? Normally a bottle of wine would be fine, I'd easily drink one and be merry but not drunk.

Blinking rapidly, the restaurant seemed to tilt, the waiters walking at a funny angle. I squeezed my eyes shut, vaguely registering Mike asking for the bill.

'I think I may have had a bit too much to drink,' I said quietly, hearing my speech slur and wishing the world would stop moving.

'Perhaps you need some air.' Mike was smiling, those teeth like jewels. He paid the waitress and left some notes on the table before discreetly walking me out of the restaurant.

'Thank you, for dinner. It's been lovely, but I think I need to go home now,' I said, my legs wholly unattached from my body.

'Absolutely, no worries. I'll get us an Uber.' Mike lowered me onto a nearby bench and tapped his phone as I watched people milling past, laughing and shouting, on their way to the next pub or club. I had no idea what the time was or even if I had my phone. I could feel the weight of my bag on my shoulder, so reached inside to check it was there. It was, although the screen was blurry.

In the car on the way home, I stared out of the window and concentrated on not being sick. My stomach contents swirled with every corner and bump in the road. Perhaps something I'd eaten hadn't agreed with me? Our driver must have thought we were a rowing couple, the atmosphere almost frosty in the back seat. Mike didn't comment on my lack of conversation, but I'd been rude. Annoyed I'd made a fool of myself on a first date. Especially when Mike had paid and been so gentlemanly. He wouldn't want to see me again now.

When we got to the house, the lamp in the lounge was shining brightly through the window. It was on a timer, and I was grateful for it as I stumbled out of the car, gulping in air like a fish and fumbling for my keys. My thoughts were disjointed, and I struggled to make sense of the situation.

Behind me, I heard a car door slam and an engine revving. My head was swimming and I staggered up the driveway, pointing my key towards the door like it was a dowsing rod leading the way. Mike appeared at my side, one hand around my shoulders, the other sliding my keys out of my fingers to open the door.

'Looks like you might need a hand.'

I tried to speak, but when I opened my mouth nothing came out. My bottom lip grew numb and an urgent need to urinate hit me. I burst through the door as soon as Mike had it open, rushing for the downstairs toilet.

In the lounge, I could hear sounds of the curtains being drawn, then Mike on the phone to someone, although I couldn't make out the words. His voice was hushed. Was he calling another cab? Unable to focus, I tried to pull up my jeans, fumbling with the zip before running my hands under the cold water at the sink. I held my hands to my eyes, dripping palms pressed over them, trying to fix my vision but everything was still fuzzy.

Making my way out of the toilet, I kicked off my boots and dragged myself along the wall around the corner to the lounge, propping myself up with my shoulder. Mike was waiting for me on the mink corduroy sofa, his hands resting on his knees. He smiled at me, eyes warm and welcoming, holding out a beckoning hand.

'I think you need to lie down.' His velvety voice danced in my ears before the room swam and I closed my eyes.

18

My mouth was full of cotton, tongue too large to fit inside. It was like I'd been eating razor blades and my throat screamed as I tried to swallow. Groaning, I opened my eyes, aware I was on the sofa, still fully clothed with the mother of all hangovers. I licked my dry lips, craving water, still trying to come to. A crack of light beamed through the curtains onto the hard wood floor, and I could hear birds singing outside, but I was strangely disorientated.

I swiped at the crust on my eyelashes and tried to sit, head pounding like someone was drilling to get inside it. At my feet lay my handbag, zip pulled open, and I reached for my phone inside as it began to ring. Was Mike checking on me? I vaguely remembered getting into a taxi and coming inside the house, but nothing else from there. How could I have got so drunk? Was the wine stronger than what I normally drank? I reached for the phone, but it slipped from my grasp and the caller rang off.

Grabbing it again, I saw a few notifications, two missed calls from a number I didn't recognise and a text from Claire asking if I'd 'sealed the deal' with Mike. We hadn't had sex, had we? No, I was sure we hadn't, although I couldn't remember a thing after getting home. I'd know, surely I'd know if we'd done the deed. My head throbbed, but nothing was amiss physically. My jeans and underwear were intact with no sign they'd been removed. Perhaps I'd passed out on the sofa and Mike had called another cab to take him home. Unless he was still here?

My eyes scooted around the room, but there was no evidence he'd even been in the house. All I could hear were the birds in the tree outside, no footsteps or movement came from upstairs, and I was sure I was alone. I'd have to message him today to apologise. Although it was probably too late and after seeing what a state I was in last night, I wouldn't have blamed him if he'd decided to run a mile.

My phone rang again, the same number as before and I slid my finger across the screen to answer.

'Hello,' I said croakily.

'Oh hello, is that Kay Massingham?' A lady's voice came down the line, shrill and sharp, making me wince.

'Yes.'

'I'm the owner of the Vauxhall you scraped last night. Thank you for leaving your details. So many people would have just driven off. It was very honest of you.'

'I'm sorry, what?' I said, trying to comprehend what she was saying, but she spoke so quickly I couldn't process the words.

'You left your business card on my windscreen last night. I found my car had a scrape on the passenger side this morning when I was taking my children out,' she said, her voice rising an octave.

The pounding in my head intensified and I closed my eyes to focus.

'I'm sorry I don't know what you're talking about,' I said, heaving myself up from the sofa.

'You drive a red car, yes? Well, there's paint down the side of my car. Do you not remember?' Her initial friendly manner had morphed into irritation.

It had to be a practical joke. My car was safely in the car park in town, I hadn't driven it home. Mike and I got a taxi. I remembered that much.

I moved to the window and pulled the curtain back, nearly dropping the phone when I saw my Skoda parked at an angle on the driveway.

'I'm sorry, I'll have to call you back,' I said, hanging up as the woman started complaining.

Mouth gaping, I threw open the front door, blinking at the sight before me. My car stood on my driveway, bodywork gleaming in the autumn sunshine. Had I gone back out to get it last night and brought it home? Surely not, I wasn't in a state to walk, let alone drive. But how else could I explain it? The car was here, and I'd left my business card on the windscreen of a vehicle I'd supposedly hit.

A chill prickled my back which had nothing to do with the temperature outside and I stepped onto the drive to survey the damage. Exactly as the woman had said, silver scrapes lined the front of my bumper, glinting in the cool sun. They weren't there yesterday, I'd have noticed. I rubbed my forehead, trying to work out what had happened. What I'd done.

The phone rang again, same number.

'Look, Ms Massingham, I really need to see you to get this sorted.'

I relented, giving her my address and going back inside to fetch my chequebook from the junk drawer. I had no memory of scraping the woman's Vauxhall, but I couldn't argue with the proof on my driveway.

If I had driven the car drunk last night and got into an accident, I could lose my licence. It would be easier to pay the woman off in the hope she wouldn't report it. She could fix the damage privately without going through her insurance.

Oh God, what had I done? If Jonathan heard about it, he'd have a field day. Another reason to add to his list as to why I was an incompetent mother who shouldn't have sole custody of our children.

By the time the woman arrived, I'd had a strong coffee, taken some painkillers for my head and ran through the shower, washing the wine from my pores. Seeing my reflection in the mirror had been a shock. I was as white as a sheet, with black smudges around my eyes as though I'd been crying. The missing hours were a mystery. Maybe Mike would be able to fill me in, if I could swallow the humiliation of calling him to find out. He hadn't called or text and I presumed he'd backed off, likely thinking he'd dodged a bullet after my behaviour last night.

'I'm very sorry, Ms...?'

'Pettigrew, Mrs Pettigrew.' She was younger than she sounded on the phone and carried a toddler on her hip, shifting from foot to foot on the driveway to jiggle the fidgety child.

'I'm so sorry about the misunderstanding. I'm on medication, you see, it can make me a bit muddled,' I lied, smiling tightly and handing over a cheque. She took it and looked at the amount.

'Two hundred and fifty pounds?' Her eyes widened.

'Yes, that should cover it. Saves going through insurance, as they always bloody put the prices up when you do. Seems silly for my mistake to cost you anything?' I smiled warmly as she looked first at the cheque and then to me, bewildered.

Her car was parked over the entrance to the drive, and I could see the red paint my car had left behind. I hoped the scrapes weren't too deep to be easily fixed.

'Let me know if you need more to cover the repairs,' I offered, adding, 'if you can get a quote and it's more than two hundred and fifty, just pop back round with the paperwork.' I didn't want her to get any ideas I was going to be easily fleeced.

'Okay, thank you. This cheque is going to clear, isn't it?' she said, eyeing me suspiciously, as if the whole transaction had been too easy and she'd prepared herself for a fight.

'Absolutely, and you know where I live after all.' I chuckled dryly, eager to get her to leave so I could carry on trying to piece the jigsaw of last night back together.

'Um, thanks. I'll bring back the rest if it's less than that,' she said, waving the cheque and backing away.

'Don't bother, sorry for the inconvenience,' I said tightly. How was I going to budget for such an amount? We'd be living on baked beans on toast if I wasn't careful, but it was cheap compared to what the accident could have cost me.

19

I watched Mrs Pettigrew load her toddler into the car and drive away, sighing with relief. She hadn't insisted on calling the police and my driving licence wasn't in danger of being revoked, for now anyway.

Back inside the house, I made another coffee. It was nearly lunchtime, but the idea of food made me nauseous. I sat at the kitchen table and scrolled through my phone, finding the number for Mike. We'd only exchanged text messages, but I knew I had to call him to thank him for last night and apologise for getting into such a state. I had no idea if he'd want to see me again, but we'd had a good time, before I'd got so drunk.

I clicked on the number and waited for it to ring. A second later, an automated voicemail kicked in and, unprepared, I left a garbled message which was part apology and part request to call me back. He must have had his phone switched off.

My thumping head had dulled to an ache, and I called Rachel to check in, knowing she was more likely to answer than Ryan.

'Hi, Mum,' she said, trying to inject enthusiasm into her voice.

'Hiya, love, just checking in. All okay?'

'Yeah fine, we're about to head out. Bowling, I think.'

'That's good, at least it's not raining,' I said, at a loss for what else to say. I wanted to ask if Monique was there, but for all I knew she'd moved into Jonathan's rental and was there all the time. I didn't want to mention her or put Rachel in a difficult position, so I was pleased when she passed the phone to Ryan.

'I hate bowling,' he grumbled.

'Well, try to enjoy it and mention to your dad you want to stay at home next weekend. I'm sure he won't mind.' No doubt he'd love the weekend to wine and dine his young girlfriend. If only she knew what she was letting herself in for. I wish someone had told me eighteen years ago.

That wasn't fair, we'd had a happy marriage, apart from the past year. We'd had two beautiful children who we adored, even if we no longer loved each other. Millions of couples separated, it wasn't uncommon, and despite Jonathan being a shit, we'd have to keep it amicable for them.

'See you later, Mum,' Ryan said, after he'd spent five minutes having a good moan. I didn't mind, it made a change from the usual monosyllabic teenager he was. In fact he must have been fed up given he'd gone on for so long.

'Just to let you know we've got a viewing booked in for Monday,' Jonathan came on the line. He was abrupt as was usual when he spoke to me now.

'That was quick, and don't worry, I'll make sure it's tidy,' I said before he could get his shot in.

'Good. Well, see you later. I'll drop the kids off tomorrow afternoon.' I didn't get a chance to say goodbye before he'd already hung up.

I laid on the sofa, my stomach still swirling, and waited for the phone to ring. Hoping Mike was going to get in touch, maybe he could tell me how my car came to be on my driveway. Staring stubbornly at my silent mobile, I was surprised when someone rang the doorbell. I prayed it wasn't Mrs Pettigrew, or the police for that matter.

'Hi,' Claire said, beaming on the doorstep. She was a little ray of sunshine.

'No spinach today?' I teased, instantly better now my best friend was here. I'd forgotten we'd made plans.

'Nope, not today. I brought my hiking boots though, fancy a walk?'

'Perhaps a short one.' I grimaced, my head still reaping the effects of last night. My body wasn't much better either.

Half an hour later, we were walking along the Worth Way, making slow progress as I filled Claire in on the details from last night and how I'd awoken on the sofa, with Mike nowhere to be seen.

'That's so weird, and the car too. What on earth did you do?'

'I wish I could remember. I'm sure we didn't have sex though,' I panted, the hill was beating me today.

'And he hasn't returned your call yet? Have you text him?' Claire asked, stopping at the side of the path to drain her water bottle. I did the same, shaking my head. 'Perhaps message him on Hinge?' she suggested.

I shrugged, I could, but I didn't want to appear clingy.

Claire already had her hand out, requesting my phone. I handed it over and watched as her mouth morphed into a frown.

'What is it?'

'His profile has gone,' she said, swiping at the screen.

'Really?' I took the phone to see for myself. Sure enough, Mike Sullivan didn't exist any more on Hinge.

'I think you've been ghosted,' she said. 'What a wanker.' Claire put her hands on her hips, outrage written all over her face.

'I can't say I'm surprised; I was a bit of a state. You should have seen me this morning. I looked a right mess. He must have wondered what he was getting himself into.' I squeezed my eyes shut for a second, cringing inwardly at the humiliation.

'But you've sunk more than a bottle of wine before, no problem,' Claire said.

'I know, and I didn't even finish the bottle. I thought it might have been the combination with something I ate, I remember feeling really sick.'

Claire stopped and turned towards me, raising her hand to shield her eyes from the glare of the sun. 'Are you sure he didn't slip something into your drink?'

I tried to remember, although everything about last night was hazy. Mike seemed so friendly, easy to talk to and honest, but it was a possibility. I'd left my drink to go to the toilet when I'd text Claire and not thought anything of it. The terrifying thing was it fit with the memory loss and how out of control I'd felt on the same amount of alcohol I'd normally consume with ease. I pressed my palm to my lips, a tremor rocketing up my legs, weakening my knees and unsteadying my balance.

Claire gripped my arm to anchor me. 'Are you okay? You're as white as a sheet,' she said, as I leaned against the fence, unable to speak.

Spiked. That sort of thing happened to young girls in night-clubs. Not mums of two in their forties out for dinner. I gulped in air as Claire soothed me, my entire body frozen to the core. The thought of being malleable, so out of it that you're totally compliant to someone's whim was horrifying. It was the sort of thing I worried about with Rachel, never thinking I'd be a target.

Eventually I calmed down and we began walking back towards the house. Linked arm in arm, both of us wrapped in our own thoughts for a while until I spoke up.

'That doesn't make any sense though, why drug someone and not have sex with them?'

'I'm positive we didn't!'

'God, for all you know he could have wanked on your cushions while you were passed out!' Claire stifled a laugh, diffusing the tension, and I wrinkled my nose.

'That's so gross,' I replied, reminding myself to check my cushions when we got home. Despite Claire trying to inject some humour into the situation, to lighten the mood, I couldn't deny I felt shaken by the experience. I'd never been so vulnerable with a stranger before.

We headed back, only having made it half the distance we'd normally walk. I wasn't in the mood. My muscles ached and my head was still foggy despite having drunk a couple of pints of water during the walk.

Back home, Claire suggested we indulge in a takeaway and stay in to watch the latest Netflix offering and I readily agreed. I didn't want to be alone in the house, still out of sorts. Something was niggling at me, but I couldn't work out what it was.

Mike's disappearance from Hinge had left a bad taste in my mouth and even if he'd ghosted me because I'd got so drunk, it didn't explain how the car had arrived on my driveway. I had no recollection of driving it, but my car had made contact with Mrs Pettigrew's Vauxhall, I'd seen the damage for myself.

It didn't make any sense and my head hurt from trying to work out what had gone on. Maybe I'd never know what happened, but considering I could have lost my licence if the police had been called and they'd breathalysed me this morning, I'd had a lucky escape. It had been worth the money spent, despite knowing I'd likely paid Mrs Pettigrew too much. I'd had one brush with the law too many in recent weeks and it wasn't something I wanted to revisit.

20

Claire stayed over, which I was grateful for. I'd happily topped up her wine glass, offering to share my bed rather than her get a taxi home. I was glad of the company. I hadn't let any alcohol pass my lips. Even the smell of the Prosecco Claire popped out to buy made me sick.

I'd pushed my rice around my plate, not fancying much of anything we'd ordered from the Chinese, but we'd still had a good evening. I nearly divulged what had happened with Simon Fox, but shame about that night's events still clung to me and I wanted to forget the whole thing. It seemed pointless to drag it up and I was anxious about exposing a side to myself Claire had never seen before despite all the years we'd known each other.

I didn't have to worry, she was happy to talk about Owen, letting slip that she was really into him. Something I'd already guessed, and I was happy for her. She was animated whenever she spoke of him, her eyes radiant. It was lovely to see, and I just hoped he wouldn't break her heart. I, on the other hand, had already had enough of online dating and was planning to delete the Hinge app as soon as Claire left. I'd had four other people like my profile, but I wasn't interested in checking them out. I'd had my fingers burnt and wasn't going to put myself out there again. If I was going to meet someone, it would be the old-fashioned way.

I found on Sunday morning my appetite had returned and I cooked us a fry-up, tucking into the eggs and bacon with gusto. So normal it emphasised how out of sorts I'd been the day before. With a clearer head and a fresh perspective, I'd texted Mike. Perhaps there was a valid reason he'd removed his profile from Hinge? Plus, the missing hours were still niggling at me. He'd not yet responded, and I feared I'd have to put the whole thing down to experience. Perhaps we'd both got away lightly?

Claire left at lunchtime, giving me time to give the house a good going-over in preparation for the viewing tomorrow. I knew I should start house-hunting but couldn't face looking at the properties I knew were outside of my budget. The twins and I would be in a shoebox compared to what we had now. It wasn't as if they could share rooms either. That wouldn't make any difference to Jonathan, who'd previously said he'd be happy for them to live with him full time. It was a decision for them to make and I hadn't pushed the topic, fearing if I made them choose, I'd be the loser.

Jonathan brought the kids back later that afternoon but didn't linger. The viewing was tomorrow at four and he'd asked the kids to make sure they were out. Rachel was going to Casey's after school, but Ryan complained to high heaven because he'd wanted to come home and vegetate in his room as he always did.

'It's just for an hour, buddy, can't you stay at school or go to the library or park or something?' Jonathan sounded exasperated and I could tell he was happy to return the twins.

'Guess I'll have to, won't I?' Ryan sulked and left the room without saying goodbye to his dad.

I knew I shouldn't have but I couldn't help it, when Jonathan rolled his eyes at me expecting solidarity, I snapped. 'Well, you are forcing them out of their own home!'

'Oh, for God's sake, Kay, what do you expect me to do?'

It was like a red rag to a bull. 'Have you considered what an important year it is for them, with their GCSEs coming up. They've got mock exams in February and all this upheaval isn't going to help. But it's not even on your radar is it, because you only ever think of yourself.'

'You know what, I don't have to listen to this, Kay. I've got a gorgeous girl getting ready for me to take her out to dinner, so I best be off.' Jonathan awarded me a smug smile and sauntered back to his car while I stood infuriated on the doorstep, my ears pounding, feeling as though I could explode.

Despite my anger at Jonathan from the day before, I'd left the house pristine when I ushered the kids out on Monday morning, having got up at the crack of dawn to make sure everything was clean and tidy. There was no way I was going to take the blame for a failure to sell the house, especially after Jonathan had already accused me of dragging my feet. Even if I didn't want any prospective buyers to make an offer.

The car felt alien when I climbed inside, having not driven it all weekend. I was sure the seat and mirror had been altered. Although I could see fine and reach the pedals, it was as though someone else had been in it. A tiny change to how far the seat had been pushed back, or perhaps I was imagining it.

'Come on, Mum, we'll be late,' Rachel said, glaring at me as I looked around the car, having not yet started the engine.

I shifted in my seat, repositioned the mirror and made my way to school. Perhaps I'd have a proper look later when I had more time.

The office was quiet when I arrived, Tim, Liam and Ed were in Birmingham as the seconded employees from Allegra were coming onboard. I hadn't bothered to wear the necklace, knowing they wouldn't be in. I would be stuck in my office all day, working on a different supplier contract so had opted for a chunky jumper and trousers. The contract was relatively straightforward, and I barely saw anyone all morning.

It was after lunch when the email from Tim came through. A global announcement of the new restructure, with attached organisation charts highlighting each department change. I scanned through them, concerned at first I wouldn't find myself there. When I opened the one for Human Resources, I saw I was at the bottom unsurprisingly and, according to the chart, I now reported into Liam. Glaring at the screen, my pulse soared, and I picked up the phone to call Tim.

'When were you going to tell me?' I said, when he answered.

Tim sighed down the phone. 'Kay, nothing's going to change, you've just got an adjustment in reporting line.'

'Yes, to Liam, who is totally unqualified for the job.' I wanted to add 'that should have been mine', but there was little point. Tim knew my feelings on the subject.

'Wind your neck in, Kay. Liam is working towards the CIPD, as you did.'

I scowled; I'd bet the company were paying for his. I'd had to fund my own qualification that I believed would give me a leg-up. How wrong was I.

'Has he any experience managing anyone?' I snapped.

'Yes, he had two staff under him when he was Sales Manager for Retail. Now is that all, Kay? Damien from Allegra is here and we're ironing out a few points.'

'What, the six months instead of three-month secondment?' I said before I could stop myself. The vein in my neck throbbed and I bit the inside of my cheek until it stung.

'Yes actually. We'll talk about that tomorrow, but for now I have to deal with this,' Tim said haughtily and ended the call.

I gaped at the phone, unable to believe he'd cut me off. Did he think the contract blunder was my fault? If Liam had let him think it was, then he'd better believe I wasn't going to take it laying down.

Fuming, I left work early, forgetting a prospective buyer was going to be visiting my house. I pulled into the road to see the Martin's branded Smart car parked in the middle of my driveway. I reversed back towards the end of the cul-de-sac and did a three-point turn, so the car was facing the other way. I could see the house in my rear-view mirror and hadn't been watching long when I saw the estate agent emerge, shaking hands with a tall, smartly dressed man.

To my horror, Simon Fox walked away from the house in my direction, smiling to himself. In a panic, I started the car and drove out of the cul-de-sac, hoping he hadn't seen me. I hid in another side road, waiting for him to walk past, back to his house at the end of the street. Lungs working overtime, I tried to calm myself as he strolled past, seemingly without a care in the world.

Simon Fox had been inside my house. That awful man who had pretty much threatened me on my driveway because I wouldn't own up to scratching his Jaguar had been in my home. Panic flared, my chest pumping because I couldn't fill my lungs with air fast enough. Him in my private space, touching my things, looking in my cupboards, made me want to vomit in the footwell.

Finding the number for Martin's from a Google search, I dialled their office and asked to be put through to the agent dealing with my viewing. After a few minutes, I heard a click and Dean answered the phone. It sounded like they'd put me through to his mobile as I could hear he was in the car.

'Mrs Massingham, we've had a good viewing. The gentleman seemed very enthusiastic,'

'Mr Fox, I know who he is,' I interrupted, 'he's not a serious buyer, he just wanted to snoop inside my home.' I could hear the wobble in my voice, after fending off the oncoming panic attack.

'Ah, you know Mr Fox. Well, he's looking to buy a second property in the area to rent out.'

'Is he bollocks,' I snapped.

'I beg your pardon, Mrs Massingham?' Dean said, taken aback.

'I don't want that man in my home again. Do you understand.'

'I'll have to speak to Mr Massingham about this,' Dean said, sounding cautious.

'You do what you need to do,' I said, rage boiling in the pit of my stomach. I hung up and sat staring out of the window. Why had Simon Fox wanted to get inside my house?

21

If I knew anything at all, I knew it wasn't a coincidence. Simon Fox had been in my house and not for the purpose of buying it. I let myself in, trepidation rising as I stared at the space which had been tainted. The air seemed different, although I knew it was my paranoia.

Starting upstairs, I moved through the rooms, taking everything in, looking for the slightest movement of furniture or any missing items. I opened every door and cupboard, but nothing looked amiss. Everything was where it was supposed to be, as I'd left it this morning. Until I returned to the kitchen and noticed in the middle of the table, a single AirPod. My scalp prickled. I hadn't left it there, had I?

No, the other one that I'd found loading the washing machine was back in its charging case on the kitchen worktop. Each tiny hair on my body stood to attention. Simon Fox had been in my house and the missing AirPod had been returned. Had I left it on his driveway that night?

I gripped the edge of the chair, feeling dizzy. The equilibrium had shifted, the house no longer felt like a safe space, the sanctuary I'd once had.

'Mum,' came a hysterical wail from the hallway and I jumped out of my skin and flew towards the front door, AirPod forgotten.

I found Rachel who'd just come in, tears streaming down her face.

'What is it, what's wrong? Where's your brother?' I asked, bombarding her with questions.

Rachel dropped her bag and flew into my outstretched arms, burying her face in my shoulder. I led her to the sofa, and she produced a crumped piece of paper, handing it over to me, her fingers shaking.

I took it, unfurling the edges and looked at the black and white image, trying to make sense of what it was. Vomit tinged my throat and I jumped up, staggering backwards.

'It's you, isn't it? I found it in my locker. It's on some website. People keep forwarding the link to me!' she sobbed.

The image was me, lying flat on my back on the sofa Rachel was sat on. Arms over my head, sprawled out with my legs open, fast asleep. The polka dot blouse I'd been wearing was unbuttoned, exposing my black lacy bra and doughy stomach which protruded over the waistband of my jeans. It was me on Friday night. Mike had taken that photo.

Tears stung my eyes, and I clamped a hand over my mouth. Unable to speak, Rachel screamed at me through her sobs.

'I mean, what the fuck, Mum! I'm completely humiliated.' Her tears made way for fury.

'I-I-I didn't know it was being taken. My eyes are closed, I'm unconscious,' I stammered, trying to piece the events together. It was strange looking at a photo of yourself that you weren't present for.

'Who took it?' she demanded, and I cringed.

'A guy,' I managed, dumbfounded at the image I held in my hands. How could I have let it happen? How could I have been so trusting to let a man I'd just met into my home? What else had he done to me while I was unconscious? Were there more photos? 'I had a date on Friday, someone from a dating app.'

Bile launched up my throat and I ran to the sink to be sick as Ryan walked in the front door, right in the middle of the drama.

'What's going on?'

'Mum had a date on Friday, he's taken pictures of her, and they are on the internet. Haven't you been sent the link?'

Ryan shook his head and took out his phone, checking his messages.

It was an utter nightmare, I'd been humiliated, the compromising photo sent around the school. The twins' friends might have seen it, their parents too.

Staggering back from the kitchen, I sank into the sofa, throat stinging, and held my head in my hands.

'Who left it in your locker?' I asked, desperately trying to focus on what to do. How I could minimise the damage.

'I don't know, but the bitches were sniggering and standing nearby when I found it.'

'What bitches?'

'Ava and her crew.' Rachel sniffed and wiped her eyes.

Ava, that name sounded familiar.

Rachel saw me grappling with the name and snapped at me. 'Ava, you asked me about her, remember? The house that was done up.'

It hit me like a mallet to the head. Ava was Simon Fox's daughter. Did Simon know Mike? Had it all been a plan to shame me?

My breath came in short gasps, and I got to my feet and paced the room, trying to work out what to do. Should I call the police? What would I report? That I let a man into my house, and he took a photo of me when I was unconscious? How would that look? I could tell them he drugged me, but there would be no proof in my system now. No evidence of a physical assault and despite the photo I still didn't believe he'd touched me. Not intimately. If only I'd been wearing the camera necklace, I could have recorded it all. My skin crawled with the violation, tongue searing with acid.

Rachel stormed upstairs, leaving the crumpled photo behind on the sofa. Ryan picked it up, dropping it as though it had burnt him once he'd seen what was on it. Without uttering a word, he threw me a look of disgust and went upstairs to his room, slamming the door behind him.

I'd never been so repulsed and had no idea what to do. I couldn't think straight. I called Mike, but again it went to voicemail. I sent messages, but they remained undelivered. Did the phone number I had for him now not exist either?

Eventually, I grabbed my car keys, shouting up the stairs to the kids, 'I'm going out, I won't be long.'

'What about dinner?' Ryan shouted back, but I didn't answer.

It was already quarter to five, but I had to do something, even if I wasn't sure what.

Driving past Simon Fox's house, I saw his car was missing. I had the urge to hammer on his door and haul Ava out by the scruff of her neck, but resisted. How could Simon have dragged his daughter into this? It was despicable. I drove on, into town, pulling up outside Fox Security Solutions on a double yellow line.

I flew out of the car and into the shop, the bell jingling like crazy. Stopping as soon I was a foot inside as though I'd walked into an invisible wall. My face caved at the sight before me. Simon, behind the counter with Mike next to him, giggling at something on Mike's phone. It had all been Simon, all of it, of course it had. Things suddenly made sense, seeing the pair of them side by side, as bold as brass.

They both looked up at the same time and saw me, their grins fading, but Simon's face morphed into a pleasant welcoming smile.

'How may I help you, madam?' he asked, looking and sounding professional as though I was just another customer.

I ignored him and directed my venom at Mike.

'How could you do that to me, to my children?' I said, tears filling my eyes.

'No idea what you're talking about,' he said, looking genuinely perplexed.

I scoffed. 'You took a photo of me, undressed me! Drugged my drink probably, snapped a pic and now it's online. My kids have seen it,' I screamed, unable to hold back.

Mike raised his palms, holding them out as though I was a stampeding bull.

'Now, hang on a minute, that's a pretty serious accusation,' Simon interjected.

I whipped my head around to face him. 'And you put him up to it? All because of your sodding car?' I could hear my voice getting louder, face puce with rage and every muscle in my body pulsing and twitching. 'You were in my house today too,' I spat.

'I'm looking to purchase an additional property, an investment,' he said, a smile dancing on his lips. I had to resist the urge to slap it off.

'Bullshit! Stay away from me and my family.' I pointed my finger at him before turning back to Mike. 'I'm calling the police.'

He raised an eyebrow. 'Why? There's no photo of you online, the link doesn't work any more, *someone* has already taken the site down.' Mike shrugged, as though it wasn't a big deal, but who knew how many people had seen the degrading image. He was calm, completely unruffled and I knew he was behind it. He'd put that photo of me online.

I opened my mouth to speak, but Mike got in first.

'I'd be careful if I were you; people in glass houses shouldn't throw stones.' Mike's smile twisted menacingly; his eyes glinted. A completely different man to the one who had taken me for dinner on Friday night.

'Are you threatening me?' I demanded, my bravado fading when he took a step forward.

'No, but when the police ask how you got home on Friday night, and someone tips them off about you driving your car, drunk, into a Vauxhall Astra, what will you say?'

Simon's eyes shone at Mike's words, and they stood side by side, feeding off each other's energy. They were so cocky, unfazed by my outrage. How did they know each other?

'I'm sure the restaurant will confirm I practically had to carry you out of there,' he continued. 'They may even have CCTV.'

I stood, gaping at them in turn, unable to believe what I was hearing.

Simon's stance relaxed and he nudged Mike's arm, letting out a snigger as his eyes roamed from my face to my feet and back again. 'You didn't shag her, did you?'

'Fuck no, I'd rather have a wank.' He laughed; his gaze lingering over my body made me feel naked and vulnerable.

Bitter tears burned, spilling down my cheeks as the humiliation washed over me. I couldn't listen to any more.

'You know, Kay, all you had to do was admit it.' Simon's voice carried over my shoulder, light as a feather as I pulled open the door to leave. I didn't bother to turn around.

22

I drove around the corner, desperate to get away from Fox Security Solutions before pulling into a side street and stopping the car. My eyes blurry from a fresh influx of tears. Self-loathing lodged in my throat, clogging my airways. I gripped the steering wheel and sobbed. What had I got involved in? Simon Fox was clearly a narcissist. His ego wouldn't allow him to let the incident with his car go. The fact I'd lied to the police and got away with the damage must have enraged him and now he was getting his own back.

How did Simon know I was on Hinge? Had Mike found me for him? He worked in IT, or so he told me. I had no idea if anything he'd said was true, or even if his name was Mike? If he did work in IT, he might know how to put up a website and take it down again. Surely there would be some sort of trail though? A link to his IP address would be traceable.

We were so vulnerable online, our social media pages giving out details that could be used against us. Simon Fox had connected with me on LinkedIn, viewed my complete work history. Hinge and Facebook had given them both access to my photos, personal information out there for anyone to find. It made me sick. I had to go to the police. They couldn't prove I was driving the car, even if Mike called them to report drunk driving. In fact, I was sure I hadn't been to get the Skoda. The realisation dawned on me then.

Mike had. He'd been in my house, had access to my keys. He hadn't drunk that much over dinner; he could have easily driven. Simon probably gave him a lift back to town. With me unconscious, he could have collected my car from the car park and crashed it on purpose. I'd given him my business card when we met for coffee; he must have left it on the windscreen of the Astra. He only had to return the keys and I'd be none the wiser.

The more I thought about it, the more it made sense. It was impossible I'd have no recollection of driving my car. What was more troubling was the lengths they'd gone to, how devious and elaborate their plan. All over a scratch in his paintwork. It seemed like a massive overreaction.

I waited until my hands stopped shaking before I made the journey home, getting stuck in the rush-hour traffic with everyone leaving the town centre. I made it back at six to find a pair of grumpy teenagers looking through the fridge for what they could scavenge.

'I'll make some pasta,' I said, putting a pan on the stove.

No one replied and our dinner, less than fifteen minutes later, was a sombre affair. Rachel and Ryan were furious with me, all they could see was I'd made a fool out of both of them. Were the rumours going around St James's that their mum was a slag; a tired divorcee desperate to get laid? A drinker, who got so out of it she allowed a man to take semi-naked photographs of her? I tried to explain, it was my first date since their dad had left and nothing had happened, but my words petered out in the silence.

I laid my fork down, unable to consume another morsel as my brain conjured images of Mike unbuttoning my blouse. My stomach was tied in knots and indecision clouded my judgement.

'I've been told the link has been removed, can you check?' I asked, my voice strained.

'Yeah, it's gone,' Ryan mumbled.

Neither of them could bear to look at me and it was like a knife to the heart.

'Can you send me the link anyway; I'm going to contact the police about it.'

Ryan tapped at his phone and mine bleeped seconds later.

'Oh, and can you please not mention this to your father,' I said, relieved when they both nodded. Jonathan was the last person I wanted to get involved. I could do without another black mark against my name. I was sure the estate agent would tell him about the angry phone call and my insistence not to allow Simon Fox anywhere near our house again.

Once their bowls were empty, the twins went back upstairs as though they couldn't stand the sight of me. I found a bottle of wine, one I'd brought but stashed at the back of the cupboard for emergencies, and poured a large glass. Stewing over the day's events at the table, I was exhausted but too wired to relax.

Claire text me a meme from *Absolutely Fabulous*, a show we both loved, and I called her, finally spilling the whole sorry story of Simon Fox. Words rushing out of my mouth at such speed, she had to ask me to repeat myself, especially when it came to revealing the damage I'd inflicted on his car.

Within an hour, she was on my doorstep, carrying more wine and an emergency packet of cigarettes that we smoked out on the patio. The twins stayed upstairs, not even bothering to come and say hello like they normally would. I really was in the doghouse.

'You definitely need to call the police, but don't tell them about scratching his car. God, Kay, I can't believe you did that!' Claire was astonished, it was something so out of character for me, she had trouble visualising it.

'I know, I regret it obviously. I'd had a terrible day and he was such a condescending prick. I'd lost the promotion and it all became a bit too much. He was the icing on the cake. I'd had a drink and just thought fuck them all.'

'I guess you didn't realise who you were dealing with,' she said, stubbing her cigarette out on the brickwork and chucking it into an empty planter.

'No. I had no idea he would take it so far. I mean it's a bit excessive, right?'

'For sure!' Claire agreed. 'And now he's been in your house, seems a bit threatening to me.'

Convinced by Claire's reaction we called the police and a pair of young male officers arrived around ten o'clock. Claire had gone home by then; she'd offered to stay, but I told her not to worry. They listened sympathetically when I told them what happened, but I wasn't sure they believed me.

'So, this Mike Sullivan, who you met on Hinge, took you out for dinner, you suspect he drugged you, brought you home and undressed you while you were unconscious to take this photo.' The dark-haired officer with bushy eyebrows held the crumpled image Rachel had brought home in his hand.

'Yes, he put it online – this is the link, here, but it's been taken down already.'

'Okay, and you've confronted him about it? He's a friend of,' he checked his notes, 'Simon Fox of Fox Security Solutions?'

I nodded. 'Yes, and all this is because Simon thinks I damaged his car.' I didn't want to admit to keying it, knowing it would only hamper my case against him.

I could see them both frowning, their eyebrows knitted tightly together. I knew how it sounded. Unrealistic. The imaginings of a neurotic woman.

'It's an extreme reaction, isn't it?' the second officer, with a deep throaty voice, asked.

'Yes.' I sighed; we weren't getting anywhere.

'And Mike Sullivan has disappeared from Hinge now?' the first officer asked, incredulity in his voice.

'Yes, but I have a number for him. It's not even ringing any more; it just goes straight through to voicemail.'

'We'll look into it for you, Mrs Massingham. Can we take this as evidence?' he asked, waving the image.

'Please do,' I said, standing to see them to the door.

'Unfortunately, too much time has passed now to test whether you had anything in your system. You should have called us the day after it happened.'

'I didn't know he'd taken the photo then,' I snapped.

They left and I had a cigarette outside, staring up at the clear night sky, watching the smoke fade into the darkness. Claire had left the packet with me, stating I needed them more than she did.

I didn't hold out much hope Mike or Simon would be charged with anything. What could I prove, and how much time would the police spend investigating? I already sensed they thought it was a waste of time. The image of me was hardly pornography and I was an adult, not a child or vulnerable person. If I pushed it, would it turn into a he said/she said scenario? If it did, who were the police most likely to believe, the neurotic single parent or the successful businessmen?

23

I hadn't slept for long when the alarm went off, shrill in my ear. I'd been tossing and turning all night, trying to figure things out. Was Mike just a pawn in Simon's revenge game? Used to reel me in, knowing I was separated from Jonathan. Did that make me an easy target? How they must have laughed at me, at my profile on Hinge. A desperate woman in her forties glad for a bit of male attention. I was easy pickings. It turned my stomach, and I was glad I'd cancelled my account and deleted the app.

Did Simon now believe I'd had a suitable enough punishment for the crime against his car or was there more to come? It was hard to understand how he could have taken things so far. Why had I yelled at him on his driveway? I'd started a chain of events which were now beyond my control. I had no idea what he was capable of, and I couldn't stop thinking about him being in my house. Every so often I got a whiff of aftershave, as though he'd marked his territory. The idea was ridiculous; was I going mad, imagining things?

I had the urge to stay in bed and pull the duvet over my head, but I got up, knowing I had to go to work. Especially if Tim wanted to talk about the Allegra contract and the length of secondment

Liam had inadvertently agreed to. There was no way I was going to be dragged down with him.

The kids were still frosty with me on the drive to school, but I listened to them talk amongst themselves, mainly about how Ava must have put the image in Rachel's locker and how she might have got it. Pulling alongside the kerb, I turned the engine off, shifting around in my seat.

'Listen, you should know. I had a bit of an altercation with Ava's dad about his car. I think that's what it stems from. However, he should never have got his daughter involved in our disagreement. Please stay away from her and if anyone winds you up about that picture, just ignore them.'

'Easy for you to say,' Ryan mumbled.

'I know, I know, but it'll soon be old news. Something else will happen and it'll be the talk of the school.'

'You don't get it, Mum! It's been so long since you've been to high school, you have no idea what it's like,' Rachel snapped and shoved open the car door to climb out.

I sighed; she was right. I knew the twins were in for a rough day, but I'd checked the website as soon as I'd woken up and the link was still unavailable. My half-naked image was no longer on the internet, to my knowledge anyway.

'Someone needs to teach Ava a lesson,' Ryan said, brushing his hair out of his eyes. I'd momentarily forgotten he was still in the car until he spoke.

'Well, it's not going to be you. Just stay away from her, Ryan. Go on, you'll be late. Have a good day.'

Ryan rolled his eyes and got out of the car, lumbering along the pavement into the mass of purple uniforms.

I contemplated visiting Simon, perhaps we could have a chat, adult to adult, and sort things out, although the idea made me nervous. When I'd visited his shop, he'd found the whole thing hilarious. It appeared he had no moral compass at all. It was a game of one-upmanship, and I was the clear loser.

Logging on to my computer when I arrived in the office, I saw Tim had requested a meeting for nine thirty. After I'd grabbed a coffee, I gathered my notes and headed for the meeting room, surprised to find Tim and Liam already there. The atmosphere weighed heavily, and Tim shuffled papers like a newsreader, clearing his throat. His jowls wobbling.

He came straight out with it. 'This Allegra contract, Kay. The secondment length was a right fuck-up and Head Office are spitting feathers.'

My knees knocked together under the table. Despite it not being my fault, I was partially responsible as the Contract Manager.

'I tried my best to renegotiate the contract, but Damien drove a hard bargain.' Aware of the flush creeping up my neck, I tried to keep my voice steady.

Liam looked at his notepad, unable to meet my eye. His pale skin looked mottled too.

'It's going to cost the company money they weren't intending to spend and unfortunately that's down to you.'

My mouth dropped open, and I glared first at Tim and then at Liam.

'Are you not going to say anything?' I said, glaring at Liam, who finally met my eyes, his face full of remorse. He parted his lips to speak, but Tim got there first.

'There's going to be an investigation into how it happened.' Tim's brow furrowed, his nostrils flaring, exposing the straggly hairs men of a certain age sprouted in all manner of places.

'Good. Then you'll see it wasn't in any way my fault,' I said, keeping my voice calm and collected, desperately trying to hide the outrage inside.

'Yes, I'm aware you sent Liam the revised contract by email.

Head Office feel you should have supplied him with a signed hard copy, which would have negated the mix-up.'

I was unable to believe my ears.

'I handed the contract to you, freshly signed by myself, the day of the Allegra phone call that you asked me to join. I brought it into your office.'

Liam stiffened. 'I'm sorry I don't remember,' he said quietly, as though he wasn't convinced.

He was no better than the others. It was the same old story, all boys together, covering each other's arses. The vein in my forehead throbbed and I gritted my teeth, clamping my mouth shut to avoid telling them where they could shove their job.

'The thing is, Kay, there was talk of amalgamating the contract role into the HR Manager role, it was part of the restructure discussion. I had to fight hard to keep you. It doesn't look good.' Tim puffed out his chest like a pigeon.

'Look, Tim, if you're trying to push me out, then fine, but you better come up with a damn good package.' I stood, indicating the meeting was over. I'd only been called in for them to lay the groundwork. I was out, they knew it and so did I. It was just a matter of how and I wasn't prepared to go down without a fight.

Back at my desk, I spent the rest of the day going through my emails involving the contract, reading every single one and forwarding those relevant to my personal email address. I knew I had a case to make and hoped I could settle without getting a solicitor involved. I could hardly use the official route and raise a grievance as the problem was my new boss, and his boss too. I knew I'd be fighting a losing battle from the outset.

I contemplated calling Damien from Allegra, perhaps asking him to write an email, covering what we discussed over the phone and the renegotiation of the contract. Although I knew Allegra wouldn't want to rock the boat, they were our supplier, and we were their customers. Tim could easily pull rank with supply chain and find another company to supply auto parts once their contract was over. They had no loyalty to me.

I couldn't believe Liam was happy to let me take the fall for his mistake. I'd misjudged his integrity and should have told Tim the day it happened, covered my own arse, but I wanted to give Liam the benefit of the doubt. I wished I'd listened to my gut. I should have seen how it would play out. Liam would be protected. For some reason, he was the golden boy, untouchable, but if they thought I'd let them walk all over me, they were sorely mistaken.

24

The twins weren't home when I got back, and I called Rachel to find out where they were. She'd gone to work on her history coursework at Casey's house and believed Ryan had gone to the supermarket. They often came home from school, via the Co-op, their bags filled with snacks and sweets I tried not to keep in the house. If it wasn't there, I couldn't eat it and trying to keep the weight off once I'd hit forty was a constant battle.

I got started on dinner and rang Claire to tell her about my day.

'That's not on, Kay, you've got to do something,' she said once I'd filled her in on my meeting with Tim and Liam.

'I know, I'm going to make them an offer, a voluntary redundancy if you like, with a bloody good package.'

'In exchange for what?' Claire asked, sounding dubious. I explained the necklace I'd bought from Simon's shop and all the footage. Almost every day I'd worn it, I'd endured some form of sexism or sexual innuendo.

Claire cackled down the phone. 'You'll have them over a barrel!'

'I hope so. I'm bricking it though,' I admitted.

'You'll be fine. Any news from the police?'

'Nope, radio silence there. I don't think they believed much of what I was saying anyway. Owen okay?' I asked, keen to change the subject.

'Yeah, he's fine, he's coming round in a bit.'

I heard a key in the door and told Claire I'd have to go. Seconds later, Ryan emerged with a full shopping bag swinging from his hand.

'Snacks?' I asked, encouraged to see he was smiling. The scowl from yesterday smoothed out.

'Yep, bought stuff for the field trip tomorrow. Can you pick me up, the coach should be back at half four?'

'Sure.' After my impromptu meeting tomorrow; Tim would no doubt be accommodating. In fact, it wouldn't surprise me if I'd be clearing my desk and swept out the back door by lunchtime.

* * *

It wasn't until later, once Rachel was home and we'd eaten, that I got my MacBook out to look at the files I'd downloaded from the necklace. Choosing what I wanted to show Tim tomorrow. My confidence grew as I watched clip after clip. There was some damning footage of several human resources faux pas. As nervous as I was, having never rocked the boat before, I relished the chance to show them what I'd gathered. The necklace had been an excellent purchase and worth every penny. The only upside of my encounter with Simon Fox.

Copying the videos to a stick, I knocked together a quick presentation, bullet-pointing the harassment I'd been subjected to, with accompanying clips. The press would have a field day if they ever got their hands on it, but they wouldn't. Not if Winston's played ball. I wasn't about to be walked over and I had no intention of making it easy. I'd had enough of that personally to go through it professionally.

I resisted the urge to have a glass of wine, trying to limit myself to weekends or emergencies. It was good to wake with a clear head and I finished my presentation before settling to watch television. Drawing the curtains to shut out the noise of the howling wind. A bored-looking Rachel came to join me, and I took the opportunity to ask her about school.

'Have you seen much of Ava?'

Rachel screwed up her face at the sound of her name. 'Not really, she's still doing it, sniggering and whispering whenever I walk past, but Casey and I just ignore her.'

'Is she the same with Ryan?' I asked, my chest aching, remembering the atrocities of being made a social pariah.

'No, she ignores him.'

I grimaced but guessed that was a good thing.

'So, there's been no more printouts in your locker?'

'No, thank God,' Rachel said.

Thank God indeed. Perhaps it had been a flash in the pan. Today's news being tomorrow's fish and chip wrapper.

'Can we watch that show with the property brothers?' Rachel asked, crossing her skinny legs beneath her. She wore an oversized sweatshirt which she huddled into.

'Sure.' I laughed and tossed the remote over to her.

'I'm sorry about how I've been, Mum,' Rachel said, her voice meek.

'It's okay,' I said, wrapping an arm around her and giving her a squeeze.

'I really thought that you pushed Dad away.'

'I didn't. I'm as sad as you are that he's gone,' I replied, the words sticking in my throat.

'Do you think you'll get back together?'

I looked at Rachel and sighed, tightening my grip around her as she laid her head on my shoulder. 'I don't think so, love.'

We watched the property show in silence, but it was nice to have a cuddle with my daughter. It seemed as soon as the teenage years hit, the twins had withdrawn from me. Time with their mum was suddenly ditched in favour of watching Netflix on their iPads or, in Ryan's case, playing Xbox online with his buddies. I didn't mind, I knew it was coming and Jonathan took more offence than I did. I told him it was the natural progression of things, but he felt they'd grown up too quickly. We couldn't force the children to spend time with us, any more than I could force Jonathan to stay when he said he wanted to leave.

At around ten, I wanted to call it a night and we went upstairs to bed. As I took off my make-up and picked a suit to wear in the morning, a text came through from Jonathan.

We've had an offer on the house. Will pop over after work tomorrow.

My heart sank and I slumped onto the bed, the only sound an echo of machine-gun fire from Ryan's room. Had there been more viewings whilst I was work? I hadn't been made aware of any, nor had I heard back from Dean. Although I guessed Jonathan was his primary contact. Still, my name was on the deeds, and I had every right to know what was going on.

Irritation itched at my skin, and I knocked on Ryan's door, opening it without waiting for an answer. His room was dark, the stale smell of Doritos and sweat hung in the air. Ryan was sat on his beanbag, headphones on, concentrating on moving his platoon through the jungle.

'Come on, time for bed. Enough Xbox for one day,' I said firmly.

Ryan gave me a withering look.

'Gotta go, guys,' he said into the microphone before pulling his headphones off.

'Thank you. Night,' I said, pulling his door shut and going back to my room.

I climbed into bed, bringing my phone with me as I tapped out a message to Jonathan.

Who from?

The frustration gave way to a lingering notion of dread which started in my toes and moved upwards through my body. The three dots appeared on the screen, to let me know Jonathan was typing and I waited for his reply. I already knew the answer before it came, my throat closing at the text on the screen.

Simon Fox.

25

Sleep didn't come for hours, the stress of the last few weeks sat leaden on my chest, weighing me down. The walls were closing in on me. Why did Simon Fox want to buy our house? I stewed on the question all night, waking bleary-eyed and not remotely ready for the day I had to come.

The only positive I could draw from the situation was that the offer was likely to be part of Simon's game. He didn't want the house, he just wanted to fuck with me. But he couldn't know I didn't want to sell. I hadn't told Mike. So, he could delay and muck us around as long as he wanted. It meant more time in the family home for me and the twins. If anything, his plan to meddle in my life had backfired. It was this that enabled me to get up and dress for the day.

I stared at my reflection in the mirror, applying mascara. Despite the dark circles under my eyes and exposed roots where I hadn't done my hair in so long, in my suit, I looked like a woman to be reckoned with. It didn't matter I was a shell of that on the inside.

Ryan rushed past my open bedroom door in jeans and a British Lions hoody, haring down the stairs so fast, I blinked to see if I'd imagined it. At the kitchen table, both him and Rachel were rapidly eating cereal. Then I remembered the field trip and why Rachel was the only one in her uniform. She'd not taken Geography for her GCSEs, choosing History instead.

'Where is it you're off to today?' I asked Ryan.

'To see a windmill, it's near Chichester I think, so not too far on the coach,' he answered, shovelling an enormous mouthful of Shreddies into his mouth.

'At least it's a day out of the classroom,' I said, putting a breakfast bar in my handbag. I never wanted to eat first thing in the morning, especially not this morning when my stomach was tied in knots.

'It's supposed to rain.' Rachel smirked, spooning the rest of her milk into her mouth.

'Shut up.' Ryan scowled at her, which made Rachel giggle.

'Now, now, children,' I said sarcastically and watched them both roll their eyes.

I put the empty bowls into the dishwasher and checked everywhere was tidy before we left. Jonathan was coming over later and though it shouldn't bother me what he thought, he no longer lived with us after all, old habits were hard to shift. I didn't want him insinuating I couldn't cope, something he'd tried before when we were discussing whom the children stayed with.

It was easier to keep them in the family home, same routines, same environment, I'd told him. Less upheaval for them, and even though I knew he wanted to take them with him, he saw sense.

* * *

The school drop-off was noticeably quieter, with many pupils coming in at nine for the field trip. Ryan said he needed to go to the library, so he was happy to come in at the normal time.

'I'll do coursework in the computer room after school, so I can get picked up too,' Rachel said, getting out of the car.

'Your legs broken?' I joked at her lack of willingness to walk.

'It's cold!' she retorted, wrinkling her nose.

I kept an eye out for Simon Fox as I drove around the roundabout, but he was absent, so, with clammy hands on the steering wheel, I made my way to work. By the time I arrived at the car park, going over what Tim was likely to say in my head, my underarms were damp with sweat. I'd deliberately worn a high-neck blouse, fixing the necklace over the top, knowing during my meeting, the blotches climbing my throat would be on display. They'd see it as a sign of weakness, and I couldn't allow that. Not today.

I tried to focus on work, I had multiple contracts to go through, but my mind wouldn't keep still, jumping around as I worked through every possible outcome once I'd presented my case. On top of that, any motivation I'd had to do my job had evaporated. What was the point of working hard, doing a good job, when you were going to get shafted anyway? Although, if things worked out as I planned, I wouldn't be the one getting shafted.

As I suspected, Tim knocked on my door around eleven. He hadn't sent a meeting invite, preferring to surprise me, but I'd worked with him for five years and knew exactly how he liked to operate.

'Got a minute?' he said with a pleasant smile. He didn't even have the decency to look sheepish.

'Sure,' I replied, undocking my laptop, checking I had the USB stick, and taking it with me.

I followed Tim to the meeting room we were in yesterday, where Liam was waiting. In contrast to Tim, Liam shifted in his seat and looked like he'd rather be anywhere else. The air conditioning had been turned on full blast and I shivered as I sat.

'Right, let's crack on with it, shall we,' Tim said, opening a folder and pulling out a sheet of paper, the print too small for me to read from where I sat.

'Let's.' I returned his fake smile with one of my own, despite my lungs straining as though they were in a vice.

'I've spoken at length with the Tunbridge Wells office about this, they believe – despite both mine and Liam's reservations – the contract role should be amalgamated with the Human Resources Manager role.' Tim cleared his throat, allowing Liam a chance to speak up.

'We've advised against this, Kay, we don't want to lose you,' he said, squirming.

I smiled tightly and forced myself to keep quiet.

'Regardless of our opinions, it is what has been decided. They are hoping you'll find this voluntary redundancy package to your liking; with stipulations you'll work with Liam for the next couple of months to bring him up to speed.'

I sniggered unable to help myself. Liam swallowed, his Adam's apple bobbing.

'So how do they choose?' I asked, trying to keep the sneer from my lips.

'What do you mean?'

'How do they choose between me and Liam?' I asked flatly. I knew the answer obviously but couldn't resist messing with them.

Liam crossed and uncrossed his legs, looking more uncomfortable with each passing minute. He didn't have what it took to manage people, he knew it and I knew it. It was likely Tim knew it too. To work in Human Resources, you had to get used to having the difficult conversations. Liam looked as though he wanted the ground to swallow him whole.

'Well, the contract position is the role going, so there isn't a choice to be made. Liam is HR Manager for the South and that's that.' Tim's eyes were icy, he didn't appreciate being questioned.

'Take a look, Kay,' he said, pushing the sheet towards me, his deep voice echoing around the paper-thin walls.

I reached across and picked it up, reading the official company letter, signed by Tim, with the terms of my voluntary redundancy. My eyes widened when I got to the figure before I set my jaw into a hard line. Six months' salary was what they were offering. I would have to teach Liam everything I knew, carry on working for these idiots for another two months, for half a year's salary? I bit the inside of my cheek, the fire in my belly bubbling intensely. I looked at Tim, sizing me up.

'It's a good offer, Kay, you've been here five years and three months. If it was compulsory, and you were given statutory redundancy pay, you would be entitled to a lot less.' Tim looked so pleased with himself, I couldn't contain it any longer.

'I've prepared something for the meeting,' I said, waking up my laptop, popping in the USB stick and connecting it to the projector.

The first slide of my presentation filled the white wall. Winston's logo looming over us. Liam and Tim both raised their eyebrows at the sudden change of direction.

'You're right, Tim, I've worked here for five years. In that time, I was promoted from your assistant to the Contract Manager role. A role which I have fulfilled, according to my appraisals on file, to an exemplary standard.'

My pulse was so fast it made me light-headed, adrenaline coursing through my veins like lightning. I was on a collision course with Winston's and I wasn't about to stop. It was like jumping off a cliff into the abyss and hoping for water beneath the mist to cushion the fall.

Tim and Liam exchanged a look, confused as to what was going on. It wasn't the meeting they thought they were going to have when they'd prepared this morning. I wasn't the Kay they expected to see when presented with such a *generous* offer, in their eyes anyway. I bet they'd hoped it would be cut and dry and they'd be in the pub celebrating by lunchtime.

'However,' I continued, 'it hasn't always been plain sailing. Winston's is a male-dominated company, in what is typically a male-dominated industry. I thought I'd give you a snapshot of what it's like to be a female employee here.'

I took a moment to centre myself and clicked to move to the next slide. A video played out right on cue.

'Careful, lads, she's on the prowl now she's single.' Gav's voice could be heard before he came into shot at the entrance of the kitchen.

Tim deflated, rubbing his forehead as he watched, bolstering me to push on.

'Most days, I've had to put up with sexual harassment or inuendo, occasionally even from the boss.'

I clicked again on the second video where Tim filled the screen.

'Maybe we'll send our glamour girl Kay to meet them.' Tim's eyes twinkled before Ed's voice chipped in.

'She'll keep them in line wearing those boots. Have you got a riding crop at home?'

The camera stayed on Tim, filming as he laughed along at Ed's comment, going so far as to slap his thigh. He'd looked so pleased with himself and I was a sniper about to reload.

'I don't think that's appropriate, do you? Let's get back to the secondment.' My voice this time.

'All right that's enough, Kay, you've made your point,' Tim snapped, narrowing his eyes at me.

Liam gaped at the screen.

'Oh, there's more,' I said, getting into the swing of it now and clicking again. Snippets of emails appeared large on the wall, sexist comments, inappropriate jokes, general misogyny all highlighted in bright yellow. Click, click, click. Ending with my email to

Liam with the amended Allegra contract, the time and date high-lighted.

'Now, Liam and I both know the Allegra contract was his mistake, not mine. He had both the soft and hard copy at the same time. I tried my best to renegotiate, but they didn't want to wriggle too far out of a contract they practically wrote themselves, that Liam signed off on.'

'What do you want, Kay?' Tim sighed, narrowing his eyes at me, and running his hand through his salt-and-pepper hair.

'Well, I don't want the media to get hold of this, it could be very awkward should that happen. Imagine the share price!'

Tim grimaced and I carried on.

'I've emailed it to you for safekeeping. Might be worth running it past Tunbridge Wells and see what they think.' I smiled tightly, keeping my composure whilst inside I gloated.

Tim shook his head and pushed his chair back abruptly. I stood too, shoulders back and chin raised to the heavens despite the quiver in my legs.

'It's a shame it's come to this,' he said as he squeezed past me to open the door.

'Yes it is, Tim, but you led the way,' I replied as he left.

Liam looked like a statue, frozen with his lips parted, as though about to speak but unable to find his voice. Ignoring him, I pulled out the lead to the projector and carried my laptop out of the meeting room. The ball was in Tim's court now, he had some damage limitation to keep him busy. After not being able to stomach breakfast, I was suddenly ravenous.

26

I didn't hear from Tim in the afternoon and left the office at quarter past four to pick up the twins. I didn't bother to tell anyone I was going; Liam hadn't been in his office next door all day and I guessed he was with Tim, trying to work out what to do with me. Despite the nagging worry over Simon Fox, and that my house was being sold from under me, I enjoyed the victory. Empowered, I walked out of the office on air.

The sensation swiftly vanished when I turned into the one-way road by the school to see an ambulance with flashing lights parked directly outside the building. Swarms of children gathered around. A group of girls hugged each other, some looked as though they were crying. Every child on the pavement wore their own clothes. Someone on the field trip had been hurt.

I stopped as soon as I could, yanking off my seat belt and throwing the car door open, sprinting towards the ambulance, all the time scanning the crowd for Ryan. When he was growing up, we were forever in Accident and Emergency. There were bumps on the head, sprained ankles, broken arms. He seemed to find trouble wherever he went. A typical boy covered in scrapes and bruises. It eased off the older he got, but the fear never left me.

I came up short when I saw Simon Fox at the back of the vehicle, leaning over a person being stretchered onto the ambulance.

'It's all right, Mum, I'm here,' came Ryan's voice behind me and I swung around, pulling him into a hug he didn't reciprocate. 'Mum, get off,' he said, sliding out of my grip. Any form of public affection from his mother was a no-no.

'What's happened?' I asked, unable to keep the panic out of my voice even though my boy was safe.

'Ava had an allergic reaction, started swelling up on the coach. It was proper funny,' he chuckled darkly.

I stared at him, tutting. 'That's not funny, Ryan.'

'She's not so pretty now though, right,' he sniggered, as I looked towards the ambulance.

Simon Fox's face was a mass of lines, and he held his hand over his mouth. The image of a desperate parent as he spoke to the paramedic. He glanced our way and our eyes locked, his rolling dark, but he wasn't looking at me. I turned to see Ryan grinning like a loon. Simon glared at him before the paramedic placed a hand on his arm and led him towards the ambulance. He climbed onboard to be with his daughter and a minute later it drove away, blue lights spinning.

'What's going on?' Rachel appeared at my side as I groaned, gesturing towards the car. I wanted to get away.

'Ava swelled up like a balloon.' Ryan laughed, blowing his cheeks out.

Rachel laughed and I baulked at their reactions. Was Ava despised that much?

I kept quiet as I drove, listening to the twins talk in the back. Ryan describing in detail about the coach journey home, revelling in the excitement Ava's allergic reaction had caused. Apparently she'd starting scratching, before her lips and face began to puff up. It wasn't until he uttered the words 'that'll teach her,' that my blood ran cold.

'What did you do, Ryan?' I asked, dread creeping up my spine, attaching itself to me like a parasite.

'Taught her a lesson, that's all. She'll think twice about fucking with us next time?' He shrugged like it was no big deal.

Rachel's mouth dropped open, glee apparent in her eyes.

'Did you do it?' she asked, as I tried to concentrate on the road.

'She's allergic to shellfish, saw it on her form on Mr Bannerman's desk. Thought I'd mess with her lunch.' Ryan reached into his backpack and pulled a half empty jar of crab paste. I could smell it from the front seat. He must have bought it from the shop yesterday.

'Oh my God, that's epic!' Rachel said, laughing her head off.

'Ryan, she could have died!' I snapped, my stomach whirling.

I cringed as they laughed, they had no idea the seriousness of the stunt he'd pulled, of what could have happened to Ava. What could still happen. Sick at the idea my boy had done that, in revenge against her. It made him no better than Simon.

'You're grounded,' I said as soon as we pulled into the driveway.

Ryan swore and I snatched the jar out of his hand as we went inside.

'Who else knows about this?' I asked, terrified his friends might have been in on it.

'No one,' he replied gruffly, slowly climbing the stairs.

'It stays that way. You better pray Ava is going to be all right. God knows what Simon will do if he thinks you, or I, were involved.' I imagined him banging on my door, threatening to beat Ryan to a pulp. Just when I hoped the war between Simon and I might be over, my son had possibly stoked the fire. We had to play dumb, pretend we had no idea how Ava had come to have an allergic reaction.

I shoved the jar to the bottom of the bin and washed my hands, rinsing away the sin which clung to them. Why had Ryan got involved? He was no doubt protecting his sister which was admirable, but he could have no idea the lengths Simon was prepared to go. Now we were all in danger if he suspected us of intentionally harming his daughter.

'He is an idiot.' Rachel laughed as she helped herself to a packet of crisps from the cupboard and began to munch on them.

'Yes, he is, and he's clueless of what kind of trouble it could have got him in. You mustn't tell anyone, Rachel, seriously, I'm worried what Ava's dad will do.'

She stopped chewing when she saw my pained expression. The gravity of the situation suddenly dawning on her.

Before she had a chance to speak, the doorbell chimed. Jonathan was early, probably hoping I would still be at work so he could come in and see the kids before I got back.

'It's your father, go and let him in, would you,' I said, clutching onto the worktop as if it was the only thing keeping me upright.

I wasn't in the mood to deal with Jonathan and hoped his visit would be brief. I couldn't tell him what had happened between me and Simon. I couldn't bear his judgement.

'Hey, Rach,' he said, stepping through the door and giving her a kiss on the top of her head.

She led her dad into the kitchen, indulging in a few minutes of small talk before making her excuses and going upstairs, taking the crisps with her.

'So, we've had a full asking price offer,' Jonathan said, his voice full of enthusiasm. Completely unaware he was being led up the garden path by Simon Fox, who I guessed was just messing us around.

'Okay,' I said, sitting at the table without offering him a drink.

He pulled a chair out and sat at the other end, his usual spot, hands clasped together. He wore a three-piece dark grey suit, and I had to admit, he looked well. It must be the younger woman.

'There are a couple of conditions though.' *Here we go.*

'And they are?' I prompted.

'Simon will be a cash buyer, with no chain and he wants the sale to go through quickly. He'll pay full asking price if we can guarantee to be out by the twenty-fifth of December.'

I closed my eyes, the room spinning. I thought Simon Fox was going to drag it out, muck us around but he was doing the opposite. 'That's just over eight weeks away! Where are we supposed to go? What about the kids, what about Christmas?' I spluttered, imagining the disappointment when they realised not only would their family Christmas be disjointed, but they wouldn't be here, in the home they loved.

Palpitations in my chest began, a steady rhythmic fluttering. It was actually happening. Simon Fox was going to buy my house.

'Kay, honestly, calm down. It's not that much of a big deal.' His flippant tone enraged me, and my nostrils flared in response.

'Not that much of a big deal? I haven't found anywhere else to live yet,' I hissed, struggling to keep my voice low. I hated arguing when the children were home. None of this was their fault and I always tried to keep the fallout to a minimum.

Jonathan gave a little shake of the head, unable to comprehend why I was so upset. 'You're overreacting. The kids can spend Christmas with me.'

27

'That's for them to decide,' I shot back, he'd stabbed me straight through the heart. I couldn't imagine spending Christmas without the twins. 'You're giving me eight weeks to not only find somewhere else to live, but to organise moving everything out of this house too. Half of your stuff is still here,' I said through gritted teeth.

'I'll help, obviously. Look, Kay, it's a good deal, we'd be silly to pass it up.' I couldn't deny Jonathan was right. Simon was offering the asking price outright and not trying to knock us down but the idea of selling my house to him tormented me.

'And what if I say no? You need my signature too, don't you?'

'Yes, of course I need your signature, half the house is yours, but we need to sell. You can't afford to live here by yourself, and I can't carry on paying for you to stay. My savings are running out. It's not personal, it's simple maths and there's no point in getting emotional about it. The sooner we get this sorted, the better.' Jonathan had hit the nail on the head, without him paying the mortgage the twins and I couldn't afford to live here. It didn't matter how much I dug my heels in. I didn't earn enough to stay.

'You ruined everything,' I said, lowering my head into my hands to disguise the onset of tears.

'I don't have time for this, Kay. Start looking for somewhere else to live, I'm going to accept the offer,' he replied coldly, getting up to leave. Jonathan hated when I got emotional, but I couldn't hold it in any longer. I didn't want to leave, and I didn't want Simon Fox getting his grubby hands on our beloved home. There had to be another way.

Once I'd pulled myself together, I broached the subject with the twins, knowing full well they weren't going to be happy. Typically, Jonathan had left me to deliver the bad news alone.

'I'm sorry, I know you don't want to go, but I can't afford this place alone,' I said.

'What if I get a job, after school and Saturday's,' Ryan offered, and my chest swelled with pride.

'No, darling, it won't be enough, and you need to concentrate on your studies anyway.' I patted his shoulder as I stood by the side of his unmade bed. Rachel lingered in the doorway, her bottom lip protruding slightly.

We were all deflated, and I knew I'd disappointed them. Adults were supposed to fix things, make everything all right, but I didn't know how. I'd failed them – me and Jonathan both had. Packing our things and finding another home in eight short weeks was overwhelming. Everything was in limbo, my job, my home, nothing was stable, and life as I knew it was hanging in the balance.

During dinner, I received a visit from the police. The same dark-haired officer with bushy eyebrows who responded to my call on Monday. I invited him in, and he reintroduced himself as Constable Matthews. I'd forgotten his name the last time he'd visited.

'I'm sorry, I didn't mean to disturb your dinner, I won't stay long,' he said, peering from the lounge through to the kitchen, where Rachel and Ryan scraped their cutlery against their plates.

We stood awkwardly for a second before I spoke.

'Have you had any luck tracking down Mike Sullivan?' I asked, getting straight to the point.

'I'm afraid not. We have spoken to Simon Fox, who says he does not know of any Mr Sullivan.'

I scoffed, of course he would.

'I saw both of them, in his shop on Monday late afternoon, together.'

'The number you gave us is no longer connected; I suspect Mike is not his real name as we cannot locate him. On speaking to Mr Fox, it appears what has happened between you and him is a civil matter and not one for the police.'

'So drugging, taking photographs and posting them online is legal then, is it?' I snapped, my hackles rising. On top of everything else today I wasn't sure I could handle another blow.

'No, it isn't, however we're struggling to find any evidence to pursue those claims. The website doesn't exist, and we cannot test you for any substances you may have been given, because of the time that has passed.' He pursed his lips, looking as frustrated as I felt.

'I have, however, asked Simon Fox to stay away from you. It's difficult as it's a "he said/she said" situation. He is claiming your allegations against him are false and you damaged his car, but again, we have no evidence to support that.'

My muscles twitched. Constable Matthews was right: I had no proof of what I knew Simon had orchestrated against me, none whatsoever. I couldn't fight him; he was too clever. Whatever I reported to the police, he would worm his way out of. Mike Sullivan could be anybody. All I had was a profile on Hinge that no longer existed and a telephone number that didn't connect. I knew nothing else about him and Simon was pretending he didn't know who he was.

I could visualise him and Constable Matthews talking, imagined Simon telling him I was the mad woman who lived down the road. A complete fantasist who'd lost the plot when her husband left her. It made my blood boil. I didn't bother telling Matthews that Simon Fox was buying my house. What would be the point?

When Thursday morning came, I'd stewed on the situation long enough. I'd decided to confront Simon at home, alone. Apologise for the car, admit liability and offer to pay the bill. If it went well, I'd ask him to retract his offer on the house, assuming it was a serious one. I wanted Simon Fox out of my life once and for all. He could tell the estate agents he'd changed his mind and Jonathan would be none the wiser. We were grown-ups, surely we could come to some sort of arrangement that benefitted the both of us.

At work, there was no mention of my presentation the day before. It seemed as though everyone was avoiding me. Even Ed made his excuses and left the kitchen as soon as I entered to make myself a coffee. Tim and Liam both had their doors shut and the bravado I'd had yesterday withered away. Not wanting to cause any drama, I too shut myself away and got on with the job. Were they trying to get me to leave with nothing? Or was a more suitable package being drawn up by the bean counters in Tunbridge Wells? I tried not to dwell on it but imagined word had got out I'd been recording some of my daily interactions. Now I was to be shunned for my betrayal.

I worked diligently until five, texting the twins to say I wouldn't be able to pick them up and they'd have to walk home.

On the way home, I stopped off at Tesco Express and bought a bunch of yellow roses in anticipation of seeing Simon. A gesture for Ava, to wish her a speedy recovery. I was sure the allergic reaction wouldn't have been that serious and the paramedics would have administered something straight away.

I parked a few houses down and got out, legs trembling as I walked towards the front door. The house was beautiful up close, the exterior walls clean and white. I stood under the archway and rang the doorbell, one of those smart ones where you could see who visited. The seconds ticked by and despite the Jaguar being in its usual spot, it seemed no one was home. I'd get a reprieve from the confrontation I wasn't looking forward to.

My neck had already mottled, sweaty palms stuck to the cellophane of the flowers as I lingered for another minute. Just as I was about to turn away, the front door swung open and Simon Fox filled the doorway, illuminated by the yellow hallway light. He was casual in jeans and a sweatshirt, but his eyes blazed with hatred. It radiated off him in waves and I took a step back, my voice faltering.

28

'These are for Ava, I heard she was ill yesterday,' I managed, holding my offering towards him.

He snatched them out of my hand, dislodging a couple of yellow petals which floated to the tarmac beneath my feet.

'Why are you here?' he spat.

'To clear the air, to apologise,' I stammered, taken aback by his hostility. It was so different from his snarky demeanour in his shop.

He glared at me before speaking.

'She could have died, you know. If they hadn't called the ambulance so quickly. Clearly the apple doesn't fall far from the tree.'

I frowned. We were talking at cross purposes. Did he assume I was apologising for Ava's allergic reaction?

'What do you mean?' I wrapped my arms around myself, shielding myself from him.

'I know it was your son.' He left the sentence hanging in the air. It wasn't an accusation; it was a statement.

'What was my son?' I asked, trying to sound confused.

'You know full well what I'm talking about.'

'I'm sorry, I have no—'

Simon cut me off, he didn't buy my wide-eyed innocence. 'I was prepared to let it go before yesterday. I'd had my fun, but now,' he said, his lip curling back to reveal gritted teeth. He was practically fizzing with anger, taking a step out of the door and onto the driveway towards me. I moved backwards instinctively. 'He poisoned her; he must have known she was allergic to shellfish.'

'That's ridiculous. How dare you accuse my son. What proof do you have?'

He scoffed but didn't answer, so I ploughed on.

'Look, I'm sorry to hear what happened to Ava on the school trip yesterday. The flowers are for her, but they are also a peace offering. I was hoping we could put *this* behind us. It's exhausting.'

He took another step forward. I stood rigid; my veins turned to ice. Was he going to hit me?

'I know it was your son because I have eyes and ears everywhere and *this* that you're talking about,' he made an oval shape with his finger, indicating the both of us, '*this* is fucking far from over.' He tossed the flowers at my feet, petals raining, before turning to go back inside and slamming the door in my face.

The sharp sting of tears pricked my eyes as I was left reeling from his words. How did he know it was Ryan? Were we in danger? He sounded like a man possessed, consumed by parental rage over the harm inflicted on his daughter. I'd be the same, we'd found common ground there, but it no longer mattered. My family were in the firing line again.

Simon Fox was clearly not a man to cross. I'd wished I'd known that at the traffic lights. I should have let him overtake me, counted to ten. I should have let it go, but it was too late to change it now. When I'd scratched his car, I'd launched a chain of events I could no longer stop.

Picking the flowers up from the ground, my legs moved of their own accord, back to the car, where I sat staring out of the window before driving away. Simon had said it was far from over but what did that mean. Just how far would he take it? Were me and the kids safe? What on earth had I got us into?

Claire sensed I was in a bit of a state when I rang her and came over that evening. The kids were upstairs when she arrived at eight; Rachel was in the bath and Ryan was doing his homework. They were both in a mood as I'd recanted my offer of them staying with me this weekend and said they had to go to their dad's. I felt safer having them away from house, especially as Simon Fox was so unpredictable. Apparently Ava hadn't been in school, but word was that she was okay and recovering at home.

'I'm here to save the day,' Claire said, bowling through the door, holding a bottle of red. For someone so petite in stature, she filled the space, whereas I'd shrunken into myself.

'Thanks for coming, I'm sorry everything is such a drama these days. You must be fed up with it.'

'Nah, it's better than *EastEnders*, I love it,' she replied, nudging my shoulder to show she was joking. 'Seriously though, I've been thinking. Crack open the wine and let's go outside for a ciggie.'

I did as she asked, pouring us both a small glass as I knew she was driving. The rest of the bottle I'd sink later.

We stood outside on the patio and, illuminated by the security light, I eyed the weeds sprouting between the slabs, another job I hadn't managed to get round to doing. Although what did it matter now, the house would be Simon's before long. He wouldn't back out of the purchase now, not when he had the opportunity to derail my life further.

'What did he say to you again, about knowing it was Ryan?'

Claire twirled her ponytail, cigarette dangling from her lips. Forehead wrinkled in concentration.

'He said, "I've got eyes and ears everywhere", or something like that.'

'Yeah, that's what's been niggling me. He owns a security company right; you even bought a necklace with a hidden camera from his shop.'

'Yeah and?' I said, taking a long drag and missing the point.

Claire sighed good-naturedly. 'He viewed the house on Monday, what if he planted something while he was here? A camera or a bug?' Claire's words hit me like a sledgehammer, and I bent over double, coughing until she slapped my back. Smoke billowed from my nose and mouth.

It made sense, there were things he knew that he shouldn't. Had he overheard how reluctant I was to move, which was why he wanted the sale pushed through so quickly? I couldn't remember if I'd mentioned it. Also, there was no way he could be certain about Ryan if he hadn't been seen messing with Ava's lunch. How else would Simon know about that?

The solar lights in the garden blinked and swam. Vomit climbed my throat, but I swallowed it down.

'Jesus,' I said, staring wide-eyed at Claire, who nodded solemnly. What if she was right?

'We'll go back inside, and you turn the radio on. Let's have a look at his website, see what he sells. Perhaps then we'll know what we could be looking for.'

I threw my arms around Claire and held her tight, standing in a spiral of cigarette smoke. 'You're so clever,' I said, overwhelmed at how much I loved my best friend at that moment.

'I do all right,' she replied with a wink.

The initial jubilation gave way then to unease, and I shuddered. Had he been watching me? The idea freaked me out; me talking with the kids, eating dinner, watching television with a glass of wine. Had he witnessed all that? Poring over every image, every word spoken so he could twist them to use against me. It made me want to stand in a hot shower and scrub my skin clean.

Back inside, my head messed with me, the imaginary stench of Simon Fox clung to everything. Claire asked Alexa to play the radio and we sat hunched over my MacBook at the kitchen table, whispering as we searched his website. There wasn't an abundance of listening devices, and the smallest camera was on the necklace I'd bought.

Claire said Simon planting a necklace camera, like the one I'd bought, wouldn't have worked. The recordings had to be downloaded every day as the memory was so small and there was no way Simon had been back, not without me knowing. It had to be a listening device we were looking for and not a camera.

'Seems there's only one option for listening remotely,' Claire whispered and pointed to a black box on the website about the size of a matchbox but thinner.

I read the description. The listening device came with a SIM card allowing you to dial in and listen remotely or be alerted when there was a voice activation. It made sense, all the other options needed recharging and content had to be downloaded directly from the device. That wouldn't work for Simon, he couldn't get in and out of the house undetected. Although it struck me that when Mike had taken my keys to retrieve my car, he could have had one cut for the house. It left me cold. Had I made us exposed, unsafe in our own home? I didn't think so. There'd been no sign anyone had been in the house when we weren't there.

'Now we search,' Claire whispered, 'it has to be here, the kitchen or lounge – that's where I'd put it,' she added over the wail of Amy Winehouse's 'Back to Black' blasting from Alexa.

She started in the kitchen, after we'd googled how best to find a listening device, first in one corner, and working in a 360-degree motion to cover every inch of the room. I moved to the lounge, scanning the possibilities. I checked the window ledge, behind the curtains, on the mantelpiece, underneath the sofa – lifting the base cushions one by one to reveal the crumbs beneath. By the time I'd got to the shelving unit, I was sure the search was ridiculous. Before this week I had no idea you could even buy such things in the UK. To me they were gadgets in James Bond films.

I reached the bookcase where I stored my favourite books. Ever the romantic, it consisted of mostly women's fiction and love stories, as well as some Jane Austen classics. Bending to look at each one in turn, I froze when I saw, on top of *Emma*, the black box I'd seen on the website. At about five millimetres thick, I hadn't noticed it lying flat on top of the pages. I hadn't picked any of the books off the shelf in days and hadn't had any cause to look there.

Was it a subliminal message? Emma was a meddler in other people's lives. Is that what Simon believed me to be? A tiny layer of dust rested on the top of the box, so I knew it hadn't been moved. I tiptoed back to the kitchen, where Claire was looking behind the storage canisters of teabags and coffee on the worktop.

'I've found it,' I hissed, beckoning her to follow me.

29

'Fuck!' Claire mouthed as she looked where I'd pointed, her eyes like saucers. She pulled my arm, and we went back outside into the cold night air.

'I don't think we should move it,' I said as soon as the back door was closed firmly behind us.

'What?' Claire rested her hands on her hips, face scrunched as though I'd suggested playing chicken on the motorway.

'He doesn't know we know, right. As soon as I remove it, he'll know I've found it. Maybe we leave it where it is, then I can feed him any information I want. Perhaps I could stop him buying the house.'

'I don't know, Kay, he fucking bugged you, he's a psycho. You need to go to the police.' Claire's teeth chattered.

'They won't help, it's personal, a vendetta. I bet there's no finger-prints on it, I have no proof he left it here on Monday when he was viewing the house.'

'You playing him at his own game sounds dangerous, we don't know what he's capable of. You need to find out more about him. I'll do some digging tomorrow at work.'

'Okay, great. I need to have a think, try to work out a plan.' I sighed.

Claire left at ten, after a welcomed change of topic. We left the radio on and closed the double doors separating the lounge and the kitchen so we wouldn't be overheard. Claire filled me in on her time spent with Owen. She hadn't got bored of him yet, which I was pleased to hear. Whenever she mentioned him, her hands became animated, eyes twinkling. Maybe he was different from the rest of the men she'd dated before, perhaps he'd be the one to go the distance. I couldn't wait to meet him, but Claire would let me know when she was ready for that.

Later, after Claire had gone, I went into the lounge and pretended to call a plumber. Telling him I believed I had a leak in my water tank, which was located in the loft, after discovering a damp patch on the bedroom ceiling. I hoped that bastard was listening to every word, squirming on his decision to buy the house. Could I make him retract his offer?

Going upstairs, I popped my head round Ryan and Rachel's bedroom doors to say goodnight. I considered whether to tell them about the listening device I'd found, but they'd likely think their mum had gone mental. It sounded far-fetched, even to me. Plus, the less they knew about my involvement with Simon Fox, the better. I didn't have to worry about what they'd say that could be overheard, the twins spent such little time in the lounge anyway and any conversations we had I could move to the kitchen. Our voices would be disguised by the radio. It would be permanently on now.

Staring at the ceiling, I considered my options. Put up a fight, dig my heels in and refuse to move, which would cause no end of problems between Jonathan and I, or find somewhere new and start again, me and the kids. It seemed sad to leave so many happy memories behind, but the stress of Simon Fox and insecurity at Winston's was going to make me ill if I wasn't careful. I didn't have the energy to take on another fight with no idea how far Simon Fox was prepared to go. If he was willing to plant a listening device in my home and get one of his friends to drug me before taking semi-naked photos to spread around, then he was capable of pretty much anything. The man had no ethics and it seemed he had to win at any cost. Now he believed Ryan had deliberately tried to poison his daughter I had to be on my guard as he'd made it clear he wasn't going to let it lie.

* * *

When I got to work on Friday, buoyed by the weekend fast approaching, I knew I had to get organised and figure out what to do. Every aspect of my life had been thrown upside down. The task of finding somewhere to live, navigating a house sale, as well as searching for a new job seemed like a list of impossible tasks. If I stopped to dwell on them, I easily became overwhelmed, so I threw myself into drafting a contract renewal for our petroleum supplier.

With my mind occupied, I wasn't prepared when Tim called me into his office after lunch. I steeled myself as though I was going into battle, believing our meeting would revolve around negotiating a better offer than the measly one he'd proposed before.

'I know you might have felt a bit in limbo this week and I wanted to thank you for your continued professionalism. I've personally had a look at the contracts you've been preparing, and your quality of work is impeccable as always.' His broad chin lifted upwards, as though he was praising his dog for rolling over or playing dead. It was a look that used to float over my head before, but now I gritted my teeth at his patronising tone.

He leaned back in his chair, fiddling with the 18k gold Parker pen he carried everywhere as though it determined his worth.

'We want you to stay, Kay, let's forget all this nonsense and we can carry on as before.'

I nearly spilt my coffee over my lap and put it on a coaster with a trembling hand.

'I beg your pardon?' I narrowed my eyes.

'Water under the bridge, wouldn't you say. We've all said and done things we're not proud of, but Winston's needs you. As you know, Liam and I have been fighting to keep you here and Head Office have finally listened.'

I scoffed, my bullshit detector going off the scale. 'Only because they know they'll have to pay me to go. I'm sorry, Tim, but surely you can't imagine we can all work together harmoniously now. I have enough emails, video and audio clips to sink Winston's, you know it and I know it. Funny that now, suddenly, they want to back out of consolidating my job with Liam's.'

Tim sighed and clasped his hands together; our meeting clearly wasn't going the way he'd hoped. I was the irritating stone in his shoe he couldn't shift.

I was positive he'd told Head Office he could smooth things over with me, make the problem go away, but I'd opened a can of worms and was in no hurry to close it again.

'What do you want, Kay? A pay rise? I'll see what I can do.'

'I want a sizeable offer of redundancy, Tim. I want the company benefits paid up, pension, health care and on top of that a glowing reference. I'm not leaving Winston's without one.' My chest puffed out, shoulders rolling back. I was no longer a woman to be messed with.

'What size redundancy are you looking for?' Tim's voice had a tiny tremor.

'Five years' salary,' I blurted.

He belly-laughed, his shirt straining. I bit my lip, trying to hold my nerve. I knew it was a ridiculous amount – they were hardly going to pay me just under a quarter of a million pounds – but I figured going in high wasn't a bad thing. I'd been playing the part of the dutiful employee, one who wouldn't say boo to a goose. I'd never stood up for myself before and could see Tim didn't know how to handle this version of me. I was prickly and unpredictable, but it had been a long time coming.

'They aren't going to pay that!'

I crossed my legs, maintaining eye contact and waiting for Tim to go on.

'So, this offer that you want, to walk away, what does that buy Winston's?'

A smile danced on my lips, and I leaned forward in my seat. 'I won't go to the press with the material I've accumulated. Winston's won't be outed as a chauvinistic, male-dominated operation that sexualises and undermines women.'

Tim's brows knitted together. 'How can we guarantee once you've been paid, you won't leak it anyway?'

I got up to leave, watching Tim raise an eyebrow at my sudden departure mid conversation. As far as I was concerned the meeting was over, Tim couldn't offer me anything on his own. He had to go back up the chain to relay my position. I turned back to him as I opened the office door.

'We'll sign a contract. I'll even draw it up for you. After all, it's what I do.' I gave him a wink and sauntered down the corridor, grinning to myself.

When I got back to my desk, my jubilation swiftly abated when I saw I had five missed calls, two from the school and three from Jonathan, while I'd been with Tim. My blood pressure spiking, I rushed to return his call. Something must have happened to one of the twins. Was it Ryan? Had Simon Fox had him beaten up or something? I silently prayed I was wrong.

It rang three times before Jonathan answered and I could tell immediately he was in the car from the traffic noise in the background.

'What's happened?' I said, not bothering with a hello.

'The school couldn't get hold of you,' he snapped. He'd always expected me to be the one to drop everything if the school called or the twins needed picking up. Assuming because he was the bread-winner, the responsibility fell automatically to me, my job wasn't as important.

'What's happened?' I snapped again.

'Ryan's been caught with weed in his locker.'

30

Within half an hour, Jonathan and I were sat in the headmaster's office in St James's High School. Ryan had been waiting in the corridor for us when we got there, hands curled into fists, eyes flashing with white hot rage. Jonathan had laid into him as soon as he got within six feet.

'How could you have been so stupid!' he'd hissed, as I tugged on his arm.

'Hang on, we don't know what happened yet!' I'd said, gripping Jonathan's blazer tightly. It could be another of Simon Fox's stunts.

'It's not mine,' Ryan had interjected, spitting his words like venom at Jonathan. Their chests were almost touching as Ryan faced his father, refusing to back down. I was in the process of separating them when the office door had opened, and Mr Lake stepped out.

'Mr and Mrs Massingham, do come in please.'

We were ushered inside, and Mr Lake resumed his position behind his enormous dark wood desk. His eyes were weary as though he'd had enough drama for one week. I glanced around the room, unchanged from when I was last there.

I'd been a pupil at St James's, although it was called Oriel back then. I was unable to stop myself from shrinking in my seat, at a desk I was so familiar sitting across from. My mother would be beside me, sniffing into a tissue as the headmistress reeled off a list of my crimes. I'd been an awful teenager. Claire and I had got up to all sorts, but somehow as an adult I'd become compliant, even submissive. How much of that had been down to marrying Jonathan, I wasn't sure.

My father was convinced I'd been the one to cause my mother to have a heart attack when I was seventeen. Once he'd uttered those words, our relationship was broken beyond repair. I had no idea where he lived now, or even if he was still alive. We hadn't spoken for years. The twins never knew their grandparents on my side, which is why I was so determined to surround them with the love and support I'd missed.

Mr Lake cleared his throat, bringing me back to the present. 'I'm afraid we found, what we believe to be, marijuana in Ryan's locker today. He denies it's his. However, I have no choice but to issue a suspension for a week. Given it's half-term next week, we'll exclude him for the following week.' Mr Lake clasped his hands together and lent forward.

Jonathan let out a loud sigh whilst I was momentarily speechless.

'Now, Ryan is a good kid, all of his teachers tell me so. Although his grades have slipped this term. I wanted to ask, have you found drugs an issue before?' Mr Lake looked from Jonathan to me, and I felt the corner of my eye twitch as the anger bubbled beneath.

'Hang on a minute, Ryan said the drugs weren't his. I mean, what are we talking about here?' I snapped.

Jonathan patted my arm in an attempt to pacify me, but I twisted away.

'Two joints in a small clear bag. The local community support officer has been in and confiscated it. She's confirmed the police won't take it any further this time and she's had a chat with Ryan. He's been given a warning and we're satisfied it won't happen again.'

'He's saying the drugs aren't his,' I repeated, enunciating each word.

'I understand, but I am unable to let the matter go without following procedure, which is a week's suspension.'

'Why was his locker searched?' I continued to argue, listening to Jonathan tut beside me.

'An anonymous tip. I'm very sorry to be passing on this news and if you need any assistance from the school in helping Ryan overcome any drug use, then please do get in touch. I know of an excellent programme for teenagers.' He leaned back in his seat, smiling as if he'd delivered us a gift before continuing. 'We'll look forward to seeing Ryan in two weeks' time.'

I opened my mouth to speak, but Jonathan rose to his feet.

'Thank you, Mr Lake. We'll take it from here. I assure you my son will not cause any further problems,' he said, pulling me upright by the top of my arm, fingers digging into my flesh as he led me from the room. 'What are you playing at?' he hissed at Ryan out in the corridor.

The pair began arguing, with Ryan protesting his innocence. I took the opportunity to poke my head back around the office door.

'Mr Lake, can you tell me if Simon Fox has been into school today?'

'Yes, he was here this morning, we had a meeting after the unfortunate field trip incident. Why do you ask?' Mr Lake looked genuinely perplexed, but I didn't grace him with an answer. My mind was too caught up in whatever game Simon Fox was playing. He wasn't going to let it go and obviously had no qualms about dragging my children into things too.

In the corridor, Ryan and his father were practically chest to chest and I had to step between them.

'You believe me, don't you, Mum?' Ryan said, almost whining.

'Yes,' I said simply, to which Jonathan scoffed and stormed down the corridor towards the exit.

Outside, it had begun to rain, the fine droplets coming down fast. Jonathan stood under the shelter, waiting for us to catch up.

'Ryan, you can spend next week with me, perhaps I can straighten you out. I'll take you home to pick up some things, I've got to let the surveyor in anyway.'

My head snapped up. 'Surveyor?'

'Yes, Kay, the surveyor is coming today.' Panic rose in my throat.

'I'll take Ryan home; you go back to work, and I'll drop him around once the surveyor is finished. Then you don't have to spend too much time out of the office.' I smiled sweetly and Jonathan narrowed his eyes before shrugging and marching towards his car without so much as a goodbye.

'You're not really going to make me spend the week with Dad, are you?' Ryan asked on the short drive back home, but I was only half listening.

My knuckles gripped the steering wheel, heckles rising at what might be waiting for me there. At least if Ryan was with his father, he'd be safe from Simon Fox. That bastard had planted drugs in my son's locker, I was sure of it. It was revenge for Ava, plain and simple. What else was the lunatic going to do?

'Mum?'

'It'll do you good to spend some time with your father, a bit of bonding. It's half-term anyway, he was always going to have you for a few days over the holiday.'

Ryan slumped lower into his seat, sulking.

When I got back to the house, the driveway was empty, so I hurried Ryan inside to pack a bag. Five minutes later, the doorbell rang, and I opened the door to find Simon Fox on my doorstep, with Dean from Martin's estate agent lagging behind. It was just as I'd expected, and I was glad I'd been home to receive them. I knew Simon would use the opportunity to get inside the house and nose around.

'Mrs Massingham,' Simon said, smirking.

'Mr Fox,' I replied, awarding him a thin smile. Under no circumstances did I want him to see his presence rattled me.

'Mrs Massingham, we're here with the surveyor, do you mind if we come in,' Dean said.

I stood aside and let the men enter, realising a short balding man with a clipboard had been hidden behind Simon's large frame.

'I'll show Mr Greaves around,' Dean said, gesturing for the surveyor to follow him upstairs.

Simon and I stood in the lounge, staring at each other, the atmosphere palpable. When the footsteps could be heard upstairs, I allowed myself to speak.

'You've had a busy day, Mr Fox.'

'Yes, it's been quite gratifying actually,' Simon sneered, rubbing his stubble, eyes sparkling with delight.

'You could have got my son in serious trouble,' I snapped, unable to control the urge to let him have it.

'My daughter could have died,' he countered. 'Nice necklace by the way.'

My hand leapt to my throat as he chuckled dryly. I saw his eyes glimpse at the bookcase behind me and my chest swelled. He didn't have as much of an upper hand as he thought he did.

Ryan thundered down the stairs, his rucksack over his shoulder, pausing at the door to the lounge.

'We were just talking about you, young man,' Simon said, turning to look at him.

'Ryan, go back upstairs.' I kept my voice calm, betraying the panic of having Ryan in the same room as Simon.

My son looked from me, to Simon, and back again. The penny slowly dropping.

'How's Ava?' he said, grinning.

Simon took a step towards him, and I raised my voice.

'Upstairs. Now!'

Ryan did as I asked, although the leer on his face remained.

'You need to watch that one.' Simon's lip curled upwards, baring his teeth.

'Stay away from my family,' I replied, in a low threatening growl.

At that moment, we were interrupted by Dean and the surveyor as they came downstairs and passed through the lounge into the kitchen. They stared at us, drawing on the animosity in the room as we continued to glare at each other.

'I hope you don't miss the damp in the corner of the kitchen, oh and outside I'm sure there's a few roof tiles missing too. We have to get buckets out when it rains,' I said loudly towards the kitchen.

31

Simon and I remained in the lounge until the survey was finished. Mentally circling each other. A lion and an antelope. Predator and prey. There was no way I was leaving him alone in the house. I would have followed him around to keep an eye on him. Eventually, when it was over, Dean thanked me for my time and ushered the surveyor out to his car. Simon was the last to leave, trying to intimidate me for as long as he could.

'I hope you found your missing AirPod, I left it on the table for you last time I was here. I discovered it on my driveway of all places.' He smiled.

'I have no idea what you're talking about,' I said through gritted teeth.

'No, of course you don't. Be seeing you,' he said, giving me a little salute.

I stood firm, holding my breath until he was out the door before slamming it shut. Slumping against the wall, I panted, lungs on fire.

Ryan emerged at the top of the stairs at the sound of the door, his expression incredulous. I pulled myself upright, hiding my distress.

'Ava's dad planted the drugs in my locker, didn't he?' Ryan said, descending the stairs, carrying his rucksack and Xbox in a carrier bag.

I closed the panelled door between the lounge and the hall, so the recording device wouldn't pick up on our voices.

'Yes.'

'Is this all about his car?' He reached the penultimate step and lowered himself onto it, staring up at me.

I nodded. Ryan waited for me to elaborate and I closed my eyes and leaned against the front door before speaking.

'I scratched his car. He knew it was me, but I wouldn't admit to it, so he posted that photo of me online to humiliate me. I thought it was over, but then you...'

'I put fish paste in her lunch.' Ryan finished my sentence, sighing and rubbing his forehead. He looked old beyond his years, as if he was the parent and I was the child.

I nodded again, swiping a tear from my cheek.

He gazed at me with pitying eyes, and it took all my strength not to sink to my knees and sob.

'And now he won't let it go?'

'No, but I'll figure something out.' I pushed away from the door, regaining composure. 'Come on, let's go.'

'Is he buying the house?' Ryan said on the way out, as I locked the front door behind us.

'Yep,' I grimaced, 'or at least he's planning to.'

'Guess we'll have to burn the place down then.' Ryan smirked and a laugh escaped my lips.

'Don't even think about it!'

I drove Ryan over to Jonathan's office. He wasn't keen to stay with his father, especially now he knew what was going on with Simon Fox. I made him promise not to tell anyone, even Rachel. The two of them as twins had a love-hate relationship, but they almost always told each other everything. I didn't want to burden Rachel as I had done with Ryan. He was deep in concentration all the way to his dad's office. Like he was trying to figure out a way out of the mess I'd created.

I parked in front of the tall building; modern diamond-shaped glass reflected our image. I saw Jonathan exit the double doors and stroll towards us.

'Maybe it won't be too bad, Mum, a new start, somewhere for the three of us. We can look together.' My heart melted at Ryan's words.

'You're right. Listen, you've got two weeks away from school, it's half-term next week and then you've got your exclusion straight after that. Do whatever work they send you, I don't want you to fall behind, okay?'

'Okay, Mum,' Ryan replied, putting up no argument, and we exchanged a smile before he got out of the car.

Jonathan tossed him the keys to the Mazda and Ryan slung his backpack over his shoulder and headed towards the car park.

I lowered my window and Jonathan bent to peer in.

'Don't be too hard on him,' I said.

'Would I?' Jonathan's eyes twinkled.

'Listen, you have to promise me something.' He raised his eyebrows and I carried on. 'If, after the survey, Simon wants to put in a lower offer, he's not having the house, it can go back on the market.'

'What is it with you and Simon Fox?' His forehead scrunched up, a bemused look upon his face.

'I mean it, Jonathan; I think he's going to try to get the house cheap. I'm not selling it to him for anything less than the full asking price. That's what he offered. Remember it's half mine too.'

'Jesus, okay! Have you started looking yet?' Jonathan stood and folded his arms across his chest.

'I will. I've got some stuff to sort out at work first.' I waited for the onslaught, but it never came. Instead, he tapped the roof of the Skoda.

'I've text Rachel. I'll pick her up after school and drop her back Sunday if she doesn't want to stay over half-term.'

'Okay,' I replied and turned the ignition, watching him follow in Ryan's footsteps towards the car park.

Back at Winston's, the office was quiet. I poked my head around Liam's door to ask where Tim was.

'He's gone to Head Office. I don't think he was very happy.'

'Well, that makes two of us,' I said, more harshly than I'd intended.

'Down with the patriarchy and all that,' Liam sniggered. Catching my glare, his ears turned pink.

'I don't think that's funny, Liam.' I turned to leave, and he jumped up from behind his desk.

'Listen, Kay, I'm sorry. I had no idea what had been going on here, or how you felt. I certainly didn't want to take anyone's job.' However, he was happy about throwing me under the bus on the Allegra contract.

My mobile rang, saving me from Liam's awkward conversation and I gestured to it before going into my office and closing the door.

'Mum, it's me.'

'Rachel, are you okay?' I said, unable to keep the panic out of my voice.

'Yeah, I'm fine. I've heard Ryan was suspended, is that true?' In the background, I could hear the shouts and laughter of children.

'Yes, he's with your dad. He should be there to pick you up,' I said, glancing at my watch, it was ten past three.

'Oh, yeah, I see him. Okay, bye, Mum, see you Sunday,' she said and without another word she hung up.

At my computer, I had lots of emails to go through, mostly to do with the petroleum supplier contract I'd been working on. I went through them in turn, adding the information to the contract where I needed to, until I spotted one I'd missed this morning from Claire.

Had a look at all the jobs available. Nothing suitable at the moment. You'd be way overqualified. Fancy dinner tonight? How about The Dragon, I love their risotto! Got some info on Fox. 6pm okay? I'll book a table and come straight from work. X

I quickly responded in agreement. The Dragon was a lovely little pub, tucked out of the way. There was a great hiking trail out the back that was a few miles, so we'd start at the pub and go on our hike, rewarding ourselves with a drink when we got back. A fluttering of excitement danced on my skin. What could she have found out about Simon?

My desk phone rang, the salesman from Upstream Petroleum wanted to talk about the wording in the contract and I was distracted from Simon for a while. At half five, the office was dead. Liam had left and I didn't hang around.

It was already dark outside, and the car park was almost empty. One of the street lights was out, the other flickered uselessly and shadows loomed in every corner. I hurried to my car; aware how vulnerable I was with no one around. Locking the doors as soon as I was inside, I was unable to shake the notion I was being watched.

By the time I arrived at The Dragon around ten to six, I was calmer. Claire's bright red Fiat 500 was already in the car park and the pub looked warm and inviting. A soft orange glow through the windows reminded me of the open fire I knew to be inside. I was looking forward to a glass of red wine to end the week.

'Over here,' Claire called as I came through the heavy wooden door, the smell of home-cooked food in the air making me salivate.

Claire had found a corner for us to tuck ourselves away in, close to the roaring fire, and she'd already ordered us two glasses of wine.

'How was your day?' I asked, sliding into the seat opposite her and squeezing her forearm.

'Knackering. That quiet morning I thought I was going to have, well one of my contractors fell out, so it was a mad rush to replace him. Bloody software testers, I tell you!' she sighed, lifting her glass. I followed suit. 'Cheers,' she said, clinking mine.

'Thanks for the drink.'

'Are you ready to order?' A rosy-cheeked girl appeared at our table, making us jump.

The fire crackled in the background, and I slipped off my jacket before scanning the paper menu.

'I'll have the mushroom risotto please,' Claire said, handing the waitress back her menu.

'I'll have the same.'

The waitress smiled and left the table.

'So, what did you find out?' I asked, leaning forward in my seat. Eager for any ammunition against Simon Fox.

'Well, Fox Security Solutions isn't his first business. According to Companies House, he's had a few. The one before was called Avenue Security. Jointly owned with a guy called George Coombs. It's no longer trading, the company dissolved in 2019.'

I leaned forward, eager to know more.

'So, I found George today, tracked him down on Facebook and messaged him. He was only too willing to talk about Simon Fox and let's just say he's not his biggest fan.'

32

Our conversation was momentarily interrupted by a large gaggle of women entering the pub squealing with laughter at something one of them must have said outside. A whoosh of cold air made me shiver in my seat.

'And?' I said, watching Claire's eyes glisten as she paused for dramatic effect.

'And he's meeting us here at seven. I said I'd buy him a pint if he gave us the lowdown on Fox.' Claire gave me a broad smile and a wink as I sank back into the wooden chair.

I took a sip of my wine, full-bodied and fruity. I had to resist the urge to take another mouthful, a large one.

'I can't believe he agreed to come,' I said, once I'd recovered.

'Neither did I really, but I thought it was worth a punt. If anyone is going to know Simon's dirty little secrets, it's going to be his ex-business partner!'

George arrived about ten minutes after we'd finished our mushroom risottos, which were delicious. At seven on the dot, an ordinary-looking man in his fifties entered the pub. His hair was thinning at the top and his skin hung loosely around his face, as though he'd lost a lot of weight rapidly. He wore a brown cable-knit jumper over a shirt and jeans and had the approachable look of a schoolteacher.

I knew better than to judge a book by its cover after what happened with Mike, but I knew Claire would have done her research before arranging to meet George. She was nothing if not thorough and we'd sought him out, not the other way around.

Claire stood straight away, waving him over.

'That's him,' she hissed, 'I recognise him from his profile photo.'

George shuffled over, glancing repeatedly at the floor so he wouldn't have to make eye contact with either of us for long. I could tell straight away the awkward-looking man pulling an extra chair over to our table of two would have been no match for Simon Fox. *Don't get ahead of yourself, Kay, you don't know what happened.*

'Pleased to meet you, George. I'm Claire and this is my friend, Kay. What can I get you to drink?'

'I'll have a pint of Bishop's Finger please. If that's okay?'

Claire beckoned the waitress over, who laid dessert menus at the edge of the table before whisking off, returning a couple of minutes later with George's pint.

'You said you know Simon Fox?' George asked, taking a sip of the dark amber liquid and licking white foam from his top lip.

'Yes, well, Kay does. He's buying her house and, well, we aren't convinced he's a legitimate buyer. There's something about him, you know.' Claire nudged me, eyes eager, prompting me to take over.

'Umm, he seems a bit, dodgy, I'm worried about getting involved with him... financially, I mean.'

It was the best I could do. Claire clearly hadn't told George anything about the situation, which I was grateful for. I was positive George was going to wonder what on earth he'd got mixed up with. Agreeing to meet two women looking for dirt on a potential buyer of their home. It was hardly normal, but he didn't bat an eyelid.

'I wouldn't go anywhere near that man if I were you. All he does is lie and cheat and steal.' George's face darkened and his demeanour changed immediately. The hand holding his pint gave a slight tremor and he took a sharp intake of breath, putting it back on the table.

'If you don't mind me asking, what happened between you?' I probed gently.

'We went into business together. He wanted us to open a security company. That's my background, you see. I worked for a firm over in Charlwood that went out of business, and he contacted me to pick my brains initially. He was all charm at first and I played right into his hands. He had ambition, the sky was the limit, and he talked a good talk. When he suggested starting up on our own, each putting in fifty grand of our own money, I agreed.' George picked at a loose thread on the sleeve of his jumper, his cheeks reddening.

Claire and I exchanged a glance but didn't speak, waiting patiently for him to continue.

'So, we launched Avenue Security. My fifty grand didn't last long, spent almost straight away on stock, which was kept in his utility room. We agreed to go online at first, with a view to expanding and renting a property in town when we'd started making a profit. I taught him everything I knew about the products on the market, what the latest technology was and what things were bestsellers for home security. Initially, it seemed to flourish, for a few months we saw a return. Then he began shutting me out, not keeping me in the loop with purchases and stock levels. He kept everything to himself.' George paused to take a mouthful of his pint, wiping his face with his sleeve.

'So, what happened?' Claire asked, her voice a sympathetic purr.

'He wouldn't answer the phone or emails. He just kind of disappeared. I had to go around his house and bang on the door numerous times. He told me the company wasn't going to survive, he'd made a bad investment and didn't have any more money to put in. Unless I could put more in the pot, Avenue Security would go under. To my knowledge, he hadn't parted with any of his cash. Everything was in his name, all the orders, the accounts, everything.' George shook his head, eyes downcast. It was still eating away at him. Simon Fox got under your skin. 'I was smart when it came to security, but not when it came to business. I told him I wasn't giving him anything and I wanted my money back, or at least part of it. He said there was nothing left. The business account was empty. He showed me the statement.'

'So, he dissolved the company?' I asked, unable to comprehend how George had let it happen. Had there been no contracts in place? No joint ownership?

'Yes. I put my trust in him and he let it go under. Or so I thought.'

I gripped the edge of the table, my eyes locked on George whose cheeks were a blaze as the penny dropped.

'He used your money to buy stock for the new company, Fox Security Solutions, didn't he?' I asked.

George nodded, visibly deflating back into his seat with watery eyes. He'd been mugged off, lied to by Simon and his money had gone up in smoke.

'Yes, but I can't prove it. He quickly launched the new company, him as the sole owner. Of course, all the profits were his alone. It wasn't long before he rented the shop in town and was making a name for himself. He undercut every local firm until they went out of business, then slowly edged his prices up.'

'Have you been to see a solicitor?' Claire asked, her brow furrowed.

'Yep, but it's small claims court and I have little to no proof. I kept some paperwork from the first orders we made, but that's it. It could cost me ten grand to take him to court and if I lose, that'll be all I have left gone. He would have taken everything.'

I sighed, wishing there was something I could do to comfort George, he was bereft. He'd been naïve but I'd seen first-hand how devious Simon could be. He was to blame, he'd been the one to cheat and steal from George. 'I'm so sorry, George, that's awful. He's a snake,' I said, the venom in my tone obvious.

'I wouldn't get involved with him at all if you can help it. He's ruthless and won't hesitate to plough through anyone standing in the way of getting what he wants.'

I swallowed the boulder in my throat. Again, I wished I could go back to that night a few weeks ago and not step a foot outside my front door. I could have drunk a bottle of wine and screamed all the expletives under the sun about the man who'd belittled me.

There was no point dwelling on it now though, I couldn't change the past.

I finished my wine, realising Claire's glass was empty too. I wanted another but had to drive.

'Is it just the two of them, Simon and his daughter?' I asked, wanting to glean as much information from George as I could.

'Yeah, his wife divorced him, took him to the cleaners apparently. It looks like he's well off – the nice car, the big house and flash clothes – but from what I hear, he's in a bit of trouble financially. Although the business is no doubt booming,' George said bitterly, draining his pint.

It didn't make any sense – if Simon Fox was buying our property and what George said was true, how could he afford it? Dean from the estate agents said he was looking for a second property to rent out. Where was he getting his money from?

33

We didn't stay at The Dragon for long after George left. He was heading off to meet a couple of mates at his local social club. I thanked him for his time, and we swapped numbers. He seemed genuinely keen to prevent anyone from going down the same path he had in getting mixed up with Simon Fox. After meeting him and listening to his story, it spurred me on to take Simon down, not just for me, but for George too.

Claire and I stood in the car park, the wind shuffling wet leaves from one corner to the next.

'Poor George,' she said, rubbing her arms to keep warm.

'I know, he didn't really stand a chance, did he.'

'We need to stop the sale going through.' Claire brushed her hair away from her face, turning into the wind.

'Or maybe not, I need to have a think about it. I'm going to call the estate agents in the morning, see if they've seen proof of a mortgage offer or something. Maybe he's stringing us along.'

'Maybe, but the survey would have cost him money, why would he have spent it if he has no intention of buying the house?' Claire frowned and I shook my head, brain firing with questions I had no answers to.

'I don't know. I need to try to dig some more. Are you off to see Owen?'

'Yeah, he's coming around for a couple of hours, but he can't stay tonight, something about a rugby tournament in the morning.'

'Have you been to his yet?'

'No, he's having an extension done at the back and the place is full of dust. He's looking forward to it being finished so he can do a big reveal. He's all excited about it, bless him.' Claire must have caught the look on my face as she quickly added, 'We've driven past though; he's showed me the house over on Plumpton Way. He got out to speak to the workman.'

I nodded and she chuckled, shaking her head at my suspicious mind. Mike had me doubting the validity of anyone met through a dating site. I had to remind myself not everyone was a weasel like him.

'Thanks for tonight, I'll ring you over the weekend,' I said, stooping to give Claire a hug.

Pulling out of the car park after her, I drummed my fingers on the steering wheel in frustration. Every time I tried to find out more about Simon Fox, new questions emerged. From tonight's chat with George, clearly the man had no qualms about dispensing with anyone who got in the way of what he wanted. More than that, he'd quite happily use them for his own needs too. He coveted my house, but why? To piss me off. It was a bit of a stretch to think he'd go so far, all because I'd scratched his precious car.

I drove past Simon's double-fronted house on the way home, slowing deliberately. The gates were closed, but through the gaps I could see the driveway was illuminated, it looked as though people were inside from the lights that were on. The house must be worth

well over half a million, especially since the front had been remod-
elled, although I had no idea what had been done to the inside.

My house in comparison when I turned into the driveway was
dark and uninviting. With the nights getting in, I had to change the
timer plug for my lamp in the lounge and make it come on earlier,
so at least it would look like someone was home. It hadn't been the
same since Jonathan left. I'd not got used to sleeping alone, especially when the twins stayed with him, I rattled around inside.
Perhaps it was time to move on.

I opened the front door, wincing at the squeaking hinges. Stepping over the threshold, I sensed I wasn't alone and whipped my
head around, surprised to find the driveway empty behind me. I
stood frozen in the hallway, looking up the stairs to the dark mass at
the top. Straining my ears to listen, but in the shadows all I could
hear was the thudding of my heart. *Stop it, Kay, there's no one there.
You're spooking yourself.*

Switching the light on I slipped off my shoes and shut the front
door, locking it behind me and trying to be as loud as possible with
no real reason why. The sound comforted me.

The lounge was the same as I'd left it. A pair of Ryan's trainers
were discarded by the sofa that he'd neglected to put away and a
mug left on the table in the kitchen. Nothing had changed since
this morning.

Turning on the lamps, I drew the curtains and put the television
on for background noise, deciding to put my pyjamas on and pour a
glass of wine. It was always hard to stop at one. Ten minutes later,
free from my work clothes, I settled on the sofa and pulled my
MacBook onto my knees, my eyes wandering to the small black box
on the bookcase. If Simon was listening in, all he would hear was
the television.

The first website I visited was Zoopla – it told me that over a
year ago the house on Dene Hill had been bought for £450,000. I

recognised Simon's house instantly, although it was prior to the refurbishment. The previous photos were still available, and I scrolled through with interest. From the décor, I assumed the previous occupants had likely been elderly. Curtains were old-fashioned floral prints, carpets a dull dusky pink, and the walls hadn't seen a coat of paint for a while. The kitchen and bathroom both needed replacing and it made sense why the price was lower than I'd expected for a house of that size. Perhaps Simon Fox had run out of money by the time he'd got to the driveway.

Leaving the site, I opened Rightmove and searched for houses in Crawley. Would I see his house listed for sale? It wasn't there, but I did find a two-bedroom terrace house close to the school which looked affordable. Googling a quick mortgage calculator, I estimated what I could afford and how much my bank would lend me, in theory, with half of the equity I would have from the sale of my home. Hypothetically, the mortgage payments looked manageable. Maybe with a decent package of voluntary redundancy from Winston's I'd be able to widen the search.

Right now, there was no way I could afford a three-bedroom by myself, and the twins were too old to share, but the house had another reception room off the kitchen that could potentially be turned into a bedroom. It was the furthest I'd got looking for somewhere for us to live since Jonathan had put the house on the market, but I couldn't bury my head in the sand any longer. If Simon was to have the house and wanted us out by Christmas, I had just over seven weeks to sort something out.

The property by the school was listed by Martin's. Perhaps I'd be able to arrange a viewing.

My mobile rang, making me jump and I sloshed red wine over my pyjamas.

'Shit!' I said, moving out to the kitchen and closing the door behind me, glass in one hand, phone in the other.

'Mum?' Rachel's voice came over the line.

'Sorry, love, I just spilt my drink. Are you okay?' I asked, surprised to hear from her. Jonathan often took the twins out for dinner on a Friday night when he had them for the weekend.

'Yeah fine, I'm upstairs. Dad and Monique are downstairs arguing.' She sighed, and I sat up straighter, my interest piqued.

'Arguing? About what?'

'Money I think. Can I come home?'

34

Rachel sounded miserable and my chest tightened.

'Of course you can come home, but you need to speak to your dad first. I've had some wine, so I can't pick you up now, but tomorrow morning if you feel the same, I'll come and get you.'

'Okay,' Rachel conceded.

'Is Ryan with you?'

'He's listening at the top of the stairs. He's so nosy!'

It must be tough for them, adjusting to not only our separation but also the introduction of a new girlfriend too.

'Have you got your homework done so you can enjoy the weekend?' I asked, changing the subject.

'Yes, Ryan's leaving his though,' she sneered, referring to his suspension.

'No surprise there. Have you got any plans for tomorrow?'

'I think Dad was talking about some water park, but I don't really fancy it, so I don't know yet.' I could almost hear Rachel rolling her eyes.

'Okay, well, let me know if you need me. I'm sure things will calm down there soon. Keep in touch, yeah?'

'Sure, Mum, will do. Love you.' Rachel rang off and my eyes filled with tears. I missed the twins when they weren't around and knowing Rachel wanted to come home was difficult to swallow.

I moved back into the lounge, my gaze falling on the black listening device. It was near on impossible to relax knowing it was there, although that was preferable to forgetting and talking freely. I smirked, an idea coming to me.

My phone back at my ear, I raised my voice. 'I know. It's such a nightmare. The neighbours on the right are such animals. Their teenager's bloody music blares at all hours and they are just plain rude when you ask them to turn it down. Don't get me started on the parking either, the number of times I've had my driveway blocked...' I ranted, keeping the charade up for a couple of minutes before telling my imaginary caller that I had to go because my programme was about to start.

Sniggering silently into my glass, I returned to the sofa, hoping Simon had enjoyed listening to the show. Shutting down my laptop, I turned up the television and poured another glass of wine from the bottle I'd opened. Unable to concentrate, I flitted between programmes, eventually giving in and going to bed at eleven. My phone had remained silent since Rachel's call, and I charged it by my bed, in case the kids wanted to get hold of me.

It was a fitful night's sleep. I kept imagining noises downstairs, something I often did when I was all too aware of being alone at night. Houses made noises I'd eventually conceded, but I was more comfortable with the twins at home with me. When I did go off, I'd dreamt Simon Fox had made me polish his car at gunpoint. I woke, sweating and tangled in the duvet. It was already eight and I got up to begin my weekend chores of cleaning and laundry.

It never ceased to amaze me how two children could wear so many clothes in one week, Rachel especially was guilty of having two or three outfits a day of a weekend on top of the different varieties of loungewear she lived in after school. There was no text or call from her overnight and I decided to leave her be. She'd soon get in touch again if she wanted to come home.

At ten, when I'd showered and dressed, I saw I had a missed call from Tim. He hadn't left a message and I had no intention of calling him back. Whatever it was could wait until Monday. Instead, I called Martin's intending to speak to Dean. The lady who answered the phone told me he didn't work Saturdays but asked if she could help. Once I'd told her who I was, she said she'd been trying to get hold of Mr Massingham. Our prospective buyer had received his survey of our property and wanted to renegotiate his offer.

'I've already spoken to Jonathan, um, Mr Massingham about this,' I quickly corrected myself. 'If Mr Fox wishes to reduce his offer we will decline and put the house back on the market,' I said stiffly.

I knew it was coming, there was no way Simon would be able to resist trying to force down the price.

'Oh, okay I'll feed that back,' the lady said, unable to keep the surprise out of her voice.

'Can you tell me if Mr Fox has a property in the chain?' I asked, hoping the inexperienced Saturday girl would happily give the information over without question.

'I understand there's another property in the chain, yes,' she hesitated, and I could hear her shuffling paper before speaking again. 'Sorry, Mrs Massingham, I'm confused, I thought you and Mr Massingham were buying another property?' she continued, a nervous giggle escaping.

My stomach lurched as the penny dropped. I wasn't buying another property, not yet, but Jonathan was. He was buying one with Monique.

'P-Perhaps my husband is,' I stammered, 'we're separated.' The bitter sting of tears clouded my vision.

'Oh, I'm sorry.' An awkward silence followed with more rustling her end.

'Is the two-bedroom by St James's still available?' I asked, pulling myself together.

'Yes, it is. Would you like me to schedule a viewing?'

'Yes please, as soon as possible.'

'The property is empty so I can take you this afternoon if it's convenient?'

A few hours later, I waited outside number 28 Goddard Close for Louise, the estate agent, to arrive with keys. The road was pleasant; an identical row of red-bricked terraced houses with white double-glazed windows lined each side. Some had picket-fenced front gardens arranged with decorative topiary balls swinging in the breeze. It appeared as though the area was looked after by its residents who took pride in their homes.

Louise arrived a few minutes later. A sturdy-looking blonde climbed out of a Fiesta, trying to disguise an expression on her face which screamed pity with an overly wide smile.

'Mrs Massingham, pleased to meet you. I'm Louise.' She shook my hand with gusto.

'Please call me Kay,' I said politely, standing aside so she could lead the way.

The house had a royal blue front door that looked new, although the front garden needed some work to bring it to the street standard, but it had potential.

'You have two numbered car parking spaces, just here,' Louise said, gesturing behind at empty spaces in front of the property. 'There's no chain, the owners have relocated to Swanage and are renting until they find somewhere to buy. I believe they can be reasonably flexible on price too. It's currently on the market for £325,000, but you'll see it's recently been updated.'

It did seem a little on the high side for a two-bedroom, but I knew I couldn't afford the jump to a three-bedroom property. Not on one salary. The whole prospect of moving out and buying somewhere alone was daunting, but I smiled, following as Louise began the tour.

Downstairs comprised of a small hallway that opened into a large living room, which housed the stairs to the first floor. At the back of the property was the kitchen which looked almost new and to a higher spec than what I was used to.

'All of the appliances are staying, pretty much everything left here is available for the buyer to keep. The owners have left their curtain poles, curtains and fitted blinds. It really is ready to move into.' Louise beamed and I smiled back, surprised to find myself matching her enthusiasm.

To the right of the kitchen was a small study and a downstairs toilet. You couldn't get a double bed in there, but I had a feeling Ryan would opt for that room.

'The garden is part patio, part artificial grass.' Louise wiggled the key in the lock, which seemed stiff, and pushed the door open to show a tidy garden with five-foot green fencing topped with trellis on all sides. 'Very easy to maintain,' she said, as I shuffled out for a second.

Back inside, I looked around, trying to take it all in. Trying to imagine me, Rachel and Ryan in the space. Thankfully the décor was neutral and therefore inoffensive, I wasn't a fan of big bold colours or feature walls. Plus, the downstairs was all dark wood flooring which would be easy to keep clean.

'It's carpeted upstairs throughout,' Louise said, as we climbed the mottled grey stairs, which flowed into both bedrooms. The master bedroom was large with fitted wardrobes and the second bedroom was also a good size. 'The family bathroom has a shower over the bath to maximise on space,' Louise continued her sales pitch, the smile never leaving her face. She let me go in alone, waiting in the hallway as I took in the glossy white suite.

'It all seems like it's been recently done,' I said, turning back towards her, catching her discreetly trying to check her phone.

'Yes, I believe so. I don't think this one will be on the market for long, as I said it's ready to move into and needs nothing doing to it.'

I cast my eyes over every inch, trying to absorb the aura from the house. I was calm, the place had a quiet to it, despite the cars going by outside. The space was safe, away from Simon's intrusion, it hadn't been smeared with his presence. As much as I didn't want to move and would never have considered it if Jonathan hadn't forced my hand, perhaps I'd found our new home.

35

I called Claire when I got home, after I'd rung the bank. I stood out in the garden with an early glass of red wine and a cigarette from the last packet she'd left behind. The trees in the next-door garden swayed precariously in the wind, but backed against the kitchen wall, I was out of the gale. The clouds had darkened to a steely grey, the sun a distant memory. A Marks and Spencer shepherd's pie was in the oven, and I was looking forward to a chilled evening watching a movie. There'd been no calls or messages from Rachel or Ryan, so I assumed last night's argument had been brushed under the carpet and neither were in a rush to return home.

I told Claire all about the house in Goddard Close and my conversation with the estate agent, and when I explained that Jonathan had a house in the chain, not Simon, I could hear her getting angry on my behalf.

'Is he not sharing the paperwork with you, Kay?'

'To be honest, I haven't really got involved. He's told me the asking price, and Simon's offer was exactly that. I guess I've been dragging my heels – so much going on at work and everything, plus not wanting to bloody move in the first place.'

'Work still the same?'

'Yep, no news on the redundancy offer yet. Although Tim did phone me today, which was random. I haven't returned his call.'

'Cheeky bugger!' Claire exclaimed.

'I know, I think maybe they are trying to backtrack and he's the messenger. They really don't want to pay me off.' I sighed. It was something I'd have to take up with Tim next week, although I wasn't looking forward to another confrontation.

'Ask Jonathan for something official, so you can keep abreast of it. Don't let him pull a fast one,' Claire said, reverting back on topic.

'I don't think he could really, not with both our names on the deeds. He just didn't tell me he was buying another house, which I'm assuming is with her.' I sucked in smoke from the cigarette, blowing it out above my head. Every time I thought about Monique, I had a stabbing sensation in my side. It pained me to think of Jonathan with another woman, despite us having been separated for months.

'Well, it's obviously with *her*, isn't it? Can't believe he's not being straight about it though. What a dick!'

'I only found out she existed a couple of weeks ago. It must have been going on before he left. I mean, you don't buy a house with someone you've been with for six months.' My chin wobbled, but I straightened, overarching my back. No longer willing to waste any tears on Jonathan or my imploding marriage.

'So, if Simon isn't selling his house, where is he getting the money from to buy yours?'

'No idea, I'm still half expecting him to pull out. I need to take the kids to Goddard Close on Monday. I called the bank when I got home – they'll lend me the sum, in principle, although it's not a formal mortgage offer. I've got to supply bank statements and payslips before they'll do that.'

'Well, that's something.' Claire yawned. 'God I've got to go out for dinner with Owen and I can't be arsed, I've got a headache. Might see if I can put him off until tomorrow.' She laughed.

'Right, it's freezing out here, I'm going back inside.'

'You'll have to have some normal conversations in the lounge, Kay, otherwise he'll get suspicious if he doesn't hear anything.'

'Last night I gave him quite a bit to hear.' I giggled, telling her about my imaginary problem neighbours. She squealed with delight.

'Anyway, I'll let you get on with blowing Owen out then, speak to you later, hon. Love you.'

A timer in the kitchen pinged and I stubbed out my cigarette, returning to dish up my dinner. I was foregoing the kitchen table, using my knees on the sofa instead. A forkful of steaming potato was halfway to my mouth when I froze. A quick glance at the bookcase as I waited for the television to come to life made every hair on my body stand to attention.

The black box was gone. Goosebumps covered my arms and my hand tremored. Lowering my fork and setting my plate aside, I jumped up to see if it had fallen down the back or slipped behind one of the books, but despite searching every shelf, sneezing as an influx of dust spiralled in the air, I couldn't find it. My tongue glued to the roof of my mouth as my search became panicked. Books tumbled off the shelf in my haste to check again. *It was here yesterday; I know it was. I saw it last night. Shit!*

Realisation dawned that Simon Fox had been in my house. Or possibly Mike Sullivan. How had they gained access? Had Mike given Simon a copy of my key? I shuddered, looking around the room as though someone was there, hiding. Why had they broken in, was it just to collect the recorder? I recalled when searching for listening devices on the internet, many of them had to be recharged or have their batteries changed. Is that why it had been removed? Or had Simon concluded it was no longer of any use? Was it only picking up the noise of the television or radio instead of useful information he could use against me? If so, could he have hidden it in another part of the house?

I moved to the front door and checked it was locked. Systematically moving from window to window and then to the back door checking the same. Upstairs, I checked the windows too, stopping to stare out onto the driveway from my bedroom window. A rain shower was in full flow, hammering the roof of my car. The hedges that lined the drive were swaying and the road was quiet, uninhabited. Everyone tucked inside their warm houses, safe and sound.

A cold sweat peppered my back as I recalled the noises I'd heard last night in bed, the floorboards creaking, movement below. Noises I'd put down to my imagination, paired with alcohol, adding to the anxiety of being alone. All the time someone had been in my house. It was either then or when I was at Goddard Close. Easier to break into someone's house under the cover of darkness though.

Claire was right. I should have called the police the moment I found the bug. I couldn't call them now, not without sounding like a mad woman. My mind whirled with possibilities. Should I go to a hotel? Was I safe here alone? I couldn't call Jonathan and I didn't want to bother Claire again. One night would be okay. I'd barricade the doors and sleep downstairs on the sofa, leaving the lights on, so anyone attempting to break in would think I was awake.

Back in the lounge, I brushed away the dust and put the books back on the shelves, checking again to make sure the listening device had gone and I wasn't going mad, but no, it had definitely gone.

My shepherd's pie was lukewarm and after one stodgy mouthful I couldn't force any more. I poured the glass of wine down the sink too. As much as I needed the numbing of alcohol, I had to be on my guard tonight in case Simon, or Mike, came back.

Resuming guard on the sofa, my brain whirred with ominous

scenarios. I couldn't switch them off and was unable to focus on anything. It was difficult to relax, my shoulders had risen to my ears, and I was on edge at the slightest sound outside. The rain slowed and one of the neighbours brought their wheelie bin back from the kerb. I peered out of the window fully expecting to find a man on my driveway.

This is ridiculous, I scolded, annoyed at Simon's ability to make me uneasy in my own home. It should be my sanctuary, but I no longer felt safe, flinching at every noise or movement, my imagination playing tricks on me. Even shadows at the back door from next-door's trees made me shudder.

Curling my knees to my chest, wrapped in a protective blanket, I let the tears fall, allowing a private moment of self-pity. An advert came on the television, interrupting my anguish. A large hardware store was offering discounted security lights to ward off the winter darkness and it struck me there was one person who might be able to help.

Snatching up my phone, I composed a text to George, asking him if he was free tomorrow as I needed some advice. Within minutes he'd responded, his Saturday night obviously as busy as mine, and we fixed a time for him to come around.

36

George arrived promptly at eleven on Sunday morning. I opened the door bleary-eyed from lack of sleep and invited him in. He looked as though he'd made an effort in jeans and a red checked shirt, whereas I was hiding my shrinking frame in a baggy jumper and unwashed hair pulled into a messy bun. I took a step back, immediately self-conscious.

'Hi, George, come in,' I said, mustering a smile. The night had been exhausting and I'd barely closed my eyes before jolting awake at foxes fighting outside or a random car door being shut. My phone gripped in my hand ready to dial the police, I'd struggled to get comfortable on the two-seater sofa and when daylight arrived my neck had a crick in it which wouldn't go away despite the hot shower. 'Would you like a cup of tea?' I asked, leading the way to the kitchen. A passing thought that I knew George as little as I'd known Mike, yet I'd invited him into my home.

'That would be lovely, thank you.' He seemed less awkward than when we'd met on Friday night. Only a sheen on his forehead betrayed his composure as we sat opposite each other at the table, nursing steaming cups of freshly made tea. I felt completely at ease. George was no threat to anyone.

'Thanks again for coming over, and for meeting us on Friday. How was the social club?' Remembering he was going on there after the pub.

'Good thanks, too much bitter, so a sore head yesterday morning, but that's the problem when the alcohol is so cheap.' He chuckled, face illuminated like I hadn't seen on Friday. Claire and I had dragged up some painful memories for him, ones which he was clearly ashamed of and had been initially embarrassed to share. My chest warmed at the change in his demeanour, and I was reluctant to mention Simon Fox again.

'I was hoping you might be able to advise me on security funnily enough. I want to put some things in place to make,' I faltered, 'well, to make this place more secure. Obviously I can't go to Fox Security.'

George looked at me quizzically. 'Has something happened? I thought you were selling?'

'I am, but I think *he's* been inside,' I admitted, my voice low.

'Simon?'

I nodded and a cloud crossed George's expression.

'I didn't realise how close you live to him.'

'Too close,' I agreed.

George stood, making his way to the front door. Was he was leaving? Reluctant to get involved.

'Let's take a look at your access points,' he said, and I felt a sudden lightness at his willingness to help.

We stood outside the house as rain spat upon us, but George surveyed each door and window with his hands on his hips. Eyes focused, he bent towards the door which I'd pulled to.

'Here, see those tiny scratches. I reckon I could get in here with a screwdriver and it looks as though someone may have tried.'

'It's uPVC!' I said. Weren't they supposed to be impenetrable?

'Yes, but it's a few years old and dropped on one side. It looks like it's been forced at some point.'

I gasped, my hand going to my throat.

'Let's have a look at the back,' George said, unruffled.

We walked around the side of the house; George seemingly satisfied with the tall back gate that locked with a deadbolt.

'The back door and the windows look fine. The front is your weak point. The long driveway with hedges either side gives cover to anyone trying to get in.'

Back inside, we drank our tea, my eyes glazed over, unable to stop picturing Simon Fox, dressed all in black, jimmying my front door in the middle of the night. It made even the tea hard to swallow.

'I get the feeling you're not telling me everything,' George said, looking at me with kind russet eyes.

I grimaced.

'Is he really buying your house?'

'Yes, but, George, I don't want to drag you into this any further.'

It was George's turn to grimace. It wasn't fair of me to open old wounds and drag him into another battle with Simon Fox. One I was likely to lose.

'If you're frightened, you should call the police,' he said gently, and for a second it looked as though he was going to reach across the table and touch my hand.

'I mean, I don't know for sure he's been in, I can't out and out accuse him. Can you recommend anything that might... discourage him coming back?'

'Absolutely, I have just the thing at home, an older-model camera doorbell. I upgraded mine recently. He'll be reluctant to break in knowing he's on camera. Deadbolts don't really work on those types of doors, but you have an internal door from the hallway into the lounge, I noticed it has a lock. Do you still have a key for it?'

I got up and moved to the junk drawer in the kitchen, pushing around the dusty utensils, batteries and phone chargers until I found some old keys.

'I think this is one of them,' I said.

George and I moved to the white panelled door, and pushed the key in. It was stiff but turned and the door locked.

'It's a secondary measure. We can't stop anyone getting upstairs from the entrance hall, but this will prevent them accessing the ground floor.' George swiped at his damp forehead, and I smiled.

'I can't thank you enough.'

'Are you around for the rest of the day? I can nip home and get the doorbell. It won't take long to fit. We can connect it to your Wi-Fi, download the app and you'll be ready to rock and roll.'

'I'm in all day.'

We finished our tea, the conversation moving to general chit-chat. George was funny, unlike the bitter man I'd met on Friday, and I relaxed in his company. He was quietly unassuming, a different breed from the Simons and Jonathans of the world.

We talked about what we both did for a living. He was interested in what I had to say and listened intently to the boring realm of contracts. His eyes lit up when he told me he'd started working for a locksmith about six months ago, bringing his security knowledge to the business while learning the skill at college.

It was nice to hear Simon hadn't broken him indefinitely. The man was rotten to the core, tainting everything and everyone he encountered.

'Right, I'll get going. See you after lunch,' George said, standing and flattening the front of his shirt where it had creased. He smiled, his cheeks reddening.

'Brilliant, thanks so much.' I followed him to the door and waved until he'd reversed off the driveway in his VW Polo.

Back inside, I glanced in the mirror and scowled at what stared back. I looked awful, but any attempt to make myself look more attractive would be obvious and I wasn't sure I wanted to send that kind of message to George. Instead, I checked my emails whilst munching on a quick sandwich. Logging on to my Office 365 account so I could look at my calendar for tomorrow and read any important emails. There were a few from Tim, late Friday and yesterday afternoon. He wanted information on the Allegra staff secondment, details that I'd finalised with Damien and Ed. Details Liam wasn't aware of. I grinned into my laptop. Tim had better get used to not being able to click his fingers and have me jump like I'd used to. I'd worked many a weekend because the workload demanded it, but it had got me nowhere. Logging off, I closed the laptop, without bothering to respond. It could wait until tomorrow, better yet he could call Ed and get the information he wanted from him.

George's visit perked me up so when he returned later that afternoon, I was surprised to find myself disappointed when the time came for him to leave again. It took an hour to install the doorbell and go through how it worked on the app. We sat with our heads together as he taught me how to view past videos and check who came to the door, going outside numerous times to ring the doorbell and speak to me through the camera. When he left, I promised to take him for a curry to say thank you, which was when he suggested the social club.

'They do a fantastic ruby on a Wednesday night.'

Before I had a chance to change my mind, I agreed, and we'd made it a date.

37

Less than half an hour later, Jonathan pulled up with the twins. I watched them come to the door on the app. The motion sensor notifying me of their arrival with a jingly chime. Surprised at how good the camera was in darkness, I silently thanked George for his kindness, determined to repay the favour.

'That's new, isn't it?' Jonathan said scornfully as soon as I opened the door, pointing to the doorbell George had fixed on the wall.

'Yep, extra security now I'm here by myself,' I replied, refusing to rise to the bait.

'Hi, Mum,' Ryan said, stooping to kiss me as he came past. Rachel doing the same.

'Hello, you two,' I replied, ruffling their hair, and laughing as they tutted and wriggled away.

I leant against the door frame, trying to fill the space. A barrier between Jonathan and the house.

'I thought you were having Ryan for the week?'

He rolled his eyes, which instantly got my back up. As though I was his nagging wife again. 'I am, I just need to pop out and see

Harry, I'll pick him up again in a bit.' He turned and walked back to his car.

Harry was Jonathan's best man at our wedding, a long-time friend who we both adored. He was having marriage problems; his wife Cherry had asked for a trial separation which had knocked him for six. It was ongoing and I guessed he'd called Jonathan for a bit of moral support. It seemed like none of us had been able to last the distance.

'Monique not around?' I called after him, unable to help myself, but he didn't respond, and I closed the door with a smirk. Clearly all was not well in paradise.

Inside, Rachel was already pulling her clothes out of her bag for me to wash and Ryan sat at the kitchen table, hand buried deep in a box of Ritz crackers.

'Have you two eaten?'

They both shook their heads, and I pulled the wok out from the cupboard under the stove.

'Sweet and sour then?'

'Okay,' they replied unenthusiastically.

Within minutes, Rachel had headed to her room to FaceTime Casey, leaving Ryan and I alone in the kitchen. A comfortable silence stretched out between us, Ryan absorbed in his phone as I tossed the chicken in the pan and weighed out basmati rice.

'How was your weekend?' I ventured.

'Did Rachel tell you Dad and Monique were fighting?' Ryan asked, no accusation in his voice, for which I was glad. I didn't want him to think I was prying or pumping him for information.

'She said she thought they were fighting about money. I expected her to ring me yesterday and ask me to pick her up.'

'Monique buggered off to her mum's Saturday morning and we didn't see her after that. Dad was well grumpy.'

I nodded, boiling the kettle and laying the table as the chicken sizzled. I didn't want to snoop any further, despite burning to know what money they were arguing about. Was it Jonathan's share of the house? Had Monique been eager to get her hands on it?

'Does she live at Dad's all the time then?' I asked.

'Think so, all her stuff is there. She's desperate to get out of the flat, always moaning it's too small, especially when we're there.'

I let the irritation wash over me.

'Did that prick show up again?' Ryan swore, changing the subject.

'If you mean Simon, then no, thankfully, he didn't, and please don't use words like that.' I sighed. I wanted the twins to feel safe at home, there was no way I was going to tell the truth and admit I suspected Simon or one of his pals of breaking in.

Ten minutes later, dinner was ready, and I called Rachel to join us. Ryan ate most of the prawn crackers and both mine and Rachel's leftover chicken. He couldn't be having a growth spurt again surely. I couldn't afford another uniform overhaul.

Rachel talked over dinner about how the water park plans had evaporated with Monique leaving to go back to her mum's and Jonathan had taken them to the arcades instead. Giving them twenty pounds each to spend on slot machines.

'It was pretty cool, I won this on a grabber machine,' Rachel said, showing me a plush octopus, which turned inside out depending on your mood.

'Did Dad ask what you're doing over half-term? I think he might have taken some time off.'

Rachel wrinkled her nose. 'Yeah, but I've made plans with Casey.'

'All week?' I said.

Rachel gave me a wicked smile. 'Yep!'

It looked as though I'd have one of the kids around for the week and I was glad of the company.

'So, I may have found a house just around the corner from St James's. I'll see if I can get a viewing tomorrow afternoon after I finish work. Ryan, I'll let you know the time and I'll collect you from Dad's so you can come and see it,' I said, capitalising on their good mood.

'Oh, all right, cool,' Ryan replied, although Rachel just nodded. She hadn't come around to the idea as quickly as her brother.

'What if we don't like it?' she asked.

'Then we won't buy it,' I replied, simply. Wishing it was as straightforward as that.

With the kids finished, they did their usual disappearing act straight after dinner, leaving me to clear up. I stacked the bowls and carried them from the table, interrupted by a call on my mobile. Claire's name flashing on the screen.

'Hiya,' I said, looking forward to telling her about George saving the day. All I could hear was raucous laughter and voices I didn't recognise. 'Hello?' I said again.

'Jonathan is here,' Claire whispered down the phone.

I frowned, pressing the phone closer to my ear to hear her over the background noise.

'Where?' I whispered back before catching myself. Why was I whispering? The recording device had gone, but I couldn't shake the notion that Simon was listening.

'At the Six Bells. I'm here with Owen, we're having dinner, but I've nipped to the toilet. Jonathan's sat alone at the bar, looks like he's waiting for someone.'

'He's gone to meet Harry,' I replied.

'Hmmm, well he's not turned up. From where we are sitting, I can see the bar, and he's been there for about twenty minutes.'

What had made Claire so suspicious she'd call me?

'I'm going to go back out. Just thought it was weird that's all, him drinking alone at the bar,' Claire said.

'Does he know you and Owen are there? Has he seen you?'

'No, I don't think so.'

'Okay, text later if you get a chance.' I hung up, letting Claire get back to her dinner.

Leaning against the worktop, I puzzled on the call. Perhaps Harry was running late or could no longer make it. Maybe Jonathan was never meeting Harry at all? I wracked my brain as to why he'd lie about it but came up with nothing. It had to be a misunderstanding.

I'd started to put the plates in the dishwasher when Claire's picture message came through. It was grainy, a picture of the bar, a row of four men, all with their backs to the camera. I could make out Jonathan by his North Face coat and the beige trousers he was wearing earlier. None of the men around him were Harry. He would have been easy to identify at well over six feet tall and built like a string bean.

I stared hard at the image, looking at the line-up. The man to Jonathan's right displayed a tiny sliver of side profile. His face was obscured by Jonathan's arm lifting his pint, but I could make out slicked-back salt-and-pepper hair. Could Jonathan be having a pint with Simon Fox?

Rooted to the spot, my stomach wound together like a coiled spring and I hunched over the sink, dropping my phone into a shallow puddle of water I'd run to rinse the wok.

'Shit!' I scrabbled to pull it out, but the screen had already gone blank. I knew I had to put it in rice to dry it out, so quickly filled a Tupperware bowl with basmati, pushing the phone deep inside and sealing it shut. 'Shit, shit, shit!' I scowled. Wishing I had the image to check again. Perhaps it wasn't Simon at all.

Jonathan said he saw him a few weeks ago, didn't he? I remembered he wasn't particularly complimentary about him either when he mentioned it. Why on earth would the two of them be having a drink together? If they were, it had to be about the house. Perhaps Jonathan was talking to Simon about renegotiating his offer after the survey. Maybe the estate agent hadn't taken my word for it, that we'd refuse and had contacted Jonathan to be sure.

Whatever it was, the idea of the two of them together made me increasingly uncomfortable. If my phone was working, I'd text Claire to see if she could get a better look or another photo, but it would take a while for my phone to dry out, if it did at all.

I straightened, holding on to the side for support until the painful knot in my stomach loosened. Moving gingerly at first, I resumed loading the dishwasher, hearing Rachel's footsteps move around her bedroom upstairs. Once the kitchen was tidy, I relented and poured myself a glass of the wine I'd opened last night. It took the edge off almost instantly and I snuck outside for a cigarette, figuring the twins would stay in their bedroom until I nudged them to get in the shower.

I hoped I'd been mistaken, and it wasn't Simon at the bar at all. If it was, then Jonathan better not have made a deal with him on the price of our home, just because he was desperate to sell quickly. Maybe his and Monique's future depended on the sale. For all I knew, she'd found her dream home, the one they were buying, and was putting pressure on Jonathan to get the chain moving.

I shook my head; it was crazy to assume anything, as in reality I knew nothing of what went on in their love nest.

Back inside, I washed my hands and popped a mint in my mouth, before spraying some perfume on my neck. Hoping it would mask the smell of tobacco. As I put the television on, the doorbell rang. With my phone dead, there had been no motion sensor chime to let me know Jonathan had returned. At least he was no longer using his key when he knew I was home.

'Ryan, your dad's back,' I called up the stairs.

Steeling myself, I opened the front door, trying to rearrange my features into something more welcoming.

Jonathan appeared harassed, shifting his weight from one foot to the other.

'Ryan ready?' he said, again without bothering to offer any pleasantries.

'He's coming. How's Harry?' I asked.

For a split second I caught the confusion on Jonathan's face, the wrinkling of his brow before he spoke.

'Harry? Yeah, he's fine. Same old, same old, you know.'

38

I bit my lip to stop myself calling Jonathan out in his lie. Maybe Harry had arrived after Claire and I had spoken, but if he had, then the pair hadn't spent much time together.

Jonathan took his phone out of his pocket and tapped at it, bored of our conversation or perhaps unable to look me in the eye.

'I hope you said hello from me,' I said, through gritted teeth.

Jonathan nodded dismissively. Could I trust him any more? Was everything that came out of his mouth a lie?

'Did the estate agent contact you about Simon lowering his offer?' I asked.

'Yeah, I refused to negotiate, as we discussed. What about you, have you been looking?'

'Yes, I think I may have found somewhere. I'm going to see if I can take the kids to view it tomorrow afternoon. I'll let you know, and I'll come and get Ryan.'

Jonathan perked up immediately; I had his full attention now. 'Brilliant. I'm sending him out with Jim Lucas, you know, my plumber mate. Think it'll do him good to get a little taste of what it's like to work for a living. He might have him for both weeks.'

'I'm sure he'll be chuffed to spend his half-term working!' I said, but it was better Ryan was doing something productive with his time than playing *Call of Duty* all day long.

Our son appeared behind me, and I moved aside to let him pass.

'See you later, Mum,' Ryan said, following his dad to the car.

I watched them go and closed the front door, making sure to lock it.

So, had Jonathan blatantly lied about meeting Harry and instead met up with Simon Fox? If Claire was right and Harry had not turned up, why had Jonathan lied about it? What was he trying to hide? Perhaps I should have called him out on it, but I didn't want to force his hand, and I didn't know for sure Harry hadn't shown or if Simon had even been there.

There were plenty of things Jonathan didn't tell me any more. After all, he'd failed to tell me he was buying a house with Monique. He could argue it was none of my business. He didn't have to tell me a thing. As each week passed, I woke every morning asking myself if today would be the day I'd receive divorce papers through the letter box. I'd accepted my marriage was beyond salvaging, but it still hurt none the less.

Jonathan was nothing like the man I'd married. Back then, he'd never been self-centred. I considered whether I'd driven him to it, to the man he'd become. I wasn't innocent of the breakdown of our relationship, but I hadn't been the instigator and until recently, despite the nasty comments, I still hoped we could work it out. Hearing about Monique had been the nail in the coffin. I knew deep in my gut he'd started seeing her before he left me, although knowing it, or even being able to prove it, didn't benefit me in any way. It might do when it came to arguing grounds for divorce, but I had a feeling Jonathan would roll over on that, happy for anything to be cited as long as the papers were signed.

The only thing Jonathan was interested in was that I was looking for somewhere else to live. He wanted this place sold, clearly needing the money. There'd been no concern as to whether what I'd found might be suitable for his children or whether I could afford it. He hadn't even bothered to ask me about it. It was likely he didn't care, it wasn't even on his radar, the selfish git.

I had to get the issue with work sorted, then perhaps I'd have some money behind me. It would give me breathing space to search for something more suitable and free up time to sort moving to a new house. Already that seemed overwhelming to organise alone, I was massively out of my depth and running out of time.

Jonathan had dealt with so much to do with the house, most of the bills and the mortgage. It never occurred to me at the time to take much notice. I was busy raising the children and trying to have a career. He took care of it, and I let him. When he first left, I let all the statements and bills pile up, not even wanting to open the envelopes. It was denial and I buried my head so far in the sand I was surprised Claire managed to help me pull it out. She was my rock, and I wouldn't have got through it without her.

39

Claire called me around ten o'clock that night. After a couple of hours drying out, I'd managed to switch my phone on again. It was seemingly unharmed, and I breathed a sigh of relief that it wasn't something else I'd have to add to my ever-growing list. As soon as it came to life I checked the photo Claire had sent, squinting at the screen to see if the man at the bar was Simon Fox. It certainly looked like it could be him.

When the phone rang, I'd said goodnight to Rachel and was getting ready for bed, taking my iPad upstairs to find something to fall asleep to, so I already had my headphones.

'Sorry for the delay, Owen's just left,' Claire explained, sounding breathless.

'He's not staying over?' I asked.

'No, he's got an early start tomorrow. Anyway, more importantly, what the fuck is Jonathan doing?'

I stifled a smile; Claire was fearlessly loyal and never shy of sniffing out a rat.

'I dropped my bloody phone in the sink. Have you still got that photo you took of him at the bar? One of the guys looked a bit like Simon Fox.'

Claire gasped. 'Shit, I deleted it, the text too. I don't know why, it made me nervous in case Owen saw what I was doing.' She laughed.

'I'll have to send it back to you. Maybe it wasn't him at all. I have no idea why the two of them would be together. Did Harry show up?' I asked.

'No, not that I saw.'

'He told me he saw Harry, that lying git. Did you say anything to Owen about it?'

'Well, only that Jonathan was there, at the bar, but then we got talking about this bloody holiday he wants to book. He wants us to go away around Christmastime, but I'm not so sure.'

'You don't fancy it?'

Claire sighed, her reaction obvious. 'Not really, it's mega expensive and I don't have any time off.'

'So, is that when you nipped to the toilet to call me?' I asked, steering the conversation back around to Jonathan.

'Yes, then I came back and took the photo, while Owen got the drinks in. I didn't take much notice of the other guys at the bar. Jonathan was only there for about twenty minutes; he didn't even finish his pint before he left.'

I drew my arms around myself protectively, rubbing the chill away.

'What is he up to?' she asked.

'Your guess is as good as mine!'

'Tell me about the trip,' I asked, changing the subject to one that wouldn't keep me awake at night.

Claire proceeded to tell me Owen had been heavily hinting about going away, either for Christmas or New Year. Claire was close to her parents and as she was single she spent every

Christmas with them. They went to Midnight Mass, and she'd cook a nut roast with all the trimmings, spoiling them with gifts. There was no way tradition would be overturned for a new boyfriend, but Owen hadn't been put off, suggesting flying somewhere to celebrate New Year instead.

'Maybe he wants to propose.' I giggled, knowing that would wind her up.

'Oh, bugger off,' Claire said. She tried to laugh, but I could hear the fear in her voice. She wouldn't admit she was a commitment-phobe, but I knew better. 'I guess it'll be hot wherever we go, so there's that. But it's such an expensive time to fly and I'm skint,' she moaned.

'Maybe he'll treat you? As a Christmas present?' I countered.

We talked for another ten minutes, as Claire griped that she'd struggle to get a bikini anywhere this time of year, not to mention the extra poundage of mince pies she'd allocated to the season. It was obvious she didn't want to go and was making excuses. Was she tiring of Owen now the novelty had worn off?

When we said goodbye, I yawned, snuggling in bed, and found a crime show to put on the iPad, removing one of my earphones so I could rest my head on the pillow comfortably. I wanted something to fill the void in my head, so I wouldn't think about Jonathan, Simon or Tim. It didn't take long to drift off, but I woke with a start to a tinkling sound, and something was illuminated in the room. The iPad battery had died, and I reached for my phone, seeing the glow through the covers.

As I looked at the screen, the chime of bells rang out again, star-tling me, and I dropped the phone like it had burnt my hand. Someone was at the front of the house. There was a chime that was a motion-sensor which was separate to the noise that came through the app when someone rang the doorbell.

Scrambling out of bed, I pulled the curtain aside and tilted the blind, peering out into the darkness, just in time to see a figure dressed in black jogging down the road. I fought the rising panic in my chest as I backed away from the window. My entire body shaking. Had Simon tried to break in?

With fumbling fingers, I grabbed the phone, clicking into the app and waiting for the video of recent activity to load. I gasped as the figure rounded the hedge, moving quickly onto the driveway and towards the front door. A few steps away, he froze, staring at the door. He was dressed in black and wearing a beanie hat pulled right down, the perfect cat burglar outfit. It might not be recognisable to anyone if they saw it, but I knew the figure was Simon.

He paused for a few seconds, midway down the drive, before turning to jog away. Was he coming to attack me? Or break in to put the recording device back? Either way, the camera doorbell had stopped him in his tracks.

My bladder loosened and I rushed to the toilet. Washing my hands with hot water which I splashed on my face before returning to the window, I shivered violently. What was the time anyway? Disorientated, I found the phone I'd dropped; it was one o'clock in the morning, the street sleeping. The only sound as I opened the window to peer onto the driveway was the rustling of trees in the wind.

I owed George much more than a curry. I had to thank him for his helpful intervention. Whatever Simon had planned tonight, he'd decided against breaking in, knowing he'd be filmed. I imagined him livid, cursing as he ran back to his double-fronted house. I'd seen him. I had proof. What I didn't know was what he intended to do once he'd got inside, although he wouldn't have been able to get to the lounge as I'd locked the internal door. However, he would have been able to come upstairs.

The thought made me shudder, especially as it was just Rachel and I alone in the house. It was time to call the police, I couldn't pretend I was safe any more and had to protect my family. Once I'd dialled 999, the police came quickly, two male uniformed officers rang the doorbell and I hurried down to greet them. Inviting them in, I asked if they wouldn't mind keeping their voices down as my daughter was asleep upstairs. They could see I was shaken, one of them insisting on making me a hot, sugary tea. I wanted a glass of red wine, but I'd wait for them to leave.

Wrapped in my robe, we sat at the kitchen table as I explained what had gone on with Simon Fox. How I was sure he was behind the photo of me that was briefly on the internet, the one I'd reported, and how I was convinced he'd been inside my house. There was little point in me mentioning the bugging device. Most of what I said was my word against his.

The two officers listened intently, one had a kindly face with big brown eyes, and he was reassuring, saying, once he'd seen the footage from the camera doorbell, he could understand why I was so upset.

'It does look suspicious, definitely. However the issue is we haven't got a crime in the act. First of all, we can't be certain from the video who that person is. And even if we could determine it is Mr Fox, we wouldn't be able to arrest him for coming onto your driveway. He didn't try the door or attempt access.'

My face crumpled, fresh tears springing to my eyes. Simon would evade the police yet again.

'However, we will go and see him. Ask him to confirm his whereabouts this evening and politely suggest to him to stay away from you. I know that's difficult as he's buying your house, you said, but we'll request everything is arranged through the solicitors and estate agents.'

I wrapped my fingers tightly around the mug, the heat burning my skin. 'What if he comes back?'

'Then you'll call us. I'm Police Constable Michael Ferron and this is my colleague Police Constable Jeff Covell. Are you able to email the footage to us for our report?'

I shook my head. 'I don't know how.'

'Here, let me show you. I have one of these at home. They are a good deterrent.' PC Covell held out his hand and I gave him my phone. He opened the app and showed me how to share the video to an email address or text message. 'I'll send this to the station so I can attach it to the report,' he said, handing me back the phone.

I yawned, lids heavy, the time on the oven was almost quarter to two. I wanted to crawl into bed and stay there.

'Would you like us to make sure the house is secure, Mrs Massingham?' PC Ferron asked, standing and hooking his thumb into the shoulder of his vest.

'No, it's fine. I've done that already. I don't think he'll be back tonight.'

'We'll warn him to stay away,' he replied.

'I think one of your colleagues did when I called before, he hasn't paid much notice,' I said, frustration rippling beneath my skin.

'Please don't hesitate to call us again if you feel under any threat.' The kindly faced officer said as I bid him goodnight at the door.

'Don't worry, I won't,' I said, trying to muster a smile. I'd already decided, as I closed the door and bolted it, if Simon Fox came back again, I'd be ready for him.

40

Thankfully, Rachel slept through the entire police visit and was clueless in the morning as to why I was so tired. I'd sacrificed breakfast for an extra ten minutes in bed, eyes stinging when I rubbed them. I'd woken to a sweary message from Claire as I'd sent her the video of Simon on my driveway last night, after the officer showed me how, before I went to sleep. Stupidly I'd turned my phone off, thinking she'd get it in the morning, but of course she'd got up earlier than me and tried to ring. Worried as she couldn't get hold of me, she left a garbled voicemail. I quickly sent her a placating message. I was fine, we were all fine, yet the saga of Simon Fox continued.

The guy was relentless, and I asked myself if Jonathan could be involved. Rage boiled in the pit of my stomach, surely he wouldn't deliberately put me and the children in danger by getting mixed up with a psycho like Simon Fox.

I had to focus; work needed my concentration. Perhaps it was one element of my life I could fix today. I'd push Tim for a figure; I couldn't go on in limbo any longer. I knew Head Office were dragging their heels, of course they were. They didn't want to pay me off. Maybe they didn't believe I was a threat? Well, I'd show them how much of a liability I could be. I was sick and tired of being pushed around by the opposite sex, overlooked, dismissed and taken advantage of.

'Mum, you'll be late,' Rachel shouted from the kitchen as I cleaned my teeth.

Washing away the toothpaste and hurrying downstairs, I fixed the onyx necklace around my neck. A glance in the mirror showed me I was presentable enough and I promised myself a strong coffee when I got into the building.

'What are you doing with your day?' I asked, watching a bleary-eyed Rachel eat her breakfast. It was likely she'd go back to bed until lunchtime.

'I'm going to Casey's for a bit, but I'll be home for dinner.'

'Okay, well have fun,' I said as I slipped out of the front door, remembering I hadn't confirmed a time for the Goddard Close viewing I was hoping to get that afternoon. It was on my list to call Louise at the estate agents and book an appointment. I could always ring Rachel later and let her know when I needed her to be around.

When I got to the office, it was bedlam, despite it being before nine. In the kitchen, I made myself a strong sweet coffee where Sarge enlightened me as to what was going on.

'Management meeting here today, so everyone is panicking as usual.' He rolled his eyes.

I couldn't help but feel the same way, although a prickle of trepidation stabbed at me. Would I have to defend myself and my actions in front of the board? With them at Tunbridge Wells, the only one I had to handle here was Tim, and I knew him so well, he didn't faze me. I couldn't say the same about the other men at the top.

My pulse accelerated as I headed back to my office, closing the door, hoping I could hide out in there. As I struggled to concentrate on what needed doing, my eyes flitted through the frosted glass to Liam. He was gathering folders, clutching them against his chest and rushing out of his office. He'd been summoned to the meeting I'd deliberately been left out of.

Checking my email, to ensure I wasn't supposed to be somewhere, I jumped when Tim opened my door, poking his head in. There was no friendly gesture, no good morning. We'd run out of pleasantries, although I wasn't surprised. I'd been a pain in his rear for the last couple of weeks and he was likely looking forward to getting shot of me.

'We've got a meeting at eleven, I've just sent you an invite.'

'Okay,' I said, trying to hide the wobble in my voice.

Tim didn't hang around, nor did he mention his emails or the information he was trying to source at the weekend.

I refreshed my email, and the meeting request came through. It had nothing in the subject line or in the body of the message, which was most irregular. How could I prepare for a meeting I knew nothing about? Checking the participants, I felt my heart sink, Peter Franks, the Chief Operating Officer, Tim and Liam were attending.

Knowing instantly it was about my presentation and threat to Winston's, anxiety struck, a lead bowling ball weighing down my stomach. They'd brought Peter in to bully me, although at least it was only him and not the entire board of directors I'd be facing. I'd heard he was a no-nonsense man. Old-school and knocking on sixty with an abrupt manner, he didn't suffer fools gladly. I was glad I'd remembered to put the camera necklace on.

I'd only met him once, at a Christmas party, the only one I'd attended. It had got rowdier as the night went on and the team had left the plush London hotel in favour of a strip club near chucking-out time. I'd made my excuses and left but I'd heard the gory details from Ed, who'd gone home to his wife after one drink while the rest of them waved tenners at girls young enough to be their daughters. I never attended another function.

Underarms damp, my office was suddenly claustrophobic, and I stepped outside to get some air, absorbing the chill in my blouse. One of the HGV drivers, Ted, gave me a roll-up and I smoked it in the car park while I rang Claire to get some advice.

'Jesus, it's all going on for you at the moment, isn't it!' she said, whistling down the line.

'I know, I'm stressed to the max. What do you think the meeting will be about?'

'Well, it's one of two things, they are either going to pay you off, or if they are really shady, try to force you out.'

'Sack me?' I said, incredulous at the idea.

'They might try.'

I gritted my teeth, turning one way and then another, embracing the cold. 'How can they? It would be illegal,' I said.

'Yes, but it's only an issue if they think you'll challenge it.'

'I'm not walking away from this fight,' I spat, tossing my roll-up, and grinding it into the concrete until it was nothing but dust.

'Good for you. Remember, you have proof of harassment, actual videos, and emails. You can prove the mistake on the contract wasn't yours, can't you?'

'Yep,' I replied. A surge of adrenaline rocketed through me. I could prove it; I could also prove I was excellent at my job. If I had to take them to court to demonstrate unfair dismissal, I wouldn't hesitate.

'Just keep calm, be clear, concise and don't get emotional, okay. You need to be level-headed. Call me after and let me know how it goes.'

'I will, thanks, Claire. I don't know what I'd do without you sometimes,' I said, a rush of love for my best friend threatening to bring me to tears. I hung up, standing tall. Every muscle flexed, I rolled my shoulders back, the adrenaline pumping around my body as though I was going into battle.

41

'Kay, thank you for joining us.' Peter slid from his seat as I entered the room. Tim and Liam did not stand, but smiled awkwardly at me, their darting eyes giving the game away. This wasn't a meeting; it was an execution.

'Thank you,' I replied, slipping into the seat across from Peter and placing my closed laptop in front of me, USB stick at the ready. I didn't know if I needed to show the presentation again, whether they fully realised what was at stake if they didn't give me what I wanted.

Tim cleared his throat, spinning that bloody gold pen in his fingers. 'Would you like a representative to attend?'

'Do I need one?' I frowned, looking about the room, but no one volunteered an answer. 'Is Ed available?' I knew Ed to be the union rep at Winston's, and although I wasn't in the union, his knowledge might be helpful. Plus if I was going to choose anyone to be on my side, he would be the only one.

'I'm afraid Ed is not in the office today, he's in Birmingham,' Tim said flatly, and I knew Ed's absence had been a calculated decision.

He'd probably been sent to Birmingham to deliberately keep him away from this meeting.

'Well, I guess I'll take my chances,' I replied, smiling tightly. I didn't trust anyone else. I considered momentarily asking to officially record the meeting, but I knew the answer would be negative. I was wearing my necklace so at least I'd have a personal account of what was said.

'Peter thought it would be a good opportunity to resolve this today, Kay, as he is in Gatwick for the Management Meeting.'

'Yes, I noticed I didn't receive an invite,' I said coldly, realising the gloves were off whether I liked it or not.

'No, well, it seems there's little point in having you attend the meeting when you're so keen to leave us,' Peter said, his voice prickly.

'I'm afraid that's incorrect, Peter. I was told my role was going to be consolidated with Liam's and I was no longer required at Winston's.'

'Yes, and you were offered a decent redundancy package, which you declined. I understand you threatened Tim for more money.'

'Threatened,' I scoffed, unable to keep the laughter from my voice, 'hardly.'

Peter looked from me to Tim and back again, Tim gave him a look that said, 'see, I told you,' as though I'd been pegged as a troublemaker.

'I didn't threaten Tim. I told him – in fact, I showed him evidence I'd collected over the past few weeks of harassment, sexual innuendo and bias from him and his staff. I offered him a chance to recalculate his figures.' I spoke slowly, the heat emanating from my skin. I had to be crimson, but I didn't let it faze me. I was in control, and I was not to be undermined, I didn't care whose boardroom we sat in.

'Well, unfortunately that figure isn't up for negotiation and I'm afraid it's been taken off the table now. The long and short of it, Kay, is you've cost the company in excess of twenty thousand pounds by messing up the Allegra contract. It should have been a three-month secondment instead of six months, as you well know.'

My mouth dropped open momentarily and I stared from Peter to Liam, whose face was ghostly. He resembled a child, shrunken in his seat wishing he was anywhere else. Still, he remained quiet, willing to throw me under the bus again, so he wouldn't have to take culpability.

'Now we'll pay your notice period, but you must leave today,' Peter continued, folding his arms across his chest and pushing himself away from the table. His last word on the matter.

My eyes blazed across at him. *Keep it together, Kay.*

I leaned forward in my seat calmly, maintaining eye contact with Peter. 'I am aware of the error in the Allegra contract, but it was not my mistake. Liam returned the contract they supplied us with initially, not the one I renegotiated. In fact, if I hadn't managed to talk Damien round, you would have been paying for pension contributions and private medical for those seconded staff too. You should be thanking me.' My leg jiggled under the table as I tried to control the outrage threatening to explode from my body like a devil possessed.

Peter blinked, obviously unaware of the error not being mine, and glared at Tim, who came to life and began to splutter.

'I don't believe that's right, as the Contract Manager, it's down to you to ensure the correct contract goes out for signing.' Tim's ears tinged pink, and I could sense the atmosphere in the room shift.

'As you know, Tim, I gave Liam the correct paper copy. I also emailed him the correct contract. Despite that, he still made the mistake of printing off the old one, signing and sending it across. I didn't see the contract again until Damien had already signed it. By then, it was damage limitation.'

'It's he said, she said,' Peter commented dismissively, waving his hand as if he could make me disappear with a flick of the wrist.

I clenched my jaw, my hand beginning to tremor. 'I assure you it's not. I have copies of the email, which is dated and timed.'

I couldn't believe they were now trying to wrangle out of paying me anything at all. Attempting to bully me into leaving. The room fell silent momentarily and I sensed the meeting wasn't going as Peter had expected.

'Filming without consent is a breach of GDPR rules, Kay, that's gross misconduct and for that we can ask you to leave immediately. However, we're trying to part amicably here. How about we reinstate the initial offer of six months' salary,' Tim suggested, beads of sweat popped onto his forehead as he looked from me to Peter, who had turned puce.

I'd had enough. Unable to keep the quiver from my voice, I barked, 'I've been here five years, Tim, worked hard and done everything asked of me. I never have a day off, no sickness, barely any holiday. I've worked well over forty hours a week since I became Contract Manager and I'm excellent at my job. Every appraisal I've had, you've marked me as outstanding. Yet I'm being made a scapegoat for Liam's cock-up.'

Tim waved a hand to stop me, but I was just getting started.

'Five years, putting up with systematic abuse from management down to the warehouse, never complaining, taking it on the chin. Well, no more. If you're firing me, I will be contacting a solicitor about unfair dismissal, and I believe I have more than enough evidence to show I've been forced out, even without the recordings.'

Sweat pooled at the base of my spine, heart banging against my ribcage. I'd never been in a situation where I'd had to stand up for myself professionally before, but knowing I was right and the injustice of what they were trying to do spurred me on. I curled my fingers into my palm, feeling the ridges of my nails against flesh.

'If that's what you feel you must do, Kay. I'll expect your desk cleared by the end of the day,' Peter said, flippantly, trying to disguise his irritation.

'I assume I'll have my dismissal in writing?'

'You'll have no such thing.' Peter slammed his fist onto the table and got up. Spritely for a man a few years away from retirement. Despite myself, I jumped at the noise, pleased to see Liam and Tim do the same.

I responded like a cornered snake, striking back with venom. 'Don't be foolish, Peter. Tim knows what I have, and how the press will have a field day with the footage I've recorded.'

'It won't be admissible in court,' he spluttered, jabbing a finger at me.

'You're right, it won't, not in a tribunal, but I guarantee the shareholders won't be happy when you're exposed as a bunch of misogynists bullying women in the workplace.'

'Revoke her access now,' Peter snapped at Tim, who leapt up and scurried from the room as though he'd been whipped.

It didn't matter, I'd forwarded on all the emails I needed.

Peter wasn't going to go down without a fight and I knew it was a battle he couldn't win. He continued to glare at me, intimidating me in stature as I remained calm and seated at the table. Underneath the cool exterior, I was jelly, unsure if my legs would hold me up when the time came to stand.

'Now get out of here,' he spat, swiping my laptop off the table.

Gripping the arm of the chair, shocked at Peter's outburst, I slowly rose to my feet on shaking legs. Liam had sunk further still into his seat and looked as though he wanted to curl into a ball when I regarded him stonily. Chin held high, I walked from the room back to my office, the temperature plummeting as soon as I exited.

Within minutes, Tim appeared at my door, dabbing his forehead with a handkerchief.

'Your dismissal in writing,' he said, handing me an envelope as though it was a bomb about to go off. 'Twelve-week notice period, along with accrued vacation, medical and pension contributions which will be paid in the next few days.' The offer had dropped from six month's salary to three, my punishment for causing a fuss.

'My solicitor will be in touch,' I replied, glaring at Tim.

Bizarrely, a wave of relief washed over me as I was escorted from my office, and although I knew I had a dispute on my hands, I was relieved the confrontation was over. No longer did I have to worry about my future at Winston's, or about climbing the corporate ladder which was only greased for those with an extra appendage I wasn't born with. I wouldn't have to suffer their idiocy, or catty remarks about my looks or the clothes I chose to wear.

My shoulders lowered as though gentle palms had been placed on them and I glided out of reception, ignoring the stares of onlookers after hearing Peter's raised voice.

42

Hands shaking on the steering wheel, I drove out of the car park and to the nearest residential street before calling Claire, who picked up after the first ring.

'Holy shit, you really gave them both barrels, didn't you,' Claire exclaimed when I relayed what had happened in the meeting.

'Can you believe they are pushing me out, with Tim knowing what I have on them?'

'It's ludicrous. What are you going to do?' she asked.

'I don't know, I feel sick. I was sure the threat of going to the press would be enough. I didn't expect them to call my bluff, but I don't think Peter, the guy at the top, has any idea what I have.' The realisation of being jobless was sinking in, panic climbing like ivy, wrapping around my limbs.

'Perhaps you need to give them another push?' Claire offered before suggesting getting advice from a solicitor might be the way forward instead.

She couldn't talk for much longer, a Teams call popped up she had to jump on, so I made my way home, a knot in my stomach like I was going to vomit. I'd start by collating everything onto the USB stick, getting all my evidence together before approaching someone for advice.

I'd momentarily forgotten all about Jonathan and Simon Fox until I arrived home to discover both of their cars blocking the driveway. I had to park down the road, which got my back up. Simon Fox's stupid enormous Jaguar filling my drive.

Storming to the house, ready to unload, they came out, shaking hands and smiling.

'What the hell is going on?' I said, steaming.

Jonathan was wide-eyed, a rabbit caught in the headlights, whereas Simon just strolled past, chuckling to himself at his predicament.

'I'll leave this one to you, mate,' he said. He climbed into his car and reversed off the driveway in one swift movement.

'It's like he already owns the place,' I seethed.

Jonathan held up his hands defensively. 'Woah, woah, calm down. What's with you?'

'He's not to be inside my house without me.' My blood pressure shot skyward, and I gritted my teeth until my gums hurt.

'What is it with you and him?' He smirked and I clenched my knuckles tightly, trying to resist the urge to punch him on the nose. I heard a neighbours' car engine purr and was reminded that my mum had taught me it wasn't decent to air your dirty laundry in public.

'Is Rachel home?' I asked, hoping she'd gone to Casey's before Simon Fox had been.

'No, she left a note to remind you she was at her friend's. What's all the panic?'

'You need to tell me what the hell is going on, Jonathan, you were drinking with Simon Fox yesterday. You lied about it, and he tried to break into my house last night. He's crazy, he's got some vendetta against me because of his ridiculous car, and I know you know.' I jabbed my finger at him, and Jonathan took a step back. I couldn't remember a time he'd ever seen me so enraged, but I couldn't stop. 'If you don't tell me what I want to know, I swear to God, I'm not moving out of this bloody house. You can get the police to remove me, kicking and screaming.' I took air in, refilling my lungs as Jonathan looked at me blankly.

'I don't know what you're on about, Kay. You've lost it.'

'Claire saw you, Jonathan, last night at the Six Bells.'

'So, you're spying on me now? Look it's over between us, Kay, you don't get to keep tabs on me any more.' His eyes narrowed to slits and we glared at each other.

'Don't flatter yourself, Monique is welcome to you. I want to know what you've cooked up with Simon Fox, that's all. He's been here, trying to get into the house. He planted a listening device.'

'Oh, come on.' Jonathan laughed, throwing his head back, clear he didn't believe a word I said.

'He's the one who put weed in Ryan's locker,' I said.

'You're mental, seriously, you need help,' Jonathan said, but he didn't sound so sure. The mention of his son rocked him, and I could see him debating whether I was telling the truth.

'Am I? I don't know what you've got going on with him, but I'm telling you, Simon Fox is a psychopath.' My head throbbed, overwhelmed with anger and the rush of adrenaline that came with it. I'd been running on high for hours now and any moment would crash.

Jonathan stood with his hands on his hips, surveying the ground as though it would give him answers. He looked confused, caught between what he thought he knew and what I was telling him. Conflicted as he knew I'd never lied to him before.

'Come back and see me when you're ready to tell the truth. I don't want you or Simon here without me, got it,' I said, heading inside and slamming the door. I contemplated asking him for his key, but he'd never hand it over willingly. He'd never relinquish control.

It took Jonathan a few minutes to leave, he shuffled around outside, tapping at his phone, and looking like he was mulling over what I'd said. I knew he was a prat, but I didn't believe he would ever put his family in harm's way, not the children.

I made a quick cup of tea and sat at the table, checking the camera doorbell to see if I could pick up on anything Simon and Jonathan had said before I got there, but there was nothing useful, only Simon's voice saying, 'Sounds good, mate,' as they shook hands. Although what *sounded good* I didn't know.

Still infuriated, but realising I wasn't going to get any further with Simon Fox right now, I turned my focus to Winston's. I downloaded the video of today's meeting from the necklace and copied it to the USB stick that already had the presentation on it. I added emails I'd forwarded from my work account to my personal one, ones about the contract, as well as the videos and other communication that could be construed as harassment.

Peter would have assumed because I no longer had access to my work email, I wouldn't have the proof required to take things further. Another man who had underestimated how far I'd go for my reputation. As much as having no permanent income filled me with dread, I was furious with the injustice.

When I'd finished, I ate a couple of breadsticks to tide me over and fixed my make-up. I'd sweated most of it off and my skin had an unappealing gleam, highlighting the bags under my eyes and lines of stress etched onto my forehead. Rachel wouldn't be home for a few hours and I considered picking up a takeaway later, as well as a bottle of red wine. I'd need it after the day I'd had.

As I drove to the supermarket, I contemplated staying in bed the following morning. How pitiful my week looked with nothing to fill it. A sour taste filled my mouth. What would I do without my job?

Once the twelve weeks were up, how would I feed us? I couldn't ask Jonathan for money, seeing as I'd torn his head off about Simon Fox. I couldn't rely on him anyway, not after he walked out. I had to stand on my own two feet.

Using the hands-free, I dialled Claire's mobile and left a message. Even if there weren't any suitable permanent jobs, perhaps she could get me some temping straight away. Anything to keep the money coming in.

Perhaps I should have taken the redundancy package they offered me, although it wasn't much better than what they gave me today. It would have bought me another three months' money though. Was I too quick to refuse it? It was hardly as attractive as they'd said, and I knew they hadn't followed the process properly.

If my role was going to be amalgamated with Liam's, surely I should have been able to apply for it. Wouldn't we have been scored against each other? It was a ruse to get me out the door.

43

I moved along the aisles, not taking anything in. My head so full, I thought it might burst. I tried to concentrate on the positives to stop me sinking into a well of despair. At least I'd be able to take a few days to start going through the house, packing things away and getting rid of junk I'd no longer need.

When Jonathan moved out, he'd only taken a handful of things, leaving most of his stuff behind. It took all my resolve not to build a bonfire in the garden with it. Stupidly I'd assumed, because he'd not taken all of it, the separation wasn't permanent. Now I would relish boxing up the rest of his belongings and leaving them out on the driveway for him to collect.

I wandered around the store aimlessly, taking in the garish orange flashing pumpkin bowls and mountains of sweets ready for Halloween in a week's time. I couldn't believe where the time had gone and that it was almost November. Christmas would be around the corner and the thought of spending it in a new home without Jonathan made my chest tighten.

I had no idea what I'd do if the kids chose to stay with him, visions of myself alone watching a Bridget Jones movie marathon and devouring a tub of Quality Street hurtled through my head. Jonathan's cruel text weeks ago of 'enjoy your dinner for one' popped from my memory and I almost erupted into a blubbering mess in the middle of the seasonal goods aisle.

I hurried away, grabbing some sweets for the twins and two bottles of Merlot for me before taking my basket to the self-service checkout, wincing when it beeped for a staff member to verify my age. It was mortifying; a woman in her forties, minutes away from ugly crying and desperate to leave the shop. The checkout lad, still a teenager, gave me a wide berth once he'd seen my watery eyes, tapping his card on the screen and scurrying away. I dashed out of the shop, a bottle in each hand, sweets wedged underarm and my receipt in my mouth.

Safe in the car, I sobbed for a while, glad the vehicles parked beside me were empty. The emotions I'd been holding in all day gushed out in a tidal wave of cries and I rested my head on the steering wheel until the hopelessness passed and I was able to see well enough to drive home.

Despite it being barely three o'clock, I cracked open the wine as soon as I was inside, pouring myself a large glass and going out into the back garden for a cigarette. Hoping the combination would settle me, but I was more on edge than ever. By the time Rachel text to say she was on her way home, my stomach was growling, and I ordered pizza, cringing as I remembered how much I'd spent that day. It would be something I'd have to rein in, especially with no job.

I told myself tomorrow was another day and by the time the third glass of red wine had been consumed I saw I had three missed calls from Tim. There was no way I was going to speak to him, not after what had happened today. For five years we'd worked together, he'd been my boss, and despite not agreeing with how he behaved at times, until recently I'd respected him. History, it seemed, didn't matter, and I'd been discarded like an old rag. How dare he treat me that way, how dare Winston's let him.

While I waited for the pizza to arrive, and for Rachel to get home, I switched on my MacBook and perused the Advisory, Conciliation and Arbitration Service website, or ACAS for short. Wanting to see where I stood legally, if in the cold light of day I wanted to take it further. Without any pay-off, I had no choice but to try to argue my case. I needed some money to tide me over until I found something else. Claire had text to say there was nothing immediately available on the temping front, but she'd keep me updated.

Wading through the information on the ACAS website, it looked as though I might have a case for unfair dismissal. There was a form I could fill out, but my eyes swam as I stared at the screen. I'd had one glass of wine too many and it would be better to wait until tomorrow, when I could focus on it sober.

'Mum, there's a guy here with pizza,' I heard a call from the front door as it opened. Rachel and dinner had arrived together, which was perfect timing as the alcohol sloshed in my empty stomach. I got up and took a meagre handful of change to give the driver a tip. Happy to be distracted from my woes.

We sat at the table, eating directly from the pizza box. I managed a couple of slices, washed down with another glass of red wine as Rachel told me about her day.

'I almost punched Ava today,' she blurted.

'When did you see Ava?' I said, the blood draining from my face.

'Me and Casey went into town on the bus, she was in Starbucks with her cronies.'

'And what happened?'

'She's spreading around that Ryan is a drug dealer, told all of her friends. Honestly, Mum, she's such a bitch!' Rachel said, tearing through another slice of pepperoni pizza.

I sighed, that girl was as much trouble as her father.

'What did you do?' I asked, unsure if I wanted to hear the answer.

'I pushed her when she got outside, told her if I heard her chatting any more shit about my brother, I'd sew her mouth shut.'

Delirious laughter escaped my lips, partly down to the wine but mostly because my daughter sounded the most 'gangster' I'd ever heard.

'Rachel, honestly, stay away from her. She's trouble, her dad is trouble, and I don't want you anywhere near either of them,' I said, quickly reverting to parent mode.

Rachel scowled and inwardly I couldn't help but be proud of her standing up for her brother as he had done for her. 'Well, she talks shit anyway. Last week at school she was telling everyone the police had been round her house and her dad was being investigated.' My ears pricked.

'Investigated for what?' I asked, and Rachel shrugged.

'No idea. Tax or something.' She wiped her mouth on a piece of kitchen roll and pushed the box away as my mind raced. 'I'm stuffed. Do you mind if I jump in the shower?' she said, getting to her feet.

'Go ahead. Have you got any coursework to do this week?'

'Yep, Casey and I are going to do our history together tomorrow.'

I nodded and Rachel went upstairs as I put the leftover pizza in the fridge.

That was interesting. Did HMRC think Simon had been evading paying tax on his business, or businesses? I didn't remember George mentioning tax, did Simon take care of all that during their start-up? I'd have to ask him on Wednesday.

My phone vibrated on the table, Ryan calling.

'Hey, kiddo, how are you?' I said, giving the sides and table a wipe as I balanced my phone between my shoulder and ear.

'Yeah good. I've been with Dad's mate, Jim; he's teaching me the basics of plumbing. He's shown me loads today. We went to a job where someone had a leak under their water tank, it had been dripping for ages and soaked through all the floorboards, it was mental.'

It took me a second to remember Jonathan had volunteered Ryan's services as first mate to Jim for half-term, maybe the week after too. It sounded as though Ryan had enjoyed his first day learning about the trade.

'Sounds good, do you think it's something you might be interesting in doing? I'm sure you can do plumbing at college.'

'Jim thinks I'm a natural, he's practically offered me an apprenticeship when I finish my GCSEs.' I'd never heard Ryan so enthusiastic about anything other than the latest *Call of Duty* release.

'I'm really pleased for you, it's good to do something productive with your time. Is Dad home yet?'

'No, he's gone round Monique's, he's left me money for a takeaway though.'

My nostrils flared, Jonathan wanted his son to stay with him and he buggered off to sort out his tiff with Monique.

'I thought we were going to view the house today?' Ryan continued.

'Shit I forgot!' I cried, slapping my hand to my forehead. With the fallout at work, I'd completely forgotten to book the viewing.

'Mum, language!' Ryan bit back sarcastically.

'I'll see if I can book one for tomorrow. It's been a really busy day,' I said, choosing my words carefully.

'Okay cool. I'm kind of excited about moving. I think it'll be good for us.'

I wanted to agree with him, but I hadn't yet come to terms with the life I was leaving behind.

44

Ryan said he was going to see what he could order on Uber Eats and I was glad as the longer I stayed on the phone with him, the larger the lump in my throat grew. The twins were growing so fast. As parents, Jonathan and I must have done something right, because they were generally good kids. Standing up for each other despite not always getting along made me proud. Family came first and we had to stick together when under attack.

Simon had been in the house. He was a threat to our family, and I had to work out why. What did he want from us? Alone in the kitchen, I cast my eye over the surfaces, moving to the lounge to check the bookcase. Surely Simon wouldn't have planted the listening device back again, not with Jonathan here, but I couldn't be positive. It wouldn't be hard to give him the slip for a few seconds. I scanned the room, looking in all the places Claire and I had searched before, but found nothing.

Pondering it further, Simon wouldn't have brought it back. His narrative was that I was mad. I could hardly be with physical proof someone had been in my house. I'd outsmarted him with the camera doorbell. Now, he couldn't come and go as he pleased, like it was his house already. We were still weeks away from that. I'd barely seen any paperwork, not a fixtures or fittings list to complete or anything to sign.

Perhaps Jonathan had done it all, keeping me out of the loop as far as possible. He wanted a quick sale as much as Simon did, or maybe it wasn't Simon who was in a rush at all. It could be they had planned to move things quickly, Simon doing Jonathan a favour. I still didn't understand why Simon wanted our house when he wasn't selling his. He was a businessman, not a property giant, a cash buyer at that. Where was his money coming from? Was Fox Security that lucrative, and now he was under investigation for tax?

None of it made sense, but I was sure Jonathan knew more than he was letting on. I hoped I'd unsettled him today, enlightening him on what Simon Fox had been up to, at least where his children were concerned.

I believed I was only seeing the tip of the iceberg where Simon's narcissistic personality was concerned. What must his wife have been like? Why would she have left Ava behind when she moved out? It was rare for a mother to do that, and alarm bells sounded in my ears. Back at my MacBook, I logged into Facebook, searching for Simon Fox, running down his friends list to find anyone with the surname Fox. Were they divorced or separated? Would she still have his surname? He had hundreds of friends and I had no idea what she was even called, but there was no one by the name of Fox.

An idea brewing, I climbed the stairs, almost bumping into Rachel wrapped in a towel crossing the hallway into the bathroom. She stood in front of the mirror combing conditioner through her waves.

'Hey, is Ava on Instagram?' I asked from the hallway. I didn't know much about the app, not being on it myself; I was too much of a dinosaur.

'She lives on there, Mum, she posts photos of herself *all* the time,' she replied, rolling her eyes. Rachel had shown me some of the pictures her friends posted, bodies turned halfway to the camera, pointing their backsides skyward. It made me cringe to see them sexualise themselves, but she'd already told me half her friends were 'doing it'. Thankfully, I hadn't seen any photos like that of Rachel and I was sure Ryan would be the first to tell me if she ever did.

Rachel finished combing her hair and picked up her phone from the side, flicking to Instagram and searching for Ava. She moved to the doorway and showed me.

'How can you see her photos then, are you friends?'

'It doesn't work like that, it's open, unless you select you only want people you allow to follow you to see your photos. She could block me, but you don't really do that unless you've got proper beef with someone.'

Rachel scrolled through photo after photo of Ava. Pouting, pointing, rude hand gestures, winking, tongue poking out. The girl loved herself.

'See, she's filtered to the max!' Rachel sneered, but I had no idea what she meant.

'Any of her and her mum?' I chanced.

She looked at me quizzically but carried on scrolling, so fast I could barely see the pictures.

'There,' she said, stopping at a selfie of Ava beside a striking blonde, both wearing sunglasses. She looked to be in her late thirties and unsurprisingly was gorgeous.

Before I even asked, Rachel clicked on Ava's mum's name, as her daughter had tagged her in the post. Nikola Gittings, not Fox, and she only had a handful of photos, mostly of a Golden Retriever called Max whom she clearly adored.

'She doesn't post much,' Rachel said, putting her phone down and moisturising her face. The steam from the bathroom was spilling out into the hallway, rolling like clouds towards the ceiling.

'Thanks, love. Open the window would you, and make sure you put the towel back,' I said, unable to count the number of times I'd picked wet towels off the banister.

Back downstairs, I typed the name Nikola Gittings into Facebook, but it appeared she didn't have an account. I put the name into google to see what came up. It directed me to a florist website, Posy Toes in Horsham. A picture of a pretty glass-fronted shop with a racing green ornate sign filled the screen, Posy Toes in large gold lettering at the top. A small snapshot of Nikola on the About Us page with the full address and contact number. I took a photo on my phone of the address and immediately decided my limited budget could stretch to a bunch of flowers.

Shutting down the MacBook, I put the television on, listening to Rachel blow-dry her hair upstairs. A comforting noise of having someone else in the house. I finished the bottle of red, toying with the idea of opening another, if I had another, but already my eyelids were heavy, tongue furred with alcohol and nicotine. It had been one hell of a day, one hell of a month. I was looking forward to putting the entire year behind me and starting again.

I picked up my phone as it occurred to me I should be looking for another job, a way to bring money into the house, but my eyes wouldn't absorb the adverts I searched for. Tomorrow, it would be better to look tomorrow. The notification of Tim's missed calls remained when I locked the screen. I hadn't bothered to delete them earlier. What had he wanted? Was he calling to rub salt in the wounds, or perhaps apologise? Either way, he hadn't left a message and I was in no hurry to talk to him. I was hurt by his betrayal. He knew the mistake was Liam's and not mine, yet he'd thrown me to the wolves anyway. Perhaps I should go to the press like I'd threatened, do an exposé on Winston's. A newspaper might pay for what I had.

The threat was one thing, but the idea made me feel dirty, like I'd never be clean again if I sold my soul for the sake of a few thousand pounds. Who would employ me after that? Knowing I was a whistle-blower. Tim had backed me into a corner, and I had bills to pay. Not to mention a mortgage to obtain on another house. No one would lend me any money without a job. I'd have to tell Jonathan I couldn't move. Although I knew what his reaction would be. He'd take the children and I'd be left on the street. We were separated and I wasn't his problem any more. He didn't have to ensure I had a roof over my head. I couldn't let that happen. If it came to losing my dignity and keeping the twins with me, then so be it.

45

I woke on the sofa, my back sore where I'd drifted off slumped over the arm, drooling down my cheek. I'd never made it to bed. The smell of stale wine permeated the room, and I opened the windows, welcoming the chill from outside. Frost covered my car, glistening in the darkness. The sun hadn't risen yet, it was just after seven in the morning, and I mourned the summer that felt a million miles away now.

One of the residents in the street worked nights and every Tuesday morning they dragged their emptied recycling bin up their driveway before going to bed. Not caring the rest of the street were still asleep. I cringed at the noise and drew the window closed.

Over a strong coffee, I debated whether to tell Rachel I'd lost my job. It took less than a second to decide against it. There was no point in worrying her and I wasn't ready for the news to filter back to Jonathan yet. I wanted to have that conversation on my own terms, if I needed to have it at all.

My stomach screamed for stodge, and I microwaved last night's pizza for breakfast, lighting a candle to disguise the smell of reheated greasy food. I hadn't been so hung-over in ages, but it had been a while since I'd polished off a whole bottle of wine by myself. I was trying to be good and stop using alcohol as a crutch, but yesterday had been an exceptionally bad day.

At nine, I was laying on the sofa when I heard Rachel get up and go into the bathroom. Getting up, I poured her an apple juice and retrieved a breakfast bar from the cupboard, before going upstairs to shower away the grime from the day before. Wine seemed to seep from my pores and even after cleaning my teeth I could still taste it at the back of my throat.

'Are you not going to work, you look a bit casual?' Rachel said, staring at my jeans and roll-neck jumper when I came downstairs.

'I'm going in late. I'm in the warehouse mostly today, it's cold in there,' I lied, ignoring the twinge of guilt. 'Did you say you were doing coursework today? Is Casey coming here?'

'No, Mum, we're going there. She has a hot tub,' Rachel replied.

'I'm going to see if I can get a viewing on that house today, so I'll text you if I get a time, will probably be around three.'

'Okay,' she replied, although the frown was evident on her face. She wanted to move as little as I did but knew it was pointless putting up a fight.

I left to get petrol, treating myself to a coffee from the machine inside the shop; concerned I might still be over the limit although I felt fine. Then I parked up in a nearby street and called the estate agents to book another viewing of Goddard Close. I knew I wouldn't be able to get a mortgage, not if I was honest about my employment situation, although I had three months' payslips I could technically provide. It was more important to see how the children felt about the place, before I even considered putting an offer in.

Tim called again while I drank my coffee, the blowers on full blast, trying to keep warm. I didn't want to return home while Rachel was there, not when I was supposed to be at work, but I did drop her a text to make sure she would be home at half two so we could go to the viewing. I let Tim go to voicemail, unsure I'd be able to talk to him without losing my temper. We never had to see each other again and Peter had made his feelings plain. There would be no payout from Winston's, not voluntarily anyway. I wanted to take a couple of days to let the dust settle while I considered what to do. Could I afford to get a solicitor and try to take them to court? If I failed, it could cost me thousands in fees. My ears pounded with the injustice of it.

I dropped a text to Jonathan to arrange to collect Ryan so we could view the house together. After a short while, he replied with a message to say Jim would drop him off at the house around half two. His tone was clipped, but I batted the annoyance away. Jonathan wouldn't change now. The niceties between us were long gone. We were only civil for the children.

When I'd finished my coffee, believing there was no way I could be over the limit, I drove to Horsham. Using the back roads and not the dual carriageway meant it was a pretty drive past fields and houses I'd never be able to afford. I didn't come to Horsham often, although I used to when the twins were smaller. Their outdoor swimming pool and adjoining park was a fun day out in the summer months, but I couldn't remember the last time I'd taken the twins swimming.

Posy Toes was on the edge of town between Horsham and Crawley, in a small parade of shops situated by a junior school. I imagined it did well with footfall there, the school traffic passing almost every day. Outside were buckets of blooms and the window display was decorated with poinsettias and fresh wreaths to hang, reminding me Christmas would soon be upon us.

I spied Nikola behind the counter serving an elderly gentleman buying red roses. I wandered in, looking at the beautiful colours, drawn to an autumnal tabletop display I imagined would look lovely in the kitchen.

'Can I help you?' came a voice from behind me.

I turned to find that in person Nikola was petite, her small frame drowned in the green apron tied double at her waist. I towered above her, realising Simon would have done the same.

'Yes, I'd like this please,' I said, smiling and pointing to the display on the side.

'Great choice,' she replied, carrying it gently to the counter.

I dug in my bag for my phone, hands clammy. How would I broach the subject of Simon Fox?

'Umm, you're Nikola Gittings, aren't you?'

'Yes, but Nik is fine.' Her face was friendly, open, and I swallowed, my throat tight.

'Did you used to be married to Simon Fox?' I asked.

The mention of his name darkened her features and she turned her back on me, lowering the flowers gently into a square box to keep them upright.

'I was,' she replied, a little stiffly.

'I'm sorry, I know this is rude of me to turn up here and ask you about him. My daughter goes to school with Ava,' I started, and she turned back around, her forehead creasing.

'You know my daughter?'

'I don't really, my daughter does though. I wanted to talk to you about Simon. I had a...' I paused, unsure how to phrase it, 'a run-in with him a few weeks ago.'

'Look, I left Simon years ago. I'm sorry, but I can't help you.' She pushed the box towards me and held out the card reader. 'That will be twenty-two pounds please.'

I tapped my phone against the reader, waiting for the beep, my body deflating. I'd come in too heavy-handed, and Nikola had shut down before my eyes. A hard exterior replacing the warm, easy-going woman I'd spoken to moments ago.

She visibly bristled as she gave me the receipt, and my cheeks coloured.

'I'm sorry, I didn't mean to cause you any distress,' I said.

'It's fine, it was a long time ago,' she replied flatly. Clearly it was anything but fine.

I carried the box towards the door and heard a sigh from behind me. Turning around, I saw Nikola's head was lowered as she gripped the counter.

'Whatever it is with Simon, don't get involved,' she said, her voice softening.

'It's too late for that.' My shoulders sagged and we stared across the shop at each other, painful memories etched on her face.

'He wouldn't let me take Ava; told the courts I was an unfit mother. Showed them evidence of drug-taking.' She laughed darkly. 'I've never touched a drug in my life. I don't even drink.'

'Why did you leave him?' I asked, my stomach clenched.

'He hit me, just once, but it was enough,' she whispered, looking down at the bench again.

The door chimed behind me, knocking the bell as someone came in, shattering the moment.

'Thank you, Nik,' I said, trying to convey I was talking about more than the flowers. Turning to leave, I caught her words over my shoulder.

'Be careful, he doesn't like to lose.'

I shuddered, turning back to ask her what she meant, but she'd focused her attention on her new customer.

I stepped out of the shop, the muscles in my neck tensing. I knew Simon Fox was dangerous, that much was obvious. I knew he was smart and once he had the bit between his teeth he wouldn't let go. What I didn't know until today was that he was violent.

46

I drove home, running the conversation with Nikola back through my mind. Simon Fox was a man who got what he wanted. He must have known, once Nikola said she was leaving, she would take Ava with her, but he'd denied her. Was it control? Did he have to be in charge all the time? Having the upper hand must be important to him. What Nikola must have gone through made my chest ache. I'd be heartbroken to have my children taken away from me, to be branded an unfit mother.

How could he have been so callous? As a father, he must have known what it would do to Nikola. Did Ava see her mother regularly? I couldn't imagine not being permitted to see Rachel, to have that bond broken because I refused to allow my husband to abuse me. I guessed she couldn't prove he'd hit her, otherwise she'd have grounds for full custody. Although it wouldn't surprise me if Simon had all sorts of people in his pocket, doing him favours. Maybe even the police had looked the other way and if they had it meant I had no allies at all, no one I could call when I was in trouble.

When I got back to the house, I got out of the car, leaning in across the front seat to get the box from Posy Toes when I heard a voice behind me.

'Mrs Massingham.' The glacial tone was instantly recognisable, and I banged my head on the roof of the car. As though thinking about him on the way home made him appear in a puff of smoke. So much for the police telling him to stay away.

'Mr Fox,' I said, trying to keep my voice light, although every inch of me wanted to run to the house and lock myself inside.

He stood on the driveway, dressed in a sharp navy suit, silver cufflinks peeking out from his sleeve. To look at, he was smart, handsome some might say, although I knew too much to ever find him attractive.

'I thought I'd pop over on the off-chance someone might be home. I'd love to do some measuring up.' His politeness caught me off guard, as though I was speaking to a different version of the Simon Fox I'd encountered numerous times before. It rendered me momentarily speechless, and I clutched my bag and the florist box to my body. There wasn't a measuring tape in sight.

'I'm sorry, but that must be arranged via Martin's. They need to be here if you want to come inside.' My voice was stilted.

A smile played on his lips before he spoke, opening his arms wide.

'Ah there's no need for that is there?'

I couldn't believe his audacity, after the way he'd spoken to me in his shop. How he'd belittled me along with Mike, or whatever his name really was.

'I'm afraid there is. I do not want you in my house, especially not unaccompanied.'

His eyes flashed with something, an expression I couldn't put my finger on. His gaze dropped to the box I was using as a shield.

'Been shopping, have you?'

My breath hitched and I stifled a cough.

'Goodbye, Mr Fox,' I managed, moving towards the door, ignoring every alarm bell in my brain that told me not to turn my back on him.

'Clock's ticking, Kay,' he called, walking back down the driveway whistling to himself as I fumbled to get the key in the lock.

The man rattled me, and I didn't buy his fake friendly manner. Why did he want to get inside the house? What was here that he wanted? Where would it stop?

I'd barely been in for five minutes, my pulse slowing after being ambushed on the driveway when the doorbell sounded, and it spiked again. Was Simon back?

Glad of the camera, I checked my phone to see who was outside, surprised to find a harassed-looking Tim staring up at the house trying to detect movement from inside.

Heat flushed through my body, and I pulled the door open so hard I was surprised it didn't come off its hinges.

'What do you want?' I snapped.

Tim's eyes bulged and he took a step back.

'You've not been answering your phone,' he said, stumbling over his words.

'I don't work for you any more, remember?' I couldn't keep the venom out of my tone. First Simon Fox and now Tim. I'd had enough of men turning up on my doorstep uninvited and unwelcome.

'I need to talk to you, can I come in?' Tim's gravelly voice was low, submissive for a change. It put me on edge.

'I don't think so, Tim. You can say what you need to out here.' I crossed my arms over my chest and watched as Tim's wayward eyebrows wriggled closer together. It was just starting to rain, and Tim looked to the heavens and lifted his coat collar.

'Have you approached the press about Winston's?'

I narrowed my eyes, and it dawned on me why Tim was at my door. Damage limitation.

'Not yet,' I replied stiffly.

'Good, good. Well, I've had a chat with Peter, you know, calmed him down and because we go way back, I've convinced him to rene-gotiate.' Tim slithered towards me like the snake he was.

'And?' I said, trying to appear uninterested as excitement bubbled in my chest.

'And, in return for your... *findings*, Peter would like to make you an offer of two and a half years' salary.'

I swallowed, calculating the figure minus tax in my head as Tim stared at me expectantly. My skin tingled as it dawned on me they were offering five times what they had previously. Peter must have realised the implications of the proof I held, and what damage it could do to Winston's for him to be willing to renegotiate.

'Obviously it would mean submitting anything you have involving Winston's to us, and there will be a non-disclosure to sign,' Tim carried on.

I tried to let the figure which would be more than a hundred thou-sand pounds sink in. Enough for a deposit, enough to pay for the move. I'd barely have any mortgage at all once the equity was split. My mouth twitched involuntarily as I imagined Peter fuming at the total U-turn. I was sure Tim hadn't done anything other than show Peter what I had. It would be a no-brainer for any company to avoid being dragged through the mud and I had so much dirt it would have been a filthy affair.

But this wasn't just about the money; it was the principle, and I wasn't about to let them steamroller me again.

'Five years, Tim, that was what I wanted, it's what I asked for.'

Tim ran a hand through his damp greying hair and rocked back on his heels. His lips parted and he was momentarily speechless.

'Kay, be reasonable,' he said eventually, trying to appeal to my better nature, but that ship had sailed long ago. I was standing my ground. I knew full well Winston's had the money. I'd read the annual reports.

'That's the price of what I have, Tim. That plus the pension, medical and benefits.' After all, the figure had to be large, large enough to counter what a tabloid newspaper might offer me for an explosive exposé. The MeToo movement was still making headlines and Winston's knew it.

My insides vibrated, pulsing with adrenaline as Tim and I stared at each other, a standoff. Rain speckled the shoulders of Tim's blazer, getting heavier by the minute.

'I'll sign it off with Peter tonight.' Tim deflated; the wind knocked out of him. I imagined Peter giving him carte blanche to get me onside and the thought alone pleased me no end.

'And if I agree to a revised figure. How long will I have to consider your offer?' I asked, pressing my lips together, enjoying the power I held.

'Tomorrow. I can arrange for legal to draft the NDA and the contract. If you can bring everything with you, say around one o'clock, we can get it done.' He grimaced, an awkwardness in his limbs betraying his solid voice.

Everything I'd had to put up with over the past five years, the jibes, innuendos, and dismissiveness of my male colleagues, I was unable to resist a final jab.

'And what if I don't accept?' I said the words with relish, my cheeks on fire.

'Well, we're hoping you will,' Tim stuttered, his pupils like little moons.

I allowed myself a moment of satisfaction. Imagining him returning to Peter, asking him for more money. He must have felt backed into a corner to send Tim around to grovel. Both of them had to be feeling emasculated and I couldn't help but savour the warm glow it gave me.

'Okay,' I said, closing the door and leaving Tim on the driveway, his tail between his legs.

I floated back into the house, elation radiating through every cell of my body. What had been a disaster yesterday might end up being my salvation.

47

It was difficult to stifle my excitement. Unable to contain it, I bounced around the house full of energy, as though I'd won the lottery. All the money worries I had could be solved with my signature. I wouldn't be tied to Jonathan financially. It gave me independence to make decisions on my own, choices I didn't have before.

Not wanting to get carried away, I called Claire, knowing she would keep my feet on the ground.

'Come over tonight, I'll do us some Quorn, mozzarella and pesto?' I offered.

'Mmmm, sounds good. Shall I come straight from work?'

'Yep, and don't forget the spinach,' I said, unable to erase the smile from my face.

'As if I would. You sound in a good mood, what's happened?'

I debated telling her, but it wouldn't be long before the kids would be home, and we'd have to set off for Goddard Close.

'I'll tell you later,' I teased.

We said goodbye and, while I remembered, I sent a quick text to George, to see if he was still on for curry night at the social club tomorrow. It conjured up images of sticky floors, dim lighting and mouldy fabric chairs, but I owed him and, to my surprise, was looking forward to it. There would be two nights of celebration – a pre-signing and a post-signing, I grinned to myself. As long as Tim could convince Peter to bow to my demands.

A little while later, Ryan let himself in, slipping off his shoes, nose buried in his phone.

'Hiya,' I called with a laugh from the kitchen table, expecting him to jump, but he barely flinched. Smiling for a change, he came and sat down. 'So how was your day?'

'Good, I quite enjoy it. Jim makes it so interesting. He's so good with his hands, I reckon he could fix anything.' He stared at me in wonder, and I swallowed the bitter pill that stuck in my throat. Ryan should feel the same way when it came to spending time with his dad. Jonathan couldn't help not being skilful when it came to DIY or mechanics, he just wasn't built that way.

'So plumbing is the way forward then, is it?' I asked, pleasantly surprised Ryan seemed to have found a sense of direction.

So far he'd floated through school, without any idea what he wanted to do afterwards. Other than gaming, there wasn't anything that stood out, an activity he really enjoyed. Rachel was different, she was already planning on doing an entry-level Beauty Tech course at college, with dreams of owning her own mobile nail and lash company.

I watched Ryan's face become animated as he talked about replacing the pipework underneath an elderly gentleman's sink that morning. Jim had let him do it himself under his supervision.

'It's gross though, all the stuff that comes out.' He mock retched and I wrinkled my nose. Fishing my hair out of the plughole in the shower was disgusting enough.

Rachel came back at quarter to three, breathless from jogging up the road from the bus stop.

'Sorry, bus was late,' she wheezed as I ushered both of them out of the door and into the car, not wanting to be late for the viewing.

This time, I parked in front of the property in one of the privately owned spaces on Goddard Close. It wouldn't be long before the twins would be learning to drive and would have cars themselves. We got out and they took in the house. Obviously smaller than what we were used to, and I wasn't sure how that would go down, but they didn't grumble.

Louise arrived in her car a few minutes later as we stood outside, her bouncy walk and enthusiasm infectious. I watched the kids carefully as she opened the front door and they stepped inside ahead of me. Interested to see their first reactions. If we were going to move, it had to be right for them as much as for me.

'It's quite nice,' said Rachel, eyebrows raised as she took in the bright airy lounge.

'Yeah,' Ryan agreed, walking through to the kitchen and disappearing into the second reception room which would need to be converted to the third bedroom.

'I was thinking one of you, or me, whatever you prefer, can have the downstairs room,' I said, following him.

'There's a toilet downstairs as well.' Ryan leaned out of the room, his hand on the door frame as Rachel went inside to have a look.

With the space empty, it was easy to visualise our things there, most I was sure would fit, some Jonathan may want to have. I looked out of the kitchen window onto the tidy back garden, trying to imagine Claire and I enjoying a glass of Pimm's in the summer. I listened for traffic, it was half-term, not peak school-run time, but it wasn't too bad.

Rachel came back into the kitchen and tried the back door which was locked.

'Oh here, let me,' Louise said, rushing forwards and unlocking it.

The twins went outside, and I followed. It was reasonably quiet; the odd loud engine of the boy racers would disturb the peace but nothing we wouldn't get used to.

'We'd be able to walk to school,' Ryan said to Rachel, who nodded thoughtfully.

'I'll let you all have a wander around. I'll be here if you need me,' Louise said, already half out of the front door with her phone in her hand.

'Shall we take a look upstairs?' I said and the twins raced ahead of me, jostling for first position.

'Careful,' I called, looking around and soaking up the atmosphere. Buying a house was almost as much about how it felt than how it looked.

I wandered into the second reception room and on into the adjacent toilet, casting my eyes around for any signs of damp or anything that would ring alarm bells. It looked like the property had been taken care of, the owners had given every room a fresh coat of paint and replaced the carpets upstairs. The dark wood floor downstairs would look lovely with a plush rug laid in front of the sofa. Even the kitchen gleamed. Could this be it? The right place for us?

'Mum,' Rachel called, and I followed her voice up the stairs where the twins waited in the master bedroom at the front of the house, overlooking the street.

'Ryan said he'd be happy downstairs and we could be up here,' she said, looking from me to Ryan and back again.

'I know it's smaller, but do you like it?' I asked, wanting to be sure they weren't just going along with it to keep me happy. It had to be right for them too.

'Yeah, Mum, it's fine. We can walk to school, and I'll be closer to Casey. She only lives around the corner.'

'What about you, Ryan? How do you feel about moving?'

'I guess it's okay. I mean, we don't have a choice, we have to move, and this place is as good as any.'

I smiled at the usual lack of enthusiasm my son normally exhibited. Rachel responded by punching him on the arm.

'Maybe we could convert the downstairs toilet to a shower room, then you'd have your own bathroom,' I suggested and Ryan shrugged.

'Yeah, I guess. At least then I wouldn't have to share the upstairs one with you two.'

'Okay, have you had a good look around?'

They both nodded.

'We may have to put some stuff in storage, but we'll see. I'll go and speak to the estate agent.'

I left them and went back downstairs to find Louise waiting patiently outside leaning against the bonnet of her car.

'Do you think they'll accept three hundred and ten thousand?' I asked watching the corners of Louise's mouth turn skyward. Goddard Close could be the new start we needed. Somewhere that was a clean slate with no history or baggage. A home where we could make happy memories, just the three of us.

48

Louise said she would go back and deliver the offer to the vendors and call me tomorrow with a response. I knew without an official mortgage offer in place, I wasn't in a position to offer anything, but I'd been told in theory what I could borrow, and that was before putting down a larger lump sum as deposit. If the money from Winston's came through, I might not need a mortgage at all. Maybe things were looking up, Goddard Close could be the escape route I needed. Away from Simon Fox and the trouble he created.

Herding the twins into the car, I took them home for dinner, whisking up a quick meal of sausages and mash so they could eat before Claire arrived. Rachel had once said we were far too cringy to be around for long and now they left us to it when we were together. To be fair, we got louder the more we drank, cackling and squealing when we got going, so I didn't blame them for wanting to disappear upstairs.

As Ryan forced a forkful of mash into his mouth, he told me he'd asked Jonathan if he could stay here for the night and if Jim could pick him up for work in the morning. Jonathan had said yes, and I was pleased to have the both of them at home with me. As the parent, I was supposed to protect them, but sometimes it was the other way around.

They ate quickly, negotiating some sweets on top of the cupboard to take upstairs. I was in such a good mood I let them, before clearing away the devastation left behind on the table.

Half an hour later, Claire arrived carrying a bag of our favourite things.

'I've been to Tesco,' she said breathlessly, her ponytail flapping in the wind behind her.

'God, it's windy out there,' I said, letting her cross the threshold as she opened the bag for me to peek inside. I glimpsed two bottles of wine, spinach, cigarettes, and chocolate and knew we were in for a good night.

'Do you mind if I leave my car here and get an Uber home,' she said, wriggling out of her coat and throwing it on the sofa.

'Or you could crash here, but either way it's fine.'

We went into the kitchen, and I put the Quorn fillets in the oven, taking the bag of spinach from her.

'So, tell me what's going on,' she asked, grabbing two glasses, and sitting at the table to open the wine. I loved the way we moved around the kitchen like an old married couple. She felt as much at home here as I did, and I hoped it would be the same when we moved.

I told Claire about my unexpected visit from Tim, the figure I'd negotiated and the house we'd viewed today which might work for the three of us. Claire listened, her eyes widening as did her grin. When I'd finally finished, she clapped her hands together.

'I'm so pleased for you. That gives you a bit of leeway doesn't it, takes the pressure off. I mean, I had a look at the jobs we've got on, Kay, but you're overqualified for all of them. They are entry-level roles and practically minimum wage. The market out there is tough.'

'I bet,' I said, relief flowing through me. I'd worried about the money situation but hadn't considered how difficult it might be to get another job quickly.

'To be honest, I was a bit panicky for you,' Claire admitted.

'Me too! At least I don't have to rush into anything now. Well, as long as it all goes to plan tomorrow. I haven't signed anything yet.' I didn't want to count my chickens. Knowing my luck, Tim had gone back to Winston's and Peter had changed his mind.

'You'll soon be in the money!'

We chinked glasses and I sat for a few minutes to have a sip of wine until the timer went off announcing the Quorn fillets were cooked.

'I love this dinner.' Claire moaned in delight, taking another mouthful of spinach and mozzarella. I had to agree, my appetite fully returned since I'd stopped drinking so much. 'What's the latest with the sly Fox?'

'Oh, he came around today too, wanted me to let him in to measure up!' I scoffed at the cheek of it and watched as she shook her head in disgust. 'I told him politely to bugger off. In fact, I saw his ex-wife this morning too. She's got a florist's shop in Horsham.'

'Is that where the flowers came from. I meant to say, they're lovely,' Claire said, pointing at the autumnal display on the table with her fork.

I nodded, scooping the last mouthful of my dinner.

'Apparently she left him because he hit her,' I said, and Claire froze, the wine glass almost at her lips. I carried on, in full swing. 'I know. I told you, he's a psycho! He got sole custody of their daughter because he convinced the courts she was an unfit mother,' I continued and watched as Claire's eyebrows inched higher towards her hairline.

'What a bastard,' she said eventually.

'The sooner I can get out of here, the better.'

Our conversation turned to George, and I told Claire we were supposed to be meeting tomorrow for dinner, although he hadn't responded to my text. I picked up my phone and frowned at it, no messages had come through. Perhaps he was busy or working late, maybe he was at his college course.

'You like him, don't you?' Claire probed, eyes twinkling.

'He's really interesting actually,' I said, face glowing. Did I like George? As a friend, but I wasn't sure there was enough of a spark for it to be anything more.

'Well, I guess that's a good start.'

'How's Owen?' I asked, changing the subject as Claire poured us a refill.

'We're taking a break,' she said, before explaining that the drama of going away for New Year had been the final straw for her. Claire didn't like to be cornered and often when she was, she ran.

The twins came down to say hello, putting the television on to watch the latest episode of a Netflix drama that sounded a lot like *Lord of the Flies*. I closed the double doors between the two rooms, so they could watch it in peace. Rain began hammering outside, thudding against the window, and we stood by the back door, open a crack, lighting cigarettes and wafting the smoke through the gap.

'I hope they don't smell it,' I whispered, before getting the giggles.

'Does this remind you of smoking in my bedroom standing on the window ledge?' Claire snorted and before we knew it we were both laughing so much at the memory of being caught by her dad, we had to cross our legs.

Our merriment ended when my phone chimed, the motion sensor going off.

'Who's that now?' I sighed. 'It's been like Piccadilly Circus in here?' Chucking the cigarette out and reaching for my phone to open the app, sure any second the doorbell would ring. Instead, a loud boom came from the front of the house.

'Mum,' shouted Ryan through the door, his panicked tone making the hair on the back of my neck stand on end.

I dropped the phone on the table and flung open the door to get to him. My maternal instinct powering me forward.

'Call the police,' Rachel screamed at me, as an almighty bang came again, from the front door.

49

'Ring the police!' I repeated back at Claire as I rushed towards the front door. Rachel and Ryan were both at the window, peaking out of the curtain into the darkness.

'Don't go out there,' Rachel cried, reaching for me.

The banging subsided, had someone tried to kick the door in?

I pulled it open to see a figure at the end of the driveway, shrouded in darkness.

'My final warning. Things don't end well for those who stick their nose into my business,' Simon Fox called. I could just about make out his voice beneath the wind, but he wasn't close enough for me to distinguish his features in the shadows. Blood drained from my face and my body went limp, knees slackened, and I gripped the frame as he turned and walked away. Blinking rapidly, I looked down at the front door which had a large dusty boot mark on it, but no damage.

'The doorbell,' Ryan said, appearing at my side and leaning out into the gloom. The wind howled, wrenching the door from my grip.

I turned to see what Ryan meant – the camera doorbell had

been smashed in, parts of it were on the floor, the rest hanging by barely attached wires to the unit George had fitted.

'Are the police coming?' I asked, as the hallway behind me filled with bodies.

'Yes, they're on their way,' Claire said, pulling me by the arm. 'Come inside and lock the door.' She'd gone pale and I shuddered as I closed and locked the door.

The mood had shifted a hundred and eighty degrees. Heart racing, I backed into the kitchen, registering the shock on the twins' faces.

'Are you okay?' I asked them, and they both nodded, mouths gaping. Lowering myself into a chair at the table, Claire pushed the wine glass towards me.

'Was that him?' she asked.

I nodded, still reeling from what had just happened.

What had he meant, *his final warning?* Warning for what?

'You've done nothing to Ava, have you?' I asked Rachel and Ryan in turn.

They both shook their heads, and I didn't doubt them. Was this because I wouldn't let him in to measure up? Was the sale not moving fast enough? The guy was a nutter, but at least I had it on camera.

'Check the app for footage,' Ryan said as the thought popped into my mind simultaneously.

Did the hardware being broken mean I'd be unable to access the footage? The video took a while to load. It buffered as it played, the video stuttering, and we all squinted at the screen as a figure rushed towards the door and kicked it. The camera suddenly went dark as though a hand had been put over it, then I heard whispering.

'Can you hear what he's saying?' Claire asked as my spine arched like a cat, fingers and toes tingling.

'Not over the wind.' I was about to scroll it back and watch again when the hand moved and something flew at the screen, causing Claire and I to cry out and lurch back in our seats like one of those joke horror videos that went viral. The video abruptly ended.

'He hit it with something, a hammer or something like that,' Ryan said, frowning.

I put the clip back to the beginning to watch again, turning the volume up full blast. Watching Simon on my driveway made my throat close, he needed locking away. I leaned in closer, concentrating on the sound. The wind whistled, a high-pitched constant screech, but I could just about make out what he was whispering.

'Sounds like, George – something about "George for me",' I said. We replayed it again.

'Say hi to George for me,' I said, my breathing turning shallow. I got up and walked away from the table, my head in my hands.

'Can I look at the video again?' Claire said, rubbing her breastbone. My normally calm and collected friend looked panicked.

'What is it?' I said, turning back, as she replayed the video two more times before clamping a hand over her mouth.

'It's the voice. I think it's Owen.' She sounded shaky and I put a hand on her shoulder. Claire had to be mistaken but before I could press her further Rachel piped up.

'The police are here.'

Through the gap in the curtains, we saw blue flashing lights and Ryan went to the door to let them in.

'It's him, I know it's him!' I shrieked, ten minutes later once they'd watched the footage and I'd explained it was Simon Fox. Police Constables Michael Ferron and Jeff Covell had responded to the call and, initially, I was pleased to see their friendly faces but their expressions changed to one of doubt when I said I knew it was Simon Fox who'd caused the damage.

'We told him to stay away from you, Mrs Massingham, but we'll head around there now.'

'It is him,' Ryan interjected.

'It could be him, but unfortunately we can't identify him from the footage this time. However, we'll go and see him now.'

'Well, you warning him to stay away hasn't made any difference. What do I need to do, get an injunction?' I shouted, rubbing the back of my neck.

'If we have reasonable cause once we've spoken to him, we'll arrest him for suspected criminal damage,' PC Covell said, rising to his feet.

I shook my head. Simon was too clever. He was too fast in the video, his figure blurry, even his voice was difficult to make out. Claire was too shell-shocked to speak, she hadn't volunteered she thought the man she'd been sleeping with, whom she called Owen, was actually Simon Fox.

Once the police had left, I turned on her.

'Why didn't you say anything?'

'What are they going to arrest him for, impersonation?' she snapped, her eyes watery.

'We're going to go upstairs,' Ryan said, steering his sister by the shoulders.

'Okay, are you sure you're both all right?'

'We're fine. Do you want us to call Dad?'

'No,' I snapped. Jonathan here would be the last thing any of us needed. Plus, he was involved with Simon somehow. I just didn't know how yet.

When they'd gone, I sat and reached across the table resting my hand over Claire's.

'Do you really think it's him?' I asked.

'I don't know,' she said weakly, reaching for her phone, but I could see her face was troubled.

'I need to call George,' I said, jumping up from the table and making the call, listening to the phone ring repeatedly before switching to voicemail. I left a garbled message and hung up, turning back around to see Claire's arm outstretched, her phone in her hand.

'I only have one photo; he hates having his photo taken,' she said, holding it up to me.

A selfie of Claire and Simon appeared on the screen, their heads resting on pillows in Claire's bed, the morning after the night before. His eyes twinkling, a look of smug satisfaction on his face.

50

I retched, the dinner I'd eaten less than two hours ago rising in my throat. Claire shook her head, mumbling to herself as she threw the phone away from her across the table, repulsed.

'Holy shit,' I said, finding no other words. Who was Simon Fox? He had to be straight up crazy. Was it a coincidence he'd been dating Claire or was he trying to get to me through my friend?

'I never sent you back that photo, the one you took of Jonathan at the bar,' I said, flicking through my messages to pull up what Claire had sent from the Six Bells.

'Here. That's Simon, isn't it, standing next to him at the bar?' I pointed to the man whose side profile was barely visible, obscured by Jonathan's raised arm drinking his pint.

'But Owen just went to the bar, he was getting us some more drinks.' She frowned at the photo, perplexed.

'Jonathan was meeting Simon, or Owen, whatever the hell he wants to call himself.'

'I should have known,' Claire mumbled, rubbing the stem of her wine glass before gulping the rest of the contents.

'How?' I asked.

'He didn't want to meet you; said he was sure you wouldn't like him, and it would be the nail in the coffin for us. He got the arse sometimes, when I chose to see you, not him. It irked me, but I brushed it off.' Claire's grimace deepened. 'Then Owen... Simon, was so forceful about going away for Christmas; unbelievably frustrated when I wouldn't change the plans I had with my parents. I didn't see what the big deal was.'

'He wants me out of the house by Christmas, those were the terms. It doesn't make sense,' I said, more confused than ever.

'So that house he showed me was never his, was it?' Claire's shoulders slumped.

'I don't think so. I'm so sorry, hon.'

'What do you think set him off tonight? You going to see his ex-wife?'

'Possibly, you dumping him probably didn't help.' I grimaced, nudging her to show I was kidding. 'Did he drive the Jaguar over to you?'

'Yes, but I didn't make the connection. Loads of people drive them now...' Claire trailed off, shaking her head.

Why would Claire guess Simon and Owen were the same person? She wouldn't, not when Simon had provided a whole other identity for Owen; a guy who was divorced, with no children, who worked in finance. Even the refurbishment of his house was plausible, especially if Claire saw him get out and speak to the workman at whatever property he stopped at. Why would she question it when she'd only been going out with him for a few weeks?

'Maybe you can get a restraining order against him?' Claire suggested, her eyes glazing over.

'That would mean I'd have to prove harassment, though, right; I mean, I can't even prove it was him tonight. He'll spin the police a story, he'll have an alibi, I bet. It's George I'm worried about,' I admitted.

'Do you think something's happened to him?'

'I don't know, I just hope he calls me back.' I sighed, getting up to pour the last dregs of wine into each of our glasses. A headache latched onto the base of my skull. 'I'm so sorry you've been dragged into this,' I said.

'It's okay, I mean at least I didn't fall for him... well not really.' Claire looked deflated and I reached for the cigarettes, lighting two and handing one to her. 'More wine,' she suggested with a weak smile.

'Definitely,' I agreed.

* * *

We drank the second bottle between us, falling into bed at ten. Claire offered to stay with me, admitting she didn't want to be alone either, and I was glad for the company. Despite not being used to having another body beside me for months, I passed out quickly, waking with a jolt at the alarm I hadn't remembered setting the night before. Tim had sent a message late last night to confirm the deal was going ahead and I breathed a sigh of relief at some good news.

Rachel and Ryan were already awake; I could hear kitchen cupboards banging downstairs and cereal being poured into bowls. Their poorly hushed tones discussing the events last night. I hoped they weren't overly worried about Simon's visit, I'd hate for them to feel unsafe in their own home. The sooner we could move to Goddard Close, the better.

'We made you coffee,' Rachel said, still in her dressing gown, delivering two cups to us when we made it downstairs.

'Thanks, angel,' Claire said, kissing the top of her head.

'You've both got red wine smiles.' Ryan sniggered as he ate his Crunchy Nut cornflakes.

Claire and I laughed at each other; we did have Joker-style red wine stains arching from the corners of our mouths. The house seemed much calmer this morning, the twins seemingly not too disturbed after last night. I hoped Simon would finally take heed of the police's warning and back off.

'How are you both doing this morning?' I asked, slurping the bitter coffee Rachel had not sugared.

'Fine,' Ryan replied, mid-chew. I glanced at Rachel, and she nodded in agreement. I wasn't sure if Ryan would have said more if his sister hadn't been present.

'What time is Jim picking you up?'

'Half eight,' said Ryan.

'I'm going to the library for when it opens,' Rachel announced, heading for the stairs.

'What are you doing today?' Claire asked, wrinkling her nose at the first sip of coffee but drinking it anyway.

'I'm going to try to find George; I'm really worried about him after what Simon said last night. Oh, and I'm going into work of course.' I eyeballed Claire, trying to convey I hadn't told the twins about losing my job.

'Oh,' she said, her lips forming the shape before giving me a discreet nod. Ryan was too busy scrolling through TikTok videos to listen to what we were saying, but I didn't want him to worry.

'Are you going into the office?' I asked and Claire shook her head.

'I think I'm going to call in sick today. I haven't had a sick day for over a year and this hangover deserves a few hours laying on the sofa.' She grimaced. I imagined the day off was more about the bombshell dropped from afar last night than about her hangover, but I didn't say anything. Claire would talk more about it when she was ready. I'd come to learn over the years that prodding her likely got you bitten.

An hour later, the house was quiet once again. Claire offered to drop Rachel off at the library before heading home and Jim had collected Ryan right on time, giving me a wave from his van. I loaded the dishwasher with the breakfast things and popped a couple of paracetamol for my headache. I had to be on top of my game today.

Tim would be expecting me at Winston's at one o'clock. I charged the necklace in case I needed it. Who knew what would be said in that meeting and it was key I was prepared. I had to remember to go through all the footage again.

I'd been so focused on what I'd gathered whilst at Winston's, I'd forgotten until now I'd been wearing it when I had a run-in with Simon. If Claire was right and I'd have to seek a restraining order of some kind, I'd need evidence of my claim Simon was a danger to me and my family. I intended to deal with that later, first I needed to handle Winston's once and for all.

Everything was downloaded to my MacBook, and I knew I had to take it with me, they would want to see deletion of the clips I'd shown them in return for the money.

I tried to call George again, but no one answered. Concerned for his safety, I was determined to find him. I didn't know where he lived, but I knew he worked for a Locksmith in Crawley and there couldn't be that many of them.

I loaded my car with my handbag and MacBook, dressed smartly for a day at the office, the weight of the necklace like a comfort blanket. As I started the engine my mobile sprang to life and I snatched it up, assuming it was George calling me back. Slumping back into my seat when I saw it was Jonathan. I didn't have the energy for another row with him.

'You have to let Simon into the house, Kay,' he hissed down the phone.

'You've got to be kidding. He came round last night and

smashed up my camera doorbell. He's not coming anywhere near the place. In fact, I'm going to get a restraining order,' I said, puffing out my chest despite the lie. Those things weren't much of a deterrent.

'For God's sake, Kay, why are you making life so difficult for me?'

'How am I? I'm trying to protect my family from that nutjob, which is more than can be said for you. I know something dodgy is going on. Why is he so desperate to get in here?'

'Forget it, I'll let him in myself,' he snapped, and the line went dead.

I pounded my fist on the cold dashboard. Over my dead body was Simon coming into the house, but Jonathan still had a key and, in the eyes of the law, the house was in his name too. If he was coming, I wanted to be around, which meant being out of the house for as short a time as possible.

Throwing the Skoda into reverse, I headed towards the first locksmith I'd earmarked to visit, only five minutes' drive away. It was an unsuccessful visit, the owner looked at me blankly when I asked after George Coombs, so I turned around and drove to the next one.

On the fifth attempt, I struck lucky. Boyce Locks was off the A road between Crawley and Horsham. It was the second to last one I had to try, and I was beginning to doubt George had been telling me the truth. Guilt seeped from every pore when the old man behind the counter rubbed at his stubble and smiled when I asked after George.

'He's in hospital, love, a mugging apparently, Sunday night at his local shops.'

My hand flew to my chest, and I gasped. 'Is he okay?'

'Yes, although he has a nasty head wound. They took his wallet and his phone. I think he might be coming out today, do you want me to give him a message for you?' he asked. The crinkles around his eyes made the man, who had to be seventy if he was a day, look kind and dependable. Just like George himself. Was it because of me? Had I caused George to end up in hospital, bringing him into my problems with Simon? The thought weighed heavy on my conscience.

'Please tell him Kay says to get well soon. Can I leave you my number? If he's not got his phone, he won't have it any more.'

He pushed a pad towards me, and I scribbled it in haste, checking it was readable.

'Will do, miss. Now is there anything else I can help you with?' he said, smiling at me over the counter, displaying yellowing nicotine-stained teeth.

'Yes, how soon can you be available to change some locks?'

51

I left the shop, my head whirling. Had Simon attacked George? What had he said last night, 'things don't end well for those that stick their nose into my business,' or something to that effect? Maybe it was a coincidence, the mugging on a dark November evening, but my gut told me otherwise. There was more to George ending up in hospital on the same day he'd fitted the doorbell for me. Had Simon known he'd helped me out and it enraged him? I hoped George wasn't badly hurt. I hadn't even asked what hospital he was at, although I didn't know him well enough to show up unannounced at his bedside. Perhaps he wouldn't even want to see me, if I'd been the one to bring trouble to his door.

I climbed back into the car and checked the time; I still had another couple of hours before I had to be at Winston's to meet with Tim so decided to go home. I'd bought another camera door-bell from Sam at Boyce Locks because he couldn't fit me in for a change of locks until Friday and I wanted to try to set it up before Jonathan or Simon visited. It didn't stop them from coming in if they really wanted to, but it had proved to be preventative, until last night anyway.

I'd watched George attach the small unit on Sunday, drilling the holes and screwing it to the wall. After that, it was all about connecting the box to the app, so I was sure I would be able to do it without help. Back at home, it took less than five minutes to fit; the holes were still there and the rawl plugs, I just had to remove what was left of the old device and screw the new one in.

Once done, I opened the app on my mobile phone and set the camera up by configuring a new device. My house was protected once again, and I hadn't needed a man to do it for me. Buoyed by my small steps to independence, I sat patiently waiting for them to arrive, watching out of the window for the Jaguar to pull up beside my car on the driveway. Like a watched pot never boiling, they didn't come and eventually I had to leave to get to Winston's on time.

Pulling into the car park was strange, although I hadn't been away for long. It was already alien, stepping into the building, something I'd done daily for years. No longer was I part of the Winston's family, if there ever was one. I was an outsider, an outcast, and as soon as I came through the door it was obvious I didn't belong. The temperature in reception was freezing, and Bernie behind the desk flared her nostrils at my arrival.

'Hi, Bernie, how are you?' I said, trying to coax a smile.

She pursed her lips and picked up the phone, dialling swiftly. 'Tim, Mrs Massingham has arrived to see you,' she said shrilly. 'Please take a seat,' she said with a wave of her hand.

Clearly there was going to be no pleasantries, so I sat on the hard leather sofa, my palms damp.

What did I have to be nervous about? In less than an hour, I was going to walk away with a signed contract and hopefully a considerably improved bank balance. The hard part had already been done, I'd pushed myself out of my comfort zone and been assertive. Anger played a big part in me standing up to Tim and to Peter, but I no longer had any emotion. The bitterness had diminished, the fight for what was fair had left me exhausted.

Tim came to collect me wearing a tight smile, but he offered no handshake.

'I'm glad you came,' he said as we climbed the stairs to the offices. I had a feeling his job may have depended on being able to take care of the situation.

The boardroom's heating system pumped out lukewarm air and I shivered as I sat, waiting to see if it would be only Tim, or whether Peter would come too.

'Peter won't be here, but I have Lorna from legal coming. I trust you've brought everything with you?' he said, reading my mind.

I pulled my MacBook from my bag and placed it on the table.

'Mrs Massingham,' Lorna said brightly as she entered.

It struck me how pleased I'd be to get rid of my married name. I no longer wanted to be a Massingham. I wanted to be Forster again. I could step out of the Massingham cage, like unzipping a suit and leaving it behind. A butterfly emerging from a cocoon.

Lorna pushed the contract across the table towards me.

'You have five years' salary and accumulated holiday, plus pension contributions and medical insurance,' Tim said, with a sigh. His eyes were sunken, face jaded, but I refused to feel any remorse.

'I'll need a full reference of course,' I said, looking from Tim to Lorna.

'Of course.' He smiled, leaving the room to presumably go and write one.

I spent fifteen minutes in silence, reading every single word. I had a couple of points to clarify with Lorna, but otherwise it was satisfactory, as though I'd written it myself. There were the expected clauses of no communication with the media or competitors on any working practices at Winston's. Also, no further communication with any Winston's employees. That wouldn't be an issue. There was also a separate non-disclosure agreement to sign, ensuring I would be liable if any evidence I'd accumulated fell into the wrong hands.

Returning to the contract, my eyes baulked at the figure in black and white I was to receive. It was such a large sum of money, I struggled to retain my composure.

Taking a deep breath, I signed my life away with a shaking hand and passed both contracts back to Lorna.

'Just Tim to sign now,' she said, smiling because she understood this meeting was awkward for all of us.

Moments later, Tim returned into the boardroom with an open A4 envelope and I pulled the complimentary reference out to read it, satisfied it would be helpful when the time came to find another job.

'Can you log on,' Tim said, placing a hand on the MacBook.

Lifting the lid, I entered my password and it whirred to life, Tim picked it up and made to leave the room with it.

'Where are you going?' I asked, frowning at him.

'It has to be wiped, Kay, it's in the contract. We have to know that you no longer have any incriminating files.'

I had read that part, but it hadn't registered that I'd lose everything.

'Tim, that has everything on it,' I spluttered. My whole life was on that laptop.

'They won't negotiate, it gets wiped or no deal. I can't sign on behalf of the company without it.'

Palpitations ricocheted around my chest. What was on it? Photos of the kids, but those were backed up, weren't they? Old CVs, Christmas lists, a novel I tried to write a few years ago that never got going. Was it really life or death to lose what was on there?

Out of the corner of my eye, Tim rolled onto the balls of his feet, watching my pained expression. I needed more time. I thought we'd delete everything together. Then it hit me. All the files from the necklace were on that laptop, nowhere else. Everything that could prove Simon was a danger, stuff I hadn't even gone through yet. I closed my eyes, the seconds ticking away.

'Kay?' Tim asked, having waited long enough.

'Okay, take it,' I said, hopelessness crashing over me like a wave. I needed the money more than I needed protection from Simon Fox. It came down to my word against his once again and that hadn't worked out for me well so far.

Lorna tapped away at her laptop, and I reread the contract again while I waited for Tim to come back. When he did, the whirring MacBook was open in his hands.

'It's taking a while to restore to factory settings.'

'It's a few years old,' I mused, perhaps I'd treat myself to a new one, a MacBook Pro. Something I'd always wanted but never been able to afford.

'Mrs Massingham has signed, can you sign on behalf of Winston's,' Lorna instructed Tim, who did as he was asked. His gold pen swiftly retrieved from his chest pocket, his signature a flourish on the page. 'The funds will be transferred into your account within the next day or so. We'll start the process today, but there's a chance it could be slightly delayed due to money-laundering checks the banks have to do.' Lorna smiled, the gap in her teeth was becoming. 'This is your copy,' she added, handing me the contract before getting to her feet. 'I'll leave you to it.' She left the room as the MacBook stopped purring and the home screen appeared.

'I'd like to say it's been a pleasure,' Tim said, brusquely.

'It's a shame, Tim, is what it is,' I replied.

'Yes, well...'

'All of this could have been avoided if you'd been the type of manager I could have come to.'

Tim raised one eyebrow, daring me to continue.

'Instead, you were too interested in being one of the lads, but they'll never accept you, Tim, not really. They'll never warm to the expensive suits, the gold pen and the fake camaraderie. You're simply not one of them.' I closed my MacBook and put it in my bag along with the contract.

Tim stared at me, a mixture of shock and amusement.

'Goodbye, Tim,' I said, standing from the table, 'have a nice life.'

52

Back in the car, my stomach stopped churning and the urge to use the toilet vanished as quickly as it had developed. I'd departed a boat in choppy seas, reaching firm ground, and could regain my balance. It was over. My working life at Winston's was finished and now my money worries would disappear. The payment would go towards the new house, with some left over to see me through the coming months as I expected it would take a while to get a new job. Plus, I didn't want to rush into anything. I knew better now than to go somewhere without researching the reputation first.

I sent Claire a text to tell her it was over and that they had paid me off, realising afterwards I'd had a missed call from Martin's. I dialled them back, putting the phone in its cradle on the dashboard and selecting speakerphone as I drove. The urge to return home was prevalent. I wanted to make sure I was there when Jonathan brought Simon back.

'Hello Martin's,' came the sing-song voice I recognised as Louise.

'Hi, Louise, it's Kay Massingham.'

'Hello, Mrs Massingham, thanks for calling me back. I'm sorry for the delay, but I've now confirmed with the vendor and I'm afraid they've rejected your offer, favouring a higher one.'

My stomach sank. 'Is there anything I can do?' I asked, desperation evident in my voice.

'They've accepted an offer of three hundred and fifteen thousand, I'm afraid, from a first-time buyer, so there's no chain,' Louise said, her imitation of sympathy unconvincing.

'What if I put in a counteroffer, the asking price, three hundred and twenty-five thousand?' I said, grasping at straws.

This piqued her interest. 'Well, I can certainly go back to the vendors and enquire, Mrs Massingham.'

'Please do, and let me know,' I replied bluntly before hanging up, my mood deteriorating. Grinding my teeth in frustration, I thew my car through its gears with little regard for the engine trying to keep up. The chime rang out from my phone, notifying me that someone was on my driveway. Was it Jonathan and Simon? I glanced repeatedly at the notification on the home screen, resisting the urge to touch it. I considered pulling over to check the app but didn't want to delay getting back to the house, especially if Simon was there, and I wasn't about to risk playing around with my phone whilst I was driving.

When I reached home, less than ten minutes later, I was just in time to see Jonathan closing the front door, a small black duffle bag thrown over his shoulder. Simon Fox wasn't with him, unless he'd left already.

I stopped the car at the edge of the drive, blocking Jonathan in and watching him scowl as I got out of the car.

'Move your car, Kay.' His voice was practically a growl and he looked harassed, his shirt ruffled, face unshaven and dark bags beneath his eyes.

'What's in the bag?' I asked, hoping he'd been to collect more of his things. It would mean less for me to pack.

'Stuff,' he replied, but the way he clutched the dusty strap tightly to his shoulder made me suspicious.

'What stuff?' I asked, narrowing my eyes. As he turned to open his car door, I pulled at the bag, the zip sliding open to reveal wads of cash.

Jonathan turned and shoved me hard in the chest and I stumbled backwards, falling to the ground, and grazing the palm of my hand.

'Jesus, Jonathan,' I cried, but he ignored me and put the bag in his car. 'What are you involved with?'

This time he turned and jabbed a finger at me, looming like a giant as I remained on the driveway. 'Keep your nose out, Kay. Remember this is still my house and I'll come and go as I fucking well please,' he barked, and I winced. I'd never been afraid of Jonathan before. He was pompous and arrogant, but he'd never laid a finger on me. 'Get up and move your car,' he said, running his hand through his wayward hair and climbing into the driver's seat of the Mazda.

The engine started and he rolled back towards me, my feet dangerously close to his wheel. I scrabbled upright and ran back to the Skoda, tears clouding my vision and an ache in my chest from where Jonathan had pushed me.

I moved the car and he reversed off the driveway, glaring at me as he turned the Mazda around and drove away. I hiccupped, tears falling fast, and slowly manoeuvred the Skoda back onto the drive. What was going on? What was he doing with that much cash? Whose was it?

I wiped away my tears and climbed out, pulling my bag and MacBook with me.

'Are you all right, love?' came a crackly voice over the hedge running down the side of the drive, separating our plot from the neighbours. It was Eileen next door; she had a cigarette dangling from her lips and rubber gardening gloves on, taking advantage of the dry afternoon.

'I'm fine thanks, Eileen,' I said, brushing the hair away from my face with the back of my hand.

'I've been meaning to call round, only I've seen the police a couple of times. I hope everything is okay?' she asked.

'Messy divorce,' I replied sadly. It was almost true, but I didn't want to go into any more details.

'Oh, I'm sorry, love, let me know if there's anything I can do. I tell you, you're better off alone. I've never been so happy since my Derek popped off.' She winked and her head ducked back below the hedge.

I laughed despite myself. Eileen was in her eighties and a bit bonkers, but as neighbours went you couldn't ask for better.

Inside, I left my bag on the table and looked around, as if I could trace where Jonathan had been, hoping the house would tell me. It looked just as I'd left it and I moved through the rooms, opening cupboards and rummaging in spaces to see if I could find anything that didn't belong.

Jonathan's bag had been full of cash, bundled up twenty-pound notes, and it must have come from inside the house. Where had he hidden it? After I spent ten minutes looking with no success, I found some flat-packed boxes under the stairs from when we moved in and decided now was as good a time as any to pack up the bastard's things. I wasn't going to allow him to treat me like he just had. I'd leave it on the driveway in full view of the neighbours. If it rained before he collected it, so be it. The sooner the house was rid of him, the better.

I lost myself in packing. First I went through the wardrobe, checking the pockets of each pair of trousers, each coat and blazer before folding them. The box was quickly full to the brim of suits, shirts, jumpers and shoes. The next box was where I chucked in all his old toiletries. Some I gifted to Ryan, but anything that was too much of a reminder of our past, I binned. I found photos of us stashed away, of when we'd first met, us beaming into the camera, Jonathan's arm slung around my shoulders, the perfect couple. Looking at them was a sucker punch to the gut and I let the tears flow freely, telling myself it was cathartic, a means to an end. I had to close a door on my marriage and say goodbye to the past. It was like ripping off a plaster and for months I'd been edging the corners away, afraid to tear the skin, but it was time to grit my teeth and bear the pain.

My mobile rang, jolting me from the memories I'd lost myself in.

'Mum, it's me,' Rachel's voice came down the line.

'Hiya, love.' I sniffed, looking at a photo of her I'd unearthed as a baby, wrapped in a pink crochet blanket.

'Do you think you could pick me up from the library?'

53

Rachel sat on the wall outside the library, her long legs in black skinny jeans crossed at the knee, a bored expression on her face.

'Cheers, Mum,' she said as she climbed in, before doing a double take at my puffy eyes. 'What's happened?' Her voice rose an octave and I felt a wave of guilt.

'Nothing, I was just boxing up your dad's stuff. Have you been at the library all day?' I asked, impressed at her diligence.

'Me and Casey had a McDonald's and shopping break at lunchtime, before hitting the books again,' she admitted, chuckling.

We chatted about her history coursework, researching The Tudors, as we drove home, with Rachel giving me side glances every few minutes to check I wasn't crying. Back at the house, when she came upstairs to see my progress, her eyes glistened, and I reminded myself again I wasn't the only victim of Jonathan leaving.

'It's for the best. A new start,' I said, trying to inject some enthusiasm into my voice. I'd not heard back from the estate agents but couldn't decide if no news was good news or the opposite. 'How about we go out for dinner tonight, what do you fancy?' I said, brushing the dust off my trousers. I should celebrate my triumph over Winston's and the freedom I now had.

'Okay, what about Smith & Westerns?' she suggested.

I agreed, and Rachel disappeared to google the menu, although I knew she'd have ribs, she always did whenever they were available.

I resumed my position knelt on the carpet, searching under the bed and through the divan drawers, but nothing remained of Jonathan's I could see. Everything had already gone from the bathrooms. His toothbrush had been used to scrub the toilet the day he walked out and then had gone in the bin.

Downstairs, I raked through the lounge and kitchen, removing books and trinkets, anything that was his or had been gifted from his mum over the years. Surprised to find how much of it I still had lying around. Stuff I'd not taken any notice of because it had always been there. Once done, I had four boxes and the rooms were cleansed, all demons exorcised. However, I still had no idea where Jonathan had been hiding the cash. I'd guessed it might have been under the stairs, but only old suitcases and bagged summer duvets were left there now.

I showered off the dust and grime, ready to go out to eat. Rachel was dolled up to the nines, filming a TikTok to send to her friends. I'd thrown on a pair of jeans and a sparkly jumper, wishing I hadn't suggested the idea of going out. My face still looked puffy despite the concealer.

Rachel's phone rang when we were in the car and I quickly guessed it was Ryan from his deep voice; he sounded annoyed.

'What is it?' I asked, pulling over at the bottom of our road.

'Ryan says can you come and get him, he's at the shops by Dad's. They've had a row or something.'

I drove towards Jonathan's ignoring the spike in my pulse, hoping he hadn't taken his bad mood out on Ryan.

Rain began to fall, but we got there before the heavens truly opened. Ryan was sheltering underneath the awning of a newsagents, illuminated by the window, and climbed in the back as soon as I parked.

'What happened?' I asked, both Rachel and I turning in our seats towards him.

'He's got the raging hump about something. I think Monique has binned him; they've been arguing on the phone. She's saying she can't live in the flat any longer. I only asked what was for dinner and he lost it, yelling I was old enough to feed myself. So I told him to fuck off, grabbed my bag and walked out. He was still shouting when I was halfway down the road.' Ryan shook his head. I pursed my lips, what was Jonathan thinking talking to Ryan like that. What was going on with him?

'We're going to Smith & Westerns,' Rachel announced. 'Come on, Mum, we'll be late,' she urged, and I turned the engine over, the windscreen wipers at full speed as we drove towards the restaurant.

They extended our reservation from two to three without a problem, the restaurant wasn't crowded as it was midweek. Ryan didn't want to talk any more about his argument with Jonathan, and I was grateful. I didn't want their dad to spoil the mood. Instead, I concentrated on enjoying dinner out with the twins, letting them order whatever they wanted.

They dominated the conversation, talking about school, the scandal of one of Ryan's mates sending an inappropriate message to his best friend's girlfriend and how it had all kicked off 'big time'. I marvelled at the whirlwind between them, the speed at which they exchanged words and how well they got on when they weren't sniping at each other.

'Did you put an offer in on that house?' Rachel asked, changing the subject.

'I did, but it was rejected. I'm waiting to hear back as I've put another one in.'

'It's a shame we have to move at all,' Ryan grumbled, stabbing his fork into a rogue chip that had escaped his plate onto the table.

'I know, I don't want to either, but it is what it is,' I replied, absent-mindedly, distracted by the waitress who had come to see if we wanted any more drinks.

Once the twins had scoffed two sundaes and were laid back in their seats patting their full stomachs, I asked for the bill. I wanted to get home and call Claire, see if she was all right after the shock of discovering who Owen really was. Had he tried to get in touch with her today? I wouldn't have put it past Claire to call him and give him what for, although I hoped for her sake she'd stay as far away from him as possible. After what he'd done to George, I didn't want to drag anyone else into my fight.

'If you wanted to hide something, where would you put it?' I asked during the drive home. It hadn't occurred to me to ask the twins before, but I remembered as a kid, I knew all the best hiding places at home.

'Under the bridge, by the church,' Rachel said immediately, as if it was the answer on a game show and she was being timed.

'I meant in the house,' I said, laughing. What could Rachel possibly be hiding under the bridge? Cigarettes and mini bottles of vodka if she was anything like Claire and I at her age.

The twins stayed silent for a minute. Rachel scrolling through her phone and Ryan staring out of the window thoughtfully before he spoke.

'The garage maybe, the loft?' he said, and a light bulb switched on in my mind.

'The loft?' I probed.

'Yeah, it's pretty empty up there. I helped Dad get the Christmas Tree down last December, remember?'

I didn't remember, but if I weren't driving I would have grabbed Ryan by the cheeks and planted a kiss on his forehead. Why hadn't I thought about the loft? I never went up there, it was always a Jonathan job, that, and various other tasks, like putting the bins out or cutting the grass.

Jonathan had looked dishevelled earlier, and there was dust on the strap of the bag. Dust from being kept somewhere like the loft.

'Why?' Ryan asked, his eyes narrowing. The boy was too inquisitive for his own good.

'No reason,' I lied.

54

I called Claire when we got back. The house was as we'd left it and I'd had no alerts from the camera doorbell to let me know Jonathan or Simon had been back. Claire yawned as she answered before telling me she'd spent a day in her comfiest clothes, laying on the sofa and watching Netflix.

'I'm surrounded by empty crisp packets and Coke cans and I'm about three clicks away from ordering an Uber Eats.' She didn't sound overly upset, but I knew she rarely let her emotions get the better of her. She wasn't cold, not by any means, but she was able to control what she projected externally, even if inside she was a mess. Out of the two of us, I was the emotional one, Claire had the stiff upper lip I coveted.

I told her about the money I'd seen Jonathan leaving the house with, how he'd pushed me over when I'd chanced a look inside the duffle bag.

'How much do you reckon was in there?'

'No idea. I mean, it wasn't a massive bag, but there were wads of twenty-pound notes. Probably around fifty grand, but I could be wrong,' I guessed, having never seen such large amounts of cash in real life, only on the television.

'Where on earth did it come from?' Claire said and between us we came up with various scenarios. A cash loan from his wealthy mother, money from the safe at the wine merchants, a payment from selling drugs or the proceeds of crime. None of them sounded plausible, not for Jonathan, the man I'd been married to for eighteen years.

'It must be Simon's,' Claire eventually conceded, although both of us were at a loss as to why Jonathan had it.

'I'm really worried it is, and if it is, why is Jonathan looking after it? Do you think he could be hiding money from the tax man or something?'

'God knows,' Claire said.

'It makes me wonder if I ever really knew him at all, the way he's acting is totally unrecognisable from the man I married.'

'I agree.'

'Have you heard from Simon?' I probed.

'No, I've blocked him anyway so he can't ring me, but half of me would like to have it out with him. I mean, what was I, a means to get to you? A bit of fun? Why would he lie about his name?' Claire said, irritation clouding her voice.

'No idea. Do you think perhaps he's got other women on the go?' I asked. It could be a reason why he would lie.

'I don't know. I mean, we were at it like rabbits, so I don't know how he had any energy left for anyone else!' She sounded indignant, but the idea of Simon Fox copulating with anyone was enough to make me gag. The man was vile. 'He never mentioned he had a kid, and obviously now I know why I never saw where he lived. I can't believe he pulled the wool over my eyes so easily,' Claire said.

'He's a master manipulator, you can't beat yourself up over it. So, did he ask about me at all then?' A sliver of unease made me fidget with my sleeve. It was a question I wasn't sure I wanted the answer to.

'Not really, I mean, yeah I mentioned you obviously, he asked me a few things now and then, but I can't imagine I gave him anything he could use against you.'

Nothing about Simon Fox made sense, right from the start. He was an enigma and one I couldn't wait to get shot of. He'd entwined himself into our family like poison ivy.

I finished my conversation with Claire, and we said goodbye. I was itching to get in the loft, despite my fear of dark damp spaces and spiders. Unfortunately, I couldn't risk it while the kids were at home. Ryan would hear me banging about and come to investigate.

'Have you heard from your father?' I asked Ryan, knocking before opening his bedroom door and getting a waft of Lynx deodorant. He was sat in his gaming chair, headset on, wiping out an army of zombies from a platform with a grenade.

'Nope,' he said, without a glance in my direction. I couldn't believe Jonathan hadn't even bothered to get in touch with me or Ryan to check he was safe. He needed to get his priorities in order, whatever was going on with him, his children had to come first.

'Okay,' I said, closing the door and swallowing my frustration.

I made a cup of tea and spent the next hour rummaging through bank statements and the files of letters, utilities payments and general household paperwork we kept in the utility room, but nothing jumped out at me. The bank statements looked normal, no massive payments in or out, and I was stumped where else to look.

Eventually I went to bed with a book, saying goodnight to the twins on my way to the bedroom, although I struggled to get into the story. My mind wandering to George and whether he'd been discharged from the hospital yet. I'd not heard from him, but I wasn't sure I would after his mugging. He could be avoiding me and who could blame him. Eventually I gave up on the book and turned out the lights but my attempts at sleep weren't forthcoming.

I kept glancing at the ceiling, was there a stash of contraband up there Jonathan had been hiding? Whatever might be up there, whether it was cash, or worse, drugs, I had to assume Simon knew it was there and that was why he was so keen to get back into the house. I hoped whatever it was, Jonathan had taken it and there would be nothing left for me to find.

* * *

Despite taking a while to doze off, I slept well, putting it down to the stress of Winston's now behind me. I checked with Ryan over breakfast if the school had sent him any work during his suspension as I'd had nothing through to my email address. I thought maybe they hadn't as it was half-term, and his suspension didn't start until next week, but when asked, he mumbled they had, but he hadn't done any of it yet as he'd been busy working with Jim.

'I'm sure you can catch up at the weekend, or in the evenings, can't you?'

'Course I will, Mum,' he replied, brushing me off.

I wanted to remind him what an important year it was for him with his GCSEs but decided he'd had enough of his dad in his ear without me joining in as well.

'Is Jim picking you up here again?'

'Yeah, in about ten minutes. I've got to run,' he said, taking his half-finished bowl of cereal to the sink and dropping it inside for the washing-up fairy to deal with later.

Rachel was still asleep, and I decided to have one more coffee before I even thought about tackling the loft. It might be safer to wait until Rachel was out of the house altogether. Sat at the table, I checked my bank account via the app on my phone, but the money from Winston's hadn't arrived yet. I hoped I wouldn't have to chase them, but Lorna did say it was subject to bank checks.

Just as I was draining the mug, my mobile rang with an unknown number.

'Hello?'

'Kay, it's George.' A whoosh of relief swept over me at the sound of his voice.

'George! Are you okay? Are you back home?'

'Yes, they discharged me yesterday afternoon. Sam popped round and gave me your number. My phone was stolen in the mugging,' he explained.

'Yes, Sam said. How are you feeling?' I asked, taking my mug to the sink and rinsing it.

'A bit bruised.' George sounded like he'd had the stuffing knocked out of him physically and mentally.

'Do you want me to pop round? Do you need anything?' I offered. George had done so much for me, fitting the camera doorbell, and checking I was safe. He was a relative stranger with a heart of gold, and I was keen to repay the favour.

'Oh, that's very kind of you. I'd love some milk; I'm gasping for a tea, but I haven't ventured outside yet. I'm a little unsteady on my feet, the knock to the head has played havoc with my balance.'

'It's no problem, give me your address and I'll see you in about half an hour.'

George relayed his address and I scribbled it onto the pad before typing it into Google Maps. The loft could wait, I had all day to rummage around.

Hopping in my car, I drove to Tesco and whizzed around the aisles, filling my basket with bread, milk, a couple of microwave meals and four cans of bitter, remembering he'd ordered that at the pub when we'd met. I had no idea what I was buying or whether he liked the brand I'd picked but hoped he'd appreciate the gesture.

I followed my phone's directions to a small, terraced property, set back from a playing field used for football and rugby games. It was a nice setting, a little cul-de-sac that seemed quiet and was well kept. George lived at number 9 in the furthest corner, and I navigated the uneven path where the patio slabs had lifted. No wonder he hadn't wanted to venture out.

I saw immediately he had a camera doorbell, similar to what he'd fitted for me, as well as a small CCTV camera mounted above the window at the front of the house. It didn't look like it had been recently installed and I wondered if everyone was more security conscious than I had been, or whether recent events had made George aware of being safe in his own home. Before I met Simon Fox, it hadn't been on my radar.

I rang the doorbell and waited, listening for footsteps. Eventually some came and when the door opened, I winced at the state of the figure in front of me.

55

'Jesus Christ, George,' I said, eyes watering at the colour of his face. George had a split across his nose, with Steri-Strips holding the skin together, as well as a black eye. His forehead was badly bruised, a dark purple colour blossomed below his hairline.

'It's not as bad as it looks,' he said, stepping back to let me in.

'Really? Because it looks terrible,' I said, trying to inject some humour. I followed the hallway towards the kitchen where I settled my carrier bag on the side. George edged behind me, reaching for the kettle. 'No, you sit down. Let me do that,' I ordered, pulling items from the bag and filling the kettle with water.

George conceded and lowered himself onto a woven lattice chair beside an old-fashioned pine dining table.

'I hit the deck with some force, knocked out one of my teeth too.' He chuckled, gesturing to his mouth where I could see a hole where his incisor should be.

'Jesus! Were you attacked from behind?' I asked.

'Yeah, struck at the back of the head.' He turned to the side, and I saw the gauze still in place.

'God, you could have been killed,' I said, wrapping my arms around myself as the kettle whistled, a chill descending my spine at what could have been.

I made our tea and put away the milk and microwave meals in the fridge before pulling out a chair opposite George.

'Thanks so much for the shopping, I can't believe you remembered I like bitter. How much do I owe you?' George asked, thrusting his hand into the pocket of his jeans.

'Nothing, don't be silly. I was supposed to be taking you out for dinner remember. This is the least I can do,' I said, waving him away before continuing. 'So, tell me what happened.'

George proceeded to recount the story of his Sunday night, where he'd gone to the local shop at around nine to pick up some bits. He'd walked as it was only around the corner, bought some milk, bread, the essentials to see him through the next few days.

'It wasn't until I came out of the shop and walked for a minute or so that I sensed someone was behind me. There's a street light that's broken on the corner of the parade, has been for ages. That's where he got me. He jumped me as I was about to turn around.' The hair on the nape of my neck lifted at George's choice of words.

'He?'

'Simon Fox,' George said, his eyes locking on mine. It made me giddy, as though the room had tilted.

'How can you be sure it was him?' I asked, my shoulders rising as I watched the vein on George's forehead throb.

'I know it was him,' he said, his breath hitching as emotion got the better of him.

'Okay, okay,' I said, placing a hand on George's forearm to pacify him.

He lowered his eyes to my hand and smiled weakly, cheeks a ruddy red.

'You have to be careful, Kay,' he warned.

'Did you tell the police it was him?'

'I can't prove it was, they aren't going to believe me when I tell them I just know it was him.' George sighed and I squeezed my lips together. I'd been in the same situation and Simon was smart, he seemed to know what he was capable of getting away with.

His luck would run out sometime though, it had to. Perhaps he needed provocation, with the right eyes watching. George was too worked up for me to tell him what the camera doorbell had recorded. What I believed to be Simon's voice, 'say hi to George for me', if that was what he'd said. The sound wasn't crystal clear, and it was hardly an admission of guilt, although I didn't doubt George's belief it was Simon who'd attacked him.

'I filled in a form online, the fraud hotline on HMRC's website. I made a report the night I met you and your friend at the pub. Talking about it again wound me up.'

'I'm sorry we dragged it up again for you,' I said solemnly.

'Why should he get away with stealing from me? Taking fifty grand of my money with no comeback. I'm sure he never paid any tax on our business, or if he did it was nothing in comparison to what he earnt.'

My jaw slackened; Simon's voice echoed at the back of my mind. *Things don't end well for those who stick their nose into my business.*

It made sense. George had to be right, Simon had caught wind of what he'd done, shopping him to HMRC. Rachel said she'd over-heard Ava telling her friends the police had been around to her house. I tried to recall the conversation, but my memory was hazy. However, hadn't she used the word tax?

'I think my ex-husband might be involved somehow.' The words slipped out before I could stop them, and George's eyes widened.

'How?'

'I don't know. I think Jonathan has been storing stuff in the house, maybe for Simon, but I'm not sure, it could be unrelated,' I said, although the words sounded hollow.

'What kind of stuff?' George asked.

'Money. I caught Jonathan leaving the house with a bag of twenty-pound notes and Simon has been...' I chose my words carefully, 'keen, to get inside.'

I didn't elaborate. George didn't need to know Simon had been round and smashed the camera doorbell he'd so kindly fitted. He had enough on his plate without worrying about me too, although looking at the state of George's face, I no longer doubted what Simon was capable of. The damage spoke for itself. George could have been killed and yet it was supposed to be a warning, like Simon turning up on my doorstep. It was no longer about a stupid scratched Jaguar; it had turned into something far more complicated.

'Listen, forget about Simon. Let the police or the tax office do their job – if there's something to find, they'll find it. I don't think he'll be back,' I said and George shook his head, wincing at the movement before lifting the mug to his lips.

'It sounds like he's got other things on his mind, and that's what worries me, Kay.'

'Don't worry about me, I'll be fine.' I smiled, staring into my mug so George wouldn't see the veneer on my face. I couldn't let him see the threat I felt.

'He's unhinged.'

'He's a bully, George, and I won't let him walk all over me,' I snapped, and George recoiled as though he'd been slapped. 'I'm sorry I wasn't implying...' I began, annoyed that yet again Simon Fox had crawled his way under my skin.

'It's fine. Just be careful,' George interrupted, standing to get a packet of chocolate digestives I'd bought and left on the counter.

'I've had enough of men walking all over me,' I said, my voice softer, trying to explain years of frustration of being dismissed and overlooked. My feelings being swept under the carpet as I wasn't important enough to warrant being listened to.

'I understand, Kay,' George said, but I couldn't bear the pity on his battered face and looked away.

Silence grew between us, and I used the opportunity to change the subject, to tell George we'd found a house we liked, although our offer hadn't been accepted yet. Louise still hadn't called me back which I took as a bad sign. Perhaps the vendors favoured a shorter chain over more money? Maybe Goddard Close wasn't to be, but trying to find somewhere else to live filled me with anxiety. Time was running out and other than packing a few boxes of Jonathan's things, I was no closer to moving out. I needed to get my act together and get myself and the twins out of that house and away from Simon Fox.

I spent the next half an hour trying to cheer George up. It wasn't only physical – the bruises on his face were easy to see – but it was clear his confidence had been dented. I suspected it might be a while before he was back to the same enthusiastic man who'd fitted my camera. That George had shrunk into himself, and I hoped it wouldn't be permanent. His eyes were still kind and his smile genuine as he talked about Sam, his manager, who'd told him to take as long as he needed to recover.

'He seems like a good boss,' I agreed, if only I'd been that lucky with Tim.

'Yeah, he is. I landed on my feet with him.'

'Everything will heal, you'll soon be up and about again,' I said, finding my hand on his arm again, this time lingering. I wasn't sure what it was, perhaps not an attraction exactly, but I was connected to George in a way I hadn't been with anyone else for a long time. He placed his rough workman's hand over mine, fingers warm and inviting.

'Then I'll take you out for dinner,' he said, eyes bright.

'I'm supposed to be taking you, remember,' I replied, cheeks reddening at the prolonged contact and what it meant.

'That's two dates then,' he said, fingers interlacing through mine.

56

My chest was feather-light and I practically floated down the path towards my car when I left George's house. Nothing more had happened between us and that was fine. A seed had been sown, something was blossoming, ever so slowly. The perfect pace for me. I was still bruised from Jonathan's betrayal. We'd been together a long time and you couldn't turn it on and off like a tap, despite how much of a shit he'd been to me.

I drove home, delighted to hear the tinkling of the motion sensor sound on my phone as I pulled onto the driveway. The camera doorbell I'd fitted was still working perfectly and I couldn't deny it gave me a sense of comfort, especially with crazies like Simon Fox a few minutes away. In a couple of days, the locks would be changed, and I'd feel even more secure.

When I got inside, satisfied that Rachel was out, I carried a kitchen chair upstairs to the hallway, climbing on it precariously to dislodge the loft hatch. I nearly dropped it when a torrent of dust fell onto my hair, visions of dead spiders, their little legs curled inwards, made me screech. Pulling myself together, I folded down the ladder Jonathan had fitted when we'd first moved in. I never went in the loft; small dark spaces were my nemesis, but Jonathan had been thrilled to discover it was part boarded and therefore good for storage. But storing what, now? I wondered.

Most of the crap up there was his. I expected to find golf clubs, boxes of old CDs from when he was a teenager he couldn't bear to part with, even though you could stream anything from your phone at the touch of a button. He had a box full of old football shirts too. I happily let him fill the space, knowing I'd never have to go up there, or so I'd thought.

Ryan was right, it was the perfect space for Jonathan to hide something from me. He knew how I felt about the loft. Every year I'd have to wait for him to get the Christmas decorations down because I couldn't bear to even open the hatch. He'd tease me relentlessly, convinced my parents must have punished me by locking me in an attic or a basement when I was a child. He said it was strange for me to have such an overwhelming hatred of a normal space. My parents hadn't of course, but I didn't like spiders, or webs, and those were in abundance in dark, damp spaces.

Steeling myself, I put my hands on the furthest rung I could reach, a tremor descending my spine to the balls of my feet. Two swift steps upward and I'd be able to reach the light switch. I pushed on, turning on the light and forcing my head into the loft cavity. Within seconds, I was completely inside, on my knees, running my fingers through my hair and looking around. It wasn't as full as I'd been led to believe, and I didn't have to look too hard either.

Right by the opening was another duffle bag, this one long, like tennis players use. It was plain black and zipped up, but as soon as I hooked my arm through the handles, the weight of it pulled me down. I quickly unzipped the bag to discover rolled fifty-pound notes this time, secured with elastic bands. I gasped; it was more money than I'd ever seen in my life.

Heaving the bag towards the edge, I pushed it through the gap, a loud thud sounding when it hit the carpet below. Desperate to get out of the loft, I climbed down the ladder, folded it up, then back onto the chair to push it back into the loft. Once the loft hatch was secure, I swept away the dust, giving my hair a shake. My skin crawled as though thousands of tiny ants scurried over me, and I brushed myself down.

Sinking to my knees, I tried to estimate how much cash was in the bag. It had to be tens of thousands, and I didn't believe it was Jonathan's. He'd got himself involved in some dodgy deal with Simon. Anger seared through my body at the risk Jonathan had put us in. Whatever he was mixed up in, it had to be illegal. People didn't keep sums of money like that hidden away. Not if they could be put in a bank.

I considered taking it, or some of it, just to spite him, but I didn't want to get my hands dirty. I wouldn't be involved in any of this; even by storing it I was guilty by association. Plus, Simon was a psychopath and I dreaded to think how far he would go to get the money back. I had no doubt he would have broken in that night if the camera wasn't up. Had Jonathan given him a key so he could come and go as he pleased when we weren't around? Or had Mike stolen one to get it cut for him? Was Simon after the money?

My mouth dried, tongue like sandpaper. That man in my house, touching my things. The idea was abhorrent. I wrenched the zip shut, and shoved at the bag, dragging it down the stairs and towards the front door. I wanted it out of my house, but first I wanted Jonathan to explain what it was doing here. Grabbing my phone, I took a photo of the bag laying in the hallway and sent it to Jonathan without explanation.

Less than a minute later, my phone began to ring accusingly.

'What the hell are you doing, Kay,' Jonathan shouted down the phone, wind howling in the background, muffling his voice.

'I could ask you the same question,' I snapped back.

'Stay there, I'm coming to get it.'

'Whose is it?'

'Mine,' Jonathan said without hesitation.

'Bullshit. It's Simon's, isn't it? Just what are you involved in, Jonathan? Why are you holding cash for him?' My tone was clipped.

'None of your fucking business,' he said. I heard a car door slam and the background noise ceased. He'd got in his car. If Jonathan was at work, he could get here in around fifteen minutes.

'It is my business, it's in my house,' I shouted, blood boiling. A sea of acid dissolving everything in its wake. I was infuriated at being kept in the dark, being lied to and fobbed off.

'You had to stick your fucking nose in, didn't you, Kay, couldn't let things lie, could you? It's all your fault anyway, you started it when you scratched his bloody car!'

I gasped; how did Jonathan know about that? I could hear his indicator, tyres screeching as he took a bend in the Mazda too fast. Adrenaline pumped around my system, heart galloping in my chest, I had to move, there was no time to wait.

'You know what, Jonathan, I'm calling the police and then I'm taking that bastard's dirty money back,' I yelled, hearing Jonathan shout, 'Kay, don't you fuc–,' down the line before I cut him off.

Thrusting my feet into my trainers, I looked around for my keys. Jonathan could be here any minute and he sounded furious. Last time I'd heard him so mad he'd pushed me over, who knew what he'd do this time. There was no time to call the police, I had to get the bag out of the house. I was going to throw it in Simon's face and make out Jonathan had told me everything. Perhaps then I'd finally get some answers.

57

I lugged the bag to the car, chucking it onto the back seat. It weighed a tonne. Throwing the car into gear, I reversed off the driveway at speed, desperate to leave the cul-de-sac and get to Simon before Jonathan arrived. My breath was raspy, head throbbing like it was going to explode and I gripped the wheel with both hands, trying to focus.

It took less than a minute to get to Simon's house, the beautiful white-painted double-fronted refurbishment, with its navy windows and door. The house of mine and Jonathan's dreams until it had been ruined with a tarmacked driveway. Although knowing Simon as I did now, I'd never look at the house in the same way again.

Simon was nowhere to be seen, but the Jaguar stood, glistening in the centre of the drive. The whole thing had started with that bloody flash car, his pride and joy which he looked to be in the middle of cleaning. A hosepipe lay discarded on the ground and puddles of water rippled in the bracing wind.

Blocking the driveway with my Skoda, I heaved the bag out of the car and limped towards the front door with it. I gave no thought to any cameras, I was happy to be recorded returning his dirty money back where it belonged. As I got closer to the door, I realised it stood ajar. Bottles of turtle wax and a shammy had been left on the doorstep. Simon was home. Why wasn't he at work? I guessed his minions were running his security empire for him. *Oh, to be so powerful.*

I gave the door a tentative push, ear cocked to listen for footsteps, but none came. Should I wait for him to come back out? I banged hard on the door with my fist, frustration erupting. I wanted to give Simon Fox a piece of my mind and I was geared up to deliver. He thought he could do crazy, but he hadn't seen unhinged yet. He'd pushed me to the edge and hell would freeze over before I backed down.

A minute passed with no response to my hammering, so I pushed the door and put one foot gingerly over the threshold, onto the plush mat. Immediately assaulted by the smell of burnt food, like toast that had been left under the grill too long. Perhaps that's what had led Simon back inside? It was lunchtime after all, and my stomach growled in response to the aroma. Ignoring it, I lifted my other foot over the step, the bag scraping the front door as I pulled it through.

The hallway was wide, a grand stripped-back wooden staircase stood in front of me with a console table to the left, an empty bowl on top for keys. The walls were a pale grey, the carpet a darker shade. It was bland, soulless and unwelcoming. No art hung on the walls, no photos of Simon or Ava graced the entrance. There was no ambience, it wasn't a home, more like a shell.

It felt dangerous to be inside and I shuddered; the sweat that had peppered my back had turned glacial. I was a lamb who had strolled into the lion's den. What was I doing?

As I was about to turn around and leave, I noticed a door to my right that stood open a few inches. I could see the floor was tiled inside and boxes piled high filling the space. George said Simon kept some of his stock at home. Perhaps, now he'd expanded, he had a warehouse somewhere, but I suspected Simon was a man who liked to keep a close eye on the things that belonged to him. Objects as well as people. A true control freak. Could I be looking at the stock he purchased when in business with George?

Leaving the duffle bag at the bottom of the stairs, I inched towards the door, pushing on the wood. It swung wide open and I jumped when a light sprang on overhead. Fearing I'd been caught red-handed, I froze, but it must have been the motion of the door, the light on a sensor. Straining my ears for movement, the silence was intimidating. No footsteps were bearing down upon me, no yelling of an intruder in the house and I was glad I'd kept my phone on silent so Jonathan's incessant calling wouldn't give me away. It didn't stop the phone pulsating repeatedly in my pocket, a reminder of his persistence.

Tiptoeing inside, Simon's stock was everywhere. Boxes of security lights, locks and alarms were piled as high as my chest. Pushed against cabinets and littering shelves that lined the walls, more stacked on top of the units that housed the washing machine and tumble dryer. Could this be what George's fifty grand had gone towards? Items yet to be sold in Simon's shop.

A whine came from the corner of the room, and I saw the scruffy dog, its sad eyes staring at me, scratching at the wire of its cage, trying to get out.

'Poor boy,' I muttered, resisting the urge to open the latch immediately. How long had it been there?

He continued to whine, seeking attention and I vowed to report Simon to the RSPCA as soon as I got out of here. That monster didn't deserve to own a dog.

I pulled my phone from my pocket and snapped a photo, then

turned to get some pictures of the piled-up boxes to show George later, getting as many of the labels as I could. Perhaps he could match the stock to what he'd ordered, prove that Simon had dissolved the company without declaring the assets he'd kept. It was a long shot but worth a try.

Focused on my phone, I nudged a box accidentally with my elbow, not realising a single light bulb sat on top. It rolled to the edge and before I could catch it, fell to the floor, smashing into pieces. The sound echoed around the room, and I cringed, holding my breath as my shoulders shot up to my ears. Eyes darting towards the door, I hastily retraced my path, sidestepping the glass as best I could.

'Well, well, well. What do we have here?' Simon Fox said, filling the doorway, manifesting like an apparition and blocking my only exit.

I opened my mouth to speak, but a high-pitched squeak came out instead. My body rigid, I was frozen to the spot, the sound of my heart thrashing in my ears.

'Would you like to tell me why you're in my house, Kay? Breaking and entering is a crime, you know,' he smirked, his tone strangely playful, as if he was talking to a child. It amazed me how calm he was when he believed he had the upper hand, turning to strike like a viper when roles were reversed.

My mouth filled with saliva, nostrils flaring indignantly. 'You'd know all about that, wouldn't you?' We stared each other down but I refused to look away. 'I didn't break in, you left your door open, and you want to know why I'm here? Well, I was delivering something that belongs to you.'

He raised one eyebrow, face still a mask of superiority. It incensed me. 'Oh?'

'A bag full of cash Jonathan has been hiding for you. He's told me everything, Simon, and I don't want your filthy money in *my* house!' I spat.

Simon's face flared with anger; brows plunging. I glimpsed him turn his head slightly, registering the bag behind him I'd left at the bottom of the stairs, as though he hadn't noticed it the first time he'd passed. So desperate to find out who was in his house he'd missed it.

'I've called the police, they're on their way. Try to dig your way out of this one,' I sneered, hoping Simon wouldn't see through my lie, and shrinking back as he took a step into the room.

The dog whined louder, seeking release from its prison, from its master, but Simon ignored him.

'You don't know anything,' he seethed, the forked vein in his forehead pulsating.

I pressed my back against the packages, some of them tumbling to the ground at my feet. His eyes were wild, crazed and I shuffled in the opposite direction, pushing boxes between us, edging back towards the door.

His lip curled into a snarl. We were opposite each other and there was no way I was getting to the door without him catching me. He rubbed his chin thoughtfully.

'You know when someone breaks into your house and attacks you, someone like the mad woman from down the road, the one that's been complaining about you to the police, it's understandable you'd retaliate.' He cupped his face, dragging nails down his cheeks and I watched as welts appeared in their wake.

I shook my head, eyes bulging, terrified at what he might do next.

'I mean, there's no contest is there, a big strong man against a woman, even one as... heavy as you. I'm sure I could cause quite a bit of damage.' He cracked his knuckles, eyes glinting in the overhead fluorescent lights. A tiny drop of blood had blossomed on his left cheek where he'd pierced the skin. He was crazy and in that second I understood how stupid I had been. How anger had blurred my reasoning, because it was clear I might not leave his house alive.

58

Simon loomed in front of me, a tower of three security light boxes between us. My breathing shallowed, waiting for him to lunge. I had to find a way to stall him, perhaps Jonathan would show up if he couldn't find me at home. Why had I come here alone and without calling the police first?

'Is that what happened with your wife?' I asked, my voice croaky. Throat so dry it hurt to speak, but I forced the words out. 'Did you tell everyone that Nikola attacked you first when you hit her?'

His eyes narrowed, the mischievous smile dissolving. He enjoyed the chase, the cat and mouse, but I could tell he loathed being stood up to. Just like any bully, and despite my bladder bulging, threatening to lose itself all over the concrete floor, I stood tall.

'Or did you flatly deny it?'

I waited for an answer, but none came.

'What am I thinking, you probably told the police she did it to herself,' I mused, watching as Simon's pupils shrank to pinpricks.

Rolling my shoulders back, I looked into the eye of the storm, no intention of backing down. I'd hit a nerve and he couldn't hide it.

'You bullied Nikola, lied to your daughter, planted drugs on her to convince the courts Ava was better off with you, but is she... really?' I ploughed on. 'Oh, I know all about you. The businesses you've had, the lives you've destroyed. I know you've been in my house, that you've been watching me, listening to my conversations.'

Simon's jaw dropped, before his face twisted in anger; teeth bared like an animal. 'You know nothing about me,' he seethed.

'Is that right, Simon, or should I call you Owen? You even wormed your way into Claire's life. Were you using her to get to me?'

Simon smirked at the mention of Claire. 'Claire was fun for a while, although I didn't get much out of her other than a roll in the sheets. Quite protective of her friends, as it turns out, plus Owen was becoming a bore. He was far too nice, too charming. I'm surprised she didn't see through it straight away.'

My nostrils flared. How dare he exploit her so casually. 'You're only interested in the people you can manipulate, the ones you can use to your advantage. You lie and you steal, you'll do anything to get ahead, with no thought for anyone. No thought for George, for Jonathan or the others you've duped.'

He let out a loud bellowing laugh, making me jump. Every muscle tensed, waiting for him to pounce, instead he jabbed a finger towards me.

'You think you know your husband do you, Kay?' His question hung in the air for a second, making its desired impact. 'He made a bargain with me to *help* you out of that house. I was only too happy to oblige, after all, you did sneak onto my driveway and vandalise my car.'

My mouth gaped at the omission, the betrayal of my husband stinging like a slap to the face. *Jonathan made a deal with him.* He was that desperate to get me to move out of our home quickly he'd asked Simon to intimidate me. He had to need the money from the sale, but was all this to do with buying a house with Monique? Was Simon buying our house part of some scam Jonathan had got involved in? None of it made any sense. My husband was a lot of things, but I'd never put him in the same league as Simon.

His eyes shone, relishing my confusion. 'His little bit of stuff – a vast improvement on you, in my opinion – has her heart set on a little cottage in Horsham. Not too far from my whore of a wife. The only thing standing in his way is you. He was only too happy to accept my offer of help.'

I stood, aghast, wishing I could put my hands over my ears so I wouldn't have to listen to any more. Still, he went on.

'I've enjoyed taking your family apart, piece by piece. Humiliating you and the twins. I was just toying with you before, but I'm done playing games, Kay. I warned you it doesn't end well for people who stick their nose into my business, and you can't seem to keep your beak out.'

Simon Fox licked his thin lips and with one swipe of his arm the boxes between us toppled and he sprang towards me. I fell backwards against the wall, stumbling to the left and tripping over the sea of boxes that sprayed the floor. Simon reached for me, but I lurched back, scrabbling on my feet, the exit in sight. Whisking past him to make my escape. The dog was barking now, clawing at the cage, desperate for freedom.

'Come here, bitch,' Simon spat, and my head jerked backwards, neck snapping as his hand grabbed clumps of hair. My back hit the floor, pain ricocheting along my shoulder blade, the air whooshing out of me like a pierced balloon. Simon's fingers found my neck and I clawed at his grip. He lifted my head, banging it back onto the concrete and stars blurred my eyes. Tiny specks of white danced across my vision.

I wheezed for air, mixing snatched breaths with coughs. Simon's face swam before my eyes and I blinked, trying to focus, my head throbbing. I raised my arms, trying to gouge at his face and eyes, but I didn't have the reach he did. He simply lifted his chin, face full of derision as I swiped, my attempts futile.

'What are you going to do now, Kay?' he jeered, his tone mocking as his fingers squeezed my windpipe and my eyes rolled.

'Dad!' A scream came from the door and Simon instantly loosened his grip, whipping his head towards his daughter. She stood in the doorway, hair bundled on top of her head, dressed in peach loungewear and fluffy socks. The colour drained from her face until she appeared ghostly, tears spurting uncontrollably. Horrified at what she was witnessing.

'Get out, Ava,' Simon shouted as I sucked in a breath, grateful for the momentary reprieve.

Thrashing beneath him, in a final last-ditch attempt to free myself, I brought a knee up into his groin. He hissed, turning back to me, spittle flying onto my face, squeezing my throat with iron fingers. My arms flailed, sweeping across the floor, trying to find a weapon, something I could use. Panic had set in; I could no longer breathe, and my heart drummed against my chest as though it would burst out at any second. The compulsion to win, to be in control, had turned Simon Fox into a murderer. I was going to die here on the tiled floor, without a chance to tell the twins how much I loved them.

'Dad, stop!' Ava cried again, her fingers tearing at her scalp, eyes like saucers.

'Get the fuck out of here,' he shouted towards her, and my heart sank as Ava and I locked eyes for a second before she disappeared from the doorway. Hope was gone.

The chill of the ceramic seeped into my clothes and my body grew numb. The fight within me dissolved and I stopped struggling despite the fire in my lungs. Hands tumbled to the floor with a bounce, and I closed my eyes, waiting for the darkness to swallow me.

Weightlessness washed over me, and I could sense I was on the edge of the abyss. The pain in my chest subsided, replaced with a cool breeze that drifted, carrying me away with it.

In the distance, the dog barked, and voices rang out, their words were muffled. I couldn't understand what they were saying, but I sensed it no longer mattered. Whoever they were, they were too late to stop Simon Fox. Too late to save the life of Kay Massingham.

59

I didn't remember much of the next few hours and was only told later I was brought back from the brink by Police Constable Jeff Covell. His lifesaving CPR until the ambulance arrived to give me oxygen allowed me to cling on.

Jeff's colleague, Michael, had been the one to pull Simon off me, to wrench his hands from my neck and thrust them behind his back, pinning him to the floor. It wasn't Jonathan who had saved me. Ava had been the one to call the police, something which must have been extremely difficult for her. She told the operator her father was strangling a woman and she couldn't make him stop. By the time they arrived, she was hysterical.

Jonathan had been leaving our house when he'd heard the sirens. He told me later he'd feared the worst, following the noise, and racing to the scene, but even he had no idea Simon was capable of such violence. As hurt as I was by his betrayal, I was glad he'd been around to take care of the twins whilst I spent a week recovering in hospital.

The doctors told me my neck was swollen internally, reducing the flow of air to my lungs and they were initially worried the carotid arteries were damaged, which could compromise blood flow to the brain. It seemed I'd been lucky to survive the attack and it took a few days before I was able to speak again.

Jonathan told the police everything, the deal he'd made with Simon that, once struck, he couldn't get out of. He'd tried to call the whole thing off when he became aware how far Simon was willing to go to keep his end of the bargain. I'd turned out to be a bit of a challenge and not easy to terrorise out of my own home. It was the reason Jonathan had been so furious with me. I wouldn't back down and he was in so deep with Simon he didn't know what to do.

It started when the two of them had bumped into each other in the pub one Friday after work. After I'd scratched his Jaguar, Simon did his research. Discovering with the help of Facebook I was married to his old college buddy. The chance meeting in the pub had likely been no such thing.

Simon and Jonathan, shared a few pints, reminiscing about college days, and bragging about how well they'd done in their respective fields since then. Simon now a successful business owner and Jonathan, as far as he'd told him, was practically running the prestigious wine merchants.

The alcohol loosening Jonathan's lips, he told Simon of his plight, moaning he needed a quick sale of the house as he was getting pressure from Monique to buy a cottage that she'd fallen in love with, and get out of the cramped flat they were renting. Their affair had started a few months before he left me, and when he moved into the flat, Monique joined him straight away.

He knew I'd dig my heels in, not wanting to uproot the twins, so when Simon sympathised, telling Jonathan that, due to our run-in, he knew how neurotic I was, Jonathan was only too keen to listen. He replayed the incident at the traffic lights, my overreaction to being cut up and subsequent damage to his car. Painting me as a demented woman who would only require a nudge to be sent over the edge.

However, in payment for getting me out of the house, he wanted Jonathan to put some money through the wine merchants, the profits from creating and dissolving his companies. Money he'd duped out of George and countless others who'd invested in business he'd subsequently folded. When HMRC began to look at Simon's accounts, he asked Jonathan to stash the cash, intending to use the funds to buy our house and sell it on a few months later for a profit.

Jonathan had drunkenly agreed but got in too deep, too quickly, and although he tried to back out, Simon already had his claws into him. When Claire saw Jonathan in the Six Bells, he'd arranged to meet Simon briefly, to call the whole thing off. Claire had no idea that Owen and Simon were the same person, so when they were standing at the bar together, it didn't occur to her they were doing anything other than ordering drinks.

Jonathan admitted he never put the cash through the company, having got cold feet and saving himself from any criminal proceedings. Instead, it had been stashed in the loft until he could return it. Simon threatened Jonathan with revealing everything if he didn't go through with the plan. By this point, HMRC had visited the house after the tip-off from George. Simon was in up to his neck and was dragging Jonathan down with him. I was the icing on the cake and my visit, claiming to know everything, tipped him over the edge. Ironic, considering I was the one portrayed as being mentally unstable.

Simon was arrested for attempted murder but charged with GBH. It was a plea deal, and he was remanded in custody awaiting sentencing. He'd thrown Mike to the wolves to try to lessen the length of time he'd serve, but investigations were ongoing.

I'd never have to see him again, not for a few years anyway. A

For Sale sign was put outside the house Jonathan and I had dreamed of owning. Ava moved in with her mum, taking Max, the dog, with her, and discovered an unlikely alliance with Rachel. It turned out Simon had been controlling, to the point of suffocating, his daughter for years. She was a pawn he exploited when he could, where it benefited him, embroiling her in his cat-and-mouse game with me.

As soon as I was discharged from hospital, the twins came home, they knew something had gone on between Jonathan and I, but not the full extent of what he'd done. I remained tight-lipped, not wanting to drive a wedge between the twins and their father. They needed their dad. I, however, felt nothing but contempt for Jonathan. What had happened eradicated anything there had been between us, despite him begging for forgiveness. He played up to how he'd been taken for a ride by Simon. But he never did know how to take responsibility for his actions. If he'd never had the affair and been so desperate to sell the house, Simon wouldn't have been able to cause so much damage in our lives.

Claire had been amazing, running around after me, ferrying me to and from the hospital, always on call for whatever I needed. She'd been plugging away at work and initiated a dialogue with a web-based manufacturer of leisure wear who was looking for a HR Manager, pencilling in an interview for me in the New Year.

A source from another recruitment company told her Winston's had replaced Tim with an experienced woman in her early fifties. He'd been pushed out due to his handling of recent internal incidents and they were looking at fresh blood to head up their team. It seemed my departure had shaken the tree right to the top and I hoped they could turn their prehistoric ways around. Even with Tim gone I was glad to be out of there and looking forward to starting a new career with a company that would appreciate me.

Claire continued to be my rock and I was glad to see her bounce back from being used by Simon. She'd brushed herself down and was already back on Hinge, talking to people, putting herself out there. I envied her resilience, but I had no intention of following in her footsteps.

George visited as soon as I was out, his head healing nicely. It was his turn to bring me shopping and he stayed for a takeaway dinner, interacting with the kids like it was second nature. They commented once he'd gone that he seemed like a nice guy, Rachel noting George's subtle attempts at flirting which sailed over my head. It gave me a warm glow to think George was interested in something potentially blossoming from our friendship but I was happy to take things slow and enjoy his company for now.

The photos I'd taken of the stock in Simon's garage had come in useful. George was able to match the serial numbers to some of the stock he'd ordered back when Avenue Security had been born. It meant he could prove Simon had dissolved the company without declaring his assets and invoked a solicitor to recover his investment into the business plus damages. We both knew Simon would fight it, he'd never roll over, but George's solicitor had convinced him he had a good case.

Jonathan pestered me for an audience and, eventually, once I was strong enough I let him come around. The boxes of his things remained in the lounge, where I'd put them, yet to be collected. He arrived in the evening, on the pretence he wanted to discuss the forthcoming Christmas arrangements with the kids. Coming into the house carrying a bottle of expensive red wine, helping himself to glasses from the cupboard.

Before, it would have irked me to see him roam about the place as though he still lived there, but now it went over my head. The twins had told me there had been no reconciliation with Monique. She had grown frustrated with Jonathan's lack of proactiveness, the honeymoon period having worn off, and moved back in with her parents. Without her there, the twins were enjoying the focus of their father's attention and time.

'I've been thinking,' Jonathan said, pouring the wine and sitting at the head of the table, his old chair. I raised an eyebrow, taking a glass from his outstretched hand and enjoying the tang as it slid down my still tender throat.

'About Christmas?' I prompted, as that was the reason for his visit.

'We don't have to sell the house,' he said, voice as smooth as silk.

I chuckled without any mirth. I had removed the sign from the driveway that morning, something Jonathan must have picked up on when he arrived. He looked at me quizzically. 'No, you're right, we don't,' I agreed, watching an eager smile spread across his face.

'I'm so very sorry, Kay, for all the Simon Fox business, everything just got out of hand. I had my head turned by Monique and I took for granted how good I had it here, with you.' His words made me queasy, as if anything could make up for him setting a monster like Simon Fox onto the mother of his children. 'It seems silly, doesn't it, we were happy here, weren't we? There's nothing stopping us from trying again... for the kids, and well, for us too.' He leant across and placed his hand on top of mine. In comparison to George's, it was cold and slippery, and I had to bite my tongue, drawing it away to place it on my lap. There was no way back for us, there never would be, he'd shown his true colours and he wasn't the man I thought he was.

'We won't be selling the house, Jonathan, because I'm going to buy you out.'

I wanted to relish it, the look of initial shock, then comprehension on Jonathan's face. That he wouldn't be worming his way back into our lives under any circumstances. I didn't need any help financially, which I was sure was his angle, and I'd already instructed a solicitor, who would petition the divorce on the basis of adultery. The papers were to be served the following week.

'How?' he spluttered.

'I've come into money, quite a lot of money,' I said simply. Knowing there was over three hundred and fifty thousand pounds sitting in my bank account, a figure, after tax, that was life-changing. It meant we could stay in the family home; the twins wouldn't have to be uprooted and life would go on as before without any financial struggle.

There was a reason the vendors of Goddard Close hadn't accepted my offer. It wasn't meant to be. Just like Jonathan and I weren't meant to be. I had to put my faith in the future and leave the past behind. Find a new job, maybe embark on a new relationship, but I had the comfort and familiarity of the house I loved and my twins whom I adored. For now, that would be enough.

ACKNOWLEDGMENTS

Firstly, I'd like to thank the superb Boldwood Team for being so supportive over what has been another tough year for many. I'm eternally grateful to be living the dream publishing with you. Caroline Ridding, thanks for being the best editor and pushing me to write the best I can. Jade Craddock, your eagle eyes are amazing. Please say you'll always be my copy editor! A big thanks to Shirley too for your fabulous proofreading prowess!

To my lovely first readers, Mum and Denise. Without your encouragement I wouldn't sit in front of the laptop every day. Knowing you are waiting for new chapters to arrive on your Kindles, because you've devoured everything I've sent, spurs me on.

A big thank you to my friends Christine and Russ Massingham for loaning me the use of their name. I hope you enjoy seeing it in print.

Thanks to Ciara Moran for swooping in to assist me with her knowledge of family law.

As always, a shout-out to the formidable Gangland Governors and Book Swap Central Facebook Groups I've come to rely on. All your wonderful members – authors and readers – have been on hand whenever I've needed a laugh or a boost. Your support is very much appreciated.

Lastly and certainly not least, thanks to my gorgeous family who have always believed in me, my amazing husband, Dean, and two beautiful daughters, Bethany and Lucy.

MORE FROM GEMMA ROGERS

We hope you enjoyed reading *The Feud*. If you did, please leave a review.

If you'd like to gift a copy, this book is also available as an ebook, digital audio download and audiobook CD.

Sign up to the Gemma Rogers mailing list for news, competitions and updates on future books:

http://bit.ly/GemmaRogersNewsletter

Explore more gritty thrillers from Gemma Rogers.

ABOUT THE AUTHOR

Gemma Rogers was inspired to write gritty thrillers by a traumatic event in her own life nearly twenty years ago. *Stalker* was her debut novel and marked the beginning of a new writing career. Gemma lives in West Sussex with her husband, two daughters and bulldog Buster.

Visit Gemma's website: www.gemmarogersauthor.co.uk

Follow Gemma on social media:

facebook.com/GemmaRogersAuthor

twitter.com/GemmaRogers79

instagram.com/gemmarogersauthor

bookbub.com/authors/gemma-rogers

ABOUT BOLDWOOD BOOKS

Boldwood Books is a fiction publishing company seeking out the best stories from around the world.

Find out more at www.boldwoodbooks.com

Sign up to the Book and Tonic newsletter for news, offers and competitions from Boldwood Books!

http://www.bit.ly/bookandtonic

We'd love to hear from you, follow us on social media:

facebook.com/BookandTonic

twitter.com/BoldwoodBooks

instagram.com/BookandTonic

Printed in Great Britain
by Amazon

81623455R00197